In Brief Authority by F. Anstey

F. Anstey was the pseudonym of Thomas Anstey Guthrie who was born in Kensington, London on August 8th, 1856, to Augusta Amherst Austen, an organist and composer, and Thomas Anstey Guthrie., a prosperous military tailor

Anstey was educated at King's College School and then at Trinity Hall, Cambridge. Although his education was first rate Anstey could only manage a third-class degree; A Gentlemen's degree as it was euphemistically known.

In 1880 he was called to the bar. However this career path rapidly fell away in his desire to become an author. The successful publication of Vice Versa, in 1882, with the premise of a substitution of a father for his schoolboy son, made his name and reputation as a refreshing and original humorist.

The following year he published a rather more serious work, The Giant's Robe. Interestingly the story is about a plagiarist and Anstey was, ironically, accused of plagiarism in writing the work. Despite good reviews both he and his public knew that his writing career was to be that of a humorist.

In the following years he published prolifically beginning with; The Black Poodle (1884), The Tinted Venus (1885), A Fallen Idol (1886), and Baboo Jabberjee B.A. (1897).

Anstey worked not only as a novelist and short story writer but was also a valued member of the staff at the humorous Punch magazine, in which his voces populi and his parodies of a reciter's stock-piece (Burglar Bill) represent perhaps his best work.

In 1901, his successful farce, The Man from Blankleys, based on a story that originally appeared in Punch, was first produced on stage at the Prince of Wales Theatre, in London.

Anstey had become a writer, and a successful one at that, of many talents.

Many more of his stories were made into plays and films over the years. Others were simply taken for the premise alone, usually with no credit to the original author.

By the end of the First World War Anstey's original publications had slowed to a crawl and he seemed rather more interested in translating and publishing some works of Moliere.

Thomas Anstey Guthrie died of pneumonia on March 10th, 1934 in London.

His self-deprecating autobiography, A Long Retrospect, was published in 1936.

Index of Contents

CHAPTER I

"THE SKIRTS OF HAPPY CHANCE"

On a certain afternoon in March Mrs. Sidney Stimpson (or rather Mrs. Sidney Wibberley-Stimpson, as a recent legacy from a distant relative had provided her with an excuse for styling herself) was sitting alone in her drawing-room at "Inglegarth," Gablehurst.

"Inglegarth" was the name she had chosen for the house on coming to live there some years before. What it exactly meant she could not have explained, but it sounded distinguished and out of the common, without being reprehensibly eccentric. Hence the choice.

Some one, she was aware, had just entered the carriage-drive, and after having rung, was now standing under the white "Queen Anne" porch; Mitchell, the rosy-cheeked and still half-trained parlour-maid, was audible in the act of "answering the door."

It being neither a First nor a Third Friday, Mrs. Stimpson was not, strictly speaking, "at home" except to very intimate friends, though she made a point of being always presentable enough to see any afternoon caller. On this occasion she was engaged in no more absorbing occupation than the study of one of the less expensive Society journals, and, having already read all that was of real interest in its columns, she was inclined to welcome a distraction.

"If you please, m'm," said Mitchell, entering, "there's a lady wishes to know if she could see you for a minute or two."

"Did you ask her to state her business, Mitchell?... No? Then you should have. Called for a subscription to something, I expect. Tell her I am particularly engaged. I suppose she didn't give any name?"

"Oh yes, m'm. She give her name—Lady 'Arriet Elmslie, it was."

"Then why on earth didn't you say so before," cried the justly exasperated Mrs. Wibberley-Stimpson, "instead of leaving her ladyship on the door-mat all this time? Really, Mitchell, you are too trying! Go and show her in at once—and be careful to say 'my lady.' And bring up tea for two as soon as you can—the silver tea-pot, mind!"

It might have been inferred from her manner that she and Lady Harriet were on terms of closest friendship, but this was not exactly the case. Mrs. Stimpson had indeed known her for a considerable time, but only by sight, and she had long ceased to consider a visit from Lady Harriet as even a possible event. Now it had actually happened, and, providentially, on an afternoon when Mitchell's cap and apron could defy inspection. But if it was the first time that an Earl's daughter had crossed Mrs. Stimpson's threshold, she was not at all the woman to allow the fact to deprive her of her self-possession.

A title had no terror for her. Before her marriage, when she was Miss Selina Prinsley, she had acted as hostess for her father, the great financier and company promoter, who had entertained lavishly up to the date of his third and final failure. Her circle then had included many who could boast of knighthoods, and even baronetcies!

And, though Lady Harriet was something of a personage at Gablehurst, and confined her acquaintance to her own particular set, there was nothing formidable or even imposing in her appearance. She was the widow of a Colonel Elmslie, and apparently left with only moderate means, judging from the almost poky house on the farther side of the Common, which she shared with an unmarried female cousin of about her own age.

So, when she was shown in, looking quite ordinary, and even a little shy, Mrs. Wibberley-Stimpson rose to receive her with perfect ease, being supported by the consciousness that she was by far the more handsomely dressed of the two. In fact her greeting was so gracious as to be rather overpowering.

"Interrupting me? Not in the very least, dear Lady Harriet! Only too delighted, I'm sure!... Now do take off your boa, and come nearer the fire. You'll find this quite a comfy chair, I think. Tea will be brought in presently.... Oh, you really must, after trapesing all that way across the Common. I can't tell you how pleased I am to see you. I've so often wished to make your acquaintance, but I couldn't take the first step, could I? So nice of you to break the ice!"

Lady Harriet submitted to these rather effusive attentions resignedly enough. She could hardly interrupt her hostess's flow of conversation without rudeness, while she had already begun to suspect that Mrs. Stimpson might form an entertaining study.

But her chief reason, after all, was that the prospect of tea had its attractions. Accordingly she attempted no further explanations of her visit just then, and was content to observe Mrs. Stimpson, while she rippled on complacently.

She saw a matron who might be about fifty, with abundant pale auburn hair, piled up, and framing her face in a sort of half aureole. The eyes were small and hazel green; the nose narrow and pointed, the wide, full-lipped mouth, which wore just then a lusciously ingratiating smile, showed white but prominent teeth. The complexion was of a uniform oatmealy tint, and, though Mrs. Wibberley-Stimpson was neither tall nor slim, she seemed to have taken some pains to preserve a waist.

"Most fortunate I happened to be at home," she was saying. "And if you had called on one of my regular days, I shouldn't have had the chance of a real talk with you. As it is, we shall be quite tête-à-tête.... Ah, here is tea—you must tell me if you like it weak, dear Lady Harriet, and I shall remember the next time you come. Yes, you find me all alone this afternoon. My eldest daughter, Edna, has gone to a lecture at her Mutual Improvement Society, on a German Philosopher called Nitchy, or some such name. She's so bookish and well-read, takes such an interest in all the latest movements—runs up to town for matinées of intellectual dramas—quite the modern type of girl. But not a blue-stocking—she's joined a Tango Class lately, and dances most beautifully, I'm told—just the figure for it. We got up a little Costume Ball here this winter—perhaps you may have heard of it?—Ah, well, my Edna was generally admitted to be the belle of the evening. A perfect Juliet, everybody said. I went as her mother—Lady Capulet, you know. I did think of going as Queen Elizabeth at one time. I've so often been told that if I ever went to a Fancy Dress Ball, I ought to go as her—or at all events as one of our English Queens. But, however, I didn't. Mr. Stimpson went as a Venetian Doge, but I do not consider myself that it was at all suitable to him."

She did not say all this without a motive. She knew that a local Historical Pageant was being arranged for the coming Summer, and that Lady Harriet was on the Committee. Also she had heard that, after rehearsals had begun, some of the principal performers had resigned their parts, and the Committee had some difficulty in finding substitutes.

It had struck her as not at all unlikely that her visitor had called with a view to ascertaining whether the services of any of the Stimpson household would be available. If she had, it was, of course very gratifying. If she had merely come in a neighbourly way, there was no harm in directing her attention to the family qualifications for a Pageant performance.

Her hearer, without betraying any sign of the mirth she inwardly felt, meekly agreed that Mrs. Stimpson was undoubtedly well fitted to impersonate a Queen, and that the costume of a Venetian Doge was rather a trying one, after which her hostess proceeded: "Perhaps you are right, dear Lady Harriet, but the worst of it was that my boy Clarence, who would have made such a handsome Romeo, insisted on going as a Pierrot! Very likely you have seen Clarence?... Oh, you would certainly have noticed him if you had—always so well turned out. He's got quite a good post as Secretary to an Insurance Co., in the City: they think so highly of him there—take his advice on everything—in fact, he practically is the Company! And only twenty-two! It's such a relief, because there was a time when it really seemed as if he'd never settle down to any regular work. Nothing would induce him to enter my husband's business—for I must tell you, Lady Harriet, we are in business. Sauces, pickles, condiments of every sort and description—wholesale, you know, not retail, so I hope you aren't too dreadfully shocked!"

Lady Harriet remarked that she saw nothing to be shocked at—several of her relations and friends were in business of various kinds, which gave Mrs. Wibberley-Stimpson the opening she required. "Society has changed its views so much lately, has it not?" she said. "Why, the youngest partner in Mr. Wibberley-Stimpson's firm is a younger son of the Earl of Fallowfields—Mr. Chervil Thistleton, and an Honourable, of course! I daresay you are acquainted with him?... Not? Quite a charming young man—

married a Miss Succory, a connection of the Restharrows, and such a sweet girl! You may have met her?... Oh, I thought—but I really hardly know her myself yet," (which was Mrs. Stimpson's method of disguising the fact that she had never met either of them in her life). "When he came into the warehouse he was perfectly amazed at the immense variety in pickles and sauces—it was quite a revelation to him. Only he can't touch pickles of any kind, which is a pity, because it prevents him from taking the interest he might in the business.... Just one of these hot cakes, dear Lady Harriet—you're making such a wretched tea!... I should like you to see my youngest child, Ruby. She's gone out to tea with some little friends of hers, but she may be back before you go. So much admired—such lovely colouring! But just a little difficult to manage. Governess after governess have I had, and none of them could do anything with her. My present one, however, she seems to have taken to. Miss Heritage, her name is—at least she was adopted as a baby by a rich widow of that name, and brought up in every luxury. But Mrs. Heritage died without making a will, and it seems she'd muddled away most of her money, and there were claims on what she left, so the poor girl had to turn out, and earn her own living. Such a sad little story, is it not? I felt it was really a charity to engage her. I'm not sure that I can keep her much longer, though. She's far too good-looking for a governess, and there's always a danger with a marriageable young man in the house, but fortunately Clarence has too much sense and principle to marry out of his own rank. I do think that's such a mistake, don't you, dear Lady Harriet? Look at the Duke of Mountravail's heir, the young Marquis of Muscombe—married only last month at a registry office to a girl who was in the chorus at the Vivacity! I hear she comes of quite a respectable family, and all that," admitted Mrs. Stimpson, who derived her information from her Society journals. "But still, can you wonder at the poor Duke and Duchess being upset by it? I've no doubt you are constantly coming across similar instances in Smart Society."

Lady Harriet disclaimed all acquaintanceship with Smart Society, which Mrs. Stimpson protested she could not believe. "I am sure you have the entrée into any set, Lady Harriet, even the smartest! Which reminds me. Have you heard anything more about that mysterious disappearance of the Dowager Duchess of Gleneagle's diamonds during her journey from the North last week? A tiara, and a dog-collar, I was told. Professional thieves, I suppose, but don't you think the Duchess's maid?—Oh, really? I made sure you would be a friend of the Duchess's—but, of course, Society is so much larger than it used to be!"

"You are a far better authority than I can pretend to be about it," Lady Harriet owned smilingly; "and really you've given me so much interesting information that I had nearly forgotten what I came to see you about. It's—well, I wanted to ask—"

"I think I can guess, Lady Harriet," put in Mrs. Stimpson, as her visitor paused for a second. "I've heard of your difficulties about getting players for the Pageant, and I'm sure I, and indeed all the family, would feel only too honoured."

"It's most kind of you," Lady Harriet interrupted, rising, "but—but that isn't why I've troubled you. It's only that I'm thinking of engaging Jane Saunders as house-parlourmaid, and she tells me she was in your service, so I called to ask about her character, don't you know."

For a moment Mrs. Wibberley-Stimpson wished she had been less precipitate, but she soon recognised that no real harm had been done. "Saunders?" she said, "yes, she left me last month. Do sit down again, dear Lady Harriet, and I'll give you all the information I possibly can. Well, when that girl first came, she had everything to learn. It was quite evident she'd never been in service before with gentlefolks. Actually brought in letters in her fingers, Lady Harriet, and knocked at sitting-room doors! And no notion of cleaning silver, and I like to see mine come up to table without a speck! However, after being with me for a while, she improved, and I can conscientiously say that she became quite competent in time. That is, for a household like ours, you know, where things are done in quite an unpretentious style."

"I don't think we are at all pretentious people either," said Lady Harriet, rising once more. "And now, Mrs. Stimpson, you have told me all I wanted to know, so I must tear myself away."

"Must you really be going? Well, Lady Harriet, I've so much enjoyed our little chat. There are so few persons in a semi-suburban neighbourhood like this, with whom one can have anything in common. So I shall hope to see more of you in future. And if," she added, after ringing for Mitchell, "I should find I've forgotten anything I ought to have told you about Saunders, I can easily pop in some morning." Lady Harriet hastened to assure her that she must not think of giving herself this trouble—after which she took her leave.

"Rather an amusing experience in its way," she was thinking. "Something to tell Joan when I get back. But oh! what an appalling woman! She's settled one thing, though. It will be quite impossible to take Jane Saunders now. A pity—because I rather liked the girl's looks!"

Meanwhile the happily unconscious Mrs. Stimpson had settled down in her chair again with the conviction that she had made a distinctly favourable impression. She allowed her eyes to wander complacently round the room, which, with its big bay window looking on the semi-circular gravel sweep, and its glazed door by the fireplace leading through a small conservatory, gay with begonias, asters, and petunias to the garden beyond, was not merely large, by Gablehurst standards, but undeniably pleasant. She regarded its various features—the white chimney-piece and over-mantel with Adam decorations in Cartonpierre, the silk fire-screen printed with Japanese photographs, the cottage-grand, on which stood a tall trumpet vase filled with branches of imitation peach blossom, the étagères ("Louis Quinze style") containing china which could not be told from genuine Dresden at a distance, the gaily patterned chintz on the couches and chairs, the water-colour sketches of Venice, and coloured terra-cotta plaques embossed on high relief with views of the Forum and St. Peter's at Rome on the walls, and numerous "nick-nacks"—an alabaster model of the Leaning Tower of Pisa, a wood carving of the Lion of Lucerne, and groups of bears from Berne—all of which were not only souvenirs of her wedding-journey, but witnesses to Continental travel and general culture.

She could see nothing that was not in the most correct taste, as Lady Harriet must have observed for herself, together with the hammered copper gong, the oak chest, and the china bowl for cards in the hall. Strange that Saunders should have been the humble means of bringing about so unexpected a meeting, but Providence chose its own instruments, and now the seed was sown, Mrs. Stimpson felt she could rely on herself for the harvest.

And so she took up the latest number of The Upper Circle, and read, to the accompaniment of alternate duologues and soliloquies by thrushes and blackbirds in the garden, until gradually she drifted into a blissful dream of being at a garden-party at Lady Harriet's and entreated, not merely by her hostess, but Royalty itself, to accept the rôle of Queen at the County Pageant!

She was in the act of doing this gracefully, when the vision was abruptly ended by the entrance of her elder daughter. Edna was by no means bad-looking, in spite of her light eyelashes and eyebrows, and the fact that the pince-nez she wore compressed her small nose in an unbecoming ridge. Her eyes were larger than her mother's, though of the same colour, and her hair was of a deeper shade of auburn. Her costume was of a kind that may be described as the floppily artistic.

"I never heard you come in, my dear," said her mother. "Did you enjoy your lecture?"

"Quite; I took pages and pages of notes. Nietzsche's Gospel of the Superman is certainly most striking."

"And what is his Gospel exactly?"

"Oh, well, he teaches that the ideal man ought to rise superior to conventional prejudices, and have the courage to do as he thinks right without deferring to ordinary ideas. To be strong in willing what he wants—all that sort of thing, you know."

"Dear me!" said Mrs. Wibberley-Stimpson dubiously. "But, if everybody acted like that, would it be quite—er—nice?"

"There's no fear of any of the men in Gablehurst being Supermen, at all events!" said Edna. "They're all perfect slaves to convention! But the lecturer explained the Nietzschean theories in such a way that he made us feel there was a great deal to be said for them.... No tea, thanks. I had mine at the Fletchers. It looks," she added, with a glance at the tea-cups, "as if you had been entertaining some one, Mother— who was it?"

"Only Lady Harriet," replied Mrs. Stimpson, with elaborate carelessness.

"What Lady Harriet?" was the intentionally provoking query.

"Really, Edna, one would think there were dozens of them! The Lady Harriet: Lady Harriet Elmslie, of course."

"Oh," said Edna. "And what did she want?"

"Well, she came to ask after Saunders' character, but she stayed to tea, and we really struck up quite an intimate friendship, discussing one thing and another. She's so quiet and unassuming, Edna—absolutely no hauteur. I'm sure you will like her. I told her about you all, and she seemed so interested. Quite between ourselves, I shouldn't be at all surprised if she got us invited to take part in the Pageant—she's on the Committee, you know."

"If I was invited, Mother, I'm not at all sure I shouldn't refuse."

"You must please yourself about that, my dear," said Mrs. Stimpson, who, perhaps, felt but little anxiety as to the result. "I shall certainly accept if the part is at all suitable."

She might have said more, if Ruby had not suddenly burst into the room. Ruby was certainly the flower of the family—an extremely engaging young person of about ten, whose mischievous golden-brown eyes had long and curling lashes, and whose vivacious face was set off by a thick mane of deepest Titian red.

"Oh, Mummy," she announced breathlessly, "I've got invitations for nearly all my animals while we're away at Eastbourne! Mucius Scævola's the most popular—everybody asked him, but I think he'll feel most at home with Daisy Williams. Vivian and Ada Porter will simply love to have Numa Pompilius, but nobody seems to want Tarquinius Superbus, so I shall turn him out in the garden, and he must catch worms for himself."

"Dearest child," said her mother, "what are these new animals of yours with the extraordinary names?"

"They're the same old animals, Mums. I've rechristened them since I began Roman History with Miss Heritage. Mucius Scævola's the Salamander, because they're indifferent to fire, like he was—though Miss Heritage says it wouldn't be kind to try with Mucius. Numa Pompilius is the Blind-worm—he used to be Kaa—and the Toad has changed from Nobbles to Tarquinius Superbus."

"I can't understand how you can keep such unpleasant pets as reptiles," said Edna.

"Because I like them," said Ruby simply. "And Bobby Williams has promised, as soon as it gets warmer, to come out on the Common with me and catch lizards. Won't it be lovely?"

"I hope you won't put one of them down anybody's neck, then, as you did to Tommy Fletcher."

"That was Mucius," Ruby admitted cheerfully. "But I didn't mean him to go so far down. And he was very good—he didn't bite Tommy anywhere."

"Little ladies don't play such tricks," said her Mother. "I hope Miss Heritage doesn't encourage your liking for these horrid creatures?"

"Oh, she doesn't mind, so long as I don't take them out of the aquarium, but she hates touching them herself."

"Did she come in with you?" her mother inquired, and was told that Miss Heritage had done so, and had gone upstairs, whereupon Ruby was ordered to go and take off her things, and stay quietly in the schoolroom till it was time to come down.

"I don't know if you noticed it, Mother," Edna began, as soon as Ruby had consented to leave them, "but Miss Heritage had a letter by the afternoon post which seemed to upset her. I went rather out of my way to ask her if she had had bad news of any kind, but she did not think proper to take me into her confidence. Perhaps she might be more open with you."

"My dear," said Mrs. Wibberley-Stimpson, with much dignity, "I take no interest whatever in Miss Heritage's private correspondence."

"Nor I," declared Edna. "I only thought that if she is in any trouble—She's so secretive, you know, Mums. I've tried more than once to get her to tell me what cosmetic she uses for her hands—and she never will own to using any at all!"

"I'm sure, Edna, you've no reason to be ashamed of your hands."

"Oh, they look all right just now," said Edna, examining them dispassionately. "But they will turn lobster colour at the most inconvenient times. Hers never do—and it does seem so unfair, considering—" She broke off here, as Daphne Heritage entered.

"Well, Miss Heritage?" said Mrs. Stimpson, as the girl hesitated on seeing Edna. "Did you wish to speak to me?"

"I did rather want your advice about something," said Daphne, who had a paper, and a small leather case in her hands; "I thought I might find you alone. It doesn't matter—it will do quite well another time."

"Don't let me prevent you, Miss Heritage," said Edna. "If you don't wish to speak to Mother before me, I've no desire to remain. I was just going up to change in any case."

She went out with a slightly huffy air, which was not entirely due to baffled curiosity, for she admired Daphne enough to resent being quietly kept at a distance.

"It's about this," explained Daphne, after Edna had made her exit—"a bill that has just been sent on to me." She gave the paper to Mrs. Stimpson as she spoke. "I don't know quite what to do about it."

She looked very young and inexperienced as she stood there, a slim girlish figure with masses of burnished hair the colour of ripe corn, braided and coiled as closely as possible round her small head, but there was no trace of timidity or subservience in her manner. In the slight form, with the milk-white skin, delicate profile and exquisite hands, there was a distinction that struck her employer as quite absurdly out of keeping with her position.

"The only thing to do about a bill, my dear," said Mrs. Stimpson, "is to pay it. But nearly thirty pounds is a large sum for you to owe your milliner."

"It's for things Mother—my adopted mother, you know—ordered for me. Stéphanie was always told to send in the account to her. But this seems to have been overlooked, and the executors have sent it on to me. Only I can't pay it myself—unless you wouldn't mind advancing me the money out of my salary."

"I couldn't possibly. You forget that it would represent over a year's salary, and it's by no means certain that you will be with me so long."

"I was afraid you wouldn't," said Daphne, with a little droop at the corners of her extremely pretty mouth. "So I brought this to show you." She held out the leather case. "It's the only jewellery I've got. It belonged to my father, I believe; he and my real mother both died when I was a baby, you know—and I never meant to part with it. But now I'm afraid I must—that is, if you think any jeweller would give as much as thirty pounds for it."

Mrs. Wibberley-Stimpson opened the case, which was much more modern than the kind of badge or pendant it contained. This was a fairly large oval stone of a milky green, deeply engraved with strangely formed letters interlaced in a cypher, and surrounded by a border of dark blue gems which Mrs. Stimpson decided instantly must be Cabochon star sapphires of quite exceptional quality. The gold chain attached to it was antique and of fine and curious workmanship.

She was convinced that the pendant must be worth considerably more than thirty pounds, though she was no doubt right in telling Daphne that no jeweller would offer so much for an ornament that was quite out of fashion. "Besides," she said, "I don't like the idea of any governess of mine going about offering jewellery for sale. Have Edna or Ruby seen you wearing this thing?" she asked with apparent irrelevance.

It appeared they had not; Daphne had never worn it herself, and she had only remembered its existence that afternoon, and found it hidden away at the back of her wardrobe.

"Well," said Mrs. Stimpson, "it is most unpleasant to me to see a young girl like you owing all this money to her milliner."

"It isn't very pleasant for me," said Daphne ruefully; "but if you won't advance the money, and I can't or mustn't sell the pendant, I don't very well see how I can help it."

"I'll tell you what I'll do," said Mrs. Stimpson. "I really oughtn't to—and under ordinary circumstances I couldn't afford it, but, as it happens, a great-uncle of mine left me a small legacy not long ago, and I haven't spent quite all of it yet. So I don't mind buying this for thirty pounds myself."

"Will you really?" cried Daphne. "How angelic of you!"

"I think it is," said Mrs. Stimpson; "but I feel myself responsible for you, to some extent. So I'll write you a cheque for the thirty pounds, and you can send it off to this milliner person at once." She went to the writing-table and filled up the cheque. "There," she said, handing it to Daphne, "put it in an envelope and direct it at once—you'll find a stamp in that box, and it can go by the next post."

"By the way, my dear," she added, as she was leaving the room, "I needn't tell you that I shall not breathe a word to a soul of our little transaction, and I should advise you, in your own interests, to keep it entirely to yourself."

"I was quite wrong about Mrs. Stimpson," Daphne told herself reproachfully, after she had slipped the letter containing bill and cheque into the letter-box in the hall. "She can be kind sometimes, and I've been a little beast to see only the comic side of her! I daresay she won't even wear that pendant."

But Mrs. Stimpson had every intention of wearing it that same evening. It is not often that one has the opportunity of doing a kindness and securing a real bargain at a single stroke; and she knew enough about jewels to be fully aware that, if the ornament was a trifle old-fashioned, she had not done at all badly over her purchase.

"It really suits me very well," she thought, as, after putting the last touches to her evening demi-toilette, she fastened the pendant round her neck. "Even better than I expected. It was lucky Miss Heritage came to me. A jeweller would have been sure to cheat her, poor child!"

And she went down to the drawing-room feeling serenely satisfied with herself.

CHAPTER II

RUSHING TO CONCLUSIONS

Mrs. Wibberley-Stimpson, as she sat in the drawing-room, where the curtains had been drawn and the lamps lighted, was occupied with a project which she was anxious to impart to her husband as soon as he returned. Some time before a dull rumble from the valley had informed her that his usual train was approaching Gablehurst station, and now she heard the click of the front gate, the crunch of his well-known step on the gravel, and the opening of the hall door.

"I want to speak to you for a moment, Sidney," she said, opening the drawing-room door. "Come in here before you go up to dress." (Mrs. Stimpson insisted on his dressing for dinner. It was customary in all really good society, and also it would prevent him from feeling awkward in evening clothes—which it never did.)

"Very well, my dear," he said, entering. "Any news with you?" which was his invariable question.

Mr. Stimpson was short and inclined to be stout. What remained of his hair was auburn and separated in the middle by a wide parting; he had close-cut whiskers of a lighter red, which met in his moustache, and if his eyes had been narrow, instead of round and filmy like a seal's, and his mouth had been firm, and not loose and slightly open, he would not have been at all a bad caricature of his Majesty King Henry the Eighth.

"Nothing—except, but I'll tell you about that afterwards. Sit down, do, and don't fidget.... Well, I've been thinking, Sidney, that we really ought to ask the Chevril Thistletons to a quiet little dinner. Not to meet any of our usual set, of course! We could have the dear Rector, who, if he is Low Church, is very well connected—and Lady Harriet Elmslie."

Mr. Stimpson showed no enthusiasm at the suggestion. "Lady Elmslie, Selina!" he cried. "But we don't know her ladyship!"

"I do wish you would learn to use titles correctly, Sidney! Lady Harriet Elmslie—not Lady Elmslie! And you shouldn't speak of her, except to servants, as 'her ladyship'; that's only done by inferiors."

"Well, my love, whatever may be the correct way of speaking of her, the fact remains that we haven't the honour of her acquaintance."

"That's just where you're mistaken! We have, or at least I have;" and she described how she had come to enjoy that privilege.

"Well," he admitted at the conclusion, "she certainly seems to have made herself exceedingly affable, but it doesn't follow that she'd come and dine, even if we asked her."

"She would if it was to meet the Thistletons."

"Perhaps so, my love, but—er—we don't know that they would come."

"Of course they would, if they knew we were expecting Lady Harriet. For goodness' sake, Sidney, don't swing your foot like that—you know I can't bear it. All you have to do is to find out from Mr. Thistleton what evenings the week after next would be most convenient, and I'll undertake the rest!"

"I—I really couldn't do that, Selina. I'm a proud man, in my way, and I don't care about exposing myself unnecessarily to a rebuff."

"Why should you be rebuffed? After all, he's only a junior partner!"

"True, my love, but that doesn't make him less stand-offish. He may be in the business, but he's not of it. I doubt myself whether even old Cramphorn would venture to invite him to dinner, and if he did, I'd bet a tidy sum that the Honourable Mr. Chevril Thistleton—"

"Mr.—not the Honourable Mr. Thistleton, Sidney," corrected his wife, who had studied all such minutiæ in a handbook written by a lady of unimpeachable authority. "The term is never employed in ordinary conversation, or on visiting cards. But, if you won't show a proper spirit, I shall write myself to Mrs. Thistleton and propose one or two dates."

"It would be no good, my love," said Mr. Stimpson, brought to bay, "because, if you must know, I—er— did approach the subject with Thistleton—and—well, his manner was not sufficiently encouraging to induce me to try it again. Not so fond of being made to feel as if I was no better than one of our own clerks. I get quite enough of that from old Cramphorn!"

"You should assert yourself more, Sidney, if you want people to respect you."

"I'm always asserting myself—but old Cramphorn never listens! Just goes on his own way. Won't hear of any changes—what was good enough when the firm started a hundred years ago is good enough for him—now I'm all for new ideas myself—Progress and so forth!"

"That's what has kept us back," said Mrs. Wibberley-Stimpson; "we should have been in a far better set here than we're ever likely to be now if you hadn't given yourself out as a violent Radical, when it's well known that all best Gablehurst people are Conservatives, and several who are not really entitled to be anything of the kind. As it is, I suppose I must be content to pass my life in this suburban hole and mix with none but second-rate people. But I certainly cannot expect Lady Harriet to come here and meet them, so there's an end of it. If she imagines I've no desire to pursue her acquaintance, it can't be helped, that's all! And now you had better go up and dress."

The whole family were assembled by the time Mr. Stimpson re-appeared—his wife was in her armchair by the standard lamp. Edna was at the writing-table revising her notes of the afternoon's lecture, and Clarence was seated close by, while Ruby was whispering earnestly to Daphne on one of the chintz couches.

"All of you down before me, eh?" said the head of the family after the usual salutations had been exchanged. "But I went up long after everybody else. And not late after all—I've taught myself to dress in well under ten minutes, you see!"

"Wish he'd taught himself not to wear a white tie with a dinner jacket!" grumbled Clarence to Edna in an undertone.

"Couldn't you tell him about it?" she replied.

"I could—but what'd be the good? He'd only turn up next time in a tail-coat and a black bow!" said Clarence gloomily. "The poor old governor's one of the people who never learn—!"

Clarence's own type was that for which the latest term is "knut." He was accepted both by his family, his intimates, and himself as an infallible guide on things in general. When consulted as to matters on which he happened to be entirely ignorant, and these were not a few—he had formed the habit of preserving a pregnant silence, as of one who could say a good deal on the subject if he were at liberty to speak. And this in itself denoted a certain degree of intelligence.

In appearance he was well built, though only of average height. He had small green eyes like his mother's; his light sandy hair had a natural ripple, and his pale face expressed nothing beyond an assured consciousness of his own superiority. And yet he was not without a certain sense of humour in matters which did not immediately concern himself, though, owing to particular circumstances, it was just then distinctly in abeyance.

"What time do you get back from the City to-morrow afternoon, my boy?" his father asked.

"Not going up at all, Pater," said Clarence. "Told them I shouldn't." He was thinking that after dinner would be quite time enough to break the news that, on receiving a severe wigging for general slackness, he had lost his temper, and offered to resign his post—an offer that had been accepted with disconcerting alacrity.

"Ah, Sidney," said Mrs. Wibberley-Stimpson, "Clarence knows how to assert himself, you see!"

"I merely asked," Mr. Stimpson explained, "because I'm taking a Saturday off myself, and I thought we could have a round or two of golf together, eh, my boy?"

"I don't mind going round with you before lunch," said Clarence. "Engaged for the afternoon; but, if you'll take my advice, Governor, you'd better practise a bit longer with the Pro before you attempt to play. No good trying to run till you can walk, don't you know, what?" (He had learnt to terminate his sentences with "what" as a kind of smart shibboleth.) "Hullo, Mater!" he broke off suddenly, as he noticed the pendant on her ample bosom, "where did you get that thing? Out of a cracker?"

"Certainly not, Clarence; I am not in the habit of wearing cheap jewellery. And this cost a considerable sum, though I daresay it is worth what I paid for it."

"Did you go much of a mucker for it, Mater?"

"If I did, Clarence, I was well able to do so, thanks to dear old Uncle Wibberley's legacy."

"I must say, Mother," said Edna, "it's far the most artistic thing I've ever known you buy."

"It isn't everybody's taste," remarked Mr. Stimpson, "but I should say myself that it wasn't a bad investment. Where did you come across it, my love?"

"My dear Sidney," replied Mrs. Wibberley-Stimpson with much majesty, "as I purchased it with my own money, where I came across it, and what I paid for it are surely matters that only concern myself."

Daphne, who could hardly avoid hearing this conversation, was impressed by the tact and delicacy it displayed. It never occurred to her that Mrs. Wibberley-Stimpson's reticence might be inspired by other motives than a generous desire to spare her feelings. "She really is quite a decent sort!" she told herself.

Clarence had not been unobservant of her—indeed it would not be too much to say that he had been acutely conscious all the time of Miss Heritage's presence.

Ever since she had become a member of the household he had alternated between the desire to impress her and the dread of becoming entangled in the toils of an artful little enchantress. It was true that since her arrival in the family she had made no effort whatever to enchant him; indeed, she had treated him with easy indifference—but this, his experience of her sex and the world told him, was probably assumed. She could hardly help knowing that he was something of a "catch" from her point of view, and scheming to ensnare him.

Perhaps Clarence, with his now dubious prospects, felt himself rather less of a catch than usual; perhaps it occurred to him that being moderately ensnared would be pleasantly exciting, since he would always know when to stop. At all events, he lounged gracefully toward the sofa, on which she and Ruby were sitting: "I say, Miss Heritage," he began, "you mustn't let my Kiddie sister bore you like this. She's been whispering away in your ear for the last ten minutes."

Daphne denied that she was being bored.

"Of course she isn't!" said Ruby; "I was finishing the story I began telling her when we were walking home. We'd got to where Daphne first meets the Fairy Prince."

"Then it's all about Miss Heritage, is it?"

"I call the heroine 'Daphne' in my story, after her—but, of course, she isn't Miss Heritage really."

"You don't seem to think it very likely that Miss Heritage will ever come across a Fairy Prince, eh!" commented Clarence, and wondered the next moment whether he mightn't have said something to commit himself.

"I hope not," said Ruby, slipping her hand affectionately through Daphne's arm, "because then she'd leave me, and I should never see her again!"

"I shouldn't worry about it just yet, darling," said Daphne, smiling. "Fairy Princes are only to be found in their own country—and it's a long way from here to Fairyland."

Clarence was noticing, not for the first time, that her full face was shaped like a shield, also that two fascinating little creases came in it when she smiled, and her pretty grey eyes had a soft sparkle in them. "I must be jolly careful," he told himself.

"I should prefer, Miss Heritage," said Mrs. Wibberley-Stimpson, who had overheard the last sentence, "that Ruby was not encouraged to fill her head with Fairy tales. I don't think them good for her."

"Oh, come, Mater!" protested Clarence, unable to resist the rôle of Champion. "Where on earth is the harm of them."

"Surely, Clarence," Edna put in instructively, "there is this harm—they give such an utterly false impression of what life really is! That's why I've never been able to take any interest in them."

"More likely," said Clarence, "because you've got no imagination."

"If I hadn't," retorted Edna, "I should hardly have got through the Poetry I have. Most of Browning and Alfred Austin, and all Ella Wheeler Wilcox! It's only the lowest degree of imagination that invents things that couldn't possibly have happened!"

"They may have left off, Edna, but they happened once," declared Ruby. "I know there used to be Fairyland somewhere, with Kings and Queens and Fairy Godmothers and enchanted castles and magicians and Ogres and Dragons and things in it. And Miss Heritage believes it, too—don't you, Miss Heritage, dear?"

"I'm much mistaken in Miss Heritage, my dear," said Mr. Stimpson gallantly, "if her head isn't too well screwed on (if she'll allow me to say so) to believe in any such stuff. All very well for the Nursery, you know, but not to be taken seriously, or ... why, what's that? Most extraordinary noise! Seems to come from outside, overhead."

They could all hear a strange kind of flapping whirr in the air, it grew nearer and louder and then suddenly ceased.

"Aeroplane," pronounced Clarence, drawing the window curtains and looking out. "Miles away by now, though. Terrific pace they travel at. Too dark to see anything."

He returned to the hearthrug, and the moment afterwards, the silence outside was broken by a shrill, clear call which seemed to come from silver trumpets.

"Very odd," said Mr. Stimpson, "some one seems to be playing trumpets on the gravel-sweep!"

"If it's one of those travelling German bands," said his wife, "you'd better send them away at once, Sidney."

But, whoever they were, they had already entered the hall, for almost immediately the drawing-room door was thrown open and two persons wearing tabards and gaily plumed hats entered and sounded another blast.

"'Pon my word, you know," gasped Mr. Stimpson, "this is really—"

The heralds stepped back as a third person entered. He was wearing a rich suit of some long-departed period, and, with his furrowed face and deep-set eyes, he rather resembled an elderly mastiff, though he did not convey the same impression of profound wisdom. He gazed round the room as though he himself were as bewildered as its other occupants, who were speechless with amazement. Then his eye fell on Mrs. Wibberley-Stimpson, and he hesitated no longer, but, advancing towards her chair, sank with some difficulty on one knee, seized her hand, and kissed it with every sign of deep respect.

"Heaven be praised!" he cried in a voice that faltered with emotion, "I have at last found the Queen we have so long sought in vain!" He spoke with some sort of foreign accent, but they all understood him perfectly. As he knelt they heard a loud crack which seemed to come from between his shoulders.

"Braces given way," whispered Clarence to Edna; "silly old ass to go kneeling in 'em!"

"Really, sir," said Mr. Stimpson, "this is most extraordinary behaviour."

"You don't understand, Sidney," said Mrs. Wibberley-Stimpson, who had recovered from her first alarm and was now in a gratified flutter; "remember what I told you about Lady Harriet and the Pageant! Pray, get up, sir," she added to the stranger, "I haven't the advantage of knowing your name."

"I am the Court Chamberlain," he said, "and my name is Treuherz von Eisenbänden."

It was unknown to Mrs. Stimpson, but she concluded that he was some Anglo-German commercial magnate, who would naturally be invited to join the Committee for any such patriotic purpose as a Pageant.

As to the excessive ceremony of his manner, that was either the proper form for the occasion, or, what was more likely, Mr. Troitz, or whatever his name was, having come fresh from a dress rehearsal, could not divest himself as yet of his assumed character. The important point was that her interview with Lady Harriet had borne fruit already, and in the shape of a pressing invitation to play the distinguished part of "Queen!" The advantages thus offered for obtaining a social footing amongst county people made it easy to overlook any trifling eccentricities where the intention was so obviously serious. "Well, Mr. Troitz," she said graciously, "since the Committee have been kind enough to ask me, I shall be very pleased to be your Queen."

"And if I may say so, Sir," said her husband, "there are few ladies in the vicinity who would prove more competent. In fact—"

"That will do, Sidney," said his wife; "if Lady Harriet and the Committee did not consider me competent to be the Queen they would not have asked me." And Mr. Stimpson said no more.

"Pardon," Mr. Treuherz said, looking at him with solemn surprise, "but—who is this?"

"This is my husband, Mr. Troitz—let me introduce him."

"Your husband. Then, he will be the King!"

"The King?" cried Mr. Stimpson, "why, really, I'm not sure that would be altogether in my line."

"Nonsense, Sidney. Of course you will be the King if they want you! And this is my son, Clarence, Mr. Troitz. My daughters, Edna and Ruby."

"A Crown Prince!" cried Treuherz, and bent low to each in turn. "And two—no, I mistake—three Princesses! Ah, it is too much for me altogether!"

It was almost too much for Ruby, who giggled helplessly, while even Daphne had to bite her lip rather hard for a moment.

"The other young lady," corrected Mrs. Wibberley-Stimpson, "is merely my daughter Ruby's governess— Miss Heritage. But if you like to find a place for her as one of my ladies of honour or something, I have no objection to her accepting a part," she added, reflecting that Miss Heritage's manners and appearance would add to the family importance, while it would be a comfort to have an attendant who could not give herself such airs as might a girl belonging to a county family.

"Naturally," said Treuherz, inclining himself again. "Any member of your Majesty's household you desire to bring."

"Very well; I suppose, Miss Heritage, you have no objection? Then you will accompany us, please. And now, Mr. Troitz, about when shall we be wanted?"

"When?" he replied. "But now! At once. Already I have the car waiting!"

"Now?" exclaimed Clarence; "rum time to rehearse—what?"

"Who said anything about rehearsing, Clarence?" said his mother impatiently. "It's necessary for them to see us and talk over the arrangements. It's not likely to take long."

"But it'll do later, my love," put in Mr. Stimpson, who did not like the idea of turning out without his dinner. "Fact is, Mr. Troitz, we were just about to sit down to dinner. Why not keep the car waiting a bit and join us? No ceremony, you know—just as you are!"

"Sire, I regret that it is impossible," he said. "I have undertaken to convey you with all possible speed. If we delay I cannot answer for what may happen."

"You hear what Mr. Troitz says, Sidney," said Mrs. Wibberley-Stimpson, alarmed at the idea of another being chosen in her absence. "What does it matter if we do dine a little late? Children, we must go and put on our things at once—your warmest cloaks, mind—we're sure to find it cold motoring. Sidney and Clarence, you had better get your coats on—we shall be down directly."

Mr. Treuherz and the heralds stood at attention in the hall. While Clarence and his father struggled into their great-coats, neither of them in a very good temper, Mr. Stimpson being annoyed at postponing his dinner for what he called "tomfoolery," and Clarence secretly sulky because his parent could not be induced to see the propriety of going up to change his tie.

"I haven't yet made out, Mother," said Edna, as they came downstairs, "exactly where we're going to— or what we're expected to do when we get there."

"It will either be The Hermitage—Lady Harriet's, you know—or Mr. Troitz's country house, wherever that is. And, of course, the Committee require to know what times will suit us for rehearsing."

"I wish you'd settle it all without me," complained Edna. "I'd much rather stay at home, and run over my lecture notes.... Well, if I must come, I shall bring my note-book with me in case I'm bored." And she ran into the drawing-room, and came back with the note-book, rather as an emblem of her own intellectual superiority than with any intention of referring to it. However, as will be found later, the manuscript proved to be of some service in the future.

Daphne and Ruby were the last to join the party in the hall, Ruby wildly excited at the unexpected jaunt and the prospects of not going to bed till ever so late, and Daphne, though a little doubtful whether Mrs. Stimpson was quite justified in bringing her, inclined to welcome almost any change from the evening routine of "Inglegarth." And then, after Mrs. Stimpson had given some hurried instructions to the hopelessly mystified Mitchell, the whole family issued out of the Queen Anne porch, and were conducted by Treuherz, who, to their intense confusion, insisted on walking backwards to the car, while the heralds performed another flourish on their silver trumpets. It was pitch-dark when they had got to the asphalt pavement outside their gates, but they could just make out the contours of the car in the light that streamed across the hedge to the stained glass front-door.

"Jolly queer-looking car," said Clarence. It was certainly unusually large, and seemed to have somewhat fantastic lines and decorations.

"Oh, never mind about the car!" cried Mrs. Wibberley-Stimpson, who was inside it already, a vague, bundled-up shape in the gloom. "It's part of the Pageant, of course! Get in, Clarence, get in! We're late as it is! and if there's a thing I detest, it's keeping people waiting!"

"All right, Mater!" said Clarence, clambering in. "I can't make out what the dickens they've done with the bonnet—but we seem to be moving, what?"

Slowly the car had begun to glide along the road. Mr. Treuherz was seated in front, probably at the steering-wheel, though none was visible. The heralds sat in the rear, and the car was of such a size that there was abundant room for the family in the centre. Some yards ahead they heard a curious dry rustle and clatter, and could distinguish a confused grey mass of forms that seemed to be clearing the way for them, though whether they were human beings it was not possible to tell till they passed a lighted street-lamp.

"Why, goodness gracious!" exclaimed Mrs. Wibberley-Stimpson, "they look like—like ostriches!"

She was mistaken here, because they were merely storks, but, before she could identify them more correctly, they all suddenly rose in the air with a whirr like that of a hundred spinning looms—and the car rose with them.

"Stop!" screamed Mrs. Wibberley-Stimpson, "Sidney, tell Mr. Troitz to stop! I insist on knowing where we are being taken to!"

Treuherz glanced over his shoulder. "Where should I conduct your Majesties," he said, "but to your own Kingdom of Märchenland?"

Mrs. Stimpson and her husband would no doubt have protested, demanded explanations, insisted upon being put down at once, had they been able; but, whether it was that the car had some peculiarly soporific tendency, or whether it was merely the sudden swift rush through the upper air, a torpor had already fallen on the whole Stimpson family. It was even questionable if they remained long enough awake to hear their destination.

Daphne, for some reason, did not fall asleep till later. She lay back in her luxuriously cushioned seat, watching the birds as they flew, spread out in a wide fan against the dusky blue evening sky. Gablehurst, with its scattered lights, artistic villa-residences, and prosaic railway station—its valley and common and wooded hills, were far below and soon left behind at an ever increasing distance. But she did not feel in the least afraid. It was odd, but, after the first surprise, she had lost all sense of strangeness in a situation so foreign to all her previous experience.

"So we're being taken to Märchenland," she was thinking. "That's the same as Fairyland, practically. At least it's where all the things they call Fairy stories really happened, and—why I can't imagine—but Mr. and Mrs. Stimpson have been chosen King and Queen! And the poor dear things have no idea of it yet! Oh, I wonder" (and here, no doubt, the little creases came into her cheeks again, for she laughed softly to herself), "I wonder what they'll say or do when they find out!" And while Daphne was still wondering, her eyelids closed gently, and she, too, was sleeping soundly.

CHAPTER III

FINE FEATHERS

Mrs. Wibberley-Stimpson was the first of her party to recover consciousness. When she did, she was greatly surprised to find that it was broad daylight, and that she was lying on a grassy slope, behind which was a forest of huge pines. Close beside her were the recumbent forms of her husband and family, which led her to the natural conclusion that the car must have met with an accident.

"Sidney!" she cried, shaking him by the shoulder. "Speak to me! You're—you're not seriously hurt, are you?"

"Eh, what?" he replied sleepily, and evidently imagining that he was comfortably in bed at home; "all right, my dear, all right! I'll get up and bring in the tea-tray presently. Lots of time.... Why, hullo!" he exclaimed, after being shaken once more, as he sat up and rubbed his eyes. "How do we all come to be here?"

The others were awake by this time. "And now we're here," put in Clarence, "where are we, eh, Mater?"

"It is no use asking me, Clarence. I know no more than you do. The last thing I remember was our all getting into the car to go and see the Pageant Committee. I've a vague recollection of ostriches—but no, I must have been dreaming them. However, the car seems to have upset somehow, only I don't see it about anywhere."

"No," said Mr. Stimpson, "or old Thingumagig, or those fellows with the trumpets either."

"Dumped us down here, and gone off with the car," said Clarence. "Looks as if we'd been the victims of a practical joke, what?"

"They would never dare to do that!" said his Mother. "I expect they have missed their way in the dark. Very careless of them. I don't know what Lady Harriet and the Committee will think of me. They'll probably ask somebody else to take the part of Queen before we can get there—for I'm sure we must be a good hundred miles away from Gablehurst!"

"The Baron said that he was taking us to Märchenland, Mrs. Stimpson," said Daphne; "and I'm almost sure that that is where we really are."

"And where may Märchenland be?" inquired Mrs. Stimpson sharply. "I never heard of it myself."

"Well," said Daphne, "it's another name for—for Fairyland, you know."

"Fairyland indeed!" replied Mrs. Wibberley-Stimpson with some irritation. "You will find it difficult to persuade me to believe that I am in Fairyland, Miss Heritage! To begin with, there is no such place, and if there was, perhaps you will kindly tell me how we could possibly have got to it?"

"Through the air," explained Daphne patiently. "That car was drawn by storks, you see—not ostriches."

"When you have quite woke up, Miss Heritage," said Mrs. Stimpson, "you will realise what nonsense you are talking."

"Whatever this place is," said Clarence, "it don't look English, somehow, to me. I mean to say—that town over there—what?" He pointed across the wide plain to a cluster of towers, spires, gables, and pinnacles which glittered and gleamed faintly through the shimmering morning haze.

"It certainly has rather a Continental appearance," observed his father.

"If it has," said Mrs. Wibberley-Stimpson, "it is only some buildings or scenery or something they have run up for the Pageant. So we haven't been taken in the wrong direction after all."

"I believe, Mummy," chirped Ruby, "Miss Heritage is right, and this is Fairyland."

"Don't be so ridiculous, child! You'll believe next that we came here in a car drawn by flying storks, I suppose!"

"D'you know, Mater," said Clarence, "I'm not so sure we mayn't have. What I mean is—there's some sort of flying machine coming along now. I grant you it isn't drawn by storks, but they're birds anyhow, and there seems to be some one in the car too."

"Nothing of the kind!" declared Mrs. Wibberley-Stimpson obstinately. "At least one may fancy one sees anything with the sun in our eyes as it is. Well, upon my word!" she added, still incredulously, as an iridescent shell-shaped chariot attached to a team of snow-white doves volplaned down from a dizzy height to a spot only a few yards away, "I really could not have—who, and what can this old person be?"

The occupant of the chariot had already got out of it, and was slowly coming towards them, supporting herself on a black crutch-handled staff. As she drew nearer they could see that she was a woman of great age. She wore a large ruff, a laced stomacher, wide quilted petticoats, and a pointed hat with a broad brim. Her expression was severe, but not unkindly, while she evidently considered herself a personage of some importance.

"She looks exactly like the Fairy Godmother in the pictures," whispered Ruby.

"Whoever she may be," said her Mother, scrambling to her feet with more haste than dignity, "I suppose I shall have to go and speak to her, as I presume I am the person she has come to meet."

However, it was Daphne who was addressed by the new-comer.

"The Court Chamberlain, Baron Treuherz von Eisenbänden, has brought me the glad tidings of your arrival, my child," she said in a high cracked voice, "and, as the high official Court Godmother to the Royal Family, I felt that I should be the first to bid you welcome."

This was more than Mrs. Wibberley-Stimpson could be expected to stand without a protest.

"Pardon me," she said, throwing back her cloak as though she were in need of air, "pardon me, Madam, but I think you are mistaking my daughter's governess for me. I am Mrs. Wibberley-Stimpson!"

The old lady turned sharply, and as her eyes fell on the matron's indignant face and heaving bosom, she instantly became deferential and almost apologetic. "You must forgive me, my dear," she said, "for not recognising you before. But at my age—I may tell you I am nearing the end of my second century—one is apt to forget the flight of Time. Or it may be that Time in your world flies more quickly than in ours. I did not stay to hear more from the Baron than that he had succeeded in finding our Queen, and, to be quite plain with you, I was unprepared to find you so mature."

Then, thought Mrs. Wibberley-Stimpson confusedly, she had been brought here for the Pageant after all. But what very odd people seemed to be getting it up!

"Baron—whatever his name is, appeared to be quite satisfied that I was suited to the part," she said coldly. "Of course, if you require someone younger—"

"There can be no manner of doubt, my dear, that you are the Queen we have been seeking, so the mere fact that you are rather older than some of us expected is of no importance whatever."

"Thank you," said Mrs. Wibberley-Stimpson. "I do not consider myself more than middle-aged, and have generally been taken for younger than I am, Mrs. —, I haven't the pleasure of knowing your name."

"Here they call me the Fairy Vogelflug; in the neighbouring Kingdom of Clairdelune my name is Voldoiseau. I have officiated as Court Godmother to the reigning Royal families in both countries for many generations."

"I thought you were a Fairy Godmother!" cried Ruby; "and I'm sure you're a good Fairy, and can do all sorts of wonderful things."

"I used to, my child, in my younger days, but my powers are not what they were, and I seldom exercise them now, because it exhausts me too severely to do so. Once there were several of us Court Godmothers, but I am the only one left, and my health is so poor that I can do little for my God-children but give them moral teaching and wise counsel. However, such good offices as I can still render shall be entirely at your service."

"You are very kind," said Mrs. Wibberley-Stimpson, resenting the other's air of patronage, "but all my children are already provided with God-parents. As you tell me you are a Fairy," she continued, "I suppose I must accept your word for it—but it will take a great deal more than that to make me believe that we are in Fairyland."

"I thought," said the Fairy, "you already knew that the name of this country is Märchenland."

It should be said here once for all that the Wibberley-Stimpsons found no difficulty in understanding, or making themselves perfectly intelligible to any Märchenlanders, although they always had a curious feeling that they were conversing in a foreign language.

"Whatever the country is called," said Mrs. Wibberley-Stimpson aggressively, "I should like some explanation of that Baron Troitz's conduct in entrapping us into coming here. I was distinctly given to understand that I had been chosen to be the Queen at our local Pageant, and that we were being taken to talk over the arrangements with the Committee. Now he has gone off in the most ungentlemanly way, and left us stranded and helpless here!"

"You must have misunderstood the good Baron," said the Fairy Vogelflug; "and he is far too loyal to desert you. He has merely hastened on to Eswareinmal, the city whose walls and towers you see yonder, to prepare for your reception. As you probably know, he has devoted himself with the most untiring zeal to his mission of seeking you out and restoring you to your inheritance."

"He never said a word about that to me—not a word. If I am really entitled to any property in this country, I should be glad to know where it is situated, and what is its exact value."

"Then," said the Fairy, "I may inform you that you are entitled, as the daughter of your late Father—our long-lost and much-lamented Prince Chrysopras—to no less a possession than the Crown of Märchenland."

"You—you don't say so!" gasped Mrs. Wibberley-Stimpson. "The Crown of—Sidney, did you hear that."

"It's some mistake, my dear," he said. "Must be! ... My wife's father, Ma'am, though in some respects— a—a remarkable character, was never a Prince—at least that I've heard of."

"It doesn't at all follow, Sidney," said his wife in a nettled tone, "that anything you don't happen to have heard of is not a fact. There always was a mystery about poor dear Papa's origin. He was most reticent about it—even with me. And I know it was rumoured that Prinsley was not his real name. So it would not surprise me in the least if Mrs. Fogleplug turned out to be right, though I cannot say till she gives us further particulars."

"I will do so most willingly," said the Fairy. "But as it will take me some time to relate them, I should strongly advise you all to sit down."

They seated themselves round her in a semicircle, and presently she began:

"You must know," she said, "that our mighty and gracious Sovereign, the late King Smaragd, was twice wedded. By his first wife he had an only son, Prince Chrysopras, a gallant and goodly prince, beloved not only by his father, but by the whole nation. Well, after mourning his first wife for a longer period than is customary, King Smaragd took to himself another, who was much younger than himself, besides being marvellously beautiful."

"And of course she hated the poor Prince," said Ruby. "Stepmothers always do in the stories."

"I have not said she hated him," said the Court Godmother, who did not like her points to be anticipated. "On the contrary, she treated him with every mark of affection, and was constantly bestowing on him gifts of the costliest description. One day she presented him with a wondrous mechanical horse, fiercer and more mettlesome than even the steeds that are born in Märchenland."

"Motor-bike, what," suggested Clarence sapiently.

"A mechanical horse is what I said," repeated the Fairy, "resembling others in shape and beauty, but made of metal. Prince Chrysopras, being a skilful and fearless horseman"

"Indeed he was!" put in Mrs. Wibberley-Stimpson. "He used to ride regularly in the Row, almost to the last. On 'Joggles,' such a dear brown fat cob. He was one of what I believe was known as 'The Liver Brigade' ... a fact which for some reason I can't pretend to fathom seems to be causing you amusement, Miss Heritage."

Daphne, whose sense of humour was occasionally an inconvenience to her, had certainly found the notion of a Fairy Prince in the Liver Brigade a little too much for her gravity. However, she attributed her lapse to the name of the horse.

"It was the name they gave it at the Livery Stables," said Mrs. Wibberley-Stimpson. "And I really cannot see myself—but we are interrupting this good lady here."

"You are," said the Fairy. "I was about to say that Prince Chrysopras was greatly delighted by his Royal Stepmother's gift, and at once leapt on the back of the strange steed."

"What I call asking for trouble," commented Clarence.

"I know what happened!" Ruby struck in eagerly. "It flew right up into the air with him, and poor Grandpapa fell off."

"If he had, none of you would be here at the moment," said the Fairy. "Don't be in such a hurry, my child. He was much too good a rider to fall off. But the horse flew up and up with him till both could no longer be seen. The remains of the steed were found long afterwards on a mountain top. But nothing more was ever seen of the Prince, who was supposed to have perished in one of our lakes."

"Then he must have fallen off after all," insisted Ruby.

"No, no, Ruby," said her mother, with a sense that, where the credit of her family was concerned, nothing was too improbable for belief; "the horse flew with him to England, or somewhere in Europe— or else he couldn't have met your dear grandmother, whom none of you ever saw, for she died long before you were born. And I expect that, after he got off, the horse flew back again, and was just able to get to Märchenland before the machinery broke down. And dear Papa very naturally would not care for people to know that he had got there by such peculiar means, which accounts for my never having heard of it before."

"Exactly," said the Fairy Vogelflug; "but King Smaragd only knew that his son was lost to him, and when he discovered that the horse was enchanted, and that his Queen had bribed the Hereditary Grand Magician to construct it, his anger knew no bounds."

"Enough to annoy anybody," said Mr. Wibberley-Stimpson. "I should certainly—"

"He ordered," the Fairy went on, without appearing to feel any interest in what Mr. Stimpson would have done in similar circumstances, "both the Queen and the Grand Magician to be enclosed in a barrel, the inside of which had been set with sharp nails, and rolled down into the lake from the top of the mountain."

"I should say myself," remarked Mr. Stimpson, "that that was going a little too far. But he certainly had great provocation."

"He also commanded that all wizards and enchanters should renounce their practices for ever, and adopt some other calling, or be banished from the Country."

"There," said Mrs. Wibberley-Stimpson approvingly, "I think he was so right. I would never encourage any of those clairvoyant people myself. And did he marry a third wife at all?"

"Not if he was wise!" said Clarence.

"No, although it grieved him sorely that he had no heir to succeed him. But towards the end of his days, he dreamed repeatedly that his son was yet living. He beheld him in these visions a wanderer in some far-off land, earning his bread as a musician, for in Music he had rare skill."

"I fancy he must have given it up when he took to Finance," said Mrs. Wibberley-Stimpson, "though he kept his taste for it. I well remember his buying a beautiful orchestrion which used to be in the Picture Gallery."

"Well," pursued the Fairy, "in further dreams it was revealed to the King that his son was married to one, who, though not of his own race or rank, was both gently born and very fair to see."

"Pollentine was the maiden name of your Grandmother on my side, my dears," explained Mrs. Stimpson to her family. "She must have been good-looking as a girl, judging by a daguerrotype I had of her. Her father was a highly distinguished Auctioneer and Estate Agent in East Croydon, as I daresay was also revealed in the King's dream."

"Of that I can say nothing," replied the Court Godmother; "but I know that further visions showed him his son as a widower with an only daughter, and later still that he was no longer living. And so much was the King impressed that he caused a search to be made for this grand-daughter of his in every country that is known to us. Even when he lay on his death-bed he did not give up hope that she would be found, and so he left his Kingdom in charge of his trusted favourite Marshal Federhelm as Regent, with strict injunctions to continue seeking for the missing Queen."

"And how," inquired Mrs. Wibberley-Stimpson, "did the Marshal manage to find me out?"

"It was not he. He soon convinced himself that all further endeavours were useless. No, it is to the devotion of our worthy Court Chamberlain, the Baron Treuherz von Eisenbänden, that your discovery is owing. He had grieved so deeply to see Märchenland without a Sovereign that, after the example of 'Faithful John,' the founder of his family, he had placed iron hoops round his chest to keep his heart from breaking."

"We heard 'em go," said Clarence; "thought it was only his braces."

"At length," continued the Fairy, "the Baron went in secret to Xuriel, the Astrologer Royal, and induced him to consult the stars. Which Xuriel did, and by much study and intricate calculation he succeeded in ascertaining the exact spot in the other world where the Queen would be discovered, and even the means by which she might be recognised."

"Ah," said Mrs. Wibberley-Stimpson, "I shall begin to believe in Astronomy after this. But even now I don't quite understand how Baron Troitz got to 'Inglegarth.'"

"That was by my assistance. I placed my travelling car at his service, with the wise storks that fly straight to any place to which they are directed, even though they may never have heard of it before. Happily for Märchenland, Xuriel's calculations have proved correct, except that he did not foresee that the Baron would bring back two Sovereigns instead of one."

"What—is the Gov'nor going to be King?" inquired Clarence. "My hat!"

"That would be ridiculous, Clarence," said his mother, "when your Father hasn't a drop of Royal blood in his veins! He can't even rank as Prince Consort!"

"Not so, my dear, not so," corrected the Fairy, "by the custom of Märchenland, anyone who weds the Sovereign shares the throne, and your husband will be as truly the King of this Country as you will be its Queen."

"Oh, is that the rule?" said Mrs. Wibberley-Stimpson, not best pleased. "Well, Sidney, I trust you will show yourself equal to your position, that is all."

"I trust so, my love," he replied uneasily. "It—it's come on me at rather short notice. However!"

"If Daddy and Mums are King and Queen," asked Ruby, "will Edna and me be Princesses?"

"Undoubtedly you will," said the Court Godmother.

"Then Clarence will be a Prince. So you see, Miss Heritage, dear, you have met a Prince after all!"

"Shut up, Kiddie!" said the new Crown Prince in some confusion.

"And what will Miss Heritage be, Mummy?"

"Miss Heritage will be what she was before, my dear—your governess."

"But I shan't want one any more—we're in Fairyland now—and Fairy Princesses haven't got to do lessons. Oh, Mums, couldn't you make Miss Heritage a Princess too? Do!"

"Why not?" said the Fairy, glancing at Daphne, whose colour had risen slightly. "Anybody might very well take her to be one as it is."

"Miss Heritage," said Mrs. Wibberley-Stimpson, "has, I am sure, too much good sense to expect a title of any kind. She will continue to be my daughter's instructress, and I may possibly find a place for her as Mistress of the Robes or something; but it's much too early to say anything definite at—Really, Edna," she broke off suddenly, "how you can sit there calmly reading as if nothing had happened!"

"I was merely running through my lecture-notes again, Mother," said Edna. "If I am a Princess," she added, for the benefit of the Court Godmother, "that is no reason why I shouldn't go on cultivating my mind."

"Now you're a Princess, my dear," replied her mother, "it doesn't signify to anybody whether your mind is cultivated or not."

"It signifies a great deal to me, mother," said Edna, and resumed the study of her notes with an air of conscious merit.

"I must say one thing, Mrs. Fogleplug," Mrs. Wibberley-Stimpson proceeded; "it would have been more considerate if I had been given proper notice, and a reasonable time to prepare for such a complete change as this. I do feel that."

She did; it was a great deprivation to her to have lost the opportunity of mentioning casually to her Gablehurst friends—and Lady Harriet especially—that she would shortly be leaving them to occupy a throne.

"Precisely my own feeling," said Mr. Stimpson, thinking regretfully how the news would have made that confounded fellow Thistleton sit up, and of the sensation it might have produced in the train to the City. "It is, to say the least of it, unfortunate that I had no time to communicate with the other members of my firm."

"And there's Clarence, too!" said his fond mother. "His Company will be quite helpless without him!"

"They may be in a bit of a hole at first," he admitted, thankful now that he had said nothing about his resignation, or the readiness with which it had been accepted. "Still, no fellow is indispensable. What?"

The Fairy explained that haste had been unavoidable, as it might have been injurious to the storks if they had remained longer in a climate to which they were unaccustomed.

"But why send storks to fetch us at all?" demanded Mrs. Wibberley-Stimpson. "Why not some more modern conveyance?... There they are again with the car—coming back for us, I expect.... Yes, I can make out Baron Troitz and the trumpeters—and there seems to be a gentleman in armour with them."

"The Regent, Marshal Federhelm," said the Fairy. "He is coming to offer his congratulations."

"Is he?" cried Mrs. Wibberley-Stimpson, scrambling to her feet again in some dismay. "A Regent! I—I wish I knew the proper way of addressing him!"

The storks by this time had brought the car to ground, and were now standing about on one leg with folded wings and an air of detachment. The Marshal alighted and advanced slowly towards the Stimpsons while the heralds sounded their trumpets.

He made a formidable and warrior-like figure in his golden half-armour of a kind unknown to antiquarians, and great jack-boots of gilded leather. He was tall, and the towering mass of waving feathers that crowned his helmet made him look taller still. His vizor was raised, showing a swarthy, hook-nosed face, with quick, restless eyes like a lizard's, a fierce moustache, and a bristling beard that spread out in a stiff black fan.

"You had better speak to him, Sidney," whispered his wife, overcome by sudden panic; "I really can't."

"Er—" began Mr. Stimpson nervously, "I believe I have the pleasure of addressing the Regent. We—we're the new King and Queen, you know, and these are the other members of the family."

The Marshal seemed a little taken aback at first, but he promptly recovered himself, and bending so low that his feathers brushed Mrs. Wibberley-Stimpson's nose, he placed in her hand a small velvet-covered baton studded with gold stars.

"Oh, thank you very much, I'm sure," she said. "It's quite charming. Has it got an address or anything inside it?"

"The symbol of my authority, your Majesty," he said, with soldierly curtness. "I have long desired to surrender it to hands more worthy to govern than mine."

"Very handsome of you to say so," replied Mr. Stimpson; "but I daresay you aren't altogether sorry to get out of it, eh?"

"It is too lofty a position, Sire, for a rough, simple warrior like myself," he said. "Nothing but a sense of duty to my country would have made me accept the Regency at all."

"I am sure," said Mrs. Wibberley-Stimpson, "we shall find you have carried on the Kingdom for us as satisfactorily as possible."

"The people appeared to think so, your Majesty. But I am forgetting the chief purpose I am here for. I have the honour to announce that the procession will shortly be on its way to escort your Majesties to your Coronation, which is to take place this morning in the great church of Eswareinmal."

"Coronation!" Mrs. Wibberley-Stimpson almost screamed. "Before we have so much as had our breakfast! And in these things we are wearing now! I never heard of anything so preposterous!"

"I don't care much myself," said Mr. Stimpson, "about being crowned on an empty—without having had something to eat—if it's only an egg."

"If they're going to crown the Guv'nor in a dinner-jacket and white tie," Clarence muttered to Edna, "we shall never hear the last of it, that's all!"

"There is nothing to make a fuss about, my dear," said the Court Godmother to Mrs. Wibberley-Stimpson, as though she were addressing a froward child; "look behind you, and you will see that everything you may require is already provided."

They looked and saw two velvet Marquees, one striped in broad bands of apple-green and mazarine blue, the other in pale rose and cream, which a party of attendants had just finished putting up. "In those pavilions," continued the Fairy, "you will find not only food prepared for you, but robes such as are fitting for a Coronation. You will have plenty of time both to eat and change your dress before the procession can possibly arrive."

"She's not likely to have got our measurements right," grumbled Mrs. Wibberley-Stimpson to her eldest daughter, as they moved towards the rose-and-cream Pavilion. "I should have much preferred to be fitted by a Court dressmaker. Such a mistake to rush things like this! I rather like that Marshal, Edna; there's something very gentlemanly and straightforward about him, though I can't see why he shouldn't wear a proper uniform instead of that absurd armour."

"Shan't be sorry to get some breakfast, my boy," Mr. Stimpson remarked, as he and Clarence were making for the other marquee; "I feel a bit peckish after being so long in the night air."

"I should like a tub first, Guv'nor."

"I'm afraid," said Mr. Stimpson, "that's expecting too much in these parts."

However, on entering, they discovered, in addition to the delicacies and gorgeous costumes laid out for them, two great crystal baths filled with steaming water which exhaled a subtle but delicious perfume.

"Doing us proud, eh, Guv'nor?" was Clarence's comment on the general luxuriousness; and his father admitted that "everything seemed to have been done regardless of expense."

While the male and female members of the Royal Party were enjoying the privacy of their respective tents, the Marshal outside was expressing his sentiments to the Court Chamberlain with much vigour and freedom.

"Well, Baron," he began, "this is a great service you have done Märchenland, and I hope you are feeling proud of yourself!"

"Oh, as for that, Marshal," modestly replied the ingenuous Baron, "I have done no more than my duty."

"The devil take you and your duty," growled the Marshal. "Why, in the name of all the fiends, couldn't you have left things as they were?"

"But, Marshal," the Baron protested, "when our learned Astrologer Royal discovered the whereabouts of our lawful Queen, you were loudest in approval of my expedition!"

"How could I oppose, after you had been gabbling and cackling about it to the whole Court, and it had even reached the ears of the people? Besides, I was given to understand that this daughter of Chrysopras's was a mere girl. If she had been—But what have you brought us?—a middle-aged matron with a husband and family!"

"I own it was not what I had expected," said the Baron; "but since it was so, what could I do but bring them all?"

"Do? Left them where they were, of course—come back and said that that little fool of a Xuriel had made a miscalculation, as he generally does!"

"I should have been a traitor had I thus denied my Queen. For, as you have seen, she bears on her breast the very jewel of her father the Prince, even as the stars foretold."

"Undoubtedly she is his daughter," the Marshal admitted reluctantly. It never occurred to him for a moment—nor would it occur to any of his countrymen—that the pendant was anything but absolutely conclusive proof of Mrs. Wibberley-Stimpson's right to the throne. Märchenland notions of what constitutes legal evidence have always been and remain elementary.

"But it's pretty plain," he went on, "that the young fool must have made a most unworthy marriage to have begotten one so utterly lacking in all queenliness and dignity."

"She will soon acquire both," the Court Chamberlain affirmed stoutly, "as she becomes more accustomed to her position."

"She may," declared the Marshal, "when a frog grows feathers. And this consort of hers! Is he a fit Monarch for Märchenland? Even you, Baron, can hardly say that for him! I may not have been beloved as Regent, but at least I have made my authority respected. But what do such a couple as this know about ruling a country? They'll make a hopeless hash of it!"

"Without guidance, perhaps," the Baron admitted; "but they will have the inestimable advantage, Marshal, of our experience and advice."

"Ha!" said the Marshal. "So they will—so they will! I was forgetting that!"

"No doubt they will submit to our guidance," went on the Baron, "and thus we shall be able to save them from any dangerous indiscretions."

"Just so," agreed the Marshal, with the flicker of a smile.

The Court Chamberlain, at all events, spoke in all sincerity. His hereditary instinct alone would have been enough to ensure his loyalty to his new Sovereigns, whatever he might think of them in private.

And they were his own "finds," which gave them an added value in his estimation, as will easily be understood by any collector of curiosities.

CHAPTER IV

CROWNED HEADS

"'Pon my word, my love," Mr. Stimpson exclaimed, as his wife came out of her pavilion in her Coronation Robes and chain, attended by the Court Godmother, "I should hardly have known you! You look majestic!—abso-lute-ly majestic!"

"I wish I could say the same of you, Sidney," she replied; "but, as I have told you more than once, legs like yours never ought to be seen except in trousers.... Considering my own and my daughter's robes are ready-made, Mrs. Fogleplug, they might be worse. As for Miss Heritage's—well, I should have thought myself that something simpler would have been more appropriate."

Daphne was naturally much less sumptuously dressed than the Members of the Royal family, but still, in her quaint double-peaked head-dress, fantastically slashed bodice, and long hanging sleeves, with her bright hair, too, waving loosely over her temples, its rich masses confined at the back by a network of pearls, she was dainty and bewitching enough to attract more than her due share of attention—Clarence's she attracted at once, while he was sustained by an agreeable conviction that his be-jewelled doublet, silken hose, white plumed velvet hat, and azure mantle set off his figure to unusual advantage.

"Tophole, Miss Heritage!" he said, strolling up with graceful languor. "I'm not joking—you really are, you know! Wish my kit suited me half as well! Can't help feeling a most awful ass in it, what?"

"Really?" she said carelessly. "How unpleasant for you! But perhaps if you left off thinking about it—!"

"Oh, I don't say it's so bad as all that!"

"I didn't suppose it was, quite."

Now this was not by any means the sort of deferential tribute he had counted upon, and he was a little ruffled by her failure to respond.

"Didn't you," he replied distantly, if somewhat lamely. "You'll excuse me mentioning it, Miss Heritage, as it's only in your own interests, but I believe it's considered the proper thing when you're addressed by—by Royalty, don't you know, to throw in a 'Your Royal Highness' occasionally. Of course, Court Etiquette and that may be all tosh, but I didn't make it, and all I mean to say is—it won't do to let it slide."

"Your Royal Highness will not have to rebuke me a second time," said Daphne, sinking to the ground in a curtsey which it is to be feared was wilfully exaggerated. "I'm afraid, sir," she added, as the two little creases in her cheeks made themselves visible, "that wasn't as low as it ought to have been, but your Royal Highness must make allowances for my want of experience."

"Oh, you'll soon get into it," he said, "with practice."

"And I shall have plenty of that, your Royal Highness."

Was she trying to pull his leg? he thought, as he moved away, and decided that she was most unlikely to venture on such presumption. No, it had been necessary to remind her of the deference due to him, and she would not forget the lesson in future. Perhaps he might unbend occasionally in private, but, on second thoughts, that would be more dangerous than ever now.

Ruby had seized Daphne and was embracing her in a burst of violent affection. "Oh, Miss Heritage, darling," she cried, "you do look such a duck in that dress—doesn't she, Mummy?"

"I see no resemblance, my dear," said her mother coldly, "between Miss Heritage and any description of poultry. And, as the procession will be here in another minute, you had better take your place quietly by me.... Really, Ruby," she added in an undertone, as the child obeyed, "you must remember you're a Princess now. It isn't at all proper for you to be seen pawing your governess about in public."

"I wasn't pawing her about, Mums!" protested Ruby; "only hugging her. And if I mayn't do that, I don't want to be a Princess at all!"

By this time the procession had arrived. It was headed by a band of knights in resplendent but rather extravagant armour, carrying lances with streaming pennons. After them rode the Courtiers on gaily caparisoned steeds, followed by a bevy of Maids of Honour on cream-coloured palfreys. A company of soldiers came next, some of whom bore heavy matchlocks of an ancient period, and the rest pikes and halberds. However, they marched with as proud and confident a step as though their weapons were of the very latest pattern—which very likely they thought they were. Following them was a State Coach, a huge, cumbrous vehicle with unglazed windows; it seemed to be of pure gold, and was drawn by sixteen milk-white horses in blue trappings.

After the procession had halted, the Court Chamberlain formally presented the members of the Royal Household, whose mere titles sounded impressively on the ear of their new Mistress. There were Prince Tapfer von Schneiderleinheimer and Prince Hansmeinigel; Baron Müllerbürschen, Baron von Bohnenranken, and Count von Daumerlingstamm; Princess Rapunzelhauser, Princess Goldernenfingerleinigen, and Princess Flachsspinnenlosburg; Baroness Belohnte von Haulemännerschen, Baroness Kluge Bauerngrosstochterheimer, and Countess Gänsehirten am Brunnen, and many others scarcely less distinguished. Never before had Mrs. Wibberley-Stimpson been in such aristocratic company, and for the moment she entirely forgot how immeasurably she was now their social superior. She had held her own triumphantly with Lady Harriet, but that was different. There was only one of her—and that one a quite ordinary and insignificant personality compared with these imposingly splendid lords and ladies-in-waiting.

Mrs. Stimpson intended to be graciously cordial, but somehow her manner was dangerously near being obsequious. "Most honoured, I'm sure, Prince!" she found herself repeating, as she ducked instinctively. "So very kind of you to come, Baron!... It's more than delightful to meet you, dear Princess—I didn't quite catch your name!... Such a privilege to make your acquaintance, Countess!"

She hoped they would take this as condescension on her part, and they were undeniably surprised by their Sovereign's excessive affability.

"Well," said Mr. Stimpson, as these amenities became exhausted and he perceived that no one was taking any notice of him, "what about making a start, hey, Mr. Marshal?"

"If your Majesties and the Princess will deign to enter the coach, we can set forth at once," was the reply.

"Get in, children, get in!" cried Mrs. Wibberley-Stimpson. "You and Ruby, Edna, must sit with your backs to the horses, and there will be plenty of room for Clarence between you."

"With all respect, Sir," said the Marshal, as Clarence was preparing to get in. "It is the custom on such an occasion as this for the Crown Prince to ride on the right of the Coach. I have arranged that a horse shall be at your Royal Highness's service."

"Thanks awfully," said Clarence, as he glanced at a spirited chestnut mare which two squires were endeavouring with some difficulty to soothe, "but—er—I think I'd rather drive." He was reflecting, as he took his seat in the coach, that he would really have to take a few riding lessons shortly, in private.

"Isn't Miss Heritage coming with us, Mummy?" called Ruby from the window.

"In the State Coach, my dear! Of course not!"

"But why not, Mater?" protested Clarence. "There's lots of room."

"Because I could not think of allowing it, Clarence. Perhaps Mrs. Fogleplug will be kind enough to give her a lift in—in her own conveyance."

"Unfortunately," replied the Court Godmother, "my car will not hold more than one person."

"Well, Miss Heritage must find her way to the Palace, then! There's no necessity for her to be present at the Coronation."

"Surely, my dear," said the Fairy, "you would not deprive her of such a privilege! I will have another saddle placed on that mare so that this fair maid of yours may ride with your other ladies in waiting."

"Of course, Mrs. Fogleplug, if you're bent on Miss Heritage making a public exhibition of herself," said Mrs. Wibberley-Stimpson, "I have nothing to say. I don't suppose she has ever been on a horse in her life!"

"Oh, but I have, Ma'am!" Daphne pleaded eagerly. "I've ridden ever since I was a child. And I'd love to ride that mare, if I may!"

"Oh, very well, Miss Heritage, ve-ry well. But remember, if you break your neck, I shall not accept any responsibility," which Daphne took as a permission. As soon as Mr. and Mrs. Wibberley-Stimpson had taken their seats, the sixteen milk-white horses began to pull and strain till eventually the great coach was on the way.

"Mummy," cried Ruby a little later, "I can see Miss Heritage! She's riding close behind. And oh, she does look so sweet on horseback!"

"Put your head in,—do, child!" said her mother sharply. "Whatever will the people think if they see a Princess hanging half out of the window like that!"

Ruby sat down rather sullenly. Clarence would have liked to put his own head out if it had been consistent with his dignity as a Prince. As it was, he could only hope that Daphne would come to no harm. "Really!" continued Mrs. Wibberley-Stimpson, "what with one's governess riding behind one's coach, and those two ridiculous bird-cars probably flapping overhead, this is quite unlike any Coronation Procession I ever heard of!"

"More like a bally Circus," remarked Clarence. "Only wants a couple of clowns with bladders on horseback and a performing elephant."

"I consider," said his mother, "that a State procession should have more solemnity about it.... How horribly this coach jolts! It can't have any springs!... There you are again, Edna, buried in that note-book! you might show a little interest in what is going on!"

"I'm sorry, mother, but it all seems to mean so little to me."

"Then all I can say is—good gracious, what a lurch! I quite thought we were over!—all I can say is that it's unnatural to be so abstracted as you are. We're getting close to Eswar—whatever they call it. If you look round you will see the walls and towers."

Edna adapted her pince-nez and turned perfunctorily for a moment. "Quite quaint!" she said, and resumed her reading.

"Picturesque, I should call it," corrected her mother. "Sidney, doesn't it put you in mind of dear lovely Lucerne?"

"Very much so, my love," he replied, "or—er—Venice" (neither of which cities, as a matter of fact, did Eswareinmal resemble in the least). "Hullo! what are we stopping for now, eh?"

It seemed they had arrived at the principal gates of the Capital, where the Burgomaster and other civic dignitaries were assembled to welcome and to do them homage, which they did with every sign of respect and loyalty. As Mrs. Wibberley-Stimpson felt unequal to the efforts of responding, that duty devolved on her husband, who presented himself at the window of the coach, and made what the reporters, had any been present, would no doubt have described as "a few gracious and appropriate remarks."

"You needn't have said that about 'doing our best to give satisfaction,' Sidney!" complained his wife after the coach had thundered over the drawbridge, and was lumbering under the massive archway into a narrow and crowded street, "for all the world as if we had been a butler and housekeeper applying for a situation!"

"It was a little unfortunate, perhaps, my dear," he admitted; "but it is so difficult to know what to say when one has to speak impromptu."

"It ought to be easy enough to know what not to say," she retorted. "Dear me, what hosts of people!" she went on, as her irritation merged into complacency. "And how pleased they all seem to see us! But no doubt, after a bachelor Regent, a whole Royal family—I love to see their happy smiling faces!"

"Grinning mugs would be nearer the mark, Mater," said Clarence; "never saw such a chuckle-headed lot of bumpkins in my life!"

"I will thank you to remember, Clarence," she replied, "that they are my loyal subjects, and will be yours at some time to come."

"I can wait for 'em," he said; "and if they're so jolly loyal, why ain't they cheering more?"

Slowly the golden coach progressed through winding streets of gabled or step-roofed houses with toppling overhanging stories, then along one side of a great square, packed with people in costume, the women recalling to Mrs. Stimpson's mind, quite inappropriately, the waitresses at the Rigi Kulm hotel on a Sunday. Then, through more narrow streets, to a smaller square, where it stopped at some steps leading to the huge West portal of a magnificent buttressed Church.

"All change here—for the Coronation!" said Clarence. "I'd better nip out first, eh, Mater?"

"Your father and I get out first, naturally, Clarence," said Mrs. Wibberley-Stimpson, and descended majestically, Mr. Stimpson following with somewhat less effect owing to an attack of cramp in his left leg. Four small pages stepped forward in pairs to carry Mr. and Mrs. Stimpson's trains, which they found a distinct convenience, and, hand in hand, they passed through the great, elaborately niched and statued doorway into the nave. The interior was thronged by all the notables of Märchenland, including the venerable President of the Council and his Councillors. Above, the light struck in shafts through the painted windows of the clerestory, tinging the haze of incense fumes with faint colours. On the high altar twinkled innumerable tapers. "Roman! as I suspected!" whispered Mrs. Wibberley-Stimpson on seeing them, and sniffing the scented atmosphere. (She had attended St. John's at Gablehurst, because the vicar, although Evangelical, was well-known to be of good family.) Under a crimson canopy in the choir were two golden chairs which they understood they were expected to sit upon, and occupied accordingly. A mitred and coped ecclesiastic, who appeared to be some kind of Bishop, then shepherded them benevolently through a series of mystic rites that, besides being hopelessly unintelligible, seemed unreasonably protracted. However, they reached the climax at last, and amidst the tumultuous acclamations of the spectators the previously anointed heads of King Sidney and Queen Selina, as they must henceforth be described, received their respective crowns.

"Ha, well," remarked King Sidney, when he and the rest of the Royal family were once more in the coach, and on their way towards the palace that was to be their future home, "we got through it most successfully on the whole. Perhaps the Bishop was a little too lavish with the anointing part of the ceremony. Still, taken altogether, it was—ah—a very solemnising affair."

"It would have been more so, Sidney," said the Queen, "if you hadn't kept on dropping your sceptre and tripping over your train. I don't wonder the Bishop got flustered. But I do wish we could have had it properly done by the dear Archbishop of Canterbury!"

"Bit out of his diocese, Märchenland, what?" said the Crown Prince.

"I'm aware of that, Clarence; and, of course, we're legally crowned, whoever did it.... Sidney, it's only just struck me, but I'm sure we ought to be bowing. Bow, children, all of you—take the time from me. Sidney, why aren't you bowing?"

"I can't, my love. It's difficult enough to keep my crown on as it is!"

"You can hold it on with one hand, can't you? You simply must bow if you don't want to be unpopular! So must you, children. Keep on with it!"

"Give us a rest, Mater," said Prince Clarence, after they had been nodding like Chinese mandarins for some minutes. "My neck's beginning to wilt already!"

Queen Selina herself was not sorry to stop. "It's certainly very fatiguing at first," she admitted; "we must practise it together in private.... Was that old Mrs. Fogleplug's dove-chariot that passed us just now? I'm afraid I shall have to put her in her place. She's rather inclined to forget herself—not only addressed me as 'my dear,' but actually attempted to kiss me after the Coronation!"

"So she did me!" said the Princess Royal, "but I hope I showed that I thought she was taking a liberty."

"She's a very worthy, well-meaning old creature, no doubt," remarked the Queen; "still, a Fairy Godmother in these days is really rather—I shall have to get her to retire—on a pension."

"She'll stick on," said Prince Clarence, "you see if she don't. Means to boss the whole show."

"I shall soon let her see that I intend to be mistress in my own Kingdom," said the Queen. "I could wish, I must say, that it was just a little more up to date! Everything so dreadfully behind the times! I haven't seen a shop yet with a plate-glass front, and not a single pillar-box!"

"Poor sort of place for Suffragettes, what?" observed Clarence.

"Frivolity apart, Clarence," remarked the Queen, "I can see already that there is much to be done here before the country can be called really civilised. We must set ourselves to raise the standard by introducing modern ideas—enlighten people's minds, and all the rest of it. And you must do your share, Sidney, as I shall do mine."

"Certainly," said the King; "I'm agreeable. All for progress myself. Always have been.... I fancy that must be our Palace up there. A truly palatial residence—replete, I've no doubt, with every convenience we can require."

The State Coach, after making a leisurely circuit of the two sides of the principal square, was now beginning the ascent of the steep zigzag road to the Palace, which stood on the terraced height of the plateau that commanded the city. The party in the coach caught glimpses of its massive but ornate towers with fantastic spires and turrets, and its great arched and columned wings of rose-tinted marble. As it was rather larger than Windsor Castle, King Sidney's commendation was fairly justified.

But Queen Selina's mind was occupied in computing the probable number of rooms, and the maids that would be required to "do" them, while she wondered aloud whether they could possibly afford to keep such a place up.

"Depend upon it, my dear," said the King, "the—ah—State will provide an ample allowance for all our expenses. I must go into that as soon as an opportunity occurs, and find out exactly what our income will be."

Little more was said after this, as the great coach creaked and groaned slowly up the winding road, and then rolled through the golden gates into the courtyard of the Palace.

On the steps of the chief entrance were Marshal Federhelm, Baron von Eisenbänden, and the Court Godmother, who, with the rest of the Royal household, had hastened on ahead to receive them. The Marshal ushered them into the Hall of Entrance, which was immense and cool. There they found the ladies and gentlemen-in-waiting drawn up in curtseying and bowing ranks. The colours of their gay costumes would have been dazzling, had they not been somewhat toned down by the subdued light from the windows, which were paned with transparent agate set in tracery of a flamboyant type. At the back rose a colossal staircase of jasper. On either side were lofty doors leading to vestibules, corridors, and reception halls.

Judged by Gablehurst standards, the general effect of the interior was hardly 'home-y' or cosy enough to be perfectly satisfactory, as Queen Selina seemed to feel, for the only comment she made was: "No china punch-bowl for visiting-cards, I see!"

"I say," the Crown Prince inquired of the Marshal, "who's the small sportsman in the extinguisher hat?" he referred to an unassuming little man with long, lint-coloured hair and pale, prominent eyes, whose shiftiness was only partly concealed by large horn spectacles. He wore black and crimson robes embroidered in gold with Zodiacal signs. "Looks like the Editor of Old Moore's Almanack."

"That, Sir," replied the Marshal, "is the learned Xuriel, our Astrologer Royal. Will your Majesties permit me to present him?" And, the Royal assent being given, he went across to fetch the sage.

"Xuriel, my friend," he said in his ear, with a slightly ironical intonation, "the august Sovereigns who owe their discovery to your learning and research are naturally anxious to express their acknowledgements. So come along and be presented, and perhaps you will produce a better impression if you can manage to look a little less like a hare with the ear-ache."

It was not, however, the prospect of being presented to Royalty that was disturbing the Astrologer Royal, but an unpleasant suspicion that the ex-Regent was, for some reason or other, a little annoyed with him.

"Your Majesties will be interested to hear," explained the Marshal, after making the presentation, "that Master Xuriel was at one time noted for his skill as a magician."

"My studies in Magic were never carried very far, your Majesties," protested the Astrologer, wriggling uncomfortably. "I—I did very little at it. And, even before it was decreed that all enchanters and sorcerers should either leave the Kingdom or take up some other profession, I had discovered that astrology was my true vocation."

"And you were right," said the Marshal heartily, "as results have shown. And doubtless there is no truth in the rumour that you still retain some proficiency in the Black Art."

"Absolutely none, your Majesties!" the Astrologer Royal declared. "What small skill I ever possessed, I have already forgotten; all my magic spells have long since been discarded."

"So I should hope," said Queen Selina severely. "Mr. Wibber—I mean, his Majesty and I are, of course, no believers in Magic, but we are determined not to allow any superstitions practices here in future—are we not, Sidney?"

"Certainly, my dear, certainly. Most undesirable. Of course, we don't object to ordinary conjuring—anything harmless of that sort. But take my advice, Sir, and stick to Astrology for the future—much more gentlemanly pursuit!"

The Astrologer Royal promised to observe this recommendation, and just then the Court Chamberlain announced that a meal had been prepared for the Royal Family in the King's Parlour, to which he offered to conduct them at once. And, as the lengthy business of the Coronation had given them all excellent appetites, they readily welcomed the proposal.

Princess Ruby, catching sight of Daphne in one of the groups, had begged that she might be included, which the Queen reluctantly granted as an exceptional indulgence.

Daphne would gladly have excused herself had that been possible; she was becoming painfully conscious of finding Mrs. Wibberley-Stimpson as a Queen irresistibly ludicrous. Once already that morning she had only just escaped detection, and she was horribly afraid now that something might happen which would lead her to betray herself by unseemly laughter. She could only pray inwardly that it would not, as she followed with Ruby to the King's Parlour.

This was a lofty hall with windows opening on to the terrace; the walls were composed of great slabs of malachite, and twisted columns of the same supported a ceiling of elaborately carved pink jade. At one end was a dais, where a table was spread with what King Sidney referred to somewhat disappointedly as "a cold snack," though he did it ample justice nevertheless.

The Marshal sat on his right hand; at his back stood the Court Chamberlain, while chubby-faced little pages served cakes of bread on bended knee, and filled the golden goblets with Märchenland's choicest wines, which the King considered "a trifle on the sour side." The Royal Household looked on from a distance—to the exquisite discomfort of the Queen.

"I really can't enjoy my food, Sidney," she complained in an undertone, "with every mouthful I take watched by all those members of the nobility!"

Suddenly she coloured with annoyance as she found she was being addressed in a gruff, strangled voice from a quarter it was difficult at first to locate. "Mr. Troitz," she demanded, "who is that ill-mannered person who seems to be trying to talk to Me with his mouth full?"

"The voice, your Majesty," he replied in the most matter-of-fact tone, "appears to proceed from the boar's head."

"How dare you try to impose on me by such a story? It's that wretched little astrologer man. Ventriloquism and Conjuring always go together, and I'll be bound he's underneath the table now!...

Well," she said, after she had satisfied herself by looking, "if he's not there, he's somewhere in the room!"

The Court Chamberlain assured her that the Astrologer Royal was not only absent, but incapable of such a liberty; it really was the boar's head that had spoken, as animals in Märchenland would on rare occasions—even after suffering decapitation.

"There was Falada, Mummy," cried Ruby eagerly. "Don't you remember? The horse that talked poetry after its head had been cut off and nailed over the arch! Miss Heritage can tell you all about it."

But Miss Heritage could not—she was far too deeply engaged in wrestling with an inward demon of unholy mirth that threatened at any moment to gain the mastery.

The head began again. But whatever felicitations, predictions, or warning it was striving to utter were rendered practically inarticulate by a large lemon that had been unfeelingly inserted between its jaws.

"Have the boar's head removed at once, Mr. Troitz," ordered Queen Selina. "I cannot and will not have it interrupting the conversation like this. It couldn't happen at all in any civilised country. Why, we shall have the cold tongue beginning next, I suppose!..."

It was here that poor Daphne's demon got the upper hand.

"You seem slightly hysterical, Miss Heritage," remarked the Queen. "Horse-exercise evidently has a very bad effect on your nerves, and I must forbid you to ride in future."

Thus was Daphne punished for her breach of etiquette. But Queen Selina had no suspicion, even then, of its real extent. She was incapable of conceiving that she could possibly seem ridiculous to one so infinitely her inferior.

CHAPTER V

DIGNITY UNDER DIFFICULTIES

The luncheon, after the removal of the too loquacious boar's head, proceeded, to Daphne's intense relief, without any further incident, and at its conclusion Queen Selina suggested a move to the terrace. One side of it faced the City far below; another the slope of the road leading immediately to the Courtyard, while from the third side steps descended by lower terraces to the Palace Gardens, which were apparently boundless. Beyond them, however, was a neglected region of groves and thickets, a sort of Wilderness, which stretched from the Garden boundaries to the edge of a plateau below which lay a wild valley, with a chain of wilder peaks and crags forming the horizon. But none of the Court had ever cared to explore the Wilderness, if they were even aware of its existence, so no more need be said of it at present.

The Royal Family leaned upon the parapet of the terrace, whence they had a bird's-eye view of the big square immediately below, and the picturesquely irregular buildings, above whose gabled red roofs grim watch-towers and quaint spires or cupolas rose here and there. Down in the square swarms of tiny figures were clustering round the public fountains, which spouted jets that, as they flashed in the afternoon sun, were seen to be of a purple hue.

"Must be wine," remarked the Crown Prince. "If it's the same tap we had at lunch, the poor devils have my sympathy!"

"I think, Sidney," said the Queen, "that we ought all to go for a drive presently—just round the principal streets. I'm sure the—a—populace would appreciate it."

"If you think it's expected of us, my love," he said. "Otherwise—well, I should have rather liked to see a little more of the Palace; we don't even know where our own bedrooms are to be yet."

"The Guv'nor's right there, Mater!" said Prince Clarence. "We'd better get settled down before we do anything else."

"Perhaps we had," Queen Selina allowed. "I'll get that good old Mrs. Fogleplug to take us round the house." And after sending for the Court Godmother, she started, accompanied by the family and several of her ladies-in-waiting, on a tour of inspection.

Possibly the suites of halls, each more magnificent than the last, the endless galleries and corridors, the walls decorated with sumptuous but bizarre hangings, the floors inlaid with marble and precious stones which were probably priceless and certainly slippery—possibly all these contributed towards the upsetting of Queen Selina's equanimity, but her manner was deplorably lacking in dignity and repose. She treated her ladies, for instance, with a politeness that came nearer subservience than ever. It was: "Pray go first, dear Princess Rapunzelhauser! After you, Baroness!... Please, Countess, I really couldn't think of preceding you!" at every doorway, till Daphne, as she noted the elevated eyebrows and covert smiles of the others, felt too much shame for her Sovereign for any thought of amusement.

However, the Queen showed more self-assertion in her treatment of the Court Godmother, which was characterised by some hauteur.

"And now, I suppose, Mrs. Fogleplug, we have seen all the Reception Rooms. We shall probably have to entertain on rather a large scale, but they appear to be fairly suitable. What I have not yet seen is a room where I could receive ordinary callers. I have always made a practice since I was first married of being 'at Home' on the first and third Fridays, and though circumstances have altered, I intend to continue it."

The Fairy, though she was rather at a loss to understand either the reason or the necessity for this, said that there was a chamber called "The Queen's Bower" which would probably meet Her Majesty's requirements, and led the way to it accordingly.

It was about sixty feet square, with a high vaulted roof of lapis-lazuli set with large diamond stars; the walls were decorated with huge frescoes representing legends, many of which Princess Ruby recognised as familiar.

"This will do, Mrs. Fogleplug," pronounced the Queen. "At least it can be made to do, with a little re-arrangement. As it is, there are none of the ordinary refinements, such as art-cushions, cake-and-bread-and-butter stand, occasional tables, and little silver knick-knacks, which a lady's boudoir of any pretensions to elegance should have. Just the trifles that express the owner, and—er—constitute Home. I must have all these provided before I can use this as a sanctum. I should certainly have expected a Palace like this to be furnished with more regard to comfort!"

"I should have expected a billiard-room or two," said Prince Clarence; "but these Courtier chaps tell me they don't even know what billiards are! Pretty sort of Palace this!"

"I think it's a perfectly lovely Palace!" Princess Ruby declared. "It hasn't got a single piano in it anywhere! I know, because I've asked."

"I'm sorry to hear it, my dear," said her Mother, "because I particularly wished Miss Heritage to get you on with your music; and, if that is impossible, I shall have to consider whether I can keep her at all."

"Oh, Mummy, you won't send her away? When you know I've never been good with anybody before, and never shall be, either!"

Queen Selina was quite alive to the advantages of retaining Daphne's services.

"Well, Ruby," she said, "I shall allow Miss Heritage to stay on, as your companion" (she had already seen her way to proposing a reduction of salary), "and she can make herself generally useful to me as well."

Ruby went dancing back to Daphne. "You're not to be my governess any more, Miss Heritage, dear," she announced, "because I shan't require one now. But I've got Mummy to let you stay on as companion. Aren't you glad?"

Daphne answered that she was—and she would certainly have been sorry to leave Märchenland quite so soon.

"And now tell me, Mr. Chamberlain—Baron Troitz, I mean," the Queen was saying. "What time do you dine here?"

"Whenever your Majesties please," was the reply.

"All the same to us," said the King affably. "No wish to put you out at all."

"Then with your permission, Sire, the Banquet will be served an hour hence in the Banqueting Hall."

"A banquet!" cried the Queen. "I would rather we dined quietly, without any fuss, on our first night here."

"It is the night of your Majesties' Coronation," the Court Chamberlain reminded her. "The Court would be deeply disappointed if so auspicious an event were not celebrated in a befitting manner."

"Oh," said the Queen. "Then it will be full dress, I suppose—with crowns?"

"I hope—not crowns," put in King Sidney, who had taken the earliest opportunity of leaving his own in a corner. "A crown is such an uncomfortable thing to eat in. At least mine is."

The Court Chamberlain gave it as his decision that crowns should certainly be worn—at least through the earlier courses of the meal.

"All you've got to do, Guv'nor," said Clarence, "is to keep yours from splashing into the soup. A bit of elastic round your chin would do that all right."

"And I presume," said the Queen, "we shall wear these robes we have on?... Oh, we shall find a change of costume upstairs? Then, as there is not too much time for dressing, I should like to see my room at once, Mrs. Fogleplug."

"Sidney," she panted a little later as, escorted by the Marshal and Baron, and followed by the Court Godmother and the ladies and lords-in-waiting, they were making the ascent of the grand staircase, "one of the first things we must do here is to put in a lift. I really can't be expected to climb all these stairs several times a day!"

"They do take it out of one, my dear," he admitted. "And a lift would certainly be a great improvement."

At the head of the staircase was a long tapestry-hung gallery in which were the doors opening into the suites of rooms prepared for Royalty.

Queen Selina, on reaching hers, could not bring herself to allow her ladies of the Bedchamber to assist at her toilet. "So very kind of you, Princess, and you, too, my dear Baroness," she protested, "but I couldn't think of troubling you—I couldn't indeed! I should feel quite ashamed to let you! I can manage perfectly well by myself—that is, Miss Heritage will come in after she has attended to Princess Ruby, and do all I require, and then she can go on and help you, Edna."

"Thank you, Mother," said Edna, "but I should prefer having some one who is more accustomed to dressing hair."

After putting Ruby into a robe of golden tissue and silken stockings and satin shoes, which, being quite as splendid as those she had just laid aside, afforded the child intense satisfaction, Daphne went to Queen Selina's Tiring Chamber—a spacious apartment with hangings of strange colours embroidered with Royal emblems. It was separated by a curtained arch, through which a glimpse could be caught of the Royal Bedchamber, with the colossal and gorgeously canopied State bed.

She found the Queen still in an early stage of her toilette and in a highly fractious state of mind.

"I expected you to be here before this, Miss Heritage," she said. "I've been waiting all this time for you to fasten me up the back, which I couldn't possibly ask any of my Court ladies to do.... I'm sure I don't know what goes on next!... Oh, do you think the—er—stomacher before the ruff?... Very well.... It's impossible to judge the effect in such a wretched light" (the chamber, it should be said, was illuminated by a number of perfumed flambeaux stuck in elaborately wrought silver sconces). "Even at 'Inglegarth' I had a pair of electric lights over my dressing-table! And how on earth any Queen can be expected to dress at a shabby tarnished old cheval-glass like this is more than I can conceive!"

Upon which a thin but silvery voice immediately responded:

"As dimly can I understand How you are Queen of Märchenland!"

"Upon my word, Miss Heritage!" exclaimed Queen Selina, with an angry flush on her oatmeal-hued cheeks, "I am surprised at such impertinence—from you!"

"It—it wasn't me, Ma'am," said Daphne, with an heroic effort to keep her countenance.

"As it was certainly not myself, and you are the only other person in the room, Miss Heritage, your denial is impudent as well as useless!"

Daphne could only point speechlessly to the mirror.

"Really, Miss Heritage! This goes beyond all—what next!"

"Reflected here there should have been A younger and far fairer Queen."

continued the voice in a doggerel as devoid of polish as the mirror itself.

"It does appear to come from—but whoever heard of a looking-glass talking?" said the mystified Queen.

"Little Snow-white's Stepmother had a mirror that answered her, Ma'am," said Daphne, "and she was a queen in Märchenland, I believe. Perhaps this is the very one!"

It would, no doubt, have proceeded to make some even more unflattering comments if Daphne had not, with much presence of mind, turned its face to the wall. How she knew that this would silence it she could not have said herself. But it certainly did.

"I have no reason for believing that any such person as Little Snow-white ever existed," said Queen Selina; "but whoever that glass belonged to, I will not have it here. I would have it smashed, if it wasn't unlucky. But it must be removed to the attics before I come up here to undress. Really, I never knew such a country as this is! Boar's heads trying to speak at luncheon, and mirrors making personal remarks, and everything so strange and unnatural! But you take it all as a matter of course, Miss Heritage; nothing seems to surprise you."

"I think, Ma'am," said Daphne, "because I've always known that, if I ever did get to Märchenland, it would be very much like this."

"Considering that you had no better means of knowing what it would be like than I had myself," replied the Queen, "I can only ascribe that to affectation.... Surely there must be more of the Crown jewellery than I have been given as yet?... Yes, there may be something in that chest.... Good gracious me! What diamonds! I don't think the dear Duchess of Gleneagles herself can have anything to approach them!... Yes, you can put me on a rivière, and two of the biggest ropes of pearls.... It won't do to go down looking dowdy. Dear me," she added, as she took up the pendant she had bought from Daphne twenty-four hours before, "to think of my giving so much money for this paltry thing! If I had known then what I do now, I should never have—but, of course, I don't mean that I should think of going back on it."

"I'm afraid, Ma'am," said Daphne, "I couldn't pay it back now; I sent the cheque last night."

"I am quite content to bear the loss, Miss Heritage. And, by the way, you may not be aware of it, but it is hardly correct or usual, in speaking to me, to call me 'Ma'am.'"

"I've always understood, Ma'am," said Daphne, "that our own Queen—in England, I mean—"

"How the Queen of England may allow herself to be addressed is entirely her own affair," said Queen Selina handsomely; "I have nothing whatever to do with that. But I am Queen of Märchenland, Miss Heritage, and I shall be obliged by your addressing me as 'Your Majesty' on all occasions."

"Certainly, your Majesty," said Daphne, executing a profound curtsey with a little smile that she was quite unable to repress. "I assure your Majesty that your Majesty may rely on my addressing your Majesty as 'Your Majesty' for the future, your Majesty."

"That is better, Miss Heritage, much better—a little overdone, but still—And now," she added, "you had better go and see if Princess Edna wants any assistance. You need not trouble to change your own dress, as, of course, you will not sit down to dinner with us."

"She's too priceless!" thought Daphne, when she was outside on the gallery, and could indulge her sense of humour in safety. "Still, I don't think I could stand her very long if it weren't for Ruby!"

"I say, Mater," the Crown Prince called out a few minutes afterwards outside his Mother's door, "how much longer are you and the Guv'nor going to be? All night?"

"You can come in, Clarence," she said. "How soon your Father will be ready, I can't say. I finished my dressing hours ago."

King Sidney, following her example, had declined the good offices of his gentlemen, and there were sounds from his dressing-room on the farther side of the Bedchamber which indicated that he was in some difficulties in consequence.

"My aunt!" exclaimed Clarence as he saw his Mother fully arrayed. "You've got 'em all on this time, Mater, and no mistake! So've you, Guv'nor," he added, as King Sidney joined them with rather a sheepish air. "Only—are you sure you've got yours on right? I mean to say—that ruff looks a bit cock-eyed."

"It's given me more trouble than any white tie, my boy—but it must do as it is."

"Ah, I got that bristly-haired chap—what's his name—Hansmeinigel—to put on mine for me. Didn't any of yours give you a hand?"

"They offered to—most kindly," said King Sidney, "but—well, I didn't altogether relish letting them dress me."

"They'd have made a jolly sight neater job of it than you have—keep still a jiff till I've tucked this tape in. There—that's more like it. And I say, you and the Mater had better hurry—you're keeping the whole Court waiting for you!"

"Why didn't you tell us before?" said the Queen in a violent flurry. "Where—where are the Court?"

"All drawn up in the Hall at the foot of the big staircase. They can't make a move till you come down, and lead the way in to dinner, you know!"

"I—I'd rather not descend all those steps in public," objected the King. "Confoundedly slippery. Er—couldn't we go by the backstairs, my love?"

"And find ourselves in our own kitchen!" said the Queen. "Certainly not, Sidney! The grand staircase is the only dignified way down, and you had better give me your arm at once."

"Very well, my dear, very well. But I'm pretty sure I shall slip."

"You must not slip, Sidney! Neither of us must slip. If we did, it would produce a very bad impression. Still, it will be safer if we go down one by one, and hold on to the banisters."

"No, I say," cried the Crown Prince, "you can't do that—might as well crawl down on all fours! Buck up, both of you. Try and throw a little swank into it!"

Their Majesties accomplished the descent amidst the congratulatory blare of the silver trumpets without actual mishap. But there was nothing in the bearing of either Sovereign that could justly be described by the term "swank," and indeed, if any fault could be found, it would have been in quite the opposite direction.

Of the banquet itself little need be said here. The numerous courses were appetising and admirably served, while, to the Queen's relief, none of the dishes showed any desire to take part in the conversation.

The members of the Court did more than look on this time, being entertained, with other guests, amongst whom were the President and Council, at cross tables below the principal one on the dais.

Clarence, seated with his family, the Ex-Regent, and the Court Godmother at the high table, wished more than once that he could have sat by Daphne, whom he could see at no great distance. He noted her perfect ease, and the pretty graciousness with which she received the attentions which her neighbours seemed only too anxious to press upon her.

"Anyone would think she'd lived with swells all her life," he thought. "She may have, for anything I know!" But, of course, even if she had, the fact did not make her his equal now.

Towards the close of the feast King Sidney, who had long since disposed of his crown underneath his chair, considered that the occasion demanded a speech. His effort might have been a greater success if he had abstained from jocularity, which was not by any means his forte. It is possible that a far happier sample of British humour would have failed to set Märchenland tables in a roar, but his hearers were either unaware that he intended to be humorous, or sensible that his purpose had not been achieved, for they listened in puzzled but depressed silence, while the effect of his facetiousness on Daphne was to render her hot and cold by turns.

The banquet over, the Court Chamberlain deferentially informed the Royal Party that they were expected to lead the procession to the Ball Room.

Clarence, who had unfortunately come away from "Inglegarth" without his cigarette-case, was longing to smoke, and hung behind for that purpose. But on applying to the Marshal, he was told that only common soldiers ever smoked in Märchenland. With some trouble a highly flavoured pipe, a tinder-box, and a pouch containing a dried herb that appeared to be the local substitute for tobacco were procured for him. However, a very short experience convinced him that duty required him to put in an appearance at the State Ball.

The Ball Room was a long, lofty hall, lit by thousands of candles set in great golden hoops; the light they gave being multiplied almost to infinity by the fact that the walls and ceiling were lined with elaborately engraved looking-glass, which, fortunately perhaps for the Queen, was dumb. When he entered, the musicians were already fiddling, piping, and fluting in a gallery high up at one end facing a raised platform, where his father and mother, looking extremely hot and uncomfortable, were seated on gorgeous chairs. A stately measure was being performed, which might have been a gavotte or minuet or pavane for anything he could say; all he knew was that the figures were quite unfamiliar to him.

But Daphne seemed to have learnt them—or had they come to her by instinct?—for she was dancing in one of the sets. He watched her lissome form as she moved through the intricate evolutions till he began to envy the Count von Daumerlingstamm, her elegant but undersized partner. However, he flattered himself that he would have no difficulty in cutting out little Daumerlingstamm.

It seemed to him that that dance would never be over, but the moment it was, he made his way to Daphne with an air that showed he was fully aware of the distinction he was conferring. "Enjoying yourself, Miss Heritage?" he said. "Don't know what that last dance was—but not much 'vim' about it, if you ask me. Tell you what—I'll get those fiddler fellows up there to play something a bit livelier, and you and I'll show this crowd a two-step, what?"

"This is a great honour, your Royal Highness," said Daphne, after sinking demurely in the regulation curtsey. "But I must not accept it until I have her Majesty's permission." ("Which I'm quite sure she won't give!" she thought to herself with much satisfaction.)

"Oh, I say—what rot! The Mater won't mind! And if she does—!"

"It would be very disagreeable for me, your Royal Highness!"

"Oh, well," he said, "I'll go and ask her."

As Daphne had anticipated, Queen Selina's refusal was most emphatic. "You ought to know, Clarence, that it's utterly out of the question!" she said. "And I'm surprised at Miss Heritage having the presumption to expect it."

"She didn't, Mater. She said I'd better ask you first."

"Then it seems she has a better sense of her position than you have of yours, Clarence. I'm told you have been seen walking about with a disgusting pipe in your mouth, and that several people were remarking on it. Now you are actually proposing to make yourself conspicuous by dancing at a State Ball with your sister's companion! I have always credited you with being a man of the world—but if this is the way you are going on—!"

He felt the sting of so unwonted a rebuke. "I daresay you're right, Mater," he acknowledged. "I'll be more careful after this."

"I hope you will, I'm sure. As Crown Prince you mustn't think of any partner under the rank of Baroness. Ask one of the Princesses first, or you'll give more offence."

"Right-oh!" was all he said, and, feeling that it would be awkward to make any explanation or excuses to Daphne, he solved the difficulty by avoiding her for the rest of the evening.

Princess Goldernenfingerleinigen, a prepossessing but not very forthcoming damsel, enjoyed the distinction of being commanded by the Crown Prince as his first partner.

He had had no experience in conversing with Princesses, and she did not exert herself either to put him more at his ease or prevent him from losing himself frequently in the mazes of the dance. Once or twice he was oppressed by a painful suspicion that he had seen her making a little grimace of self-pity at the Countess Gänsehirtin. But elaborately engraved mirrors are not very trustworthy, and he might have been mistaken. Still, he was thankful when the dance, in which he was conscious of having done himself so little credit, came to an end.

"Edna, old girl," he remarked subsequently to the Princess Royal, "I call this a rotten ball. Can't stick dancing with any more of these Princesses!"

Princess Edna, it appeared, had been no more favourably impressed by the Courtiers.

"They've simply no conversation," she complained, "and no ideas about any serious subjects!"

"No, I've noticed that," he said; "and they think they're the only people who can dance! I tell you what—you and I'll show 'em how we do the Tango. That'll make 'em open their eyes!"

It did. As has already been said, both he and Edna, as persons who could not afford to be out of the movement, had taken lessons that winter in the recent importation from dubious Argentine dancing-saloons. They danced it now with conscientious care, Prince Clarence exhibiting as much abandon as a man could who was dancing with his sister.

But the Court were not sufficiently enlightened to appreciate the performance. They evidently considered it not only uncouth and undignified, but more than a little improper, and their general attitude conveyed that the couple were committing one of those temporary indiscretions which it was not only etiquette but charity to pass over in silence.

"Capital!" said King Sidney, clapping his hands at the conclusion. "Uncommonly well they dance together, eh, my dear—never seen them do it before."

"And you will never see them do it again, Sidney," replied the Queen; "for I'm much mistaken if they haven't broken up the Ball!"

She was not very far wrong, for although, after some minutes of awestruck silence, dancing was resumed, it was carried on with a restraint and gloom that soon decided the Royal Family to retire from the Ball Room.

The Queen forbore from expressing her sentiments just then either to her son or daughter, with the latter of whom, indeed, she seldom, if ever, ventured to find fault. But she felt that her first evening in the Palace had not been a brilliant success.

This feeling impelled her to be more ingratiating than ever to her ladies of the Bedchamber, whose services in disrobing her she was compelled to accept, though under protest.

"So much obliged!" she said, as they finally withdrew with glacial ceremony. "Quite ashamed to have troubled you, really! Good-night, dear Princess, good-night. We shall breakfast at 8.30. But en famille, you know—quite en famille—so don't dream of coming down!"

"I hope, Sidney," she began later, as he joined her in the Royal Bedchamber, "I hope you have treated the gentlemen who undressed you with proper consideration. It is so important.... Good gracious! What's that you've got on? A night-cap?"

"Those—er—noblemen seemed to consider it the correct thing, my love, and they've put me on this night-gown, too."

"I see they have. Embroidered all over with impossible animals. You look a perfect sight in it!"

"I'm told they're—er—hippogriffs, my dear, the—ah—Royal Crest or emblem or something. I should have much preferred pyjamas myself. But it seems they are not procurable here."

"Everything in this country is in a disgracefully backward state!" declared the Queen; "and I can see I shall have hard work to bring it up to my ideas of what is proper. I shall begin by putting that old Mrs. Fogleplug in her proper place."

"I should be careful, my dear," advised King Sidney. "After all, you know, she's by way of being a Fairy."

"So she says! But, Fairy or no Fairy, she's much too familiar. And if she cannot conform to my rules, she will have to go, that's all."

"Well, my dear, I daresay when you put it to her like that," began the King, who had by this time succeeded in clambering into the immense bed, and whose head was already buried in an enormous pillow. "As I was saying," he continued hazily, "put it to her in—in that way, and—and—no doubt ... very probably ... no reason to suppose ... any...." But here his voice sank into an unintelligible murmur, until it rose presently into his first, but not by any means last, snore in the character of monarch.

CHAPTER VI

CARES OF STATE

Queen Selina was as good as her word. The first thing after breakfast the next morning she retired to her Bower, and sent a summons to the Court Godmother, desiring her immediate attendance. King Sidney was engaged in interviewing the Lord Treasurer on the subject of the Royal revenue. The Crown Prince and Princess Edna were strolling on the terrace, and Daphne had discovered the board and pieces of a game something between Chess and Halma, the rules of which she and Princess Ruby were learning under the instruction of the Countess von Haulemännerschen. So that the Queen, having taken care not to disturb any of her ladies-in-waiting, could count upon being able to deal faithfully with the obnoxious old Fairy without fear of interruption.

"Well, my dear," began the latter, as soon as she appeared, "I hope you passed a comfortable night?"

"I don't know when I passed a more uncomfortable one, Mrs. Fogleplug. That is one of the things I wished to speak to you about. After being accustomed as I have to a spring mattress, all those great feather beds made it simply impossible to get a wink of sleep!"

"That," said the Fairy, "is one of the penalties of being of the blood Royal. An ancestress of yours slept in that very bed, my dear, ages ago, before even I can remember—or I should rather say she tried to sleep, but could not, owing to a pea that had somehow got under the lowest feather-bed of all. It was certainly very careless if the pea has never been removed."

"It would also show, Mrs. Fogleplug, that during all those ages the bed can never have been properly aired. I should have thought it would have been your business to see to that."

"Then you would be entirely mistaken, my dear, for it is not. And, as I notice that you find a difficulty in pronouncing my name correctly, I may suggest that it would be simpler in future to call me by my proper title, which is, 'High Court Godmother,' or 'Court Godmother,' if you prefer it."

"And while we are on the subject of titles," said Queen Selina, "I may mention that it is customary to address a Queen as 'Your Majesty,' and not as 'my dear.'"

"It has always been my habit with Sovereigns, and I have never heard it objected to till now."

"Well, I object to it. But—and this is what I sent for you about—there are other matters I object to even more. I intend to regulate my household on a thoroughly modern and English system, and I cannot have any member of it careering about in the air in outlandish cars drawn by birds. If you must have a conveyance you must be content with a brougham or a victoria, for I shall insist on your putting down both those bird-cars."

"You seem to forget that, but for one of them, you would never have come into your Kingdom!"

"That may or may not be. At any rate there is no further necessity for them, and—well, it just comes to this, Madam, either they go or you do."

The old Fairy's eyes smouldered with anger, and her nut-cracker mouth and chin champed for a few seconds before she replied.

"I have occupied rooms in this Palace—when not at the Palace of Clairdelune—for over a century and a half, and I have no intention of giving them up. I shall also continue to use the vehicles which I find most convenient."

"Oh?" said the Queen, "will you? We shall see about that!"

"We shall," the Court Godmother retorted. "I don't think you quite realise yet whom you have to deal with. I may be getting on in years, but both here and at Clairdelune I am accustomed to being treated with more deference and respect than you seem disposed to pay me. You see, they know that, although I have not used the full powers I possess as a Fairy for many years past, I have not lost them altogether. I might see fit to employ them once more—on any person who was rash enough to incur my displeasure. And ingratitude and pride are the failings which I always made it my particular business to correct. You would find it more to your advantage to be on good terms with me." There was no mistaking the veiled threat, and Queen Selina no longer doubted the Fairy's abilities to carry it out. She was worsted, and her only course was to give in gracefully.

"My dear Court Godmother!" she cried, "you quite misunderstood me! I'd no wish to interfere with any of your habits—not in the very slightest degree. All I meant was that, perhaps, at your age, a more ordinary carriage than your present ones might be—er—safer, you know!"

"I am quite capable of looking after my own safety, thank you. But, though you are our beloved Prince's daughter, you have been brought up in ignorance of the ways of this country, so I am the more willing to overlook treatment to which I feel sure I shall not have to draw your attention again. And now, as we quite understand one another, my dear, we will say no more about it. By the way, I hear you haven't sent for any of your ladies-in-waiting this morning. How is that?"

"I—I didn't quite like to, Court Godmother. We're—well, hardly intimate as yet. They are so reserved and distant—especially that Princess Rapunzelhauser. But, of course, she comes of a very high family."

"She is descended from the famous Rapunzel, whose story is no doubt familiar to you.... No? Well, her father was a poor cottager who was caught by an old witch stealing radishes from her garden. She let him off on condition that he gave up to her the child his wife was expecting. Rapunzel was the child, and in due time was claimed by the witch, who shut her up in a lofty tower. However, she had the most wonderful hair, so long that when she let it down from the top window it touched the ground, and so thick that the Prince whom she subsequently married was able to climb up by it, and make love to her."

"Now you mention it, I have some faint recollection—and so Princess Rapunzelhauser is descended from her! Well, that would account for—but Princess Goldenenfinger—something, now, she does look as if she had some good blood in her veins."

"The best in Märchenland. An ancestor of hers was King of one of the smaller Kingdoms into which the country was divided in those days. One day when out hunting he found a woodcutter's daughter living all alone in a hollow tree, and fell violently in love with her."

"A woodcutter's daughter? Dear me! Then, of course, marriage was out of the question."

"Not at all! they were married and had children. Unfortunately there was an estrangement between the King and Queen later as she was accused of having murdered them, and condemned to be burnt to death."

"It only shows what a mistake it is to marry beneath one."

"This marriage ended happily. It was discovered, just in time, that the children were alive after all."

"Still," said the Queen, "it is not a pleasant thing to have happened in any family. I should like to hear something about the pedigrees of my other ladies-in-waiting."

The Court Godmother was quite ready to give her all the information she could. Princess Flachspinnenlosburg, it appeared, traced her descent from the incorrigibly lazy daughter of a poor and not over scrupulous mother; Baroness Belohnte von Haulemännerschen from similarly humble folk, whose daughter was servant of all work to seven dwarfs, and afterwards married the King of one of the petty states before mentioned; Baroness von Bauerngrosstochterheimer's ancestor was a peasant; Countess Gänsehirten am Brunnen's ancestress a goose-girl—and so on through the entire list. Queen Selina then became curious as to the origin of the gentlemen of her Court, and found that many of their forbears were sullied by the taint of Trade. The founders of both Prince Tapfer von Schneiderleinberg's and Count Daumerlingenstamm's houses were tailors; Baron von Bohnenranken derived his title from a speculator who, after a remarkably unsuccessful venture in cattle, had made a colossal coup in beans. As for Prince Hansmeinigel, his pretensions to high descent were even more questionable—at least, if it was actually the fact, as the Fairy stated, that the first of his progenitors was not only the son of a poor father, but also suffered the additional social disadvantage of being a hedgehog from the waist upwards; added to which he seemed to have cherished an eccentric passion for playing the bagpipes while riding on a cock. It is true that, after his marriage with a Princess, he became a less impossible member of Society—still, as the Queen very rightly felt, there are some things which can never be altogether lived down.

"I'm much obliged to you for telling me all this, Court Godmother," she said, at the end; "most interesting, I'm sure. And so useful to know who everybody really is!"

It was something of a disillusion to find that her Court was so largely composed of parvenus, but, on the other hand, it enabled her to face her ladies-in-waiting in future without any distressing sense of inferiority.

She was on the point of summoning them when the King suddenly burst into her bower. "Selina, my love," he began, with suppressed excitement, "if you'll tell this good woman to go, I've something to say to you."

"Oblige me, Sidney," replied the Queen, "by not alluding to the High Court Godmother again as a good woman; we may consider ourselves very fortunate that she is doing us the honour of residing under our roof, and you will be good enough to show her proper respect."

"Oh, sorry, I'm sure; I thought you said—but if that's how it is, I apologise for interrupting you."

"I have said all I have to say," said the Court Godmother, "so there is no need for me to remain any longer." And with that she hobbled out of the room.

"I suppose you got your way about those—ah—bird-chariots, my dear?" he asked, "as you don't seem to have sacked her!"

"She seemed so upset at the idea of giving them up that I said she might keep them. I shall certainly not 'sack' her, as you call it. Now I've come to know her better, I find she is a good, faithful old soul who is much too useful to part with, and you must be very careful to be civil to her in future. What was it you wanted to say to me?"

"The Lord Treasurer and I have been going into our private resources," he said. "I thought perhaps you might like to come with me to my Counting-house and—and have a look at 'em, my dear."

She was only too eager to do so. "Tell me, Sidney," she gasped, as they hurried through various corridors to the wing in which the King's Counting-house was situated. "Shall we—shall we have enough to live on decently?"

"I don't know what you will think," he replied, with an irrepressible chuckle, "but I should call it affluence myself—positive affluence, my love!"

They arrived at a heavily clamped door, where the Marshal, the Treasurer, and Prince Clarence and Princess Edna were waiting for them. "Two steps down," said King Sidney after unlocking the door.

"And here we are!" he cried triumphantly, as they entered.

The Counting-house was a huge barrel-roofed chamber lighted from windows protected by elaborate scroll-work bars. Upon shelves all round the walls, and piled in heaps on the floor, were sacks, "Every blessed one," explained the King, "chock full of gold ducats! What do you think of that, eh, my love?"

"I think, Sidney," she replied, "that I am the person who should have the key."

"There's one for each of us," he said. "Here's yours. And on that table there you'll find purses laid out, and a little gold shovel to fill them with. I've filled mine. Whenever our funds are running low, you see, we've only to come down here and help ourselves."

"Good biz!" said the Crown Prince, beginning to fill one of the purses. "I shall fill my pockets as well—save another journey, what?"

"Some of us do not possess pockets, Clarence," said his mother. "And I must make it a rule that no one is to take out more than a purseful at a time, and only after satisfying me that the money is required for some legitimate purpose."

"I don't think such precautions are at all necessary, my dear," said King Sidney. "Marshal Federhelm seems to have put by a good deal while he was Regent. And besides, there's plenty more where this comes from, you know!"

"And where does it come from?" inquired the Queen.

"Why, the Treasurer tells me, we've a mine of our own in the Golden Mountains a few miles from here—a mine that is practically—ah—inexhaustible. I rather thought of driving over to see it some day."

"Let's all go!" said the Crown Prince. "Why not this afternoon? It'll be something to do!"

Queen Selina was pleased to approve the suggestion. "We certainly ought to show that we are interested in industrial concerns," she said. "All the best Sovereigns do. I can't help wishing, though, that poor dear Papa could have come with us. He knew so much about gold mines."

"Just as well for us he can't," said Clarence, "because he'd be the Boss, then! I say, I've got an idea. Why not take one of those sacks in the coach with us and chuck money out of the window to the crowd, what?"

"Look too much as if we were out for a beanfeast, my boy," objected his father.

"And what's the matter with a beanfeast? Believe me, it will make us jolly popular and be a lot better fun than just bowing to the blighters."

"And far less fatiguing," said Edna.

"There's something in what Clarence says," said the Queen. "It would increase our popularity—and that is so important. Of course we shouldn't make a practice of it, but we can quite afford it, just for once— what do you think, Mr. Marshal?"

The Marshal thought it was an excellent notion.

The Golden Mountains were not much more than a couple of leagues from Eswareinmal, and the roads being tolerably good, a lighter vehicle than the State Coach and six sturdy horses accomplished the journey in very good time. In the streets they passed through and at various villages along the valley, crowds had collected, and the enthusiasm with which they scrambled for the coins that were showered from the carriage windows proved how fully they appreciated the benefits of an established Monarchy.

"Don't throw any more now, children," counselled Queen Selina as they neared the mine. "We must keep some for the dear miners. Sidney, be sure to ask some questions about the machinery, and whether they're all happy and comfortable. And do it tactfully, because I've always heard miners are such a very independent and intelligent class."

Perhaps even so short a residence in Märchenland as theirs might have prepared the Royal party for the unusual. But it was an undeniable shock to them all to find, on arrival at the mine, not only that the method of working was primitive to the last degree, but that it was entirely conducted by diminutive beings who were unmistakable Yellow Gnomes. The interior of the mine resounded with the blows of pickaxes, but the inevitable trumpeters had no sooner announced that the Sovereigns had left their coach than all work was suspended. The miners swarmed up from their tunnellings, literally tumbling over one another in their haste to behold the countenances of Royalty.

"They seem—ah—a remarkable lively lot," observed King Sidney as some of the Gnomes turned somersaults and Catherine wheels around their visitors, while the more retiring stood unassumingly in the background on their heads. "A bit undersized, and, judging from their complexions, I should say the work had affected their livers. But it may only be due to the gold-dust."

"They don't seem to realise a bit who we are!" complained Queen Selina. "Sidney, did you see that? One of the little wretches has just taken a flying leap over my very head!"

The Baron, who had followed in another coach, explained that these demonstrations were merely intended to express loyal delight.

"Oh, if you say so, Baron," she said. "But anyone might easily mistake it for impertinence. If it was not hopeless to expect an intelligent answer from people who seem unable to stay right side up for a single moment, I should like to know what wages they receive and what they live on."

The Court Chamberlain informed her that the Gnomes got no wages and required little in the way of food, their favourite diet, he believed, being earth.

"Revolting!" was her comment. "No wonder they look so unwell! Still, their living cannot cost much, so I should think, Sidney, if we gave the—er—foreman a gold piece to be divided amongst them, that would be amply sufficient."

King Sidney thereupon presented a ducat to the most important-looking Gnome, who immediately let it drop indifferently.

"Wonder why he did that?" said the King. "Doesn't he think it's enough?"

"Knows too much about how it's made, I expect," said Clarence. "Like the chap at the Marmalade factory."

"Well, it's a pity to waste it," said his father, picking up the coin. "I should like to see them at work before we go."

His wish having been conveyed to the Head Gnome, the whole band rushed, yelping and screeching, back into the galleries, seized their picks, and began hacking at the gold which gleamed in veins of incredible richness through the rocky walls and roof of the caves. But perhaps their efforts would have been more effective if they had not been quite so apt to get in one another's way.

The visitors then inspected the furnace where the ore was melted, and the Mint where it was stamped into big fat coins. These were put up in sacks for transmission to the Royal Treasury, but, as a fresh batch had been delivered only recently, the supply in hand at the Mint was not very large just then.

"I did like those Gnomes!" said Princess Ruby on the way home. "Didn't you, Mummy?"

"I should have liked them better, my dear, if they had been more like fellow-Christians. Sidney, I shall insist on their wearing some civilised costume."

"By all means, my love, if we continue to employ them. But I rather think it would be better to get rid of them altogether."

"Get rid of them, Sidney? What in the world for?"

"Well, you see, my dear, at the last General Election I took a somewhat prominent part in denouncing the Conservatives for employing Chinese labour in the South African mines. It would be very awkward if people at Gablehurst found out that our entire income was derived from—er—'Yellow Slavery.'"

"Stuff and nonsense, Sidney! Who do you suppose is likely to tell them?"

"You never know how things get about," he said uneasily. "And, as a consistent Radical, it—it goes against my conscience."

"Conscience, indeed! My dear good Sidney, if you go and get rid of those Gnomes, who seem perfectly happy and contented, there'll be no one to dig the gold!"

"We could hire full-grown white labourers, my dear. Of course at a living wage, but, as they would work more systematically, they would obtain a far larger output, so we should make a handsome profit by the change."

"Ah, when you put it like that, Sidney, it makes all the difference. I could see for myself that those hideous little horrors weren't taking their work seriously."

"There's to be a State Council to-morrow morning," said the King. "It would be a good opportunity to inform them that we do not intend to countenance slavery any longer."

"That ought to have an excellent effect," Queen Selina replied. "I shouldn't wonder if it made us more popular than ever.... Why, we're back in the city already!... How delighted the dear people seem to see us!... Yes, Children, you can empty the sack. The love of one's subjects is well worth the money—and it's not as if we were ever likely to miss it!"

The next morning after breakfast the King and Queen held their first State Council, Prince Clarence, of whose business capacity both his parents had a great opinion, being given a seat at the board. There were, it appeared, various measures on the agenda which, as the President explained, were of the highest political importance, being concerned with the settlement of such matters as the precise number of cherries that were to be strung on a stick and sold for a groschen at old women's fruit-stalls; the dimensions of the piece of jam that a huckster should be permitted to put in his porridge; whether the watchmen's horns really needed new mouthpieces, and, if so, whether these should be of ivory or bone. Questions which had to be given the fullest consideration and debated at prodigious length before the Sovereigns could be asked to affix their signatures and seals to the decrees.

Clarence fidgeted with undisguised impatience, and King Sidney was more than once under the necessity of raising the golden hand at the end of his sceptre to his lips in order to conceal an irrepressible yawn. But at last the state business was disposed of, and the King was able to introduce his own. It was clear from the vehement wagging of the Councillors' white beards while he was announcing the Royal intention to emancipate all Gnomes at present in the Gold mine, that they regarded the new departure with no great favour. The President himself, although he admitted that it concerned the Sovereigns more closely than any other person, pointed out certain objections which he begged their Majesties to ponder. And Councillor after Councillor rose and protested against the scheme with the utmost solemnity and prolixity.

Queen Selina, who was now far more eager than the King to have the mine reorganised on a more paying principle, would have answered the critics herself, if Clarence had not induced her to leave the reply in his hands.

"Well," he said, rising, "have you all done? No other gentleman wish to hear himself talk?... All right then. Now I'll have my little say. Of course, what the venerable old Father Christmas in the chair told you was perfectly correct. If we choose to set these little beggars free, it's no business of anybody but ourselves. The Guv'nor—that is to say, his Majesty—was merely telling you about it—not asking what you thought about it. Sorry if you don't approve, but we shall get over it in time. And really, your objections, if you won't mind my saying so, are absolutely footling. All they amount to is—because Gold Mines here always have been worked by gangs of Yellow Gnomes, therefore they must be for all time. Now that's just the kind of fine old crusted pig-headed Conservativism that's kept this the stick-in-the-mud Country it is! Look at the sort of business you've been wasting our time in jawing about to-day— why, in the country We came from, a Rural District Council would have settled it all in five minutes if they thought it worth bothering about at all. Street lanterns and watchmen's horns and old women's sweet-stalls indeed! If you could only walk through—I won't say one of our Cities, that might be too much of a shock for you—but through an ordinary suburb such as we lived in, and saw how things were done there, it would open your eyes a bit, I can tell you! You've been marking time all these centuries while other Kingdoms have been making progress. I'll tell you about some of the things we've learnt to do and use, just as an ordinary matter of course—and you haven't so much as heard of."

Here he gave them a vivid description of the chief inventions and discoveries of the last eighty years, from the steam-engine to the aeroplane, which latter, he declared, put their sixty-stork-power car completely in the shade.

"If it is the fact," said the President, "that the inhabitants of your Royal Highness's Country can work such marvels, you must be even mightier magicians than were they whom our late King so wisely suppressed."

"You're wrong there, old bird!" said Clarence cheerfully; "no Magic about it whatever. All done by brains and enterprise, but—and this is what I am trying to knock into your heads—if we'd been governed by a set of stuffy old fossils like yourselves—if you'll allow me the expression—we should never have got a blessed thing so much as started!"

Many, if not most of the Council were sceptical as to the possibility of such inventions as Clarence had described, but the good old Baron assured them that, even during the short time he was in England, and although it was night, he had witnessed many of them with his own eyes, thanks to the powerful illuminants which made darkness almost as light as day. He exhorted his hearers to count themselves fortunate in having gained Sovereigns who possessed such wondrous powers, since their faithful subjects would assuredly now enjoy the benefits of them.

"Aye," said the ex-Regent—though possibly not in such good faith as the Baron. "We shall indeed have reason to congratulate ourselves if his Royal Highness will graciously teach us how to construct one of these fire-and-smoke-breathing engines that draw a line of waggons along roads of iron, or even a mast that will send messages through a thousand leagues of air."

"You don't want much, do you, dear old boy?" said Clarence. "You don't suppose I can show you how to build a railway train when you haven't got any of the bally materials or appliances, do you?"

"Your Royal Highness has but to name them, and they shall be procured."

"They're not to be got here," replied Clarence. "If I tried to tell you what they were, you wouldn't be any the wiser!" He spoke nothing but the truth, for he had but the sketchiest acquaintance with the composition of any kind of machinery.

"Perhaps His Majesty," suggested the Marshal, who had long ago taken King Sidney's measure, "is better able to instruct us in these mighty secrets?"

"H'm, well, to tell you the truth," confessed the King, "although I've been in the habit of using railways, motors, electric light, telephones, and so forth constantly, I can't pretend to more than a general notion of how they work. Couldn't make any of 'em, you know. Not my line of business!"

"If that is indeed the case," said the President, "we find it the more difficult to understand why his Royal Highness should have reproached us for an ignorance which is no greater than either his own or your Majesty's."

"I wasn't reproaching you," said the Crown Prince, a little awkwardly, "I was only telling you how differently things are managed where we come from. But after all, that isn't the point, so we'll say no more about it. Let's get back to the Gnomes. One of you—I think it was the gentleman with the grey topknot—objected that there was no other useful way of employing them, except in the mine. Well, of course, we've thought all that out," he declared, though, as a matter of fact, the idea had only just struck him. "We intend to set 'em to work at laying out a golf links, and when they've done that, we shall keep 'em on as caddies. They're such nippy little devils that they ought to be jolly useful.... Ah, naturally, you wouldn't know what Golf is. Well, Golf happens to be a thing I do know something about. I can teach you that right enough. It's simply the greatest game going, and you'll be grateful to me for introducing it. Don't worry," he added, as some of the Council expressed dissent, "nobody's asking you to learn unless you like. I shouldn't say myself that any of you—except perhaps the Marshal—was very likely to shape into a 'plus' man. I fancy he's got the makings of a golfer in him, though, and, once I've got the course laid out and given him a lesson or two, I bet you'll see he'll be as keen as mustard."

Before the Council broke up, the ex-Regent undertook that, as soon as Clarence had selected the ground, the Gnomes should be removed from their present quarters, and placed under the Crown Prince's directions.

"Never again, Sidney," declared the Queen afterwards, "will you and I sit through one of those tiresome councils! We'll leave them to manage their own silly business, and if there's anything that requires our signatures, they can bring the papers to us, and we'll sign them in our own rooms. If there should be any difficulty, we can always ask the Marshal—he's so very sympathetic and helpful."

"Very," said the King, "oh, very—that is, I half fancied now and then—but I believe he means us well. Yes, on the whole, my dear, I think he's a person we can trust."

"You needn't think about it, Sidney," she replied; "you can feel absolutely certain that there's nothing that man wouldn't do for us!"

CHAPTER VII

A GAME THEY DID NOT UNDERSTAND

With regard to the Royal visit to the Gold Mine, it should be mentioned that, on returning to the Palace, the Queen and Princess Ruby had met Daphne in one of the galleries. Ruby ran to her impulsively: "Oh, Miss Heritage!" she cried, "we've had a ripping afternoon. Such fun throwing money to the people, and seeing them scramble for it! We saw the Gold Mine. And all the darling little Gnomes! You would have loved them! I do wish you had come with us!"

"I fully intended to have arranged for you to do so, Miss Heritage," said Queen Selina, with unwonted graciousness. "But with so much to think of—! Do you happen to know where my other ladies-in-waiting are?... In the Tapestry Chamber? Then I must get you to show me to it, for I don't know my way yet about this immense house.... Through here? Yes, you will accompany me—in fact, I particularly desire you to be present."

At her entrance the Maids of Honour all rose from their seats and made obeisances which, but for the Court Godmother's revelations of their ancestries, would have occasioned their Sovereign agonies of embarrassment. But she felt she could face them now without mauvaise honte, and indeed with all the assurance of superiority.

"You may sit down, girls," she said, and although they found it hard to believe at first that they could be the persons thus addressed, they sat down.

"And what are you all about?" she inquired. "Embroidery, is it? The pattern seems rather large.... Oh, tapestry? I see. I prefer a bright, cheerful paper on the walls to any tapestry myself. Only collects dust. Now if you were to knit some warm woollen jerseys for those wretched little Gnomes, who are really in want of them, you would be doing something useful. But that wasn't what I—ah, to be sure, I remember now. I looked in to tell you, girls, that I have appointed Miss Heritage here as my First Lady-in-waiting. You will be careful to address her in future as 'Lady Daphne,' and treat her in all respects as your equal in rank.... I don't know why you should look so surprised." (If they did, it was merely that any such recommendation should be thought necessary.) "Miss Heritage's parentage may, it is true, be obscure— but not more so, from all I have been told, than that of most of your own ancestresses. Indeed, I am much mistaken if she has not a better claim to be considered a lady than any of them. Not that I think mere birth of any importance myself, but I object to people giving themselves airs without some real ground for it. I am not alluding to Lady Daphne, whom I have always found perfectly well-behaved and unpretentious."

This was not perhaps the surest way of endearing Daphne to her new companions, but then Queen Selina was less concerned to effect that than to make them pay for the excessive deference she had so mistakenly shown them in the past.

However, in their simplicity it had never occurred to them that they had any cause to be ashamed of their descent, and so they never imagined that their Royal Mistress could insult them with it, and her shafts missed the target.

Fortunately for Daphne, too, she was already the object of a secret schwärmerei that left no room in their sentimental bosoms for jealousy or ill-feeling.

But, not being aware of this as yet, she was rendered only unhappy by this sudden rise in the Royal favour. Her one consolation was the certainty that it would not be very long before she was again in disgrace.

On the afternoon of the day on which the State Council had been held, the Crown Prince explored the surrounding country with a view to selecting a golf course.

He found a district which was in every way suitable for his purpose—a stretch of undulating land in a valley behind the plateau on which the Palace stood, abounding in natural hazards, and affording great facilities for artificial ones—in short, an ideal site for any links. He began laying it out the next morning. The Gnomes were brought out of the mine and conducted to the spot. The general idea was conveyed to a Gnome who seemed, on the whole, less devoid of intelligence than his fellows, and they all set to work with more activity than immediate result. However, they seemed to take kindly to their new industry, and Clarence was very well pleased with them. He had had no experience in golf-architecture himself, but the nature of the ground was such that it required but little to turn it into a very sporting course indeed, and, if the Gnomes did not do much else, they constructed some remarkably cunning bunkers.

While they were thus engaged he ordered several sets of clubs to be made from rough designs of his own by a master artificer in Eswareinmal, who carried them out with considerable skill and fidelity. The implements he produced may not have been quite according to Club standards, but they were fairly serviceable. The balls seemed at first likely to be the main difficulty, but some were discovered on the toy-stalls in the market square which, though not of rubber, were composed of a substance that proved an admirable substitute. They were certainly open to one objection that, in ordinary circumstances, might have disqualified them—they cost considerably under a farthing each. But Clarence got over that by paying a ducat apiece for them. And then, as the work progressed but slowly, he was forced to wait with what patience he could until the links were ready for practising on.

It does not take long for most people to get accustomed to any surroundings, no matter how novel, and Queen Selina and her family soon became acclimatised. Now that her household had lost their terrors for her, she began to enjoy the sensation of being a Queen and inspiring reverence and awe wherever she went, though she could have wished to be the ruler of a Kingdom that was not quite so outré as Märchenland. However, she felt she must take it as it was, and in a short time she had almost forgotten that there ever had been a period when she had not occupied a throne.

Princess Edna, though she frequently protested that her rank had no charms for her, was ready enough to assert it on all occasions, and exercised authority over the unfortunate ladies-in-waiting to a degree that might have rendered their lives a burden to them if they had been able to take her as seriously as she did herself, which they were not.

"Mother," she remarked one day, "I've been quite shocked to find how appallingly ignorant our Maids of Honour are. Fancy, they've never heard of Shakespeare, or Ibsen, or Bernard Shaw, or—well, anybody!"

"My dear," said the Queen, "what can you expect from such a set of giggling, empty-headed minxes?"

"I know. Still, I feel it a duty to do what I can to improve their minds. I shall bring down my note-book this afternoon. It's got all my notes on those lectures on English Literature I attended last Autumn. I thought I'd read them aloud to them. It would give them a very good general idea of the subject. Enough, at least, to enable them to talk about it without exposing themselves."

"I'm sure, Edna dear, it's most sweet of you to trouble about them."

"Oh, since I have to live with a Court, I must try and raise it to a more intellectual level."

And so that afternoon, while the ladies of the Court were engaged, under the Queen's supervision, in knitting little woollen garments of shattering hues for the unsuspecting Gnomes, the Princess Royal produced her note-book and read aloud extracts which gave an impressionist bird's-eye view of English Literature from the fourteenth to the close of the nineteenth Century.

No doubt the lecturer had given his audience credit for some previous acquaintance with the subject, and it may be that Princess Edna's method of note-taking had been a trifle desultory; it was certain that the ladies-in-waiting found a difficulty in assimilating the scraps of literary pemmican she dispensed to them.

They received with polite but languid attention such items as that: "Shakespeare stands supreme among dramatists for consummate knowledge of the human heart"; that: "as Ralph Roister Doister is the first pure comedy, so The Vicar of Wakefield may be termed the first idyllic English novel"; that: "while Byron possessed more intellect than imagination, Shelley, on the contrary, was rather imaginative than intellectual"; and even the statement that: "Browning's 'Ring and the Book' contains upwards of twenty-one thousand lines" left them unmoved.

It is true they were more interested in hearing that it was: "after he had come under the spell of Petrarch and Boccaccio that Chaucer produced his wondrous Tales," but it appeared their interest was due to some slight misapprehension. Daphne felt the fearful joy of suppressed mirth combined with the danger of detection as she heard Edna explaining with laborious patience that she had not intended to convey that the Poet had been afflicted by a pair of enchanters with any caudal appendages whatever.

But the Princess Royal could not conceal her disgust when her final extract, which was to the effect that: "during the closing decade of the Nineteenth Century England became once more a 'nest of singing birds,' as was apparent from the stream of fresh and melodious strains issuing from, among other sources, 'The Bodley Head,'" was greeted with a ripple of girlish laughter from her hearers. It seemed that this incontrovertible statement of fact had somehow aroused reminiscences of another head which, if fresh, had not been precisely melodious on the luncheon board after the Coronation.

Princess Edna waited with cold dignity until the last giggle was no longer audible before announcing that she was willing to answer any questions they might wish to ask her. Upon which Baroness Kluge von Bauerngrosstochterheimer begged that they might be favoured with the outline of one of the romances written by the Poet Shakespeare, who they had been informed by her was so unsurpassed as a story-teller.

Now Edna was undoubtedly well versed in the Literature of her native land. She could not only have given with tolerable accuracy the names and dates of the principal authors of each century, but a list of their best-known works, and an estimate of the rank assigned to them by modern criticism. She had even, impelled by an almost morbid conscientiousness, consulted the works themselves, and could honestly assert that she had read every single play of Shakespeare's all through, though her private preference was for a more advanced and psychological form of drama.

And yet on this occasion she chose to parry the Baroness's very reasonable request. "Shakespeare," she said, in her most superior tone, "did not write romances. He wrote plays."

"Will your Royal Highness please," said the Baroness, "to tell us about one of them?"

For the life of her Edna could not just then summon up a clear recollection of the plot of any Shakespearian comedy or tragedy—and it is quite possible that there are many persons as highly educated as she who might be equally at a loss.

"With so prolific a writer as Shakespeare," she hedged, "it is difficult to single out any particular play."

She was so plainly embarrassed that Daphne felt impelled to come to the rescue.

"I think, Ma'am," she said, "they would like the story of The Merchant of Venice!"

"I should hardly call it suitable myself to such an audience as this," replied Edna, who was possibly confusing it with Othello. "No, Miss Heritage, I really think something less—less objectionable would be—There's As you like it, now, quite a pleasant play. I think I can remember the outline of that. Let me see. Yes, it's about a girl called "Rosalind," who dressed up as a boy and ran away into a forest, where she met Ferdinand—or was it Bassanio?—anyway, the name is of no consequence. Well, and he carved her name on all the trees, and so they fell in love, and in the end they were married, you know."

As drama this appeared to strike the ladies-in-waiting as lacking in incident, and the Baroness von Haulemännerschen openly declared that an ancestress of hers who also ran away into a forest had the far more exciting experience of being poisoned by a jealous Queen and enclosed by dwarfs in a glass coffin.

"Oh, very well!" said Edna; "if you are going to compare your own silly traditions with works of genius, I give you up as hopeless!"

And this was the beginning and the end of the Princess Royal's attempt to infuse Culture into Court Circles.

She had certainly failed signally to inspire her ladies with any enthusiasm for English Literature, though, strangely enough, Daphne succeeded later in giving them a more favourable impression of its quality.

Edna was, of course, incomparably more widely read, but then Daphne knew such authors as she had read well enough to be able to give a very full and clear account of her favourite books, and to repeat many of her best loved poems from memory.

It is quite possible that much of the pleasure her companions took in hearing her do so was due to her own personality. They were not, it must be confessed, a highly intellectual or cultivated set of young women, but one and all regarded Daphne with a whole-hearted adoration which would have given Princess Edna, had she condescended to notice it, a lower opinion than ever of their intelligence.

The links were at last in a sufficiently advanced stage for practice at the first nine of the eighteen holes, and Clarence undertook to instruct the Marshal in the mysteries of the game. The Marshal, though slightly handicapped by insisting on playing in a breastplate and high boots, was so much encouraged by the success which most beginners at golf experience that he at once became an ardent votary. He tried to make converts of the Courtiers, but they preferred to keep an open mind and remain spectators for the present.

Prince Tapfer von Schneiderleinberg indeed went so far as to say that golf seemed to him to be without the element of danger which all genuine sport should possess. He modified that opinion, it is true, after incautiously standing close behind the Marshal when he was driving off from the tee, but it did not alter his prejudices against the game.

King Sidney practised most assiduously in private, and found he improved in his driving under Clarence's tuition. The Gnomes had been established in a kind of compound near the links, but their unfortunate tendency to bolt with the club-bags and purloin every ball they found rather impaired their usefulness as caddies. Marshal Federhelm treated his with regrettable inhumanity.

There was still a good deal of "ground under repair" on the course, but the day was drawing near when the links could be formally opened. The Marshal was anxious to celebrate the occasion by challenging his Royal Master to play him a single, a challenge which was conveyed through the Crown Prince.

"Well, what do you think, my boy," asked King Sidney. "Can I beat him?"

"I think you ought to, Guv'nor. He fancies himself at it—but he's pretty rotten."

"In that case, you can tell him I accept," said the King.

But on the morning before the day, Clarence, after watching his parent top and slice and foozle through a whole round without intermission, became less sanguine.

"I tell you what it is, Guv'nor," he said, frankly, "the Marshal's been shaping a bit better these last few days, and it's my belief he can give you a stroke a hole and win easy."

"After all," said the King, "I'm not sure there isn't a certain loss of dignity—playing with my own subject, don't you know."

"It won't do to let him lick you, certainly," agreed Clarence.

"Quite so, my boy, quite so. I was thinking—I might be prevented by sudden business—I could go and sit with the Council, you know."

"He'd only want you to fix another day for playing him. It's no use, Guv'nor, you can't get out of it now. Perhaps you'd do better if you played with a different sort of ball. I must see if I can't get you one or two."

And that evening he brought his father half a dozen. "They're specially marked," he said, "so you can't make a mistake over them, and I fancy you'll find they travel better than any of the Marshal's."

"You've got those golf balls I gave you?" he asked the King at breakfast next morning. "Mind you don't forget to take 'em."

"I shan't forget, my boy. But what I'm most troubled about is my swing—there's something wrong with it, only I can't find out what."

"I think it a great pity myself," said Queen Selina, "that you ever agreed to play this match at all. If you are beaten it will certainly lower your prestige. But I am sure the dear Marshal has too much tact not to let you win."

"Don't you worry, Mater," said Clarence. "The Guv'nor's going to win on his own, hands down!"

"I sincerely hope so. It will be a sad blow to the Throne if he does not."

These remarks did not help much to steady King Sidney's nerves when he met the Marshal on the links, where, as Monarch, he naturally had the honour. A large crowd of onlookers from the Court had collected, and the players had decided to dispense with caddies under the circumstances.

The first hole was only about a hundred and sixty yards; a deep gully lay between, and on either side of the approach were beds of tall rushes.

King Sidney addressed his ball for some time in agonising indecision before he finally drove off. A cloud of sand rose; the ball was nowhere to be seen, and, taught by experience, he looked behind for it.

"Jolly good shot!" cried Clarence. "Right on the green!"

"Is it, my boy?" said the King. "I can't see it there myself."

"No more can I," Clarence owned, "but I bet you what you like you're on the pretty, anyway. Your drive, Marshal."

The Marshal smote a mighty blow, and his ball likewise vanished. Clarence was of opinion that it had gone over the boundary, but the Marshal was so certain that it was on the green that he declined to search for it.

"Funny," said Clarence disappointedly, as they neared the pin, "I don't see your ball anywhere, Pater. Nor yet the Marshal's."

"I fancy mine isn't very far away, my boy," said the King hopefully.

One of the Courtiers who had gone to the hole, called out to say that he could see a ball marked with a Royal Crown wedged in by the pin.

"By George, Guv'nor!" cried Clarence, "you've holed it in one!"

"Ah," said King Sidney, "I thought I'd got the right direction."

But the next moment both of them were depressed by the announcement that the Marshal's ball had also landed in the hole. The Courtier had naturally mentioned his Sovereign's achievement first, but there could be no possible doubt that the Marshal had succeeded in equalling it.

To have holed out at a hundred and sixty yards is not by any means an unprecedented feat, but that two players should have done it in succession was at least a rather remarkable coincidence. It was a severe disappointment to the King, who had serious doubts of his own ability to repeat such a performance.

The next hole was a long one, some six hundred yards, over undulating land with patches of bog; the green was on a hillock protected by artfully devised bunkers, and the approach was full of difficulties.

The Marshal was given the honour, and, as before, none could follow the flight of his ball, though he declared with the greatest confidence that it was straight for the green. King Sidney's drive did not look very promising, but Clarence assured him that it was probably a longer one than he thought.

But neither player could locate his ball as they trudged on, and, though it seemed unlikely that either could have reached the green, they did not stop to search on the way to it. Still, when they arrived there each of them was obviously astonished by the discovery that the other had holed out once more. Even had the distance been less, it seemed to them that this was stretching the long arm of coincidence almost too far, but they did not say so; in fact, they both thought it wiser to abstain from any comment at all. The next hole was some three hundred and fifty yards, with several extremely tricky hazards, but, contrary to all reasonable expectations, both King Sidney and the Marshal distinguished themselves by doing it in one.

At this the King felt bound to make some comment. "Very even game this, Marshal, so far," he said.

"Very even indeed, Sire!" said the Marshal curtly, and turned aside to curse under his breath.

However, after they had played the fourth and fifth holes with precisely the same result, King Sidney became suspicious. "Clarence, my boy," he said, taking him aside. "It strikes me there's something rather odd about his play. I can't understand it!"

"I can," said Clarence; "it's plain enough. Haven't you noticed he's been using a mashie—the same mashie every time? Well, he's bribed or bullied that pop-eyed little swine of an Astrologer to enchant it for him—that's what he's done!"

"What a confounded low, ungentlemanly trick!" spluttered King Sidney in high indignation. "Just when I was beginning to find my form at last, too! I shall decline to go on with the match. And what's more, when we do get a Golf Club started, I'll have him blackballed for it!"

"I wouldn't make a row about it if I were you," advised Clarence.

"Not make a row? When he's taking an unfair advantage of me by using this infernal Magic?—which is unlawful, by Gad, don't you forget that! Why shouldn't I denounce such trickery?"

"Because," said the Crown Prince, "he might say something disagreeable about it being a case of Pot and Kettle, don't you know."

"Let him!" cried the King. "Let him! I defy him to prove that I've had anything done to my clubs!"

"Not the clubs," said Clarence; "it's those balls I gave you. I hadn't meant to tell you, but p'raps I'd better now. I paid that little sweep to put a spell on 'em. Of course I'd no idea he'd go and overdo it like this. If he'd been anything of a Golfer he'd have known most of these holes couldn't be done under three or four. And now he's given you both away, blast him!"

"It—it's most unfortunate!" said King Sidney. "I—I don't quite see what to do about it."

"Simple enough," said his son, "pretend not to notice anything and play it out."

"I suppose I must, my boy, I suppose I must. But I know I shan't play so well after this—it's quite put me off my game!"

"No, it hasn't, Guv'nor. You'll play up all right, at least if Xuriel knows his job."

Xuriel apparently did know his job, for the King's ball continued to be as foozle-proof as the Marshal's mashie.

It would be tedious to describe any further holes. When a bewitched mashie is pitted against an enchanted ball, there can obviously be none of the alternations and vicissitudes of Fortune which constitute the charm of Golf.

When they were at the turn, having halved every hole up to the ninth, the Marshal had had enough of it. "We are too well matched, Sire," he said, "and to proceed would only be to waste your Majesty's time, which is of far more value than my own."

"H'm, well, perhaps we'd better call it a draw and have done with it," said the King.

The Court had witnessed the game without excitement or astonishment. They saw no particular reason why the balls should fail to reach the hole in one stroke, and did not care in the least whether they failed or not. The only impressions they received were that Golf was too monotonous and too easy a pastime to have any attractions for them, and that nothing should induce them to indulge in it against such invincible champions as his Majesty and the Ex-Regent.

"I must say, my boy," said the King to his son, as they walked back to the Palace together, "I wish you hadn't gone to that magician fellow. It makes it so very awkward for me."

"It would have been a jolly sight more awkward if I hadn't. Just think of the licking you'd have had, what?"

"Yes, yes—but there's your Mother. She's so set against Magic of any kind. I really don't know what I'm to say to her."

"Well," said Clarence, "I should hope, Guv'nor, you wouldn't be such a jay as to say anything."

"It might be only distressing her unnecessarily," said the King.

"Sidney!" exclaimed the Queen when they met, "I can see by your face that you've been beaten after all!"

"Not at all, my love, not at all. Far from it!"

"Then you've won?"

"Well—er—not exactly won, my dear. We—we finished up all square."

"Considering how long you've been learning, that's as bad as if you'd lost. Now, mind what I say, Sidney, you must never attempt to play golf again after this. I cannot have you making yourself ridiculous!"

"I think you're right, my dear," he said meekly. "In fact, I had already decided to give it up."

Clarence clung to his Golf as long as he could, but he found it dreary work going round the course alone. None of the Courtiers could be induced to learn the game, and he felt a natural reluctance to take on the Marshal as an antagonist, even if the latter had continued to be keen. But he had conceived a strong distaste for the game, and it was rumoured that there had been a stormy interview between him and the Astrologer Royal, who kept his bed for several days afterwards.

And Clarence, as the Yellow Gnomes were impossible as caddies, had to carry his own clubs, which he particularly detested. So in course of time he ceased to visit the links, and thus deprived himself of his only form of open-air exercise.

There was nothing much for him to do, except to lounge and loaf aimlessly about the Palace, with a depressed suspicion that he was not inspiring the full amount of respect that was due to his position as Crown Prince. It would have been a distraction to make advances to Daphne, but, after his somewhat cavalier treatment of her at the Ball, he could not be sure how they would be received. Moreover, either by her own management or his Royal Mother's, he was never given a chance of seeing her except in public.

He found a resource in gambling with the gentlemen of the Royal Household. They played for high stakes, but no higher, seeing that he could replenish his purse as often as it was emptied, than he could well afford. His visits to the sacks of gold in the King's Counting-house became more and more frequent, but he would have derived more enjoyment from cards if he had won occasionally.

One afternoon when, the usual card-players being absent on some hunting expedition, he was left to his own devices, he wandered forlornly through a suite of empty halls till he drifted out upon a balcony that overlooked the Palace gardens.

And then, as he stepped through the window, his heart gave a sudden leap. At the corner of the balcony he had just recognised Daphne. She was quite alone, and he recognised that the opportunity, half-feared, half-desired, had come at last.

CHAPTER VIII

"A STEED THAT KNOWS HIS RIDER"

Daphne turned and saw Prince Clarence almost immediately, and, after making the prescribed curtsey, was about to retreat indoors when he stopped her.

"I say, Lady Daphne," he remonstrated, "don't run away like that!"

"Your Royal Highness will be good enough to excuse me," she said; "I ought to be with Princess Ruby by this time."

"She's all right—trying to teach the Pages hockey in the Entrance Court. And—look here, you needn't be so beastly formal—with me, you know."

"I may remind your Royal Highness that you desired me to observe the strictest etiquette."

"Did I? I only meant in public. Let's drop it just now, anyway. I've been wanting to get a talk with you. You see, you're the only person here I can really talk to; and if you only knew how awfully hipped and depressed I'm feeling—"

"Are you?" she said. "I'm sorry." And there was certainly pity in the soft grey eyes which rested on him for a moment or two.

"I give you my word," he went on, "there are times when I almost wish myself back at the office again. There were things to be done there, even if I didn't do 'em. Here there's nothing—except cards. It wouldn't be so bad if the chaps here only knew Auction—I could hold my own at that. But you couldn't play bridge with the sort of packs they've got in this God-forsaken country. So they've taught me a bally game they call 'Krebsgriff,' and I've lost over two sacks of ducats at it already. Anyone would think after that they'd treat me as a pal, but not a bit of it!"

"Perhaps, Sir, they're afraid of being rebuked for such presumption."

"Perhaps, but I don't think it's that. They're polite enough and all that, to my face, but they don't look up to me, you know!"

"Why should they?" Daphne thought, but all she said was, "That's very sad."

"Isn't it?" he said; "they don't give me a chance to show what I can do. I could knock their silly heads off at golf, and they won't even learn! And now I can't get a game; and this afternoon, when I was feeling inclined for cards, they all go off to the forest without a word to me, hunting beastly boars and bears, and I'm left without a soul to speak to."

"They might have asked you to do them the honour of coming too," said Daphne.

"I couldn't very well have gone if they had. You see, they hunt boars and that on horseback here, and riding's a thing I've never gone in for."

"It's not too late to begin, Sir."

"Well, to tell you the truth, I did think at one time of taking a few lessons. But I don't know. You see, it would get about, and—well, people would think it rather ridiculous."

"I should have thought—" began Daphne; "no, I mustn't say any more."

"Oh, go on, Lady Daphne, don't mind me! What would you have thought?"

"Well," said Daphne boldly, "that nothing could be so ridiculous as a Crown Prince who can't sit a horse."

"I daresay I could as well as any other fellow, if I tried."

"No doubt, sir, but if you never do try."

"I would, if I thought you cared."

"Of course I care, Prince Clarence," said Daphne. "Naturally, I should like to see you doing everything that other Princes do. You really aren't, so far, you know. I suppose I oughtn't to have said that—I couldn't help it."

"That's all right," he said. "There's one thing," he added, thinking aloud, "if I did learn to ride decently, you and I might go out riding together, what?"

"It's rather early to talk about that," said Daphne, "when you haven't even begun to learn."

"I know, but I will begin. For your sake."

"No, Prince Clarence, for your own," she replied, "though I shall be glad, too. And now, I mustn't stay here any longer."

Why, he asked himself, after she had gone, was she so keen on his cutting a figure at Court? The answer was obvious—he had interested and impressed her more than he could have hoped. But that, he shrewdly perceived, only made it more necessary for him to be wary. She was certainly a most fascinating girl, but if she had any ambitious designs on him, she would find that he was quite capable of taking care of himself. Still, she was right about his riding. Every Prince ought to be able to ride. It would not take him long to learn. And when he could ride he would go out hunting. She would think a lot more of him when she saw him returning in triumph with a few boars and bears as trophies of the chase.

Accordingly he took the earliest opportunity of mentioning to his family that he intended to take lessons in horsemanship, which both the King and Queen considered an admirable idea. The Marshal was consulted, and though he opposed it at first, on the ground that anything which might affect the succession to the throne was to be avoided, he gave way in the end, and undertook to act himself as Clarence's riding master. Clarence was prudent enough to stipulate that none of his family should be present while he was undergoing instruction, and the Court were not to be informed that he was having any lessons at all until he had completed the course and become an accomplished equestrian.

"Well, my boy," said the King, when the Crown Prince entered the Royal Parlour after his private lessons in the Palace tiltyard. "Well, and how did you get on, hey?"

"Never got on at all," Clarence reluctantly admitted. "Not likely I should, when there wasn't a bally gee in the stables that would let me come near him!"

"Clarence!" cried his mother, "you don't mean to say you've been there all this time without riding a single horse!"

"I'd have ridden 'em right enough, if they'd let me get on 'em—but they wouldn't."

"And pray what was the Marshal about?" inquired the Queen.

"Well, he was laughing most of the time; it's my belief he'd had 'em all gingered up beforehand."

"I'm quite sure, Clarence, he would be incapable of such conduct as that. Why should he?"

"I don't know," he said. "But I won't have him about again. I'll get some one else to teach me."

"But, my dear boy, nobody can teach you much if you can't even manage to get on a horse's back. You'll only get hurt if you try any more, and you will be far wiser to give it up altogether."

"Not much, Mater!" he declared; "I'm not so easily bested as all that. Now I've begun I mean to go on with it."

And he went on; for, to do Clarence justice, want of pluck was not among his defects. But he was obliged to admit that the Marshal was not fairly accountable for the horses' behaviour, since they were quite as unmanageable when he was no longer there.

They were spirited creatures, but perfectly docile until they caught sight of Clarence, when they immediately became as vicious as the most untameable bronco. If he contrived occasionally to get hoisted into the saddle, he never remained there long enough to put the Royal Chief Huntsman's instructions into practice, and he began at last to have serious doubts whether Nature had ever intended him to shine as a horseman.

He said nothing of these ignominious experiences to Daphne, partly because he never found an opportunity, though more from a fear of being laughed at. But he could not keep them from his family, and so Daphne came to hear of his repeated failures through Princess Ruby. She did not laugh at them, however; she was even a little touched. She thought more of him for his attempts to follow her unlucky suggestion than if he had never attempted anything at all, and fully believed that if he persevered he would conquer in the end.

His Royal Mother was so perturbed and alarmed that at last she made a confidant of the Court Godmother, who was about to depart on her annual visit to the Court of Clairdelune. "He will go on with it!" Queen Selina lamented, "and I know he'll break his neck before long! It does seem so strange that those horrible horses should behave like this with Clarence and nobody else. When his poor dear Grandfather was such a good rider, too! I can't think why they should, Court Godmother, can you?"

The Fairy Vogelflug thought privately that the reason was not very far to see. The horses of the Royal stud were, she knew, of an exceptional aristocratic breed. Now poor Clarence, though of Royal blood on his mother's side, unfortunately had little of the air and appearance which these intelligent and observant animals probably connected with a true Prince. It was more than likely that they had failed to recognise that he was a Prince at all, and so resented being called upon to carry him.

But, though she could be out-spoken enough on occasion, she felt that this was hardly an explanation she could give to his mother. "Well, my dear," she said, "it's very trying for you, of course. But I don't know that there's anything I can do."

"I—I thought perhaps," said Queen Selina, with some natural hesitation, "that you, as a Fairy, might—er—know some quite simple little spell which—"

"As I have told you before," interrupted the Fairy, "I make a point of using my knowledge of Magic as seldom as I can nowadays. I have my health to consider. And, in any case, I am acquainted with no spell for making a Prince into a horseman. Princes in Märchenland," she added, rather unkindly, "have never needed such aids."

But, after all, she was anxious that this Royal family, whom she had been largely responsible for importing, should do her as much credit as possible, and so she applied herself to think of something that might be of help to the unfortunate Crown Prince. A means occurred to her at length, but as she was by no means sure that it would be effectual, she was careful not to commit herself.

She did not even mention it till she was on the point of starting for Clairdelune, and then, before she stepped into her dove-chariot, she suddenly said to the Queen, á propos of nothing in particular, "By the way, my dear, that jewel you were wearing when you first came—I haven't seen you with it for a long while—how is that?"

"Well, you see, Court Godmother, my Crown jewels seem to suit me so much better."

"Then, if you don't want that pendant yourself, you had better give it to your son."

"To Clarence?" cried the Queen. "Why, what use would it be to him?"

"It is a jewel which any Prince might be proud to wear," said the Fairy; "and I should strongly advise you to see that he wears it. Not merely now and then, but constantly. It may—mind, I don't say it will—but it may bring him better luck than he has enjoyed as yet."

"But really, Godmother, I can't quite believe that a thing—" began the Queen, when the Fairy cut her short unceremoniously.

"I've no time to stay here arguing about it," she said; "my doves will be catching cold if they stand about any longer. By all means don't take my advice if you don't believe in it; I merely thought you might find it worth trying—but you must please yourself. And now, with your permission, I'll take my leave of you."

At a sign from her, the team of doves fluttered up in a snow-white cloud and winged their flight to the neighbouring Kingdom of Clairdelune, where she had another Royal Godson, Prince Mirliflor, in whose affairs she took a keener interest than she could in Clarence's.

"Old people have such queer ideas," thought Queen Selina, as the chariot rapidly receded from sight. "As if that twopenny-halfpenny pendant of Miss Heritage's could—but the Court Godmother will be annoyed if I don't follow her advice—and it's best not to offend the old creature. I'll go up and see if it's still in my jewel case."

It was, and she brought it down in time to intercept Clarence as he was starting in rather low spirits for another crowded hour of anything but glorious life in the Riding Court.

"Clarence, my boy," she said, "I want you to oblige me by wearing this in future."

"What—that thing you bought before we came away!" he replied. "I say, Mater, you don't expect me to go about with a woman's pendant on my manly bosom!"

"Your Godmother Vogelflug thinks it is quite a fit ornament for a Prince," urged his mother, "and—and she as much as said that it would bring you good-luck."

"Did she, though? Well, I could do with a bit of that for a change." And he allowed her to fasten the chain round his neck. "By Gad, makes me feel like a Good Forester or a Member of the Ancient Order of Buffaloes or something!" he remarked.

"Never mind," she said; "and it really doesn't look so very out of place. But remember, Clarence, if it's to do any good, you must wear it always."

"Right-oh!" he said; "and now I'll go and take my usual morning toss, what?"

Half an hour later, he came into the Royal Parlour, where his family were assembled, Daphne being with them. He looked round the circle with a satisfied air, and then said in a tone of studied carelessness, "If you've nothing better to do just now, all of you, you may as well look in at the Riding Court in a few minutes, and see how I'm getting on. I—er—should like Lady Daphne to come, too, and the whole Court. Tell 'em to hurry up. You'll find me down there ready for you." He was gone before they had recovered from their surprise.

"Dear me," said the King, "I'm not quite sure that it would be wise to have the Court looking on just yet, eh, my dear?"

"I have every confidence in Clarence," said the Queen. "He would not have suggested that they should attend unless—but perhaps a smaller audience, of just ourselves, might be less trying for him."

So it was only the Royal family and Daphne that went down to the Riding Court, where, to Queen Selina's alarm, some very formidable-looking jumps had been put up.

"He's never going to be rash enough to try to get over those!" she said. "Tell him he's not to run such risks. I can't allow him to!"

Just then Clarence cantered in on a high-spirited mare, over which he seemed to have complete control. He put her at obstacle after obstacle, and surmounted all of them with the greatest ease. To prove that he was equally at home on any mount, he had several other horses brought in, and over each he showed the same mastery, and a seat with which Daphne, who was critical in such matters, could find no fault.

"You young dog!" said his father, when the exhibition was over and Clarence had dismounted. "So you've been taking us in all this time, pretending you couldn't stick on a horse for more than a few seconds, hey?"

"Oh, well," he said modestly, "I didn't like to say too much. Fact is, it's only quite lately that I've felt what you might call at home on a gee."

The Stud grooms could have testified how very lately this was if they had thought proper to do so—which, of course, they did not.

"It only shows what can be done with a little perseverance," said Queen Selina. "Clarence, you will be able to ride through the City now!"

He managed to get Daphne to himself for a few minutes on the way back to the Palace.

"Well, Lady Daphne," he began, "I've done what I could to please you, and I hope you are satisfied, what?"

"Indeed I am, Prince Clarence," she said warmly, for he had risen several places in her esteem during the past hour. "And I congratulate you most heartily. And now things will be ever so much pleasanter for you, won't they?" As she spoke she noticed the pendant, which, of course, she recognised immediately.

"Ah, you're looking at this," he said. "Daresay it strikes you as funny my wearing it?"

"Not at all, Sir," she replied; "it isn't really a woman's ornament." She did not tell him how she knew it was not, for she had not forgotten her undertaking to say nothing about it.

"Well, it was the Mater's," he said. "She's made me promise to wear it always. Thinks it may bring me luck."

"I hope it will, Prince Clarence," she said, quite sincerely; and, as the Queen happened to look back just then and summon her sharply to her side, that was all that passed between him and Daphne on that occasion.

She was rather pleased than otherwise that he should be the possessor of the pendant. As has been said, she had never known her father, so there were no tender associations attaching to it. And she had been a little afraid that Mrs. Wibberley-Stimpson had only bought it out of consideration for her. It was some relief that she had found a use for it. Daphne was, of course, quite unaware who her unknown father had been or that the pendant was a badge of his princely rank; and both the Queen and her son had no suspicion of the truth. Nor did either of them connect it with his suddenly acquired mastery of the whole art of horsemanship, Queen Selina believing that his reports of previous unsuccess had been intended to increase the surprise of his triumph, while Clarence naturally found it easy to persuade himself that he had been learning more from his disheartening failures than he had been conscious of at the time. He certainly did not hide his new talent in a napkin, but organised riding excursions of the lords and ladies of the Royal household, at the head of which he made a very gay and gallant appearance on a prancing bay palfrey. Only there was one thorn in his luxuriously padded saddle. He had hoped that he might have the pleasure of commanding Daphne to ride by his side on these excursions, but, though she accompanied them, it was never on horseback. Queen Selina, it seemed, had developed such a preference for her first lady-in-waiting's society that she was always required to accompany her in the Royal coach.

Daphne would willingly have dispensed with this and other signs of the marked favour with which her Sovereign was overwhelming her just then. She had no illusions as to the motives. The Queen thought—most mistakenly, as it happened—that making a favourite of Daphne was the surest method of snubbing and annoying her other ladies-in-waiting, for whom she had begun to conceive a hearty dislike.

The dislike was certainly reciprocated. They resented their Royal Mistress's insolence as much as they despised her previous obsequiousness. They accepted the fact that she was their Queen, but, among themselves, they did not pretend any respect for her, as was manifest from their habit of referring to her in private as "Mother Schwellenposch!" Edna, who was scarcely more beloved, was known as "Princess Four-eyes," in allusion to her pince-nez. Daphne found it hard at times to refrain from joining them in this irreverence, but, while she saw the Queen's and Edna's weak points as clearly as her companions—and indeed more clearly than any of them—her sense of loyalty kept her silent. She might laugh when she was alone, and frequently did, but that was a relief to her feelings for which she felt she need not reproach herself very severely. Another reason for Queen Selina's insistence on Daphne's company in the coach was, as she was fully aware, the desire to keep her at a safe distance from the Crown Prince—a needless precaution which had its amusing side for her.

Still, she often longed to be on a horse instead of being shut up in a great lumbering vehicle with the Queen and the Princess Royal, even if Princess Ruby's presence did something to make things less dull. On one of these expeditions Queen Selina had once more provided herself with a sack of gold from which she and the Princesses scattered largesse.

"You may throw a little if you like, Miss Heritage," said the Queen graciously. (She reserved the title "Lady Daphne" for occasions when the Court was present.)

"I'd rather not, your Majesty," she replied. "I mean," she explained, "it's not as if it was my money."

"I should have thought," said Edna, "that that was all the more reason for throwing it away." And as she spoke she flung a handful to a stout old citizen, who glared with indignation—not at her, however, but at the nimbler and needier persons who had grabbed most of the coins before he could stoop to pick them up.

Daphne felt rather ashamed of these proceedings, which seemed to her not merely undignified, but likely to demoralise the public. But she said nothing.

"We're not doing this out of ostentation, Miss Heritage," explained the Queen, who seemed to have divined something of her sentiments. "It's policy. You may have noticed that we've not been nearly so well received lately. Why, I don't know, unless there's any ill-feeling about those detestable little Gnomes."

There was a good deal. The Gnomes, having no employment on the golf-links, had recently broken out of their compound and found their way into Eswareinmal, where they made themselves very much at home. They quartered themselves on several of the householders, and, having discovered that cooked food was more palatable than earth, they had no diffidence in helping themselves. In other respects they were inoffensive and inclined to be sociable, but, even in Märchenland, the most harmless and playful Yellow Gnome is not considered a desirable addition to any respectable family. The citizens one and all regarded their visitors as intolerable nuisances for which they had to thank their Sovereigns.

"It was his Majesty's idea to free them," the Queen went on. "I was always in favour of keeping them in the mine, where they were out of mischief. And they certainly mustn't be allowed to run about loose any longer. They ought to learn some sort of discipline. Perhaps the best thing would be to train them as Boy Scouts.... Have you caught cold, Miss Heritage? You seem troubled by a most distressing cough."

King Sidney himself had begun to doubt whether the enfranchisement of the Yellow Gnomes was quite one of his happiest inspirations. Such Märchenlanders as had been induced to enter the mine were demanding wages which left but a small margin for profit, especially when it was considered that, if their methods of working were more systematic than their predecessors', they somehow got very much less gold. No sacks at all had been delivered of late, and the shelves of the Royal Counting-house were beginning to look ominously bare.

He forced himself to mention this to the Queen after the drive that afternoon, and point out the necessity for being rather more economical than they had been hitherto. "I'm sure, Sidney," she protested, "no one can say I am extravagant! It was absolutely necessary to have the whole Palace done up—I had to order some new dresses, as I couldn't be expected to wear ready-made robes in my position, and one or two tiaras and things from the Court Goldsmith, whose charges certainly were disgracefully high. Then the household expenses come to several sacks a week, try as I may to keep them down!"

"I daresay, my love, I daresay—but I hear there was another sack emptied only this afternoon—and we really can't go on like this!"

"Then I shall have to give up driving out altogether, Sidney. You've no idea how unpopular you've made us all by releasing those wretched little Gnomes. The people object to having to associate with them—and I'm sure I don't wonder. You simply must find some way of getting rid of them!"

"The Court Chamberlain tells me a certain number could be taken on the Palace Kitchens as extra scullions."

"And we shall have them getting upstairs and running about all over the Palace!"

"Oh no, my dear; there will be strict orders against that. But, to return to our expenses, I'm afraid Clarence hasn't been as careful as he might have been, and I shall have to speak to him very—"

"No, you will not, Sidney. I won't have you scolding Clarence just when he's doing so well—riding and going out hunting and making himself a social leader. You can give him a hint to be less extravagant if you like—but no more. But the first thing you have to do, is to settle the trouble about those Gnomes. You'd better ask the Marshal if he can suggest anything."

The Marshal's solution was simple but practical. There was, it seemed, a marshy tract at a considerable distance from the capital which needed draining and reclaiming—a work which the more able-bodied of the Gnomes could carry out under strict control. So the majority were deported to the Märchenlands, the remainder being employed in the Royal Kitchens as supernumerary and highly incompetent scullions.

Whether a damp climate would suit the Gnomes' constitutions was not a matter of general concern. Most of them had been supplied with jerseys, which, if they made them look more hideous little objects than ever, had been knitted expressly for them by the Queen and her ladies-in-waiting—and what more could they possibly want?

The citizens of Eswareinmal witnessed the exodus of the gnomes with profound relief, but without any outburst of gratitude to their Sovereign. It had somehow been allowed to transpire that they owed their deliverance entirely to the statesmanship of the ex-Regent.

CHAPTER IX

THE PLEASURES OF THE TABLE

King Sidney's remonstrances to Clarence on his extravagances were put in too mild a form to offend. "Perhaps I have got through rather a lot lately," the Crown Prince admitted. "Not that I spend much on myself—precious little chance in a bally place like this. It mostly goes in tips. You see, the peasants about here think anything under a purse of gold stingy. But it certainly struck me the last time I went to the Counting-house that what sacks there were looked a bit flabby. When do you expect some more in?"

"The Lord Treasurer thinks one or two may be delivered in a week or so—but we shall want considerably more than that to pay our way, and I don't see myself where it's to come from."

"I suppose," said Clarence, "it wouldn't quite do to have the gates melted down, or the thrones; but there's any amount of other gold furniture knocking about—what's the matter with coining that?"

"It did occur to me," confessed King Sidney, "but the Court Chamberlain says they're only silver gilt, and that's no good here, you know."

"Well," said Clarence, "it's pretty clear that we shall all be in the cart if we can't find some way to raise the wind."

A day or two later he burst into the Royal Parlour where his father was sitting disconsolately alone. "I've found it, Guv'nor," he announced triumphantly.

"Eh, my boy, found, what?"

"The way to raise the wind. I've been in to see little Pop-Eye—you know, the Astrologer Royal."

"Xuriel? I haven't seen him since that—er—match I played with the Marshal."

"I daresay not. The Marshal saw him, though—and he hasn't been fit to be seen in public since. Well, it seems he's been pottering away at Magic all this time on the quiet—and quite lately he's come upon an old spell-book of his father's and tried some of the formulas in it. And he's turned out one little thing that's simply it. I bought it of him on the spot. I'll have it brought in here for you to see."

When it was brought it was not much to look at, being just an ordinary round table of the plainest design.

"Ah, but you wait," said Clarence. "Just say to it 'Little table, be laid.'"

"Really, my boy," protested his father, who had evidently forgotten his Grimm's Fairy Tales, "I can't bring myself to—"

"Try it, Guv'nor—and see what happens."

"Oh well, it's all nonsense—all nonsense—but—er—'Little table be laid.'"

Instantly the table was covered with a snowy linen cloth and laid with a daintily prepared meal for one person, including a small flagon of wine and a knife and even a two-pronged fork.

"Neat, isn't it?" remarked Clarence. "The little joker wouldn't part with it at first—afraid of getting into more hot water about it."

"I don't suppose for a moment the food's genuine," said the King. "Well," he pronounced, after trying it, "I'm bound to say it's quite tasty—really very tasty indeed. I think I'll have a little more—ate so little at lunch. The wine isn't at all bad either—sort of Moselle flavour. It would be awkward if your mother were to come in just now, eh?"

"If you've done," said Clarence, "all you've got to say is: 'Little table, be cleared.'"

The King repeated the words, and the table became bare as before.

"Highly ingenious," he said; "but all the same, my boy, considering the cuisine we have in the Palace already, it seems a waste of money to buy it."

"But there's money in it, Guv'nor—money enough to make us all millionaires if we go the right way to work it! Listen to me. Xuriel says he could easily make any quantity of these tables—produce 'em in all styles and sizes, to dine any number, if you and the Mater will only give him a free hand."

"I think you're forgetting, my boy," said King Sidney with dignity, "that there is a law—a law which your mother and I think a very wise and salutary one—against the practice of anything in the nature of—ah—Magic in our dominions."

"Oh, I know that," said Clarence. "But you can alter it easily enough, can't you?"

"No doubt we could. But why should we?"

"Do you mean to say you don't see why? And you've been a business man all your life! Of course, we shouldn't give Xuriel such a concession as this except on our own terms. He's willing to let us take two-thirds of the selling price of every table he sells. And they'll sell like hot cakes! Why, there won't be a family in all Märchenland that can afford to be without one. They'll pay any price we like to put on such an article as this. Just think of it, Dad! No expenses—no risk—and a bigger income than we could ever hope for from any bally mine. You can't let a chance like that slip through your fingers!"

"I quite see the possibilities, my boy!" said the King; "and in fact—but I can't decide one way or the other till I know what your Mother thinks of it."

Queen Selina took an unexpectedly broad-minded view of the scheme as soon as she fully understood its advantages.

"Of course," she said, "nothing would induce me to encourage any enterprise that was based on Sorcery. But the Astrologer Royal is far too respectable a little man to have anything to do with that. And these tables would be such a boon to so many hundreds! We cannot leave that out of consideration. The dear people will be so grateful to us for allowing them to be placed within the reach of the humblest. I daresay Mr. Xuriel would supply them on the hire system. And as for there being any Magic about the process—if there is, it's quite harmless, and it's much more probable that it can be accounted for by purely natural causes which unscientific persons like ourselves can't be expected to understand. After all, who really knows?"

"And who really cares?" added Clarence, "so long as the tables sell. It's lucky the Guv'nor and I have had a business training. We shall be able to check Master Xuriel's accounts—he'll do us in the eye if he can, I'll bet. We'd better start it as a private company. The Patent Self-supplying Tables Co., Limited. Under Royal Patronage, what?"

"I cannot have any in the Palace," objected the Queen. "The chefs would make such a fuss if I did. And another thing, Clarence—it mustn't on any account be known that we take a share of the profits. A Royal Family has to be so very careful that its actions are not misinterpreted."

"We'll be sleeping partners, Mater," said the Crown Prince, "and I don't fancy Master Xuriel will be such a fool as to give us away. So far as the Public'll know, we're interested in the venture on strictly philanthropic principles."

"And that will be quite true," added Queen Selina, "for I can conscientiously say that I wouldn't be connected with it if I didn't feel it was for the general advantage."

Thus was the "Patent Self-supplying Tables Co., Ltd.," founded. A large disused granary in the City was adapted as an Emporium, and the Astrologer Royal, after working day and night for a week, filled it with an extensive stock of dining-tables which were graduated to suit the needs of every class of purchaser.

As Clarence had predicted, they met with a ready sale, for, although Märchenlanders had a tradition of the existence of such tables, they had never expected to be able to procure one for themselves by cash payment.

It was obvious to all that an article which simplified housekeeping by rendering both cook and kitchen fire superfluous was cheap at almost any price, and the demand was so great that Xuriel had to work harder than ever to keep pace with it.

And everybody expressed the greatest satisfaction with the tables when delivered—except, indeed, those citizens who earned their livelihood as provision-dealers. They protested that they were being ruined by what they chose to call unfair competition, and even sent a deputation to the Palace to represent their grievances.

"Show them into the Hall of Audience," said King Sidney, when he was told of their arrival, "and tell them I will be with them presently and hear anything they may have to say."

After he had done so he addressed them in a paternal manner, but with sound common-sense. It was very unfortunate, he admitted, but it was one of these cases where a small minority had to suffer for the benefit of the community at large. As a constitutional and democratic Monarch, he could not interfere to restrict the production of articles that increased the comfort and well-being of the vast majority of his beloved subjects. The deputation had his sincere sympathy, but he could do no more than offer them his advice, which was to escape the starvation they seemed—a little unnecessarily, if he might say so— to apprehend by immediately investing their savings in these self-supplying tables. He added that, from all he could hear, he thought it very probable that the prices would go up very shortly.

The deputation then thanked him and withdrew. Such dealers as could afford the outlay followed his advice, and very soon the sacks in the Sovereign's Counting-house were fuller than ever, and all danger of a Royal bankruptcy was happily at an end, while the Family had the additional pleasure of finding themselves popular once more.

Strictly speaking, the Astrologer Royal had not been authorised to employ his occult skill in producing any objects but the self-supplying dinner-tables, though it was rumoured that his industry was not entirely confined to these. He certainly sold the Crown Prince a sword with which he could face undismayed the fiercest of bears and boars, while the old Court Chamberlain bought a silk skull-cap that he found most useful on occasions when he did not desire to attract attention. But, perhaps from unwillingness to get Xuriel into trouble, neither of them made any mention of these purchases.

Clarence should have been satisfied, for his feats in the saddle and his daring in the forest, where he slew every wild beast he encountered, had rendered him a hero in the eyes of the populace, and even of the Court. And yet he was very far from being satisfied—for what was the good of his glory if it brought him no nearer Daphne? He hoped it was making an impression, but he could not be certain, because he never succeeded in getting a moment alone with her. When she was not in attendance on his Mother she was either with Ruby or the ladies-in-waiting, or, worse still, surrounded by courtiers who had not the tact to withdraw on his appearance. And although she did not seem to show a preference for any one in particular, that did not prevent him from being furiously jealous of them all.

One afternoon Daphne received a message by one of the pages that she was wanted at once in the Hall of Audience by Princess Edna. But when she obeyed the summons the only person she found in the hall was the Crown Prince in hunting costume, with high boots and a plumed hat.

"It's all right," he called out as she hesitated, "Edna will be here directly.... You look as if you didn't believe me."

"I'm afraid I don't, your Royal Highness," said Daphne.

"Don't you? Well, you're right. It was not Edna that sent for you. It was me."

"You might have sent for me in your own name, Prince Clarence."

"I daresay! And then you'd have got out of coming! I've something I particularly want to say to you. And I say—do sit down. It's like this," he proceeded, after Daphne had sat down on one of the benches, "I never seem to see anything of you now—what with all those Courtier chaps always hanging about you. I wonder you let 'em. You wouldn't if you knew as much about 'em as I do. Why, that fellow Hansmeinigel's ancestor was half a hedgehog—a beastly common ordinary hedgehog, by Gad!—and as for young Bohnenranken—"

"Your Royal Highness may spare yourself the trouble of going on," said Daphne. "I know all about their descent already—from themselves. They're not in the least ashamed of their ancestors—indeed they're very proud of them."

"More than I should be if they were mine. Anyhow, there isn't one of 'em that's fit for you to make a pal of."

"You would have more right to say that, Prince Clarence, if I had ever shown the slightest inclination to treat them as 'pals.'"

"You can look higher than bounders like them. And I must say I feel a bit hurt, that you haven't taken more notice of all I've been doing to please you. I mean, learning to ride as I've done, and leading an active life, and all that."

"I really thought your Royal Highness was doing it for your own pleasure. But of course I've noticed the change, and if I've had any share in bringing it about, I'm very glad."

"And is that all I'm to get by it? I want a lot more than that. I want you!"

"Don't be absurd, Prince Clarence," said Daphne. "You know very well you would never be allowed to marry me, even if I—"

"Oh, of course, I know that. But—but, you see, I—er—well, I wasn't thinking of marriage exactly."

"Then," said Daphne, with ominous quietness, "would your Royal Highness be good enough to explain what you were thinking of exactly?"

"Well," he said, "my idea was something more in the nature of a—what do you call it?—a morganatic alliance. Of course even that would have to be kept dark because of the Mater, but—"

Daphne rose. "Prince Clarence," she said, "is it because I have been your sister's Governess that you think you have the right to insult me like this?"

"It isn't an insult," he protested; "you don't understand. I assure you it's quite the usual thing in cases like ours. You'd be none the less thought of—rather the other way about. So why take this narrow-minded, prudish view of it? I didn't expect it—from you, you know!"

"Probably," said Daphne, "you don't expect to get your ears boxed—but you will, if you dare to say any more."

"Oh, do you think you'd better?" he asked. "I mean—smacking a Crown Prince's head—well, it's a jolly serious offence, you know—what?"

"I suppose," she said scornfully, "you think I should deserve to be executed for it."

"It would make a good 'par' in the papers," he replied, "if we had any papers here. Something of this sort: 'The execution of Lady Daphne took place yesterday in the Market Square. There was no hitch, everything, including Lady Daphne's head, going off with the greatest éclat. The Crown Prince was expected to be present, but was unavoidably detained out hunting.'... Ah, you're laughing! You're not so very angry with me after all!"

"I was," said Daphne; "but, after all, you don't know any better, and it really isn't worth while. Still, as it seems I can't expect any consideration from your Royal Highness, it will be impossible for me to remain in her Majesty's service."

He began to realise at last how deeply he had offended her, and to desire a reconciliation on almost any terms.

"No, I say," he pleaded, "don't take it like that. I—I made a mistake. I'll never do it again. I swear I won't! Now won't you stay?"

Daphne looked at him for a moment before she replied. "I wouldn't stay, Prince Clarence," she said, "if I didn't believe you really are a little sorry and ashamed of yourself. And I will only stay now on condition that you never try to speak to me again except in public."

He had a sudden sense of what this would be to him—he might almost as well lose her altogether. There was only one way of obtaining her full forgiveness and the privilege of being alone with her as often as he wished. Of course he would have to pay pretty dearly for it—but, hang it, she was worth making some sacrifice for! He might be able to get round his people after all.... Yes, he'd take the plunge, whatever it cost him.

"But—but look here," he began desperately, "suppose—suppose I ask you"—he was on the point of adding, "to be my wife," when the words died on his lips as he saw that his mother had just entered the Audience Chamber. "Not now," he broke off heartily, "some other time."

Queen Selina regarded Daphne with cold displeasure for a moment or two before speaking. "I was not aware, Miss Heritage," she said, "that your duties required you to be in this part of the Palace at any time."

"I had a summons, your Majesty," explained Daphne, "which I understood was from the Princess Royal, to come to her in the Hall of Audience, or I should not be here."

"If her Royal Highness had required you at all, Miss Heritage, I think it more likely, on the whole, that she would have sent for you to my Bower, where she has been sitting with me all the afternoon. But I will find out if the message came from her."

Daphne bit her lip.

"It did not, your Majesty," she said; "I know now that it was given to me—by mistake."

"A mistake, Miss Heritage, which I trust will not happen again. And, as it is the hour when you should be in attendance on Princess Ruby, I will ask you to go to her at once."

"She wasn't to blame, Mater," said Clarence, after Daphne had left the Hall. "It was all my fault. I sent her that message."

"It's very chivalrous of you, Clarence, to take the blame on yourself," replied his Mother; "but don't imagine you can deceive me. I know very well you are much too clever and wideawake to do anything so compromising. That girl is doing her best to entrap you into some rash promise. I've suspected it for some time."

"No, I don't think so, really, Mater. Just before you came in she was asking me to promise not to speak to her again, except in public."

"And didn't you see that was just her artful way of leading you on? But of course you did! As if you could fail to see through such an obvious trick as that."

Now Clarence came to think of it, it was pretty obvious. He shuddered to remember how very nearly he had been taken in by it. But the shrewdest man is liable to lose his head for the moment. Fortunately he had recovered his in time.

"Well, Mater," he said, "I wasn't born yesterday, you know. I flatter myself I'm up to most moves on the board. And you may depend upon it if she's had any designs on me—mind you, I don't say she has—but if she has, she sees now that they'll never come to anything. She's given me up as a hopeless proposition."

This statement was inspired less by any personal conviction than by the dread that without such reassurance his anxious Mother might dismiss Daphne on the spot.

Queen Selina did not dismiss Daphne, whose powers of keeping Ruby amused and the ladies-in-waiting in good humour were too valuable to be dispensed with unless it was absolutely necessary. But she was allowed to see in many ways that she had fallen from favour. One of these was she was no longer invited to take part in the daily drives, a deprivation which would alone have consoled her for much worse penalties.

And she was freed from any further importunities from the Crown Prince, who kept his side of the compact by maintaining a cold and lofty dignity. Clarence intended this to convey that his eyes were at last open to her designs, and that it would be useless for her to seek to beguile him any longer. But as Daphne was quite guiltless of any designs at all, she was merely grateful to him for leaving her in peace.

Queen Selina generally left it to the Marshal to direct her excursions, and he always rode beside the Royal coach. One afternoon he had conducted her and her eldest daughter by a road across a fertile plain dotted with pleasant villages and isolated farmhouses, towards the outlying spurs of a range of mountains.

On one of these spurs the Queen happened to notice a large castle, whose grim-looking keep and towers were surrounded by a high and far-extending wall, while at its rear rose a frowning black crag.

"Tell me, Marshal," she said, "whose place is that, and who lives there?"

"That is Castle Drachenstolz, your Majesty," he said. "It has belonged for many centuries to a Count who chose, at some time during the previous reign, to change the original family name to that of von Rubenfresser. It's present occupant is the last of the race, the young Count Ruprecht."

"Really!" said the Queen, "considering the Count is so near a neighbour of ours, he might have had the civility to call, or at least leave cards, on us before now!"

"He would no doubt be happy to present himself at Court, Madam, if he were not under strict orders never to go outside his Castle walls."

"But why not?"

"His parents were accused, whether justly or not I cannot say, of certain malpractices, and the late King, your Majesty's gracious grandfather, ordered them both to be put to death. Burnt alive, if I remember rightly. This youth, being a mere infant at that period, was allowed to live, but in semi-confinement within his ancestral walls, with a custodian (who is now removed), and a few old family retainers, who are the only persons he has ever been permitted to see."

"And is there anything against the young Count himself?"

"Nothing whatever," replied the Marshal. "He has been brought up in the simplest manner and on the strictest principles, and by all accounts, is a most amiable and excellent young man."

"It seems rather hard that he should have been a prisoner all these years," said Princess Edna, "for no fault of his own."

"It does seem hard, your Royal Highness, and, in fact, while I was Regent I was on the point of ordering him to be allowed at large, when—when I was relieved of all responsibility. However, his lot is not a very severe one. The estate is large, and he can drive or walk anywhere within its boundaries. I understand that he spends much of his time in his kitchen garden, where he has brought the art of forcing certain vegetables to truly wonderful perfection."

The young Count did not sound from this description particularly exciting, even to Edna, but still she could not get him and his undeserved captivity out of her thoughts, and, as soon as she got back to the Palace, she attacked the King on the subject.

"It's all very well, father," she concluded indignantly, "but in these days you simply can't keep that young man shut up for life just because my great-grandfather chose to have his parents burnt alive—most likely for no reason at all."

"I don't want to keep him shut up, my dear. Never heard of him before. I am quite willing to set him free if I am satisfied that it's the right thing to do."

"Of course it's the right thing to do, Sidney," said his wife; "and, what's more, it will be very popular. Just one of these gracious little acts of clemency that go home to people's hearts. The Marshal quite agreed with me about that."

"Oh, very well," said the King, "I'll send a herald over to tell him he needn't consider himself a prisoner for the future."

"We owe him more than that, Sidney," said the Queen; "we ought at least to ask him over to lunch."

"Yes, we might do that," agreed Edna; "not that he's likely to accept."

"He cannot refuse a Royal command, my love," said her mother.

The Count did not refuse. On the appointed day Clarence and his sisters saw from one of the windows a dilapidated sable coach drawn by eight very ancient coal-black horses turn into the Courtyard.

"Only wants a few undertaker's men in weepers to be a really classy funeral!" was the Crown Prince's tribute to this equipage. "'Come to bury Cæsar, not to praise him,' as Hamlet or some other Shakespearian Johnny says, what?"

When the young Count von Rubenfresser was ushered into the Royal presence his entrance made a slight sensation. Nobody had been prepared for the fact that he was much nearer seven than six feet in height. Otherwise there was nothing alarming about him; he wore his flaxen hair rather long and arranged over the centre of his head in a sort of roll; his china-blue eyes (which Ruby said afterwards was "plain all round, like a fish's eyes") were singularly candid; he had a clear, fresh complexion, full red lips, and magnificent teeth. He wore a rich suit of sable as deep as his coach. "Magog in mourning," Clarence christened him in an undertone.

It was curious that he should have inspired Daphne at first sight with a vague repulsion, and that Ruby should have felt a similar antipathy, though, with her, it took the form of a violent fit of the giggles—but so it was. Daphne was thankful that she was able to remain at a distance from him, as she was not lunching at the Royal Table.

He was shy at first, as most persons would be if the first meal they had ever eaten away from their own home had to be consumed in the presence of Royalty, but he had been evidently trained to observe the ordinary table etiquette, and as he became more at ease he talked fluently enough, though at times with a naïveté that was almost childlike, and increased Clarence's resolve to pull his leg whenever he saw an opportunity.

"Your Majesties must pardon my asking the question," he said, in his thin, piping voice, as he helped himself to a cutlet, "but is this what is called meat?"

"So we're given to understand by the butcher, Count," replied Clarence. "Why do you want to know?"

"Because," he replied, "I've often heard of meat, but this is the first time I've ever seen it. Do you know," he went on presently, "I like meat. I shall have some more."

"I should, if I were you," advised Clarence; "it may make you grow!" which reduced Ruby to silent convulsions.

"Do you really think it will?" inquired the Count, either not noticing, or tactfully disregarding, Princess Ruby's lapse from good manners. "It might. My poor dear Father and Mother were both great meat-eaters, I believe, before they took to vegetarianism, which was quite late in life. I cannot remember seeing them, but I've always understood that they were much taller than I am."

"You don't say so," returned Clarence. "Must have been most interesting people to meet."

"They were, your Royal Highness. Though, unfortunately, I cannot speak of my own knowledge. As your Majesties may be aware, during the short time they were spared to me I was too young to appreciate their society."

"Well, well, Count," said Queen Selina, perceiving that this was delicate ground, "it's all very sad, but you must try not to think about it now. The Marshal tells me you give a great deal of your time to growing vegetables. How do tomatoes do with you?"

"I don't pay any attention to tomatoes, your Majesty," he replied, with a blush that few tomatoes could have outdone. "My efforts have been chiefly directed to pumpkins. I have reared some particularly fine ones. I am very fond of pumpkins."

"Jolly little things, ain't they?" put in Clarence. "So playful!"

"Are they?" said the Count with perfect simplicity. "I did not know that. But then I have never attempted to play with my pumpkins."

"Haven't you?" said Clarence. "Well, you get 'em to play kiss-in-the-ring with you, and you'll find out how frisky they can be!"

"I do not know anything about kissing," he confessed, "except that it is very wrong."

"Not pumpkins," said the Crown Prince. "There's no harm in that! Ask the bishop!"

"I say, old girl," he remarked to Princess Edna, after their visitor had taken his departure, "what on earth induced the Mater to tell that lanky overgrown lout we should be pleased to see him any time he cared to drop in? We shall have the beggar running in and out here like a bally rabbit, you see if we don't!"

"Not if you intend to go on insulting him, Clarence, as you did to-day at lunch," replied Edna coldly.

"Why, I was only ragging him. Who could help ragging such a champion mug as that?"

"There is more—far more—in him than you are capable of seeing, Clarence. And, even from a physical point of view, he is immeasurably your superior."

"I admit I shouldn't have a look in with him if we were both candidates for a Freak Show," he conceded. "On the other hand, no one can say I'm gone at the knees."

"It's a pity, Clarence, that you're so narrow as you are!" she said.

"D'you mean round the chest or calves?" he asked. "Because I'm quite up to the average measurements."

"I meant, so insular in your prejudices. You were almost rude to the poor Count. When he was our guest, too!"

"I expect," he said, "that if he's ever our guest again, I shall be a bit more insular. I can't stick the beggar, somehow!"

CHAPTER X

THE BLONDE BEAST

The Count was not slow to take advantage of his permis de circuler; his coal-black horses and coach were soon a familiar spectacle in the streets of Eswareinmal, where he had discovered the delights of promiscuous shopping. He ordered a self-supplying dinner-table of the best quality—to be paid for by monthly instalments—from the Astrologer Royal, with whom he struck up a sort of friendship. Nor did he neglect to avail himself of his general invitation to the Palace, where he dropped in so frequently as almost to justify Clarence's prediction. Queen Selina gave him occasional hints that she had not expected him quite so often, but hints were thrown away on the Count's ingenuous nature—he seemed to take it for granted that he was always welcome.

Princess Edna certainly never discouraged his visits. She had been struck from the first by his great stature and powerful physique, which were just what she imagined that Nietzsche's ideal Superman would possess. It has already been mentioned that she had been attending lectures on the Nietzschean philosophy.

Those were the days—not so very long ago, though they seem remote enough now—when a certain class of high-browed and serious persons accepted works of modern German philosophers as containing a new gospel which none who desired intellectual freedom, enlightenment, and efficiency could afford to neglect. The theories of "the Will to Power" and of Might being equivalent to Right are already hopelessly discredited in this country by recent exhibitions of the way in which they work out in practice. But it was not so then, and Edna, who liked to feel that she was one of the elect and in the advance guard of Culture, readily imbibed as much of the Nietzschean doctrine as could be boiled down for her in a single lecture. She would not, of course, have thought of regulating her own actions on such principles, any more than, in all probability, did their author himself. But she was very anxious to see some one else do so, and the young Count seemed to have been formed by Nature for Nietzsche's typical "Blond Beast," if he only chose to divulge his possibilities. Unfortunately, he did not seem even to suspect them; he remained quite oppressively mild and amiable. She very nearly gave him up in despair once when he timidly presented her with a pair of mittens which he had knitted for her himself. However, a day came when she saw him under a less discouraging aspect.

They were at lunch, to which he had invited himself as usual, and Ruby had asked her brother how it was that in all his hunting expeditions he had never managed to slay a dragon.

"Never saw one to slay, Kiddie," he replied. "They seem scarce about here."

The Court Chamberlain, from behind the King's chair, took it upon himself to explain that there were no longer any dragons in existence, the few that remained having been exterminated by the late King's orders.

"Oh!" exclaimed Ruby, "I did so want to see a dragon! And now I never shall!"

"If you wish it, little Princess," said Count von Rubenfresser kindly, "you shall see mine."

"Yours!" cried Ruby, quite forgetting her dislike for him in her excitement. "Have you really got a dragon—a real live one?"

"A real live one—and almost full-grown," he replied. "My poor dear Father had a pair, but they were killed. Mine is the last of the breed. I discovered it myself when I was a child in a cave close to the castle. At that time it was only an egg."

"Hatch it yourself?" inquired Clarence.

"Only partially," said the young Count; "the sun did the rest." (It was perhaps as well for Daphne that she was not at the table just then.) "I begged that its life might be spared, and it was. So Tützi and I have grown up together."

"Tootsie!" remarked Clarence sotto voce, "what a dashed silly-ass name for a dragon!"

"And will you show us him?" asked Ruby eagerly. "Mummy, couldn't we go to the Count's castle and see his dragon? This afternoon?"

"I should rather like to see it myself," said her Father. "No idea there were such things. What do you say to our driving back with the Count and having a look at it, eh, my love?"

"I think, Sidney," replied the Queen, "we certainly ought to do so."

So, to Ruby's delight, the State coach was ordered to take the Royal Family to Drachenstolz, and the party set out shortly after lunch. Clarence accompanied them on horseback, while the Count followed in his sombre vehicle. Daphne was left behind, and the Court, although invited to join the party, begged with singular unanimity that they might be excused.

On arriving at the Castle the visitors were first taken over the interior, which was ill-lighted and rather depressing, after which the Count led them through a spacious courtyard to the kitchen-garden, where the Queen deigned to compliment him on the huge size of the vegetable marrows and pumpkins that were ripening in the sun.

"If there should be a Harvest Festival at the Church, Count," she said graciously, "I'm sure some of those would come in very nicely for it!"

They then passed over a rough tract of ground towards a rocky cliff that formed part of the Castle boundary. In this cliff was a deep cavern, on one side of which was a stout staple with a chain attached, only a portion of which was visible. Here their young host stopped and gave a low whistle. Instantly there was a rattle of the chain, and the next moment all but the Count and Ruby hastily retreated as a great horny head with distended nostrils and lidless eyes was protruded from the opening.

"Don't be alarmed!" said the Count, calmly unfastening the chain and leading the creature out into the open. "Tützi is perfectly tame, as you can see."

It may or may not have been full-grown, but it was large enough at all events to be a fairly fearful wildfowl, with its huge leathery wings, crested spine, formidable talons, and restless tail. The colour of its scales was extraordinarily rich, ranging from deepest purple and azure through vivid green to orange and pale yellow, and fully justified King Sidney in remarking—from a safe distance—that "it appeared to be in very good condition."

But there was no doubt about its tameness. It suffered Ruby, who showed no fear of it whatever, to stroke it on its plated beak, and even to scratch it behind its bristly ears, with every sign of satisfaction.

"Ruby!" shrieked the horrified Queen, "come away at once! I'm sure it isn't safe to tease that dreadful thing!"

"I'm not teasing him, Mummy," replied Ruby, whose eccentric penchant for reptiles was now being gratified beyond her wildest dreams. "He loves being tickled. Can't you hear him purring?"

As the noise the brute was making would have drowned that of the most powerful dynamo, the question was almost unnecessary. Count Ruprecht next made his dragon exhibit the few accomplishments it had learnt, which were of the simplest, consisting in sitting up, rolling over and shamming death, and reviving to utter three terrific snorts, supposed to be loyal cheers, all at the proper word of command. He concluded by mounting its back and riding it several times round the enclosure, after which he lay between its forepaws, while it licked his face with its huge flickering forked tongue.

"Capital!" cried Clarence, apparently unimpressed, though he did not venture very near the beast. "You've only to teach it to jump through a hoop, and you'd make quite a decent Music-hall 'turn' together. What do you feed it on, eh? Sop—or canary-seed?"

To which the Count did not vouchsafe any reply.

"I've been most interested, I'm sure, my dear Count," said the Queen, after he had chained it up again. "And it's quite a thing to have seen—once. But we really can't allow you to go on keeping such a creature as that—can we, Sidney?"

"Certainly not, my love," said the King. "It's against the law, you know, Count, against the law."

"Is it, your Majesty?" said the Count. "I—I had no idea of that—no one ever told me so!"

"Well, it is, you know. You must put an end to it—have it destroyed. Painlessly, if you like, but—well, you've got to get rid of it somehow."

"In your own interest, Count," urged the Queen. "Just think how unpopular you would be with your neighbours if it broke loose!"

"I should not like to be unpopular," he said. "And if your Majesties insist on slaying the only living creature that loves me—!"

"What?" put in Clarence unfeelingly, "don't the hearse—I mean the carriage-horses love you?"

But again the Count took no notice of the question.

"It's too bad of you, Father!" cried Edna indignantly; "yes, and you too, Mother! To come here at Count Ruprecht's invitation, to see his dragon and then tell him to destroy it! I think it perfectly disgraceful of you, and you will get a very bad name in the country when people hear of it. When you happen to be Sovereigns you might at least behave as such!"

"Well, well, my dear," said her Mother, who had not considered the question from this side before, "we merely threw it out as a suggestion—nothing more. And if the Count will undertake to keep his dragon under proper control, that is all we shall require of him."

The Count willingly gave this undertaking, and the visit ended without any loss of cordiality on either side.

"We've seen the dragon, Miss Heritage!" Ruby announced with sparkling eyes on her return. "And he is such a darling! Do you know, I don't think the Count can be quite so horrid after all, or Tützi wouldn't be fond of him. Only fancy, Mums and Daddy wanted the Count to have him killed! But Edna made them say he needn't. Aren't you glad?... Oh, I forgot—you never really loved my newts. But you would Tützi—he's quite dry, you know—not the least bit clammy.... Do you think there's time before dinner for me to run down and play with the Gnomes?"

"My dearest!" cried Daphne, "surely your Mother doesn't approve of your doing that?"

"She wouldn't mind if she knew. They're yellow—but quite nice. Much better fun than those fat little muffs of pages, who are too afraid of spoiling their clothes to play at anything rough. You don't mind my having a game of 'I spy' with the Gnomes—just till it's time to dress for dinner—do you, Miss Heritage?"

"Well, darling," said Daphne, "I'm not allowed any authority over you now, you know. But I'm quite sure that if her Majesty ever hears of your running about with Yellow Gnomes, she will blame me for it, and probably send me away."

"Oh, then I won't any more. Only it will be rather dull without them. I almost wish sometimes I had lessons to do. But there's nothing for me to learn. I can understand everything everybody says, and they understand me. And there aren't any pianos, and History and Geography are no earthly good here, and I know more Arithmetic as it is than I shall ever want now I'm a Princess. Princess Flachspinnenlos promised to show me how to work a spinning-wheel some day, but she's not very good at it herself, and anyhow, I'm sure it will be frightfully boring. Still, I'd rather give up the Gnomes than lose you, Miss Heritage, dearest!"

She spoke with feeling, for it meant abandoning a cherished scheme of hers for inciting them to steal up during dinner and pinch the pages' legs.

Daphne was sorry for the poor little tomboy Princess, of whom she had grown to be really fond. There was little she could do for her, however, beyond being with her as often as she could; and the Queen had shown a tendency of late to discourage even this.

Edna looked forward with interest to the Count's next visit; his performances with the dragon had impressed her greatly in his favour, and she had begun to think that he might have the makings of a Superman in him after all. It might be time to begin his education, and she prepared herself for the task by running through her lecture notes on Nietzsche once more.

When he called he was shown by her command to the chamber which served as her boudoir, where, rather to the scandal of some of the Court ladies, she received him in private.

He looked taller than ever as he sat doubled up on a low seat. "I came to thank you, Princess," he began, "for persuading your exalted parents to spare my poor dear Tützi. Of course I don't want to break the law, but he is chained up, and besides, he is such a good dragon that I'm sure nobody could object to my keeping him."

"Why are you so anxious not to break the law?"

"Because it's wrong to break laws."

"And do you never do anything wrong?"

"Never. My tutors taught me that people who do wrong are always punished for it. I shouldn't like to be punished at all."

"Still, you must have wanted to do bad things now and then."

"Now and then I have," he confessed. "Especially lately. But I never do them. You see, bad people are never really liked."

"Do you know, Count, what the great German philosopher Nietzsche would call such goodness as yours? He would say it was 'slave-morality.' You only do what other people tell you is right because you're afraid of what they would think of you if you didn't. You have courage enough to master Tützi, but you daren't defy what Nietzsche so finely terms 'the Great Dragon of the Law,' which says: 'Thou shalt'—'Thou shalt not.'"

"What?" he said in surprise. "Is there another dragon besides Tützi? And one that can talk, too! I never heard of him!"

"Nietzsche was speaking metaphorically, of course," said Edna impatiently. "He meant the human laws and customs and prejudices which a true Superman should soar above. I think you ought to be more of a Superman."

"Ought I?" he said, open-mouthed. "What sort of things does a—one of those gentlemen—do?"

"Well," said Edna, after refreshing her memory by her notes, "you should begin by 'hating and despising the ideals of the average man'! You should create your own Truth—your own Morality. Obey only your primordial instincts—the Will to Power."

"I wonder if I could do all that."

"Of course you can, if you are strong enough—and I believe you are."

"And what else ought I to do, Princess?"

"Well, let me see—oh, yes, you should 'act towards slave or stranger exactly as you think fit.' You should be 'an intrepid experimentalist, ceaselessly looking for new forms of existence.' You must 'be able to bear the sight of others' pain, remembering that you cannot attain the height of greatness—'"

"I've grown taller lately," he interjected, "a great deal taller; haven't you noticed it?"

"'Attain the height of greatness,'" resumed Edna severely, "if you do not feel within yourself both the will and the power to inflict great suffering! And 'through it all you must exhibit the joyous innocence of a child that is amusing itself.' Do you understand?"

"I think I do. It means I must do whatever I feel inclined, without minding what people say. Shall you be pleased with me, Princess, if I do that?"

"I shall at least respect you more than I can do while you form your conduct entirely on Sunday School standards."

"Then I'll try," he said. "Yes, I will certainly try. Do you know, I think I shall rather like being what your great teacher with a name like a sneeze calls a Superman."

"Then make yourself one," she said, "for I am quite sure that you have the power."

Probably she did not know herself exactly what she wanted him to be; it did not mean much more than the admiration for the prehistoric male brute to which the more advanced type of young woman seems peculiarly prone. But when he left she felt that she had made a most promising convert, and had every reason to be satisfied with the success of her afternoon.

As much could not be said with regard to her Mother, who remonstrated with her after the Count's departure as strongly as she dared.

"I shouldn't see him alone like that, again, my love," she said anxiously. "It might put ideas into people's heads. Indeed I'm not sure that, as it is, some of the Court don't think there must be something between you."

"It's perfectly indifferent to me what they think, Mother," was the lofty reply. "As a matter of fact, there is nothing whatever between us. I am merely doing what I can to make him a little more civilised."

"There would be no objection to that, my dear. Only it does look so very like encouraging him, you know. And it's so necessary to be careful just now. I'm afraid the People think we are making far too much of that young man. I noticed they looked very black that day we drove over to Drachenstolz. I really think it would be better if the next time he calls you would be 'not at home' to him."

"My dear Mother," returned Edna, "I am old enough to have the right to choose my own friends, and I shall certainly decline to drop them just because the Court chooses to make my friendships a subject for foolish gossip."

Queen Selina did not venture to pursue the conversation any farther, but she was more relieved than she would once have thought possible when she heard that the Court Godmother had returned from Clairdelune. According to strict etiquette, it was for the Fairy to attend her Mistress and report herself, but the Queen waived all ceremony by paying the first visit. She went at once, and unattended, to the apartments in one of the towers that had been assigned to the Court Godmother, who, without seeming at all overwhelmed by such condescension, received her with more benignity than usual. "Thank you, my dear," she said, in answer to the Queen's inquiries, "I am tolerably well, and feel no ill effects from my journey. And I think," she added complacently, "you will agree that I have spent my time at Clairdelune not altogether unprofitably. But you shall hear all about it presently. Tell me how things have been going on here while I have been away. As satisfactorily, I trust, as possible?"

"Oh, quite—quite—that is, I've been just a little worried lately about that young Count Rubenfresser. He has taken to coming here oftener than I think quite desirable."

"Coming here?" repeated the Fairy, with surprise. "Why, I thought he was never allowed outside his Castle!"

"Not till lately. My poor dear Grandfather seems to have been very severe both on him and his parents. But the Marshal spoke so highly of the poor young man, and recommended so strongly that he should be given his freedom, that his Majesty and I decided to do it."

"Oh," said the Fairy. "Well, of course, if the Marshal thinks it safe!" She suspected the ex-Regent of cherishing some resentment against her still for the part she had taken in bringing back the Sovereigns to supersede him, and she had no wish to run counter to him again. So, whatever she might think of the wisdom of his advice, she was far too prudent an old person to express her doubts. "But I gather," she went on, "that you don't approve of the young Count yourself, my dear?"

"Oh, he seems gentlemanly enough—though rather taller than the average. The only reason that I disapprove of him is that I'm afraid he comes here so often on Edna's account."

"You don't mean," said the Court Godmother, in some alarm, "that she shows any—?"

"Oh, dear me, no! Not the slightest! She thinks he requires civilising, and is trying to do it for him, that's all. But I can't get her to see that the notice she takes of him is liable to be misunderstood. Not only by him—but by everybody, you know."

"Oh well, my dear, if it's no worse than that, you needn't trouble yourself about it. And now for my news. You've heard me speak of Prince Mirliflor of Clairdelune, King Tournesol's only son?"

Queen Selina had heard her speak of him so often that she instinctively prepared herself for half an hour of ennui.

"A charming young man. I don't say he hasn't his faults, but I shall make it my business to cure him of them all in time. I was one of the three Godmothers at his christening—the other two have gone years ago—I forget what their gifts were—Courage and Good-looks, I think. I gave him what I still consider a most useful present for any infant prince—a complete set of the highest ideals."

"How nice!" murmured Queen Selina absently, for her attention was beginning to wander already. "Most neat and appropriate, I'm sure."

"They would have been," said the old Fairy, "if he'd made use of them sensibly, as I intended. But that is just what he hasn't done. For instance, although he's been of an age to marry these three years, he's refused to look at every eligible Princess that has been suggested to him because, if you please, she doesn't happen to come up to his ideal of beauty!"

"Dear me," said the Queen, concealing a yawn, "you don't say so, Court Godmother!"

"My dear," said the Fairy irritably, "it's nonsense to tell me I don't say what I've just said! And, as I was about to tell you, his conduct caused the greatest disappointment and annoyance to his father, who is naturally anxious that his line should not die out. So he begged me to use my influence. Well, I saw, of course, that the only way was to appeal to another of the ideals I had given him—his ideal of Duty. I put it to him that he owed it not only to his father, but his country, to choose a bride without any further shilly-shallying."

"And what did he say?" asked the Queen, with more interest, as she had begun to see what was coming.

"Don't be in such a hurry," said the Fairy; "I haven't finished what I said yet. I told him that personal beauty was of very little consequence in a bride, and that what he needed was a sensible girl who would be clever enough to keep him from having too high an opinion of himself—which, I may say, has always been one of his failings. I added that your Edna was just the very person for him."

"How kind of you to put in a word for her!" said Queen Selina. "And—was it any good?"

"So much so that, to his father's great joy, he recognised that it was his imperative duty to seek the hand of such a paragon of wisdom and learning. And I am empowered by him to prepare you for his arrival in the course of a day or two, in the character of the Princess Royal's suitor. So you see," she concluded, "I haven't been at Clairdelune all this time for nothing."

"Indeed you have not, dear Court Godmother; and I'm most grateful, I'm sure, for all the trouble you must have taken. Fancy our Edna the Queen of Clairdelune some day! Not that she isn't fitted for any position. How pleased she will be when she hears of this, dear thing! So will his Majesty—and Clarence too! He and dear Prince Mirliflor will be able to go out hunting together. For—I forgot to tell you—since you have deserted us, Clarence has learnt to ride most beautifully!"

"Has he indeed?" said the Fairy. "Then I was right after all. I thought it just possible that, if you could persuade him to wear that jewel—"

"Do you mean that pendant of mine? He does wear it, but that has nothing whatever to do with his riding. He'd taught himself to ride long before I gave it to him. He was only pretending he couldn't, as a joke."

"He may say so, my dear—but, all the same, if it hadn't been for that jewel—"

"Really, Court Godmother," said Queen Selina, who naturally resented anything that detracted from her son's credit, "it astonishes me to find anyone so—so clear-headed as you are in most things still clinging to these superstitious ideas. As if the mere fact of wearing a piece of jewellery could suddenly make anyone into a good rider!"

"It depends upon what the piece of jewellery is," said the Fairy.

Queen Selina saw her way to an absolutely crushing rejoinder. "Well, this particular piece of jewellery," she said, "happens to be a paltry ornament which I bought from Miss Heritage before I ever heard of Märchenland."

Her shot had certainly told. "What?" faltered the Court Godmother, obviously out of countenance. "Did I understand you to say you bought that jewel—and from the Lady Daphne?"

"I prefer to call her Miss Heritage—the other is merely a courtesy title. Yes, I did buy it from her. She was in difficulties at the time, and I gave her thirty pounds for it, which was a good deal more than anybody else would have done."

"And—and—have you told this to any other person—the—the Marshal, for instance?"

"My dear Court Godmother, I am not in the habit of proclaiming my acts of charity—for it was an act of charity!"

"An act of charity," said the Fairy drily, "which I should strongly advise you to keep to yourself."

"I intend to," replied the Queen, as she rose with much dignity, though her face was redder than usual. "I should never have mentioned it at all, even to you, Court Godmother, if I hadn't felt it necessary. Of course, in my present position, I should never dream of buying jewellery from one of my own ladies-in-waiting. But it was different then. I hadn't come into my Kingdom, and Miss Heritage was only my governess; and anyway, it was a perfectly fair bargain, so my conscience is absolutely clear. Still," she added, turning on the threshold, "perhaps you will admit now that you were just a little mistaken in attaching any importance to wearing that pendant?"

"Yes," said the Fairy, completely crestfallen and subdued, "I made a mistake—a great mistake—I admit that."

"I thought you would!" returned the Queen triumphantly. "And now I must go to dear Edna and tell her the news about Prince Mirliflor."

She had no suspicion of the state of mind in which, by her unconscious revelation, she was leaving the unhappy Court Godmother, who was so stunned that it was some time before she could think out the situation at all clearly.

The present Sovereigns of Märchenland, it seemed, were nothing but impostors! Innocent impostors, no doubt—but that did not lessen her own responsibility for helping to place them on the throne. If she made the truth known, would the people—worse still, would the ex-Regent—believe that she and the Baron and the Astrologer Royal had not been deceiving them from the first? She recognised now that they had been too ready to accept the wearer of Prince Chrysopras's jewelled badge as the sought-for Queen without some further inquiry—and yet who in all Märchenland would have dreamed of making any? How could anyone have supposed that Queen Selina had merely become the possessor of the jewel by purchasing it from that little Lady Daphne? It seemed to follow that Lady Daphne must be the true Queen. The Fairy remembered now that she had taken her to be so at their first meeting. If only she had thought then of asking a question or two, the mistake might have been discovered before matters had gone too far—but, in her unfortunate anxiety to see a legitimate sovereign ruling Märchenland once more she had taken everything for granted. How could she put it right now without appearing either a traitress to the Kingdom, or at least a foolish old Fairy who ought to have known her own business better? That was a bitter reflection for an autocratic dame who had long been accustomed to consider that age and experience had endowed her with a wisdom which was absolutely infallible.

There was just one faint hope to which she clung. She had been mistaken once—why should she not be mistaken again? Lady Daphne might herself have bought the pendant from some third person. In that case she would have no better claim to the throne than Queen Selina, and matters could be left as they were—which would relieve the Fairy of the unpleasant necessity of having to admit that she was liable to error.

She could not rest till she knew more, and so, as soon as she felt equal to any action, she took her crutch-handled staff, hobbled down the winding steps, and then up more stairs and along a succession of corridors, until she reached the door of the chamber she had been told was Daphne's.

"I shall know very soon now!" she told herself. "And, after all, there's nothing to be uneasy about. Whoever this girl may be, it's most unlikely that she will turn out to be any relation of poor Chrysopras'."

But, in spite of these reassurances, it was a very tremulous hand that rapped at the door, and the Court Godmother's heart sank as she heard a clear sweet voice inviting her to enter.

It would have been such a relief, just then, to find that Daphne was not in her room.

CHAPTER XI

A WAY OUT

Daphne was rather surprised to see the Court Godmother enter, for she had not honoured her by any special notice since her first arrival. But she was pleased, and touched as well, by a visit which she knew must have cost the old Fairy considerable effort.

"I thought I'd come up and see how you were getting on, my dear," began the latter, after sinking into the chair Daphne had brought forward for her, and recovering her breath. "I hope you are happy here—and—and well treated?"

"Quite, thanks, Court Godmother," said Daphne.

"But you shouldn't sit moping here by yourself like this."

"Her Majesty doesn't like me to come down until she sends for me," explained Daphne; "and she hasn't to-day. But I haven't been moping, Court Godmother; I've been listening to the swallows. They're discussing their plans for the winter, and they can't make up their minds where to go, poor darlings!"

"That's only what you fancy they're talking about," said the Fairy sharply; for the gift of understanding bird-language is comparatively rare, and only possessed by those who have a strain of Fairy blood in their descent. "You can't possibly know!"

"I didn't till I came here, and then I suddenly found I could. Princess Ruby declares I make it all up—but I don't. I can even understand what some of the animals have to say, and its rather fun sometimes. The other morning in the Gardens I heard a tortoise telling a squirrel—"

"I daresay, I daresay," interrupted the Court Godmother, who had not come there to hear the small talk of any tortoise; "I find their conversation wearisome myself—and so will you when you've been here a little longer. And so you're comfortable here, are you?" she went on, looking round the chamber, which had walls of mother-o'-pearl with hangings of delicate shimmering blue-green at the window and round the small ivory four-post bed. "Well, this room looks very cool and pleasant. And you've pretty dresses to wear, it seems. I like that one you have on—most becoming, though it wants an ornament of some kind to set it off. But perhaps you don't care for jewellery?"

"I do," said Daphne, "very much. But I haven't any now, you see."

"But you had once, hadn't you? I seem to recollect the Queen telling me she bought something—a pendant, I fancy she said—from you before you came to Märchenland. Or was it somebody else?"

"No, it was me," said Daphne. "It was very decent of her, because I was in rather a hole just then—with a debt I couldn't possibly have paid otherwise—and the pendant was no use to me, you see—not a thing I could ever have worn."

"So you wasted your money in buying an ornament which was unsuited to you, eh?"

"I didn't buy it, Court Godmother," said Daphne, and proceeded to explain—much as she had done at "Inglegarth"—how it came into her possession. The Fairy questioned her about her father, but she had little information to give. Even his name was uncertain, as it seemed he had only moved into his last rooms shortly before his death. All his landlady could say was that it was something foreign which she could not pronounce. But she had gathered from certain things he had let fall that he had led a wandering life as a musician, and had at one period been a riding-master. She believed that, in the latter capacity, he had met his young wife, Daphne's mother, and that it had been a runaway marriage. She died soon after giving birth to Daphne, and left him so broken-hearted that he did not care to make any fight against illness when it came to him, but rather welcomed a death that meant re-union. "But all I really know," concluded Daphne, "is that that pendant belonged to him, and that my adopted Mother took care of it for me till I was grown up. And I think he would not have minded my selling it when I wanted the money so badly."

"Well, whether he would have minded or not," said the Fairy, "you did sell it—and a sorry bargain you made of it, too! I'll be bound, now, that you've told the whole Court about it long ago!"

"I have told no one, Court Godmother," said Daphne. "Why should I tell them about my own private affairs? I shouldn't have said anything to you, if you hadn't heard of it already from her Majesty."

"You were wise to hold your tongue," remarked the Fairy, greatly relieved. "For I may tell you that, if the Court once heard that the Queen bought that jewel from you, it would prejudice them very seriously against her. And I am sure you would not wish that."

"Of course I shouldn't wish it," said Daphne, a little haughtily. "Though how I could prejudice her Majesty by telling anybody of an instance of her kindness to me, I really don't know. She's scarcely worn the pendant herself, and now she's given it to Prince Clarence. But nobody knows that it was once mine, and you can be quite sure that nobody ever will, from me."

"In a Court like this, my child," said the Fairy, almost apologetically, "one cannot be too careful. But I can see you are to be trusted." And, after some conversation on less dangerous subjects, she retired.

Her worst fears had been confirmed; she could no longer doubt that Daphne was Prince Chrysopras's daughter. She wondered now how she could ever have doubted it. But this constituted her Daphne's official Godmother. As such, was it not her duty to see that she had her rights?

If she did her duty to her godchild it might entail very unpleasant consequences to herself—consequences from which she felt herself shrinking as much as ever. Might they not be avoided? Daphne evidently had no suspicion of her claims. And, as the Fairy reminded herself, "What the eye does not miss the heart will not grieve for." The child was quite happy and contented as she was. If the Marshal still had any ambition to resume his power, he would have no scruples about removing any rival.

"I should only be exposing her to danger," thought the Court Godmother. And there were the poor King and Queen to be considered, and the Baron and the Astrologer Royal, who would all go down in the general débâcle if the truth were allowed to come out. She was bound to think of them. So far as she could see, the only result of disclosure would be to establish the Marshal as Monarch—and they had had quite enough of him as Regent.

So, as it is seldom difficult to discover insuperable objections to any course that one has strong personal reasons for avoiding, the Fairy easily persuaded herself that she owed it to others to remain silent. The secret was safe enough. Both Queen Selina and Daphne could be depended on not to betray it now. It was better for everybody concerned—particularly the Court Godmother—that it should remain unknown for ever.

Still, her conscience smote her a little with regard to Daphne. She was so well fitted to be a Queen—it seemed hard that she should forfeit the crown that was rightfully hers. "But that's entirely her own fault!" the Fairy told herself. "Xuriel read the stars quite correctly. He foretold not only the very spot where she would be discovered, but the sign by which she was to be recognised. If she chose to part with the jewel to another, she must take the consequences. I'm not responsible!"

And yet, after all, Daphne was her god-daughter, if she could not be openly acknowledged as such. Something must be done to make up to the poor child for all she had lost. And here the Fairy had a positively brilliant idea—why not marry her to Mirliflor? But almost immediately she remembered with dismay that she had been making a very different matrimonial arrangement for him. That, however, was before she knew what she knew now. The case was entirely altered—she could not possibly allow him to commit himself to an alliance with a daughter of these usurpers. That must be prevented at all hazards, and fortunately he had taken no irretrievable step as yet. "Unless I'm much mistaken," she thought, "he will forget all about Princess Edna if he once sees Lady Daphne. She ought to be lovely enough to satisfy even his ideal. But if he doesn't see her soon, it may be too late to save him."

Like most Fairy Godmothers, she possessed the power of impressing any protégé of hers who was not more than a couple of hundred leagues away with a perfectly distinct vision of anybody or anything she chose. She had made not a few matches by this means in her best days, and some of them had not turned out at all badly. But it was a long time since she had last exercised any of her occult faculties. To do so demanded a concentration of will-power and psychic force which told on her more and more severely as she advanced in years, and she had resolved to abstain from any practices that might shorten the life to which she had every intention of clinging as long as possible.

"But I must risk it—just for this once," she decided. "Yes, I'll make him dream of her this very night."

Meanwhile Queen Selina had informed her daughter of the brilliant future that awaited her, and was not a little annoyed at Edna's failure to express the least enthusiasm.

"I wish Godmother wouldn't meddle like this in my affairs," she said. "I suppose I shall have to see this Prince Mirliflor now if he comes; but it is not at all likely that he will have any of the qualities that appeal to me."

"My love!" remonstrated Queen Selina. "He will be the King of Clairdelune some day!"

"He may be, Mother," returned Edna. "But that is a consideration which I shall not allow to affect me in the slightest."

"Of course not, my dear," said her Mother, feeling that Edna could be safely trusted to look after her own interests. "You are free to decide exactly as you please. I shall put no pressure on you whatever."

"My dear Mother," returned Edna, "you would gain nothing by it if you did."

That night the Court Godmother retired early, and spent a long and strenuous vigil in calling up a vivid recollection of Daphne as she had seen her that afternoon, and imprinting the vision on her godson's sleeping brain. She was unwell in consequence all the next day, but she was easier in her mind after having prevented any untoward effects her counsels might have had upon Mirliflor. It was rather a strain upon her to face the Royal Family again, but she forced herself, for her own sake, to treat them with as much outward respect as before.

She had begun to think that the worst was over when an envoy suddenly arrived in hot haste from Clairdelune bearing a formal proposal from Prince Mirliflor for Princess Edna's hand, and the information that he was following shortly to plead his suit in person.

He had also entrusted the messenger with a short despatch to his Godmother, which she read with impotent fury. It was a somewhat involved and incoherent letter, expressing his thanks for the vision, for which he could not doubt he was indebted to her, but intimating that she had convinced him so forcibly that Princess Edna possessed qualities infinitely more precious than the most exquisite beauty, that his determination to win her had already been irrevocably fixed.

"Prefers her to Lady Daphne, does he?" she said to herself, as she realised that she would be forced to speak out now if he was to be saved from such an alliance. "Then he must marry her, that's all! I can't and won't turn all Märchenland topsy-turvy on his account! I've done all I could for him, and I shall leave him to go his own way. I'll go up to bed before he arrives, and I expect it will be a long time before I'm able to come down, for I feel sure I am going to be ill—and little wonder!"

Queen Selina was so elated by the Prince's message that she ordered it to be publicly announced at once. The Court, whom she informed herself, expressed the greatest delight, and, as for the old Court Chamberlain von Eisenbänden, he was almost lyrical in his jubilation.

"This is indeed a glorious day, Madam!" he cried. "It has long been my dream to see the reigning houses of Märchenland and Clairdelune united, but of late I had begun to despair that it would ever be accomplished! And from all I have heard of Prince Mirliflor, her Royal Highness is almost as much to be felicitated as he!"

"Thank you, Baron," replied the Queen. "We are all most pleased about it. Though I shall be very lonely without her. You see," she added, raising her voice for the benefit of such of her ladies-in-waiting as happened to be within hearing, "there is no one else here who is any companion for me. I can't make intimate friends of any of my ladies, as I could of the dear old Duchess of Gleneagles, for instance, or even the Marchioness of Muscombe. Ah, my dear Baron, our English aristocracy! You've nothing to approach them in a country like this—nothing!"

"I can well understand," he said, "that your Majesty must feel the loss of such society."

"I miss it, Baron," Queen Selina confessed, without untruthfulness, seeing that she always had missed it. "It is only natural that I should. The Duchess is such a sweet woman—a true grande dame! And the Marchioness, though only a peeress by marriage, such a clever, talented creature! They would both have so rejoiced to hear of our dear Edna's engagement—she was such a favourite of theirs, you know! I remember the Duchess always prophesied that she would make a brilliant marriage."

These particulars were thrown in mainly for the edification of the Court, but Queen Selina had almost brought herself to believe them, and, in any case, none of her own family was at hand just then, so she was safe from contradiction.

The announcement of Prince Mirlinor's proposal had no sooner reached Count Rubenfresser's ears than he drove over to the Palace, to ascertain from Edna herself whether the report had any truth in it. He succeeded in obtaining a private interview, and at once put his question.

"It is only true so far as that the Prince has proposed to me by letter," Edna informed him. "Whether I shall accept him when he appears will depend entirely upon circumstances."

"You won't accept him, Princess," said the Count, drawing himself up to his full height, which was now well over seven feet. "Or, if you do, he will never wed you. I shall see to that!"

"Really, Count!" protested Princess Edna, feeling secretly rather pleased. "I don't quite see what it has to do with you."

"Don't you?" he replied. "I might want to marry you myself. I've been thinking of it lately."

"Have you?" said Edna, not so pleased. "That is very good of you. But has it never occurred to you that I might have a voice in the matter?"

"You would have to belong to me, if I wanted you badly enough," he said calmly.

"And you're not sure yet if you do want me badly enough, but, in the meantime, you would prevent anyone else from marrying me if you could—is that it?"

"That's exactly it!" he said, gratified at being so thoroughly understood.

"Well, can't you see how selfish that is of you?"

"It's splendid being selfish," he said, "and not really so difficult after all—when you try."

"And how do you suppose you could prevent me from marrying Prince Mirliflor if I thought proper to accept him?"

"Oh, that would be easy. I should only have to unchain Tützi, and send him to kill the Prince for me. Tützi's so intelligent and obedient that he'll do everything I tell him."

"I think you forget, Count, that it's against the law to let that dragon loose."

"I know," he said; "but I've no respect for human laws any more. I'm not going to obey anything in future, except my own instincts."

"I'm sure you don't mean that. And if you really sent that dragon to kill anybody—especially anyone who had done nothing to offend you—it would be very wicked indeed."

"Other people might think so," he said. "I shouldn't myself—and that's all that really matters. I'm going to make my own morality for the future. I want to be a Superman, like that learned man you told me about with the odd name. Aren't you glad I'm taking your advice?"

"Of course I am pleased," said Edna, "that you should be more independent and unconventional and assert yourself—which is all that Nietzsche really meant. You mustn't carry it too far, you know."

"But you said I couldn't be really great unless I felt the will and the power to inflict great suffering," he said; "and that's just what I do feel."

"Yes, but you can feel the will and the power without actually inflicting suffering," said Edna instructively. "Nietzsche never intended that. And if you set that horrid dragon of yours at the Prince, you would inflict very great suffering indeed."

"I shouldn't mind that," he said.

"Perhaps not—but Father and Mother would. And you would be imprisoned again, and lose your dragon as well. But I don't suppose for a moment you are serious. It would be too absurd of you to threaten violence to a Prince before I've ever seen him or made up my mind to accept him—which most likely I shall not do."

"That is true," he said, rather as if he were glad of an excuse for not taking any immediate action. "Yes, I will wait till I hear whether he is betrothed to you or not. But if I find he is, I shall have to clear him out of my path somehow or other."

He left Edna with the consciousness that she had been more than usually interested. The Count was certainly developing. She liked his new air of self-confident domination. It would be rather thrilling, she thought, to be wooed in this masterful way. But he had taken some pains to let her see that he was not sure yet whether she was worth the trouble of wooing! That was insulting, of course, but he might alter his opinion in time—and then she would know how to avenge herself. She wondered if Prince Mirliflor would be ardent and domineering enough to carry her by storm, and caught herself hoping he might be.

But when, shortly afterwards, she heard that he was just entering the Courtyard of the Palace with his suite, she was seized by a sudden panic. "You go down and speak to him, Mother," she implored the Queen. "I—I can't see him just yet. And make him understand that I must get to know him better before I can give him a definite answer."

Queen Selina bustled down to the State Reception Hall, where she arrived in a highly flurried condition, just after the Prince and his brilliant retinue had been ushered in.

"My dear Prince!" she began. "This is really too kind! So delighted by your proposal—we all are—dear Edna especially. We feel it such a compliment. My husband—his Majesty, I mean—will be in directly, but Edna has asked me to make her apologies for not coming down for a few minutes. The poor child—naturally—is feeling a little shy and overcome."

"Madam," said the Prince, whose comely face and gallant bearing had already won him the sympathies of those of the Court who were present, and particularly the Court Chamberlain's, "I count each minute a month until I have the happiness of looking upon the enchanting face that has haunted me constantly from the moment I beheld it in a vision."

"In a vision?" cried the Queen. "How very odd! But how did you know, Prince, it was our Edna?"

"I will attempt to describe my vision, Madam," he replied, "and, though my poor words cannot hope to do it justice, they will at least convince you that it was indeed the Princess whom I was permitted to see."

He described her as well as he could, though with a growing bewilderment that the lady of his dream should have a Mother who so little resembled her.

Queen Selina listened to his rhapsody with misgivings. With every allowance for the fervour of a lover who was also a Fairy Prince, even maternal partiality could not blind her to the fact that his description would be far less incorrect as applied to that Heritage girl than to the Princess Edna.

"It certainly suggests dear Edna, Prince," she remarked, with a mental note that Daphne must be kept out of his way. "Except, perhaps in one or two respects; but then you can't expect to see people in dreams looking exactly like themselves, can you? I'll run up and bring her down to you—and, if a Mother may say so, I don't think you'll be very disappointed."

But it was to Daphne's chamber that she went first. "Oh, Miss Heritage," she began, quite pleasantly, "I'm going to ask you to do something for me. I don't at all like the effect of those jewels they've sewn on to the front of my satin-brocade. I'm sure they would look much better on my cloth-of-gold skirt. Would you mind getting both skirts from my wardrobe and just making the necessary alterations for me? You had better set to work at once, as I may be requiring the cloth-of-gold very shortly. And as time is pressing, I will tell them to bring all your meals up here till the work is done. It's so important that I can't trust any of the regular ladies-in-waiting with it."

"That disposes of her for at least a week," she reflected, as she went on to Princess Edna's apartments. "And everything ought to be settled long before that!"

When, a little later, she smilingly re-entered the Reception Hall with one arm affectionately placed round her reluctant daughter's waist, it cannot be denied that the Prince was very much disappointed indeed. The vision had not prepared him for Edna's pince-nez, among other matters, and altogether he felt that his Godmother had exaggerated the Princess's personal attractions to a most unscrupulous degree. But this he had sufficient self-command to conceal. In fact, he rather overdid it, though it was only to himself that his courtly greeting sounded fulsome and insincere.

But if Edna detected no extravagance in his homage, she was none the more pleased with it. It made her feel awkward and self-conscious. She set him down in her own mind as "too finicking," while his good looks did not happen to be of a type that appealed to her.

Still, they got through the first interview fairly well, though both were relieved when a message came from the Court Godmother that she was feeling too indisposed to leave her apartments, but would be glad to see him as soon as he was at liberty. He had himself conducted to her at once, and was not a little aggrieved, as well as surprised, by the asperity of his reception.

"Well," she said peevishly; "so you've seen your Princess, have you? And now I suppose it is all settled between you?"

"Not yet," he said stiffly. "I believe she is reserving her answer till we are better acquainted."

"But you don't expect it will be unfavourable, do you?"

"Do you, Godmother? I can't think you would have urged me to present myself here to be publicly humiliated."

"Oh, there's no doubt she will accept you," she said, with a sharp twinge. "You need have no apprehensions on that score. And, as you no longer consider beauty indispensable, I daresay she will be as satisfactory a helpmate as you could wish."

"I daresay," he agreed dully; and then his pent-up grievance suddenly broke out in spite of him. "With all respect to you, Godmother Voldoiseau," he said, "I don't consider you've treated me fairly over this! You persuaded me that it was my duty to marry at once, and that there were better and more permanent qualities than beauty. I'm not complaining of that—I am quite ready to believe that the Princess Edna is as learned and admirable a lady as you gave me to understand, while she is not without good looks of a kind. But why send me a vision representing her as a miracle of loveliness? That is a deception which I can't understand, and I confess I find hard to forgive!"

How could she have foreseen that he would be foolish enough to imagine that the vision represented Edna? But the worst of it was that the Fairy could not explain her real intention just then without landing herself in fresh difficulties. So she sought refuge in prevarication.

"I send you a vision!" she said. "I don't know what you're talking about, Mirliflor. A vision, indeed!"

"Didn't it come from you?" he asked lamely. "I—I made sure it must have."

"You had no business to make sure of anything of the kind. And if you choose to dream that your future bride is more beautiful than she happens to be, I don't see why you should put the blame on me! But the truth is you're longing for some excuse for getting out of this marriage. Come, Mirliflor, you know you are—and you had better say so frankly."

"It is not so, Godmother," he replied; "I'm quite prepared to obey your wishes. After all, since I must marry, I am not likely to find a more advantageous match than this. Besides, I couldn't possibly back out of it now—even if I desired."

"And what," asked the Fairy, "if you actually meet the Princess of your dreams?" She was ignorant of the Queen's man[oe]uvre, and so thought he could not well fail to come across Daphne that very evening.

"That is so likely!" he said bitterly. "A mere creation of my own mind—an ideal that I ought to have known would never be realised! No, Godmother, since there is no hope of that, it matters little to me whom I marry!"

"Listen to me, Mirliflor," said the Fairy impatiently. "I—I'm not so bent on this alliance as I was. Never mind why—but I'm not. And—and—if you would rather withdraw, it's not too late. I see nothing to prevent you."

"Nothing to prevent me!" replied Mirliflor indignantly. "There is my honour! What Prince with any sense of honour at all could propose to a Princess and then inform her that he finds, after a personal interview, that he has changed his intentions? You of all people, Godmother Voldoiseau, should know that we cannot do these things!"

"Those ideals again!" said the exasperated Fairy. "You'll drive me out of all patience directly! But there— I've said all I could, and if you will be pig-headed, you must. And now I'll ask you to go away, as I'm really not well enough to bear any more conversation."

He had not been gone more than ten minutes when there was another knock at her door, and this time it was Princess Edna herself who entered.

"So it's you, is it?" snapped the Court Godmother, with none of her customary urbanity. And then, recollecting the necessity of keeping up appearances, threw in a belated "my dear." "Well, I hear you are taking time before you put Mirliflor out of suspense, but I presume you've already decided to accept him?"

"That's what I came to consult you about, Court Godmother," replied Edna. "I don't feel that I—he is at all a person I could ever be happy with. He is not on the same intellectual plane with me—we should have nothing whatever in common. He seems to have none of the qualities that would make me respect and look up to a man."

Relieved though she was, the Fairy still resented any disparagement of her favourite godson from such a quarter.

"Hoity-toity!" she exclaimed—an expression which, if it ever was popular, is no longer used by anyone but Fairy Godmothers—and even the Fairy only indulged in it under extreme provocation. "Let me tell you that Mirliflor is not generally regarded as ineligible. But, no doubt, my dear," she added acidly, "you have every right to be fastidious." She was greatly tempted to let her know that Mirliflor would be anything but broken-hearted by a refusal, but prudence warned her that she had better not. "And may I ask what you propose to say to him?"

"Oh," said Edna, "I suppose I shall have to tell him to-night that I find I don't like him enough to marry him."

"And give everybody to understand that he is personally displeasing to you! Indeed you will not!" said the old Fairy imperiously. "Other persons' feelings have to be considered as well as your own. Mine, for one. Mirliflor would never forgive me for exposing him to such humiliation. Nor would his father, King Tournesol, for that matter, and I can't afford to quarrel with either of them. You can't get rid of an unwelcome suitor like that—at all events, not in Märchenland!"

"Can't I?" said Edna. "Then how am I to get rid of him?"

"A Princess of high breeding," replied the Fairy, "finds some means of tempering her refusal so as to avoid wounding her suitor's pride; and I may tell you Mirliflor has more than his share of that. The usual method here is to accept him, on condition that he succeeds in answering some question so difficult that it is no disgrace if he fails to answer it."

"Do you mean something in the nature of a riddle?" asked Edna.

"Well, a riddle will do. Yes, there are precedents for that. A riddle would be quite in accordance with Court etiquette. Ask him a riddle if you like."

"I'm afraid I am not very familiar with riddles," said Edna. "I have never found them particularly amusing myself. But I must try and remember one. It needn't be so very difficult, because he doesn't seem to me clever enough to guess any riddle."

"Quite clever enough not to try!" was on the tip of the Fairy's tongue, though she did not say it. "I've no doubt, my dear," she replied, "that any riddle you may ask Mirliflor will be quite beyond his power to answer."

"Thank you very much for your advice, Court Godmother," said Edna. "I daresay I shall be able to remember a riddle of some sort by this evening."

The Fairy felt that she had extricated herself from her dilemma with considerable tact and ingenuity. Not only had she delivered her godson from the slight of being summarily rejected by this upstart girl, but she had saved herself from all necessity to make any compromising disclosures.

"Yes," she told herself complacently, "I've really got myself and Mirliflor out of it very neatly indeed. I mayn't be quite as quick-witted as I was in my prime—but I'm not in my dotage just yet!"

CHAPTER XII

UNWELCOME ANNOUNCEMENTS

Princess Edna took the earliest opportunity of acting on the Fairy Vogelflug's suggestion. At the conclusion of the banquet that evening, she requested King Sidney to order the silver trumpets to be flourished, and when this had been done and an expectant hush fell upon the assembly, she rose. After regarding the Prince, who sat on her right, with a graciousness which, enhanced as it was by her pince-nez, struck terror into his very soul, she began in a high, clear tone:

"You all know, I think," she said, "that his Royal Highness Prince Mirliflor of Clairdelune has done me the great honour of asking me to be his wife, and that I have promised him my answer this evening. That answer I am now about to give. Prince Mirliflor, you have impressed me so favourably that, although I had previously no thought of marrying, I have decided to accept you." At this the whole Court broke out in frantic and rapturous applause, for they had been most anxious for the Prince to succeed in his project—if only for the reason that it would entail the removal of Princess "Four-eyes" to Clairdelune. The King exclaimed, "Quite right! Sensible girl!" and Queen Selina assured the Prince that he had won a treasure. Clarence, who had taken a liking to his new brother-in-law, which was not entirely reciprocated, rose and clapped him heartily on the back, while the old Court Chamberlain could scarcely contain his pride and joy. Edna held up her hand for silence. "Wait, please!" she said; "I haven't finished. I said I would accept you, Prince Mirliflor, and so I will—on condition that you are able to give the correct answer to a question I am about to ask you."

There was a murmur of disappointment at this, though it was generally recognised that the Princess's action was quite en règle. The Prince, feeling that it was at least a reprieve, begged her to put the question without keeping him in any further suspense.

"My question is this," said Edna: "Why did the sausage roll?"

"Hang it all, Edna!" cried Clarence, "you're not going to chuck him unless he can guess a rotten riddle like that!"

"Of course not!" said her anxious Mother. "Don't be alarmed, dear Prince Mirliflor. She doesn't mean it seriously. It—it's a little joke, that's all!"

"It's not a joke, Mother," said Edna; "I'm perfectly serious. I am sure Prince Mirliflor is so clever that he will have no difficulty in guessing the riddle. If he can't—well, I shall be very sorry, but—I shall not be able to marry him."

"Alas, Princess!" said Mirliflor, "but it passes my poor wit to discover why the sausage rolled."

"Will your Majesties pardon me," struck in the Court Chamberlain, "if I humbly offer a suggestion. Such a problem as her Royal Highness has propounded cannot be solved in a moment. It is only just to his Royal Highness Prince Mirliflor that he should be given a night to reflect before delivering his answer."

"Certainly," said the King; "you must see that yourself, Edna. Give him a chance—every chance!"

"I have no objection, Father," said Edna. "The Prince shall have till to-morrow morning to think it over—but I can give him no longer."

"It's an infernal shame, Mirliflor!" said Clarence. "I haven't an idea why the bally sausage rolled, or I'd tell you, dear old chap!"

"I am sure you would, my dear Prince Clarence!" Mirliflor assured him; "but, believe me, I am none the less grateful to you."

Queen Selina did all she could think of to persuade her daughter to alter her decision, and, when this failed, to extract the answer to the momentous conundrum, which Edna knew her mother too well to confide to her, so that at length she was obliged to take up her bedroom taper and retreat, with a Parthian prediction that such folly would be bitterly repented in the future.

Edna's next visitor was the Court Godmother, on whose entrance she at once informed her waiting-women that she would not require their further services that night. "Well, Godmother," she began, as soon as they were alone together, "I did as you advised, you see. And—you don't think Prince Mirliflor can possibly find out the answer, do you?"

"My good girl," said the Fairy, "I'd defy the Astrologer Royal himself to find it out, if he consulted all the stars and all his mystic books into the bargain! How the dickens did you come to invent such a riddle as that?"

"I didn't invent it," said Edna; "I heard it a long time ago—at the Theatre—in some silly play. I've forgotten what the play was about—but I remembered the riddle."

"Are you sure you remember the answer? I have heard of sausages talking occasionally, and I daresay they can roll, but I fail to see what intelligible reason any sausage could give for doing it."

"It's a catch," explained Edna. "It's like this. Why did the sausage roll? Because it saw the jam-turnover. Now do you see?"

"I can't say I do, my dear. It seems senseless to me. But that's all the better—the more idiotic it is, the less chance of its being guessed. Yes, on the whole, I don't think you could have thought of a better one."

Shortly afterwards Prince Mirliflor, just as he was about to extinguish the flambeaux and turn into bed, was startled to see his door opening by some mysterious means. He was more startled still when the figure of the old Court Chamberlain suddenly materialised in the centre of the room.

"Your Royal Highness will forgive my intrusion," said the Baron, "when I explain the object of this visit. My reason for suggesting that the Princess should grant you a night to answer her question was that I felt convinced that she would be unable to refrain from telling it to some person—her mother, most probably. So I resolved by means of this" (and here he exhibited a small skull-cap of purple silk) "to penetrate unseen to the Princess's apartments and overhear her conversation. To my disappointment, she would reveal nothing to Her Majesty, but by-and-by the Court Godmother paid the Princess a visit, in the course of which I, remaining, of course, invisible, succeeded in learning the secret on which your Royal Highness's happiness and the hopes of all Märchenland depend. The answer, it seems—though I must admit I can make little of it myself—is—"

"Stop, Baron!" interrupted Prince Mirliflor, "I refuse—do you hear?—I refuse to take advantage of any information obtained in such a disreputable manner—I insist on your leaving this room at once without another word!"

"But, sire, hear me! This is not a case for being over-scrupulous. In love, as in war, all is fair. And the answer is—'Because—'"

"Will you get out?" cried the Prince, stopping both his ears. "I won't hear you. I can't, as you can see. And if you don't clear out at once, I'll strike this gong for the guard!"

The Baron, seeing that he could do no more, hastily put on his cap again and disappeared. "What a pity," he thought, "that such a fine young Prince should be so priggish when his own interests are concerned!"

But although Mirliflor's code of honour was undoubtedly high, it is quite possible that he might not have stopped his ears quite so hermetically if Princess Edna had only borne a closer resemblance to his vision of her.

As it was, even if the Baron had forced him to hear the answer, it would have made no difference, since he had not the least intention of profiting by it, and so he slept soundly, with no apprehensions concerning what the morrow might bring him.

Shortly after breakfast the next day the Court filled the body of the Hall of Audience, on the dais of which the King and Queen presently appeared and took their thrones, Prince Mirliflor and the members of the Royal Family being accommodated with lower seats on the same platform.

"Now, Prince Mirliflor," remarked Edna sweetly, "you have been given a night to consider the answer to my question. I hope you have found it?"

The Prince was about to confess his utter inability to do so, when, to his extreme annoyance, he found that the Baron, who had stationed himself behind his chair, was whispering discreetly into his ear. "Will you be kind enough to leave me alone, Baron?" he said in a savage undertone. "I've told you already that I don't desire any interference in my affairs. Oblige me by holding your tongue!"

"Certainly, your Royal Highness," said the Baron obsequiously, "your wishes shall be obeyed.... His Royal Highness, Madam," he said aloud, "begs me to make his excuses. He feels too much agitated to speak for himself, but instructs me to say that he believes the reason why the sausage rolled was because it had seen the jam pasty. And," he added confidently, "your Royal Highness will, I am sure, be gracious enough to admit that Prince Mirliflor has answered her question with absolute correctness."

Mirliflor's attempts to deny that he had offered any solution whatever were unheard in the tumult of acclamation which followed the Court Chamberlain's announcement.

"He hasn't given the correct answer!" declared Edna, as soon as silence could be obtained. "He ought to have said 'the jam turnover'—not the 'jam pasty'!"

"Oh, come, my dear!" said her father. "That's splitting hairs, you know. He was near enough. What's the difference?"

"None that I can see," pronounced the Queen. "Both are pastry, and both contain jam. Yes, Prince Mirliflor, you have won the dear child, as I'm sure you richly deserved to!"

"How can you say that, Mother?" cried Edna, scarlet with vexation. "When his answer utterly missed the point? And, anyhow, it was given by proxy, so it doesn't count!"

"H'm—ha!" said King Sydney, "that's rather a ticklish question! What do you think, my love?" and he consulted the Queen in undertones for a minute or two. "Well," he announced presently, "her Majesty and myself both consider that the Prince's answer should be adjudged correct, and that its having been given by proxy is—ah—no disqualification whatever. Still, to avoid all appearance of favouritism, we propose to refer the case to the final decision of our Council."

"I say!" protested Clarence in a horrified whisper, "you're never going to leave it to those old pumps?"

"It's quite safe, my boy," said the King. "They won't give it against him!"

So, after the Councillors had filed out to deliberate, Clarence devoted himself to keeping up Mirliflor's spirits, though the latter could not be induced to see that he had no cause for uneasiness.

But King Sidney had not been mistaken in his prediction; after a short absence the Councillors filed in again and reported that they were unanimously of opinion that Prince Mirliflor had succeeded.

"There, my dear," said the King to the Princess Royal, as soon as the shouts of joy had quieted down, "you've got the Council's decision. Give the Prince your hand, and let's have no more bother about it."

"I won't!" declared Edna, losing all self-control in her rage and disappointment. "He hasn't won me fairly. I've been tricked into this, and it's all the Court Godmother's doing!"

No accusation could well be more unjust, but it was difficult for the Fairy to disprove it without declaring that she had done her utmost to hinder the match—and this would have been impolitic just then.

"My doing, forsooth!" she repeated. "If you really believe that, you were never more mistaken in your life!"

"Oh no, I'm not mistaken!" said Edna. "It was you who suggested my asking the riddles—and you were the only person I told the answer. If you did not tell him, I should like to know who did!"

"May I remind you, Princess," said Mirliflor, "that the answer was not made by me?"

"You let the Baron answer for you, which is just as bad!" retorted Edna. "And I absolutely refuse to be trapped and cheated into marrying anybody!"

"My conscience at least is clear," he said. "But I am to understand that you decline to marry me, Princess—is that so?"

"Certainly I do. Nothing would induce me to accept you after this! I don't care what Father and Mother or the Council or anyone says! When—if—I marry I intend to choose for myself. And you are about the last person, Prince Mirliflor, I should ever dream of choosing!"

"I am desolated to hear it, Princess," he replied, with admirable patience and resignation. "But since I have the misfortune to be so obnoxious to you, the only service I can render you now is to relieve you of my presence as soon as possible."

Queen Selina implored him to stay to lunch, and even held out hopes that Edna might relent in time—but all her entreaties were in vain. To her infinite chagrin and the general lamentation, he insisted on leaving the Palace within an hour. He said no farewell to his Godmother, who for her part was glad to escape a private interview with him, but he took his leave of his host and hostess with all due outward courtesy, though inwardly fuming with rage and impatience to quit a place where he considered he had been so wantonly insulted.

Count von Rubenfresser must have got wind from some quarter of the Prince's discomfiture, for on the very next day he turned up at the Palace about lunch time, according to his previous habit, and Queen Selina, though far from delighted at his appearance, could hardly avoid inviting him to remain. His manner at table was considerably more assured, and his appetite, if anything, heartier than usual, but even so he seemed, to all but Princess Edna, an indifferent substitute for the Prince whose departure they were still mourning.

Edna, however, seemed to make a point of treating him with marked favour, so much so that, when lunch was over and the Royal Family had removed to the Terrace, it was rather with disgust than surprise that they discovered that the Princess Royal and the Count had stolen off together to a secluded part of the gardens.

Whether amour propre had incited her to make a special effort to overcome his hesitation, or absence and jealousy had quickened his somewhat lagging ardour, none could say with any certainty, but when they eventually re-appeared, Queen Selina observed with positive horror that they were walking hand-in-hand.

"It's quite all right, Mother," said Edna, as they came within speaking distance; "Ruprecht and I are engaged."

"Engaged!" spluttered King Sidney. "You've got to get your Mother's consent for that, you know. And we couldn't hear of it. Not for a moment! Eh, my love?"

"Of course not!" said the Queen. "Entirely out of the question!"

"We expected this," remarked Edna calmly. "But no amount of opposition will make the slightest difference to us—will it, Ruprecht?"

"Not the slightest," he replied. "At least—to ME."

"But think, my dear, only think!" the distressed Queen entreated Edna. "After you've just made us all so unpopular by refusing a Prince, you simply can't go and engage yourself to some one whose position is so far beneath your own!"

"Ruprecht is above me in every sense," said Edna; "and because I'm a Princess by no wish of mine is no reason why I should sacrifice myself for reasons of state. I utterly and entirely deny that any parents, no matter what their position in life, have the right nowadays to dictate to their children whom they should marry or not marry. Of course, I would rather you were sensible enough to recognise our engagement, but if you aren't, I shall simply marry Ruprecht just the same."

Queen Selina reflected. If she refused consent, it would only end in a still worse situation. And, after all, she would have been proud enough in her Gablehurst days to be able to announce her daughter's engagement to a real Count with a fine and ancient castle.

"Well," she said, "if it's understood that there must be no thought of marriage for at least a year—"

"Oh, Ruprecht will wait a year for me—won't you, Ruprecht? But the engagement must be proclaimed at once—we insist on that. And now you may kiss Mother, Ruprecht, and tell her that you already look on yourself as her son."

The Count stooped to give his prospective Mother-in-law an amateurish embrace, while Ruby fled, fearing that her own turn would come next. "Good Lord, Edna!" said Clarence, drawing her aside, "have you gone dotty or what? To go and chuck a real good sort like Mirliflor, and then take this overgrown bounder—it beats me what you can see in the beggar!"

"I see a man, Clarence, whom I feel I can really look up to."

"You'll have the devil of a way to look up, if he goes on growing much longer. He's shot up lately like a bally beanstalk!"

"You are jealous because he makes you feel so small. I glory in his being so big. He is just my idea of a superman!"

"Strike out 'man' and substitute 'swine'!" said Clarence, "and I'm with you!"

"There's no need to descend to vulgarity, Clarence. And it seems a pity you should be so prejudiced against him when he is only anxious to prove the affection he feels for you!"

"Oh, is he? Well, if he comes pawing me about, he'll find out what my sentiments are!"

"I should advise you to be civil to him—for your own sake," said Edna coldly, "because he's rather a powerful person."

Queen Selina had no option but to inform the Court of the engagement without delay, and the general consternation it caused could only find expression in chilling silence.

To the Court Godmother she tried to present the matter as favourably as possible. "I don't pretend," she said, "that it is quite all we could desire from a mere worldly point of view. But in a case of true love on both sides such as this, his Majesty and I both feel that it would not be right to interfere. And you know what dear Edna can be when she's once set her mind on anything. Besides," she concluded, "we've insisted on their being engaged for a year—a good deal may happen before then."

"It may," agreed the Fairy; "and I shall be very much surprised if it doesn't. But, so far as I am concerned, Princess Edna may bestow her hand as she pleases. I shall never go out of my way to find her a suitor again, I can assure you!"

It had already occurred to her that the Royal Family might very shortly find Märchenland too hot to hold them, which would relieve her of all responsibility for them. So she saw no reason for interfering with any of their proceedings.

Ruby rushed excitedly up to Daphne's chamber, where she had been hurting her pretty fingers by laboriously unpicking the innumerable jewels from one of the Queen's robes and sewing them on to another. "Oh, Miss Heritage, dear," she began, "it's such ages since I've seen you, and I've such lots to tell you about. Just fancy! Edna's engaged!... No, not Prince Mirliflor! She sent him away the day before yesterday. I can't think why—when he was so perfectly ripping. It's Count Rubenfresser."

"Oh, Ruby!" cried Daphne in dismay. "Not to him! How can she?"

"I don't know—but she is. Mums doesn't like it, of course, but she's had to give in, and they'll be married in a year. Isn't it awful? There's only one advantage about it that I can see—Tützi will be one of the family now.... Oh, and you needn't go on sewing any more. Mummy said after lunch that she'd forgotten to tell you she won't want the skirt altered after all, and that you might come down again as usual now."

So Daphne made her re-appearance that evening, and was welcomed by the Court with as much effusion as if they had not seen her for weeks. The Count was there, his towering form more splendidly apparelled, as became his new rôle of an accepted suitor, and she soon learnt that she was by no means alone in loathing the thought of the engagement. Princess Edna was in such high good humour that she not only deigned to single out Daphne by her notice, but actually offered to present her to her fiancé— an honour from which Daphne had the courage to beg that she might be excused.

"I see how it is, Miss Heritage," said Edna, with a frown, "You can't understand my rejecting a Prince and preferring some one of so far inferior a rank. I really should not have thought you would be quite so snobbish as that!"

"It isn't that, Princess Edna," said Daphne desperately. "It's because—I'm sure—I can't explain why, but I am sure he's bad—really bad!"

"If you mean by that—that he is not a pattern of virtue like Prince Mirliflor," said Edna, "he is none the worse for it, in my eyes!"

"I meant more—much more than that. But I ought not to have said anything."

"Oh, pray go on. In fact, I insist on it."

"Well, then, Princess Edna," said Daphne undauntedly, "not only I, but almost everybody at Court, think that a marriage with Count von Rubenfresser would be a horrible mistake."

"So you have joined the league against him, have you, Miss Heritage?" said Edna. "But, of course, you would condemn anyone who failed to conform to your prim, governessy little notions of right and wrong. I might have known as much! I am only sorry I should have gone out of my way to offer you a privilege you are so incapable of appreciating. You may now retire."

Daphne retreated accordingly. She knew very well that she would have been wiser in her own interests to hold her tongue, and she had certainly done no good by speaking. But for no earthly inducement would she have allowed herself to be presented to that detestable Count. She had been almost forced to speak plainly, if only in the faint hope of opening Edna's eyes to a sense of what she was doing. And though she had failed, she did not in the least regret having spoken. If the other ladies-in-waiting had known of her protest she would have been more idolised by them than ever, but a lingering sense of loyalty kept her from saying anything that might increase their disaffection for "Princess Four-Eyes."

Perhaps the person in the Royal Household who felt the engagement most acutely was the old Court Chamberlain. Queen Selina, returning from a drive the next day, discovered him weeping, or rather absolutely blubbering, in a darker corner of one of the passages. "I can't help it, your Majesty," he said, almost inarticulate with emotion. "That the Princess should have scorned such a consort as Prince Mirliflor for one whose parentage—it's too much to bear! I think my old heart would break if I had not once more put a hoop around it. If your Majesty only knew how your subjects detest such an alliance as this!"

"I don't see what it has to do with them, Baron," said the Queen. "But they have certainly been less respectful lately. I'm afraid we shall have to take a sack of gold out again on our next drive. I was most alarmed this afternoon by a rude person throwing something into the coach which I quite thought at first was a bomb. However, it turned out to be only a particularly fine turnip, though it very narrowly missed his Majesty's nose. Of course, as the Marshal assures us, it may have been intended merely as a humble sort of offering, but I should like to feel surer about it than I do. And—strictly between ourselves, Baron—I should be only too thankful if this engagement was broken off. But what can I do? The Princess won't listen to me!"

"Perchance," said the Baron, "she would allow herself to be influenced by the noble ladies whom your Majesty spoke of."

"The Duchess of Gleneagles and the Marchioness of Muscombe? Ah, my dear Baron, she might, if they were only here! I know they would do their best to persuade her. But what is the use of thinking of that, when they are both so far away?"

"And doubtless your Majesty is in ignorance of their very whereabouts."

"Oh, they would be in London just now," said the Queen, not displeased to exhibit her knowledge. "The dear Duchess travelled down from the North sometime ago to her town residence in Stratford Place— had her tiara stolen on the journey, Baron—and came to tell me about it at once, poor soul! And—yes, the Muscombes must be back in that cosy little flat of theirs in Mount Street by this time. They always spend Easter in London, you know."

"In London!" sighed the Baron. "That is truly a far cry from our Märchenland! But your Majesty can see that, in my present spirits, I should make but a sorry figure at Court. Have I your leave to absent myself for a brief period!"

"By all means—as long as you like," said the Queen, who rightly considered that a Court Chamberlain in constant floods of tears would do little to relieve the prevailing depression. And so the Baron did not appear that evening, which might have excited some remark if anyone had happened to notice his absence.

On the following morning Queen Selina paid a surprise visit to the Tapestry Chamber, where her ladies were more or less busy in embroidering "chair-backs" (she was too much in the movement not to know that the term "antimacassars" was a solecism). It was an industry she had lately invented for them, and they held it in healthy abhorrence.

She had not had at all a good night, and was consequently inclined to be aggressive. "Good morning, girls," she began, "I fancy I heard, just before I came in, one of you mentioning a person of the name of 'Old Mother Schwellenposch.' The speaker, if I'm not mistaken, was Baroness Bauerngrosstochterheimer."

"It was, your Majesty," admitted the Baroness, rising and curtseying.

"And who, may I ask, is this Mother—whatever-her-name is? Some vulgar acquaintance of yours, I presume?"

"If your Majesty is so pleased to describe her, it is not for me to protest," was the Baroness's demure reply, followed by suppressed but quite audible giggles from her companions.

"Why you should all snigger in that excessively unladylike way is best known to yourselves," said Queen Selina. "But I can make allowances for you, considering who your ancestresses were! It's true I had hoped when I first came here that, if I could not expect quite the sort of society I had been accustomed to, I should at least have people about me of ordinary refinement! As it is, I often wonder what my dear friends the Duchess of Gleneagles and the Marchioness of Muscombe would say if they knew the class of persons I have to associate with. I can fancy how they would pity me. When one has enjoyed the privilege of intimacy with really great ladies like them, one is all the more apt to notice the difference.... Is that you, Baron? Returned so soon? But you shouldn't come bursting in like this without asking for an audience. That is quite against my rules!"

"Your Majesty will, I feel sure, pardon the intrusion when you hear my tidings," said the Baron. "I have the honour to inform your Majesty that your high-born friends, the Grand Duchess of Gleneagles and the Margravine of Muscombe, are now in the Palace!"

"The—the Duchess? And the Marchioness?" cried the Queen. "Nonsense, Baron! It must be some silly mistake of yours. How could they possibly get here?"

"In the stork-car, your Majesty," he explained. "I brought them myself. As they are still sunk in sleep, I have had them laid on couches in one of the vestibules, and instructed the Lady Daphne to remain in attendance."

"Good gracious!" said Queen Selina faintly. She was painfully conscious that her face must be expressing dismay rather than delight, and that her ladies-in-waiting had not failed to notice it. "What a—what a delightful surprise! And Lady Daphne with them, did you say? I—I'll go to them at once!"

If the poor Court Chamberlain had expected any gratitude from his Sovereign when they got outside, he received none. She did not speak to him at all—possibly because she could not trust herself, and she hurried towards the great Entrance Hall at a pace which left him hopelessly in the rear. As she went she vainly endeavoured to think of any possible excuse or apology that she could offer her distinguished visitors, but her chief anxiety was that she might not arrive until after they had awaked, and Miss Heritage had anticipated her explanations.

CHAPTER XIII

WHAT THE PIGEON SAID

Daphne was passing through the upper gallery, on her way to join the other ladies-in-waiting in the Tapestry Chamber, when she heard a commotion in the great hall below, and, looking down over the balustrade, was astonished to see two inanimate female forms being carried by attendants into the vestibule. Baron von Eisenbänden, who was directing them, caught sight of her and beckoned. On descending the jasper staircase, she found him beaming with satisfaction, surrounded by a host of courtiers, guards, and pages.

"All will be well now, my Lady Daphne," he whispered confidentially. "I have brought hither two noble dames to persuade the Princess to renounce this ill-omened alliance—the Grand Duchess of Gleneagle and Margravine of Muscombe, her Majesty's dearest and most intimate friends. She will surely be overjoyed when I announce their arrival."

Somehow Daphne could not share his certainty. Queen Selina had been careful not to dwell too much, in her presence, on these aristocratic acquaintances, and they certainly had not visited "Inglegarth" while she had been an inmate of the household.

"If I were you, Baron," she said diplomatically, "I should send away all these people before I told her Majesty. I am sure she would rather welcome her friends in private."

He accepted the suggestion, cleared the hall, and bustled away, after committing the still unconscious visitors to Daphne's care.

She found them laid side by side on couches in the vestibule, which was a lofty chamber, panelled in ivory and ebony, with inset opals of enormous size and a ceiling of dull silver. The Duchess was a short, spare, grey-haired and rather homely-looking woman in a black demi-toilette with priceless old lace. Lady Muscombe was about twenty-six, tall, with a beautiful figure and a pale, piquant face; she wore a rose charmeuse gown that scintillated with paillettes; her luxuriant, but just then slightly dishevelled, chestnut hair was confined in a sparkling band, from which drooped a crushed pink plume.

As they seemed on the point of awaking, Daphne, thinking that they would probably prefer to do so unobserved, discreetly left them to themselves.

Lady Muscombe was the first to recover. She sat up, stretched her white and shapely arms, and yawned widely, revealing her perfect teeth, as she regarded the Duchess with sleepy brown eyes.

"I suppose you are the Duchess of Gleneagles?" she said. "And, if you don't mind, I should rather like to know why you've brought me here—wherever it is."

"I?" said the Duchess. "I've had nothing to do with bringing you. Don't even know who you are—though you seem to have got hold of my name."

"Why, I married Muscombe—the Marquis, don't you know. I dare say you knew before that I was Verity Stilton of the Vivacity. I was working my way up to quite important parts. You may have seen me in some of them?"

"I have not had that advantage. I seldom visit a theatre, and when I do—"

"You like to go and see something stuffy? I know. And I expect you've got quite a wrong idea of Musical Comedy. Most of us in the Chorus at the Vivacity were ladies by birth. And we didn't mix with the others, off the stage. We were most particular, too. I assure you I never went to sup alone with Nibbles—I call Muscombe 'Nibbles,' you know—he's so exactly like a white mouse—I never supped with him alone till after we were regularly engaged."

"That is most interesting," said the Duchess, "and entirely to your credit, but it doesn't explain how we came to be here together."

"All I can say is that a queerly dressed old freak suddenly burst into my flat, just as I was going to dine at the Carlton, and told me you were waiting outside in a car to take me on a visit to the Queen."

"And did not that strike you as slightly improbable?"

"Oh, for anything I knew, you might be another of Nibbles's aunts. I haven't nearly worked through all his relations yet. But I said at once that I couldn't throw over my Carlton party to oblige any Duchess on earth. And then the old creature put on a cap and vanished. And the next thing I knew was that a cloak was thrown over my head and I was being lifted up and bundled out kicking—and that's all I remember. I don't know what they thought of me in Mount Street, or why nobody interfered."

"Much the same thing happened to me," said the Duchess. "Only I was told that the Queen wished to see me at once on an urgent matter. Of course, as the messenger's appearance did not inspire me with confidence, I insisted on seeing his credentials. And then he disappeared, and I found myself caught up and carried off. I suppose none of my people were in the hall, or else they were too afraid to come to my rescue. And Stratford Place is very quiet, so my smothered cries attracted no attention. Besides, I fancy I must have been chloroformed."

"I expect we both were. Nibbles would be furious if he knew—luckily he doesn't. We had a tiff, and he went off to Monte, all on his little lone. But I wish I had any idea where we are."

"I have certainly no recollection of ever having been in such a place as this before in my life," said the Duchess.

Daphne returned in time to offer what explanations she could.

"I know it must seem a little strange at first," she said, coming forward, "but this is the Palace of the Queen of Märchenland."

"Märchenland?" repeated the Duchess. "And where may that be? Never heard of such a country!"

"Well," said Daphne, "it's a long way from everywhere, and it's the place where most of the stories one used to think were only Fairy Tales really happened."

"I never expected to find myself in Fairyland," the Duchess remarked. "Tell me—are you the Queen of this country? You look as if you might be."

"Oh no," replied Daphne, with a little laugh. "I'm only one of her ladies-in-waiting. She hasn't long been Queen. We were all carried here from England in a big car drawn by flying storks—the one that brought you, I expect. I don't know, of course," she added dubiously, "but you may have met Queen Selina when she lived at Gablehurst—her former name was Mrs. Wibberley-Stimpson."

"Wibberley-Stimpson?" repeated the Duchess thoughtfully. "No, I can't say I remember anyone of that name."

"Nor I," said Lady Muscombe languidly. "Don't know any one at Gablehurst."

"But if she is half as charming as you, my dear," added the Duchess graciously, "it will give me much pleasure to make her acquaintance, though I am curious to know why she seems to have taken so much trouble to cultivate mine."

At this moment Queen Selina herself arrived, very much out of breath. "Your Grace!" she began, "My lady Marchioness!"

"Ah, here is the housekeeper!" said the Duchess, before Daphne could enlighten her. "Can you tell us, my good woman, when and where her Majesty will receive us?"

"I—I am her Majesty!" said Queen Selina, wishing she had devoted more pains to her morning toilet.

"Oh, to be sure," said the Duchess. "You must forgive my blunder, Ma'am, but my sight is not what it was."

"It is of no consequence, my dear Duchess—pray don't mention it. Miss Heritage, I find I shall require that skirt after all. You will be good enough to see to it at once, and not come down till it is finished," said the Queen sharply, feeling it more imperative than ever to prevent any account of this meeting from being communicated to the Court.... "No, Baron, I shall not require you," she went on, as he appeared at the entrance. "You have done quite enough." And Daphne and the Baron withdrew accordingly.

"I'm so distressed, your Grace, by this unfortunate—er—contretemps," said Queen Selina, as soon as she had her guests to herself. "I really hardly know how to apologise. I'm afraid my old Court Chamberlain has taken a most unpardonable liberty."

"Well, Ma'am," said the Duchess, "there's no doubt he kidnapped both myself and this lady here. On false pretences, too! I don't know yet whether he was acting on your instructions?"

"Most decidedly not! Indeed I should never have ventured. The fact is, he must have confused you with two other ladies of title who are great friends of mine. I expect he heard me mention them, and—it was most stupid and careless of him, I know—but he must have concluded I wanted to see them, and brought you by mistake."

"I see," said the Duchess; "though I don't understand how he came to know our names and addresses, as he must have done to find us."

"Oh," said Queen Selina, with much presence of mind, "you're both of you public characters, you know. He's such an old blunderer, he probably couldn't find the right people, and thought you would do as well."

"I can only say," replied the Duchess, "that that impression of his has put me to a great deal of personal inconvenience."

"I was carried off without a chance of ringing them up at the Carlton, where I ought to have dined last night!" complained Lady Muscombe.

"If your Majesty will get a new Chamberlain—one who isn't an absolute idiot," said the Duchess severely, "your house-party would be in less danger of being recruited in this irregular manner."

"But I assure you I'm delighted to see your Grace, and you too, of course, Lady Muscombe! I hope, now you are here, you will stay as long as ever you can. Such a pleasure always to his Majesty and myself to welcome any of our own country-women! And now I will take you up to your rooms, and you will no doubt be glad of a little rest before you come down to lunch and meet the family."

"I cannot possibly appear at lunch in this dress," said the Duchess; "but I shall be glad if you will send me up some food, and then I must really start for home."

"So must I," declared Lady Muscombe; "there'll be a fuss if I'm not back soon—and I simply couldn't stay in any house without a single trunk, or a maid either! It isn't giving me a fair chance!"

"I'm afraid the storks won't be fit for such a long return journey just yet," said their hostess; "and it would be a pity to leave without seeing something of Märchenland, so I hope you will remain for at least a night, as a favour to me. I see no one of any real distinction now! And as for clothes, I can lend you all you require. You will excuse their being out of the fashion—we don't get the latest Paris models here."

"You're very kind," said the Duchess. "Then I will accept your hospitality for the present."

"So will I—er—your Majesty, thanks," said Lady Muscombe. "It will be something to tell Muscombe—when we're on speaking terms again."

"So very nice and friendly of you both!" said Queen Selina as she escorted them across the hall to the foot of the immense staircase. "I must apologise for asking you to come up all these steps, but there's no such thing as a lift here. The Astrologer Royal offered to try and procure us a flying carpet—but, of course, I wouldn't hear of that."

"Well," said the Duchess, as she toiled up, "this is certainly a wonderful Palace you live in—I have never seen one so splendid in my life!"

"Ah, my dear Duchess, it's much too large to be really comfortable, and all the arrangements, too, so unlike our English ways! I'm afraid I shall never get things done here according to my ideas.... This is your room, dear Duchess, and yours is next, Marchioness. I will send some of my waiting-women to you with everything necessary. You will find us assembled in the Throne Room before lunch.... Oh, and there's just one thing. My Court have got an impression—I'm sure I don't know why—that we're quite old friends. If you wouldn't mind—er—addressing me as 'Selina' now and then.... Not at all, I assure you, I should consider it a compliment—from you.... Then I shall hope to see you later on in the Throne Room.... It's in the left wing, down the great corridor; you can't miss it because of the trumpeters at the doors."

After an interval the two visitors made their appearance in the Throne Room, arrayed in magnificent but rather fantastic robes of velvet and brocade with long hanging sleeves lined with ermine—a costume which suited Lady Muscombe better than the Duchess.

Queen Selina advanced to welcome them effusively. "So you've found your way here!" she said. "How very well you both look in those dresses! Most becoming, I assure you. By the bye, my dear Duchess, did you ever recover that tiara you lost in the train?"

"I never did lose it," replied the Duchess, "I believe some story got into the papers, but it was a down-right lie."

"So glad! I must tell you that I don't as a rule wear my crown at lunch, but I thought, to-day being a gala occasion—"

"Quite right!" said the Duchess. "And quite regal!"

"I could lend both of you tiaras, if it would make you feel more at your ease."

"I feel perfectly at ease as I am, thank you," replied the Duchess shortly.

"Nibbles gave me one of the family fenders," said the Marchioness, "but I never wear it—it gives me such a headache."

"Ah, dear Lady Muscombe, I can sympathise with you—but I have to put up with my headaches. I want you to come and shake hands with my husband—His Majesty, you know."

"Charmed," said the Duchess. "Is that His Majesty with the—er—auburn whiskers and moustache? I thought it must be.... How d'you do, sir?"

"Thank you, your Grace, I'm very tolerably well," said King Sidney, who was not entirely at his ease in welcoming such distinguished guests—especially as he was far from clear as to how and why they came to be there. "Glad you found time to—er—look us up. Hardly had time to settle down here ourselves yet—so you must take us as you find us."

"I never expected to find you all so magnificent, I can assure you," replied the Duchess.

"Oh, well," he said, "my wife likes living in style. And of course when you are Royalties, so to speak, you've got to do the thing well."

"That is my eldest daughter, Edna, Duchess, the Princess Royal ... yes, over there, with the eye-glasses. Edna, my love, come and tell her Grace how delighted you are to see her, and Lady Muscombe too."

"How do you do, my dear? You're looking well," said the complaisant old lady, preparing to embrace her hostess's daughter.... "Oh, if you prefer me to kiss your hand, ma'am—"

"You shouldn't be so formal, Edna!" said her mother. "Not with such an old friend as the Duchess. This, Duchess, is my son, the Crown Prince Clarence, and here is my youngest daughter, Princess Ruby."

"I must tell you about Edna, my dear Duchess," said Queen Selina, drawing her apart after these presentations had been effected. "She has only just become engaged—to a neighbour of ours, young Count von Rubenfresser. From a merely worldly point of view she might have done much better. In fact, Prince Mirliflor of Clairdelune came here to propose to her, but she rejected him. Wouldn't hear of anyone but the Count! So as His Majesty and I do not approve of forcing our children's hearts, we have let her have her own way."

"It seems quite a romance," observed the Duchess.

"Quite. And of course the Count comes of a very old family. I forget what the original title was, but they've had Castle Drachenstolz for centuries. Such a picturesque old place! And—actually, Duchess!— Count Ruprecht has a pet dragon there—it's the only one left in Märchenland now, and as it's rather a curiosity in its way, and quite inoffensive, we see no objection to his keeping it. You will probably meet the Count to-day, he generally drives over to luncheon now—so devoted to dear Edna! And such a height, too!"

"I shall be interested to meet him," said the Duchess. "He must be rather a remarkable person."

Meanwhile Clarence was engaged in making himself agreeable to Lady Muscombe. "Funny thing, Marchioness," he remarked, "but I seem to know your face quite well."

"Perhaps you've seem me on picture-postcards," she said, "or else at the Vivacity. Before I married I was Verity Stilton, you know."

"Oh," he stammered in confusion, "I—I wasn't aware—or else—of course. Sorry!"

"Why on earth should you be? You don't suppose I'm ashamed of having been on the stage? I should soon have got to the front if I had stayed. I was offered one of the best parts in 'The Girl from Greenland,' and I threw it up to marry Muscombe. His people know perfectly well that I sacrificed my career for his sake." (It might be added that if they did not, it was no fault of Lady Muscombe's.)

"I remember you," he said. "I used to go to the Vivacity before the Mater came to the throne."

"Ah, you haven't been a Royalty long, have you? Weren't you a Wobbly-something or other before that?"

"Wibberley-Stimpson was the family name," he corrected.

"I knew it was something like that. And when you were—one of those, what did you do with yourself?"

"I was in Finance," he replied largely. "In the City, don't you know, what?"

"Really?" she drawled. "That accounts for my not remembering you. Somehow, at the Vivacity, we didn't know any City men. All this must be rather a change for you, isn't it?"

"It was a bit, at first, but we soon got into it. Except the Guv'nor, who's never taken very kindly to it—hasn't had the training, what?"

"And you have? I see. And what does a Fairy Crown Prince have to do?"

"Well," he said, "I do a lot of riding and hunting. Mostly boar about here. The Guv'nor don't ride, nor does Edna. Can't induce them to get on a horse. So I have to represent the family."

"I expect you're no end of a nut here," she said.

"Oh, really, Marchioness, you're pulling my leg!"

"Am I? I've never pulled a Fairy Prince's leg before, so it's quite a new experience for me. But one expects new experiences in Fairyland—if this really is Fairyland, which I can't quite believe!"

"Oh, it's Fairyland right enough, though, mind you, it isn't the place it was. Nothing like the magic that there used to be. Most of it died out. Still, we've got a sort of old Fairy Godmother, as part of the Palace fixtures—goes about in a car drawn by doves—give you my word she does! She has another old turn-out, with storks. We came here in that—and I expect you did."

"Yes, and I see the old gentleman over there who carried me off by main force. He doesn't look as if he was such a good hand at abductions!"

"He looks pretty much the blithering old idiot he is," said Clarence. "If I'd only known he was going to London I'd have told him to get me a few thousand cigarettes—they've none here of course. But I expect he'd only have brought 'Woodbines,' or the wrong sort anyhow!"

"Does he always bring the wrong sort?" inquired Lady Muscombe.

"Well," said Clarence, crudely enough, "he didn't make much mistake about you, Marchioness!"

"That's exactly what I expected from you!" she said. "By the way, what has become of the lovely person who was with the Duchess and me when we first woke up? I think your mother called her Hermitage. I don't see her anywhere here."

"Heritage—Lady Daphne, as we call her now. She used to be my kiddie-sister's governess."

"Oh? Well, she's quite the sweetest thing I've seen—don't you think she is, yourself?"

"Not since you came!" was his gallant reply.

"It's lucky Muscombe can't hear you paying me compliments of that sort," she said. "If he did he'd want your blood. And why isn't that Lady Daphne here? I'm dying to see her again. Duchess," she added, as the elder lady, having escaped from her hostess, came towards them, "I've been asking the Prince why that charming little Heritage creature isn't here. You would like to see her, wouldn't you?"

"Certainly," said the Duchess. "Where is she?"

"We'll ask the Court Godmother," said Clarence (it had already struck him that it might give Daphne a higher opinion of him if she could see the terms he was on with a real English Marchioness). "She'll know." But the Fairy could only say that she supposed Lady Daphne was remaining in her own rooms for some reason.

"I wish you'd get her to come down, Court Godmother," said Clarence. "These ladies would like to see her."

"I will go and fetch her myself," said the Fairy, who was pleased, in spite of herself, that her unacknowledged god-daughter should be in such request.

She found Daphne engaged in sewing the great pierced jewels in an intricate pattern on the skirt of the royal robe.

"Why, how's this?" exclaimed she. "At work! When they will be sitting down to table directly! The Prince and our two noble guests have asked me to come and see what is keeping you."

"This," said Daphne, touching the skirt on her knee. "Her Majesty has sent me up to finish it, and forbidden me to come down till it's done."

"Then," said the Fairy, "she ought to be ashamed of herself!"

"Oh, I don't mind a bit, Court Godmother. They'll bring me something to eat presently, and I'd much rather be here than have to meet that odious Count Ruprecht! Court Godmother," she added, with a little anxious line on her forehead, "I'd better tell you, though I dare say you'll think it silly—but I'm rather worried by a conversation I overheard just now between two pigeons on the roof."

"You shouldn't pay any attention to anything pigeons say—it's generally love-talk; and very foolish at that."

"They weren't making love. They were talking about the Count. The first pigeon said, 'The Count has come here again. I have just seen his big coach in the courtyard,' and the second pigeon said, 'There is nothing in that.'"

"Well, one of them had some sense, anyway!" remarked the Fairy.

"Ah, but wait. 'Indeed there is something,' said the other bird. 'There is a big sack in the coach, and I know what is inside the sack, too.' 'And what may that be?' the second one asked. 'All I can tell you,' said the first, 'is that, if the Princess only knew as much about it as I do, there wouldn't be any marriage!' They flew away after that, but I've been wondering ever since whether he mayn't have murdered somebody."

"If he had," said the Fairy, "he wouldn't be very likely to bring the body out to lunch with him. You shouldn't be so uncharitable, my child. And, as for birds, I should have thought you knew what busybodies they are, and what scandals they make out of nothing at all."

"Then you think it's all right?" said Daphne, relieved. "But all the same, I can't trust the Count."

"Nobody asks you to. I don't trust him myself, if it comes to that. But, whatever he may or may not be is no affair of yours or mine. Princess Edna will find out in time what a mistake she has made."

"If only she doesn't find it out too late!" said Daphne.

"She'll have herself to thank, whatever happens. I shan't interfere again. I'm tired of trying to help anyone. I never get anything but ingratitude for it."

CHAPTER XIV

BAG AND BAGGAGE

The Court Godmother returned to the Throne-room. She had not attached much importance to what Daphne had told her, but, even if she had, she would have belittled it in her extreme desire to avoid any action that might entail inconvenience to herself.

In the Throne-room, Count Rubenfresser had just been announced.

"Yes, Duchess," said Queen Selina, in answer to an astonished inquiry. "That is dear Edna's fiancé. A fine young man, is he not?"

"Heavens! I should think he was! I should call him a giant myself," replied the Duchess bluntly.

"I told you he was rather tall. I think he's grown since his engagement. How do you do, my dear Ruprecht? Come and be introduced to my old friend the Duchess of Gleneagles, who is so very anxious to make your acquaintance."

"I don't much care about knowing old women," said the Count, who had no great love for his future mother-in-law, and had become much less deferential of late.

"But this one's a Duchess, Ruprecht!" whispered the agonised Queen. "Edna, my love, perhaps you had better—" and eventually he submitted with a slight scowl to be led up and presented by his fiancée.

"I hear I am to congratulate you—er—Count Fresser," said the Duchess. "You are certainly a fortunate man to have won a Princess."

"Not more fortunate than she," he replied. "She wanted a Superman, as she calls it. I am doing all I can to become one."

"If she isn't satisfied with you as you are, she must be hard to please."

"She is satisfied enough," he said. "Now it is for her to please me. She knows that by this time—don't you, Edna?"

"Yes, Ruprecht dear, yes," said Edna, hastily. "Of course I do. This is how he's taken to bullying me, Duchess," she added lightly. "Don't you think it's too bad of him?"

"It seems a little early to begin. You shouldn't allow it."

"Oh, but I like him to!" said Edna, pressing the Count's great arm.

"In that case, my dear," said the Duchess, "you have every prospect of a happy future!"

A blast from the silver trumpets here proclaimed that luncheon was served.

"Lunch, at last, eh?" said King Sidney, bustling up to the Duchess. "Permit me to offer your Grace my arm. Clarence, my boy, you take in her ladyship here. Selina, my love, if you will lead the way with the Marshal."

The Count followed with Edna, and the Fairy Vogelflug arrived in time to bring up the rear with Princess Ruby.

"It's a most extraordinary thing," said the King, after they had sat down to lunch in the hall with the malachite columns, "a most extraordinary thing, that, when we have company like this, there should be no more than six pages to wait on us! We generally have at least a dozen. What's become of all the rest of you?" he asked a page.

"I cannot say, sire," answered the boy. "They were waiting in the courtyard to receive His Excellency the Count, but have not yet returned."

King Sidney told the Court Chamberlain to send for them at once, but the messenger returned with the information that the missing pages were nowhere to be seen.

"Must have run off before I arrived," said the Count, laughing boisterously. "Played truant, the young rascals!"

The Fairy, however, recollected Daphne's story of the sack, and was seized with suspicion. Was it possible that the royal pages—? If so, she felt something ought to be done—though not by her. She was too cautious an old person to take unnecessary risks, and decided to employ a deputy.

"Ruby, my child," she whispered to the little Princess, who was sitting next to her, "I believe the Count has brought a present for you. It's in a sack in his coach. Ask him what it is."

"I don't want to know," objected Ruby, "I wouldn't take any present from him—except Tützi, perhaps."

"I may be wrong," said the Court Godmother, "perhaps it isn't for you after all. But I'm sure it would make him very uncomfortable if you asked him, before everybody, what he happens to have in that sack of his."

"If I was sure of that," said Ruby, "I'd ask him like a shot!"

"You may depend on it. And more than that, Lady Daphne is particularly anxious to know."

"Oh, if Miss Heritage wants me to, all right!" said Ruby. "I say, Count Rubenfresser," she called across the table, "I want to ask you something."

"If it's a riddle, little Princess," replied the Count, with his mouth full, "I give it up beforehand."

"It isn't a riddle. It's this: What have you got inside that sack?"

"Sack?" said the Count blankly. "I don't understand. I have no sack here."

"I don't mean here. I mean the sack that's inside your coach."

"Ruby, my dear," interposed her mother, "you mustn't be so inquisitive. It's very rude."

"I know he has got a sack there, Mummy," insisted Ruby, "and I do want to know what he's got in it."

"Hear me rag my precious brother-in-law," said Clarence aside to Lady Muscombe. "A sack, eh?" he said aloud. "What do you bring a sack out to lunch for—scraps?"

"For shame, Clarence!" cried Edna.

"It's not a sack, as it happens," said the Count sulkily. "It's a long bag—and what I use it for is entirely my own business."

"I don't know so much about that," retorted Clarence. "With such a lot of plate in the Palace!"

"Clarence!" cried Edna again. "This is too outrageous of you!"

"Much!" put in Lady Muscombe. "As if the Count couldn't bring his clubs with him if he's going on to golf somewhere!" she said to Clarence in an undertone. "And of course he'd want a very long case for them! You really must behave more decently!"

"I mean having this out with the beggar," he replied. "Count, her ladyship suggests that you may have golf clubs in that bag of yours. Is that so?"

"And if I have," said the Count. "Why shouldn't I?"

"Because you don't play golf. No one does here—now, and I'll take my oath you can't tell a brassey from a putter. You never owned a set of clubs in your life!"

"Really, my boy!" said King Sidney nervously. "A scene like this! Before our guests! It won't do, you know. Drop it!"

"Yes," said Lady Muscombe, laying her pretty but slightly over-manicured fingers on Clarence's sleeve. "You're only making everybody uncomfortable. Talk to me instead!"

"Presently," he said. "If you really have got golf clubs, Count, I should like to have a look at them after lunch."

"I never said I had got those things," replied the Count, with a wonderful command over his temper. "And if you want to know what is in the bag, I don't mind telling you—only a few pumpkins from my own gardens."

"You mean to say you make such pets of your bally pumpkins that you take 'em out driving with you? That's such a likely story!"

"Clarence," said the Queen, "I will not have poor Ruprecht badgered like this. If he chooses to carry pumpkins with him—as we do gold sometimes—and distribute them to deserving persons, it is so much the more to his credit."

"He'd get 'em buzzed back at his head pretty soon, if he did!" replied the impenitent Clarence. "He's not exactly the object of general adoration in these parts, as he jolly well knows.... Anything upset you, Marchioness?" he inquired of Lady Muscombe, who was giggling with a quite un-peeress-like lack of restraint.

"Nothing," she said faintly. "Only the—the pumpkins. You really are rather a funny Royal Family, you know!"

"I'm sorry to make myself unpleasant, Mater," said Clarence, returning to the charge. "But I can't swallow those pumpkins. I want the sack brought in so that we can satisfy ourselves what there is in it." The Court Chamberlain, in the hope that the contents, whatever they might be, would at least serve to compromise the Count, instantly despatched one of the pages to fetch the bag.

"Baron," said the Queen angrily, "it is for Us to give orders—not you!"

"Your Majesty must pardon my presumption," he said, as the pages had already obeyed him. "I was merely carrying out the wishes of His Royal Highness the Crown Prince."

"I shall die if this goes on much longer! I know I shall!" gasped Lady Muscombe.

"Ha!" cried Clarence, as the pages staggered in with a huge distended sack. "Leave it alone, I'll open it myself."

"Surely not without asking the owner's permission?" said the Duchess, who had hitherto witnessed the scene in silent and dignified amazement.

"You can open it if you like!" said the Count, with a confident smile. "And then you will see what a fuss you have made about nothing."

Clarence cut the cord, and opened the sack. The moment he did so his jaw fell. "I own up," he said. "I was wrong. They are pumpkins!"

"And if you are a gentleman, Clarence," cried Edna, "you will apologise to Ruprecht at once!"

"There may be something else underneath," he said, lifting a pumpkin suspiciously in both hands. "Hullo! My hat! What's this I've got hold of?" he exclaimed, as the vegetable suddenly developed, the moment it was clear of the sack, into one of the chubbiest of the royal pages. "Very odd!" he remarked, as he set the boy down. "Let's have the lot out." He tilted the sack, and as each pumpkin rolled out upon the sardonyx pavement, a bewildered page sprang up in its stead.

"Quite a clever trick!" said Lady Muscombe. "Even Maskelyne and Devant couldn't beat that!"

"After all, it wasn't so very much of a change!" was Ruby's comment.

"What do you boys mean by playing at being pumpkins in this way?" demanded King Sidney. "I must have an explanation of this. Speak out, one of you!"

"If it please you, sire," said the first page, sinking on one knee, "When His Excellency the Count arrived he invited us to get inside the sack, at the bottom of which he told us we should find sweetmeats. And we crawled in—and I don't remember any more till I fell out just now."

"Just count these boys, Baron, will you?" said the King. "The whole dozen correct? Good. And now, sir," he added, turning to the Count, "I should like to hear what you have got to say."

"Allow me, sire," interrupted Marshal Federhelm, as Count Ruprecht seemed content to smile blandly. "His Excellency no doubt intended to afford your Majesties a little harmless diversion."

"That was all," said the Count. "This is a magic sack which has the property of turning anything inside it into whatever its owner wishes. I thought it might amuse you."

"Liar!" struck in Clarence. "You wouldn't have said a word about it but for Ruby! You meant to take those pumpkins—I mean pages—away with you. You know you did! I don't know what the Guv'nor and Mater think of it—but I consider myself it was a confounded liberty!"

"Well, well," said the King, "it was a mistake no doubt. But there's been no harm done, so perhaps we'd better leave it at that—for the present, you know, for the present."

But the Court Chamberlain could not allow such an opportunity to escape him. "Forgive me, sire," he said eagerly, "but your Majesties are evidently unacquainted with his Excellency's family history. The motive for his indiscretion will perhaps be better understood when I mention that his parents' title was formerly Bubenfresser, and that they were executed by command of the late King as being notorious ogres."

"So that was his game, was it?" cried Clarence. "Bagged our pages, meaning to gobble 'em up when he got 'em home! Am I to have an Ogre for a brother-in-law?"

At this there was a general cry of horror.

"Marshal," said the King, "you must have known all about this—and you gave that fellow an excellent character!"

"I had no reason to believe otherwise, sire," replied the ex-Regent smoothly. "He had been brought up as a strict vegetarian, and I cannot think that, if he had not acquired a taste for meat at your Majesty's table, he would ever have developed these—er—hereditary proclivities."

"He hasn't developed them!" declared Edna. "It's false! Ruprecht, deny it! Tell them you are no Ogre!"

"Really, ma'am," said the Duchess to Queen Selina, "I must ask your permission to leave the table. I don't feel as if I ought to be present at a family dispute of this intimate nature."

"Pray don't go, my dear Duchess!" the Queen implored her. "Not till you've heard what the Count has to say."

The Count rose and folded his arms in proud defiance. "I'm not an Ogre," he said sulkily.

"I knew it—I knew it!" cried Edna. "Appearances were against him, that's all!"

"Not an Ogre yet," went on the Count. "But I hope to be one as soon as I get the chance."

"No, no, Ruprecht!" protested Edna. "You don't mean it—you know you don't!"

"What!" said the Count, scowling at her. "Are you going to turn round on me like this, after encouraging me as you did?"

"You will not find it easy to persuade me," said the Duchess, "that the Princess would ever have urged you to become an Ogre."

"Urged him, indeed!" cried Edna wildly. "I had no suspicion—I never said a single word that could possibly—"

"Didn't you say I was to follow the teachings of your great master with the name I never can pronounce?" he demanded. "Didn't you tell me to make my own morality and obey my own instincts, without caring what people thought or what suffering I inflicted? You know you did! And that's all I've done. My instincts told me that those pages were my natural provender. I had a perfect right to take them if I could. The only people who would condemn me would be just those average conventional persons for whom you have such a contempt. I expected better things from you!"

"I cannot sit here another moment," declared the Duchess, rising. "It is making me positively ill!"

"And me!" added Lady Muscombe. "I've been on the point of fainting several times. I must say," she told Clarence, "this is quite the weirdest lunch I ever sat through!"

"We will all leave, Duchess," said the Queen. "I assure you I entirely share your sentiments, and perhaps by this time even Edna—"

"I loathe him, Mother!" she said, shuddering; "I only hope I shall never see his face again!"

"You hear that, sir?" said King Sidney, with more firmness than he usually showed. "And, as the Princess Edna—er—voices the general feeling, perhaps you'll see the propriety of getting out of this at once?"

"It seems to me," said the Count, "that you are all making a great fuss about nothing. If I'd eaten any of your pages I could understand it. But I haven't—I never got the chance."

"Thanks to Clarence!" put in Queen Selina. "He saved the poor boys!"

"It was Miss Heritage, really, Mummy!" corrected Ruby jealously. "She wanted to know about the sack, or I shouldn't have asked."

"Miss Heritage!" muttered Edna. "Ah! I might have known it!"

"Now just you be off to that castle of yours," said the King, addressing the discomfited but quite unrepentant Ogre. "And mind you keep inside it for the future. You will see that he does that, Marshal? I don't want any scandal about this business, but if I have any more trouble from you, I shall be forced— well, to take some very strong measures."

"I'm just going," said the Ogre calmly. "May I have my bag?"

"Confound your impudence, no!" returned the King, "I shall have the beastly thing destroyed."

"Then I think you ought to give me back some of the money I paid for it," said the Ogre. "I bought it from Master Xuriel, and I know you get two-thirds the price of any article he sells. He told me so."

"You—you infamous scoundrel!" cried King Sidney, turning extremely red, perhaps with anger. "Marshal, see this ruffian off the premises—and look here, just send for that rascally astrologer, will you? I'll make short work of him!"

"Farewell, then, to your Majesties," said the Ogre, with a jaunty wave of his big hand. "And farewell to you, Princess Edna. If I have not been as much of a Superman as I could wish, you may still find that I have profited by your teachings."

The old Court Chamberlain's chest gave a loud crack as the Count swaggered out.

"Thank goodness he's gone!" said Queen Selina. "Really, my dear Duchess, and you, dear Lady Muscombe, I simply can't say how distressed I am that anything so unpleasant should have occurred while you were under our roof. I do hope you won't blame me. I always disliked the Count myself—but I should never have dreamed of asking him to meet you if I had known the sort of person he really was!"

"Indeed, Ma'am," said the Duchess, "I can quite believe that."

"And, after all," said Lady Muscombe languidly, "I dare say there are lots of people in town—in houses where they don't keep a page, I mean—who'd be glad enough to get him to come and dine. Society is so much less exclusive than it used to be."

"That," remarked the Duchess, "entirely depends on what you mean by 'Society.' And now, Ma'am," she continued to her hostess, "as the birds—I think you mentioned that they were storks—which brought us here should be rested by this time, I shall be obliged if you will order the car to take me back as soon as I have changed my dress."

"And me, too, if you don't mind," said Lady Muscombe. "I must get home before Nibbles does."

"Oh, but you mustn't leave us so soon!" protested Queen Selina in dismay. "To come all this way for such a miserable little visit!"

"A flying visit, let us call it," said the Duchess. "But, candidly, this country of yours doesn't suit me. I don't feel safe with characters such as Ogres and Giants and Dragons about."

"But I assure your Grace there are very very few—hardly any, in fact!"

"There are more than my nerves can stand," said the Duchess, firmly, and Queen Selina, though deeply mortified by her guests' eagerness to go, found that she could no longer detain them.

The Court Chamberlain and his attendants brought the stork car to the palace door by the time the visitors had resumed their former costumes.

"Good-bye, dear Duchess!" said the Queen. "So charmed to have seen you, even for so short a time. I hope some day you will come again."

"I think it improbable," was the grim reply. "And if you'll allow me to say so, Ma'am, when I do stay anywhere, I prefer a house where I can be sure of the sort of people I am likely to meet."

"I say, Marchioness," cried Clarence, as he joined them on the steps, "you're not really going, are you? I wish you'd stay on a bit. We were getting on thundering well together, you and I!"

"Very sad, isn't it?" she answered, with a charming but slightly mocking grimace. "But Nibbles wouldn't like me to stop here philandering with Fairy Princes—even if they aren't quite the real thing. Good-bye, Ma'am," she added, with a gay little nod, as she stepped into the car, where the Duchess was already seated. "Thanks so much for having me! It's a wonderful house to stay in—and a most interesting experience."

"I have an impression," said the Duchess drowsily, "that I shall wake up presently and find all this has been a dream. I trust so, but, if not, would you mind telling this elderly gentleman to set me down in some unfrequented part—not Stratford Place, where I should attract more attention than is at all desirable."

"That's a good idea, Duchess!" said Lady Muscombe. "He can drop us on Clapham Common, and we can share a taxi home."

Queen Selina kissed her hand affectionately to them both as the storks spread their great wings and the car slowly rose. But her salute was not returned—principally for the reason that both ladies had already closed their eyes in slumber.

"And we might have made those two women our friends for life!" she lamented, as she went indoors. "I hope, Edna, my love, you see now what comes of getting your own way?"

"If I have been mistaken for once," said Edna, in a spiritless tone, "you needn't rub it in, Mother. I can't imagine now what I could ever have seen in that detestable creature."

"Nor I—especially as you could see nothing in Prince Mirliflor, who really was—no, my dear, I'm only speaking for your good. If I was sure you regretted your treatment of him, I might perhaps find some way—"

"I dare say I should act differently if he asked me again. But he won't. This dreadful story is sure to get round to him somehow. Of course I'm glad Ruprecht has been found out in time. But he need not have been exposed so publicly! I do resent that. And you heard what Ruby said? Miss Heritage was at the bottom of it. She deliberately planned this to humiliate me! And if you have the smallest consideration for me, Mother, you will forbid her to appear at Court after this."

"I'm afraid she is a designing young person," admitted the Queen, "and I have thought more than once lately of sending her home to England."

"Then do it, Mother. If you don't, I shall simply refuse to appear in public myself, sooner than meet her."

"She shall go, my dear. I'll see the Court Godmother about it at once. And don't let yourself get too downhearted over the other affair—Prince Mirliflor, I mean. I've great hopes we can put that right."

"I've just left poor darling Edna," she began, as soon as she found the Fairy alone; "all this has been a terrible shock to her, as you may imagine. But it seems I was right in thinking she never really cared for that unspeakable man. He terrified her into accepting him. And, between ourselves, Godmother, I fancy that, if you could induce Prince Mirliflor to come forward again, he would not be sent away a second time."

"So I should imagine, myself," said the Fairy drily. "But, as it happens, owing to the result of my previous efforts, I have lost all influence with Mirliflor. He and I have fallen out."

"But you could easily make it up with him. You might say she was really in love with him from the first, only she wished to put him to the proof—something of that sort. Tell him how delighted we should all be to see him again. There's another little matter I wished to speak to you about. Edna has taken the strongest dislike to that Miss Heritage, who I must say has acted most unwarrantably. I have made up my mind to part with her, and I thought, if you would arrange to have her taken back to England as soon as the car returns to-morrow—"

"Stop," said the Fairy, "I must have time to think over that." She had, it is true, renounced all further interference in anybody's affairs, but habit was too strong for her. Her old brain was busying itself once more with the scheme she had abandoned—a scheme that would certainly not be assisted by Daphne's expulsion from Märchenland. So she temporised.

"Yes," she said at last, "I quite see from what you tell me, that Lady Daphne cannot remain at Court any longer. The difficulty is that I can't send her back to England just yet. My storks will not be fit for so long a flight again for a fortnight at the very least. I'm not going to have them killed on her account. I could do this for you. I could establish her in a little pavilion in a distant part of the palace grounds and keep her there, under my own eyes, till the storks are ready for another journey. It's a very secluded place— almost a wilderness—and none of the Court ever go near it."

"That seems an excellent plan," said the Queen. "But I shouldn't care for them to know that she is a prisoner. They had better be told that she has resigned her situation and left the Palace. And—you won't forget my little hint—about Prince Mirliflor, you know?"

"I will bear it in mind. In fact, if you can spare me for a day or two, I thought of going over to Clairdelune in the dove-chariot to-morrow and having a little chat with him."

"Oh, by all means do!" said the Queen gratefully. "So kind of you to take so much trouble!"

"It's more on his account than yours," replied the Fairy, with a candour that might have been intended as complimentary. "But I don't guarantee that anything will come of it—at all events for a considerable time."

"Indeed I quite understand that—that his wound can hardly be expected to heal just yet."

The Fairy lost no time in conveying Daphne to the secret pavilion without the knowledge of any of the Court. It was quite fit for occupation, and supplied with all that was necessary for comfort; the Court Godmother provided her with an attendant, and even procured some ancient volumes of Märchenland history with which Daphne could beguile her solitude.

That night the Court Godmother summoned up all her energies to send Mirliflor another vision of Daphne. It was the best vision she had ever transmitted, but it was terribly exhausting work, and she grumbled bitterly to herself that the scheme she had in hand should demand these excessive exertions.

But it was one of the good old-fashioned schemes which have always been beloved by romantic but didactic Fairy Godmothers. It would test the characters of Mirliflor and Daphne, and be valuable moral discipline for both, while, if they came through it triumphantly, they would be amply compensated for any temporary inconvenience. She had not engaged in an affair of this kind for at least a century and a quarter, and she was looking forward to a highly interesting and enjoyable experience. First she must regain her influence over Mirliflor, but she thought she would not find much difficulty in doing that.

The Astrologer Royal had been duly summoned before the King to explain his dealings with the Ogre-Count. But he not unwisely preferred to disappear instead, taking with him his books of spells and other apparatus. It was reported that he had found refuge at Drachenstolz.

"Gone there, has he?" said King Sidney to the Marshal. "Better send someone to arrest him."

"It would need an army, sire," said the Marshal, "and a long siege, to enter the Castle."

"Oh, is that so?" said the King. "Well, then, have guards posted all round to see that they don't get out. After all, so long as we keep them boxed up there, they can't do any mischief." And the guards were posted accordingly.

Poor Ruby was almost broken-hearted on hearing from her mother that her beloved Miss Heritage had gone back to England without so much as a word of farewell. The Court received the news with murmurs, and a strong suspicion that she had not left of her own free will.

Clarence was in the deepest dejection. It was true that he had made no advance of late in his pursuit of her, but so long as she remained there had always been hope. Now that she was gone for ever, even his riding and hunting became uninteresting and purposeless. What was the use of excelling in them when she was not there to hear of his prowess?

Early that afternoon he returned from the forest, and, after spending a few minutes in his own apartments, came down to his father's private cabinet with a gloomy and slightly startled expression. He found King Sidney alone and in better spirits than usual.

"Back from your hunting already, my boy?" he said.

"Had enough of it," said Clarence. "Felt a bit off it to-day, somehow."

"Ah, your mother and I are just in from a drive. There's no doubt this—er—rupture with that disgusting fellow has brought about an enormous improvement in the public feeling. We were cheered, my boy, actually cheered!"

"It may be some time before you're cheered again, Guv'nor," said Clarence. "I mean, you made a grand mistake in letting that little perisher Xuriel sell those tables of his 'Under Royal patronage,' and I'm afraid you'll hear of it before long."

"Eh, why, what's wrong with them? They seemed to give perfect satisfaction. Have there been any complaints?"

"There'll be lots if they all go like mine has. When I came in just now I was feeling a bit peckish, so I got out my table. It laid itself right enough, only the wine was stiff with wriggly things like tadpoles—and, when I lifted the dish-cover, I'm hanged if there weren't a couple of great fat snakes under it, hissing like tea-kettles! And I paid the beggar a sack and a half of ducats for that table!"

"Most untradesmanlike!" said King Sidney indignantly. "Of course you can make him return the money! No, you can't, though, I forgot—the fellow's bolted!"

"I wasn't thinking so much of that," said Clarence, "but suppose all the other johnnies who've bought tables find they're wrong 'uns, and want their money back—from us?"

"They wouldn't have a leg to stand on, my boy. It's a clear case of 'Caveat emptor.' But, after all, there's no reason at present to suppose the other tables are—hem—in a similar condition to yours."

"It's to be hoped not," said Clarence. "There'll be the devil's own row if they are."

Unfortunately it soon appeared that they were, and the numerous persons in Eswareinmal who had purchased them felt their grievance so strongly that they sent a large and somewhat turbulent deputation to demand an audience from His Majesty.

King Sidney received them, indeed he could not very well avoid doing so, as they forced their way to his presence. He did his best to reason with them, pointing out the undeniable fact that no guarantee had been given that the tables would last for ever, and that it was scarcely surprising if, after being in constant use, they should begin to show symptoms of wear and tear—a phrase which had the effect of infuriating them almost to madness. Nor were they pacified when he quoted his maxim of "Caveat emptor," and pointed out that, if people would invest in magic tables, some degree of trickery was only to be expected. His arguments were lost on them. They had discovered somehow that the greater part of their purchase money had gone to swell the Royal revenues, and they clamoured for instant restitution.

So finally the King had recourse to his usual expedient. "Don't let us have a row about this little matter, gentlemen," he said. "I'm anxious to meet you if I can, and I tell you what I'll do. I'll have the Council summoned at once. You can lay your claims before them, and if they can see their way to granting you any compensation, we shall be as good friends as ever again."

King Sidney's idea had been that the Council, if they decreed any compensation at all, would do so from funds belonging to the State. It appeared, however, that they did not consider this to be within their powers. They decided that, as the Sovereign had enjoyed the greater part of the profit on the sales of the self-supplying tables, he was bound to refund the money, proportionate deductions being made for the period during which each table had been in proper order. This required elaborate calculations, but the Lord Treasurer had a wonderful head for figures, and worked them out to such effect that there was only moderate grumbling on the part of the creditors, all of whom received rather more than their due, while a good many had never bought a table at all.

So, on the whole, the decision satisfied all except the Royal Family.

"It's easy to be generous with other people's money!" said the King. "But this business has nearly cleared us out. That confounded Treasurer hasn't left us more than a dozen sacks or so to go on with.

He's suggested that I might try to get a loan from the King of Goldenbergenland. I'm told he's wealthy, so perhaps he'd be willing to oblige a fellow-monarch, if I gave him the mine as security."

"That mine?" said Clarence. "Why, it doesn't cover its working expenses—and never will, with the wages we pay those miner-johnnies!"

"Most exorbitant," said the King; "I've been thinking of—hem—bringing back those yellow gnomes. They wouldn't want wages—and the mine would be healthier for them than those marshes they're draining."

"It might," agreed Clarence, "if there were any of the poor little beggars left. But I believe the climate has been too much for 'em."

"Has it, though? I'm afraid they must have neglected to take proper precautions. Very ungrateful, after all I've done for them! But it's no use trying to benefit that class of persons. I see that now."

Clarence still wore his pendant, though he rode less and less frequently. The Marshal told him that there was excellent carp-fishing to be had on the Crystal Lake a few miles from Eswareinmal, and he took up this sport, making solitary expeditions to the lake, from which he returned in better spirits for a time. But even this occupation soon palled, and the whole Court were struck by his increasing dejection, which, rightly or wrongly, they attributed to the absence of Lady Daphne.

CHAPTER XV

"RIVEN WITH VAIN ENDEAVOUR"

After a few hours' flight the Fairy Vogelflug's team of doves had safely deposited her at the entrance to the Palace of King Tournesol. She ascertained that Prince Mirliflor was within and went at once to his apartments. He received her with his usual respect, but there was a reserve in his manner which showed that the memory of his late fiasco was still rankling. His reserve increased perceptibly after she had explained the purpose of her visit. He altogether declined to consider a second matrimonial venture on her recommendation, hinting as politely as possible that her idea of a suitable consort for him was too unlikely to correspond with his own. "You mean with the ideal of your visions?" she said. "And you saw her again last night. Now didn't you, Mirliflor?"

"I did," he said; "but how did you know that?"

"How did I know? Because I sent you the vision, of course. I sent you the former one, too, though there were reasons why I couldn't tell you so till now."

"And why do you tantalise me by making me dream of an unattainable perfection?" he asked hotly. "Can you suppose that anything short of it will ever content me now? Since I cannot hope to find so sweet and fair a Princess in all the world, I am only the more resolved to live and die unmarried!"

"She exists, or I could not have shown her to you in a vision. You have only to do exactly as I tell you, Mirliflor, and you shall see her, and win her, if you can."

"You said all that about the other one, Godmother Voldoiseau," he replied. "No, it's no good. I really can't trust you again."

"Don't be obstinate, Mirliflor, or you'll put me in a passion, and that's dangerous at my age. I grant you I was wrong about Princess Edna. But I'm not wrong now. I assure you that, if you saw this girl, you would own that she was no less fair than she appeared in your visions."

"But if there indeed lives so lovely a Princess," he said, "how comes it that I have never heard of her existence?"

"She is no Princess, Mirliflor. Merely a poor friendless girl I have chosen to protect."

"So much the better," he said. "She is the less likely to refuse me."

"Because you are a Prince? Just so—but I don't intend that she shall accept you for any such reason. I shall not allow you to see her at all unless you promise not to reveal your rank, or even your real name, to her until I give you leave to do so."

"You have my word, Godmother," he replied. "After all, it may be that, even without rank or title, I shall succeed in obtaining favour in her eyes."

"You trust to your good looks—but those, too, you must consent to sacrifice. Love that is based on mere outward appearance soon passes. I have to be very careful now how I exercise any magic power whatever—each time it takes more and more out of me, and even sending you these visions taxed me most severely. Still, I will make another effort and change you into a less comely form."

"I suppose you are proposing to turn me into a beast of some kind?" he said. "If so, I cry off. I know it succeeded with an ancestor of ours—but that was centuries ago, and I'm not inclined to undertake the risk myself."

"I'm not asking you to undertake it. The form you would assume would be human, and not in the least repulsive. In strict fairness I ought to transform the girl as well, but as I know very well that, if I did, you would never so much as look at her, I must leave her as she is. Only if you don't consent to be transformed yourself, you will never see her at all."

"But what if I let myself be transformed and find out when I see her that she doesn't resemble my vision?"

"You need not fear that. But if, when you see her, you wish to withdraw, I will bring you back here and restore you to your own shape again, and thus you will be none the worse."

"Well," he said, "on those terms I agree." Upon which the Fairy began her incantations, and, after one or two failures, succeeded in remembering the precise formula and accomplishing the metamorphosis.

"I knew it would come back to me in time," she remarked, exhausted but gratified. "I shall suffer for it later—but it's certainly a highly successful piece of work—as you will see if you go and look at yourself in that mirror."

When he looked it was a complete stranger that he saw reflected. A young man of his own height and figure, but with features that, without being absolutely plain, were quite ordinary. His own curling brown locks were replaced by short black hair, and his complexion had deepened from its original slight bronze to a swarthy hue. Even his silk and velvet suit had suffered a change and was now a coarse leather jerkin with hose and sleeves of russet cloth.

"You might just as well have made a beast of me outright!" he said bitterly. "I should have been as likely to win the heart of any maiden as I am now."

"My dear Mirliflor," retorted the Fairy, "if, as you are now, you cannot win this girl by your own worth, it will either be because she is not worth winning or you have not sufficient worth to deserve her."

"And how," he asked, "am I to set about winning her?"

"You will start at once for Eswareinmal—on horseback if you like, provided your horse and his trappings are not too fine. You will leave him outside the City, and find your way to one of the side entrances of the Palace, where you will ask an attendant to inform me that 'Giroflé'—as you will henceforth call yourself—has arrived in obedience to my summons. I will arrange that you shall see this girl, and it will then be for you to say whether you will go any further or not in this enterprise. You had better leave the Palace without seeing the King, your father, and I will explain to him that there were good and sufficient reasons for your secret departure."

However, when she did obtain an audience from King Tournesol, she saw that he was not in a mood that promised a favourable reception to any further matrimonial project on Mirliflor's behalf—at all events from her. So she merely informed him that Mirliflor had left Clairdelune to seek a bride for himself, and that he might be absent for some time. She did not mention his transformation, and was disingenuous enough to agree with the King that the Prince had behaved most unfilially in departing without permission. But King Tournesol was too glad that his son's thoughts had again turned to marriage to be very seriously angry, and the Fairy left him in tolerable good humour, and got back to Eswareinmal long before Mirliflor, who reached the Palace at last, after a journey of entirely unfamiliar discomfort and a total lack of the deference and attention he had always hitherto received as of right. He made his way in an aggrieved and rather rebellious frame of mind to a side entrance and, on inquiring for the Court Godmother, was taken at once to her apartments. After hearing his tale of hardships, which she merely said were extremely good for him, she led him down by a private staircase to the gardens at the back of the Palace, and through them, by a postern gate of which she had the key, to an uncultivated region of glades and groves. Here she ordered him to conceal himself behind a thicket at the edge of a clearing, and to remain there till she gave him leave to come out. He waited for what seemed an interminable time—and then his patience was rewarded. The Fairy returned with the very lady of his visions. This time at least his Godmother had not deceived him—the living reality was even more radiantly beautiful than his dream! They passed and repassed him several times, and, if he had not seen Daphne, the mere sound of her gay sweet voice would have been enough to enslave him. But he could see her perfectly well, and note the animation of her every gesture, the easy grace with which she moved, and her pretty tenderness for the old woman who was leaning on her strong young arm. When would the Fairy see fit to call him forth and present him to this adorable being? And yet, inconsistently enough, he was dreading the moment. How could he hope, changed as he was now, that those bright eyes would regard him with any interest whatever? But, as it happened, they did not regard him at all on this occasion, for, after a few more turns up and down the clearing, the Fairy retired with her protégée, and presently re-appeared alone.

"Well," she said, as Mirliflor came forward at her summons, "now you have seen her, what is your decision?"

"I stay here," he replied, "and will submit to anything as long as there is a chance of gaining her."

"I expected as much," she said. "And I have arranged that you shall be employed here as one of the Royal under-gardeners."

"An under-gardener!" he exclaimed. "Really, Godmother, that is not giving me a fair chance! And I've never done any gardening in my life!"

"Then it is high time you began," she said calmly. "It will not only give you a greater respect for manual labour, but subdue your pride."

"You have left me nothing I can be proud of. And what opportunity shall I have of even seeing her?"

"You will be given the key which will admit you to the grounds, and the pavilion in which she lives is not far from here. As to opportunities of meeting her, you must make them for yourself. Those are my conditions," said the despotic old Fairy, "and if you don't choose to accept them, you may as well return to Clairdelune at once, for I shall take care that you never see her again."

"Oh, I accept," he said. "I can't help myself. Only, it does seem to me, Godmother, that if you're really anxious that I should succeed, you might make it easier for me than this!"

"No doubt," she said. "But if it was easy there would be no merit in success. I am putting her to the test, remember, as well as you, and until I see how you both come through it, I cannot be certain that you are really fitted for one another."

She had, as a matter of fact, quite made up her mind that they should marry, but she could not resist such an opening for one of the practical moral lessons which, as a Fairy Godmother of the fine old didactic type, she had often brought to an effectively instructive dénoûment.

But if she was enjoying herself over the probation, it is more than can be said for the unhappy Mirliflor. It is true that, owing to the Court Godmother's protection, he was treated by the Head Gardener with some indulgence, but, nevertheless, he had to work much harder and longer than he liked. Sometimes, however, he was sent to the outlying part of the gardens, where he was under no supervision, and then it was easy to slip away to the postern gate, which his key enabled him to enter, and he was not long in discovering the pavilion which sheltered his divinity. He wore a big apron and carried a pair of garden shears with which he lopped and trimmed a shrub now and then by way of accounting for his intrusion, and sometimes he was rewarded by a glimpse of her. But that was all, for, with a diffidence he had never known before, he did not venture near enough to speak. The fact was that he was morbidly self-conscious about his altered appearance. If the Fairy had only let him retain his own form, he thought, he would not have hesitated a moment, but her disdain was more than he could bring himself to face, and so he watched from afar, and when she wandered out would follow at a distance, keeping her in view, while remaining unseen himself. It was, as he felt, not precisely the way to conduct a courtship, and he despised himself for his want of courage. But he always hoped that something might happen to bring them together, though it seemed less and less likely that anything would.

Daphne, meanwhile, was growing resigned to her exclusion from the Palace, which she chiefly regretted because she could see nothing of Ruby, the one member of the Royal Family for whom she could feel any real affection. She expected to hear at any moment that the car was ready to take her back to England, where she would have to find employment if she could.

The Queen had certainly furnished her with a character; "Miss Heritage," the reference stated, "has been for some months in the service of Her Majesty Queen Selina of Märchenland as Governess-companion to Her Majesty's younger daughter, Princess Ruby. Her Majesty could not conscientiously recommend Miss Heritage as a teacher for advanced pupils, but has no doubt that she would be fairly competent to undertake a situation as Nursery Governess."

That was all—and Daphne did not think it would do much for her. And besides, people might want to know who the Queen of Märchenland was—which would be awkward to explain. But perhaps the Court Godmother would see that she was not sent home without funds enough to support her till she could get an engagement. She would be rather sorry to leave Märchenland, which, queer country as it was in some ways, she had come to look upon her home. However, she did not worry much about the future, being content to enjoy her present restful life as long as she might.

She was comfortable enough in the Pavilion, where she was well looked after by an elderly taciturn attendant, one of the Court Godmother's own waiting-women.

The old Fairy herself came from time to time to inquire after Daphne's health and bring her news of the Court, and her visits were welcome. When alone Daphne spent much of her time over the ancient Chronicles, which the Fairy had provided for her, and which she found strangely fascinating. Or when she was disinclined to read or embroider, she would explore the grounds about the Pavilion, which were wild and neglected enough to impart a sense of adventure to her wanderings. Often, as she walked and worked or read, her thoughts would drift into dreams—the dreams that come to most girls—of a Prince Charming who would discover her in her retreat, and be her champion and deliverer. In a country like this, such a dream was less unlikely to come true than elsewhere, and yet she always ended by laughing at herself for indulging it.

The Prince (for of course he must be a Prince!) would have to make haste if he was to find her still in Märchenland. But even if he came in time, she thought, it would be useless—his arrival would be reported at once to the Queen. For she had lately become aware that she was being watched by someone who was obviously not the gardener he tried to appear, and whom she had more than once detected in the act of following her in secret. He must be either a spy, or a guard with orders to prevent her escape—as if she were likely to attempt it when there was no place to which she could escape! She had made no complaint to the Court Godmother, being unwilling to trouble the old Fairy with a matter of so little importance. But she took her revenge on the spy by making his task as difficult as she could. If she detected him in time lying in wait in the bushes by the front of the Pavilion, she would slip out at the back, and reach her favourite haunts by a roundabout path screened by yew hedges, while he imagined her to be still indoors. He was really such an unsuspicious spy that there was hardly any fun in baffling him. She had done so with the usual success one hot afternoon, and was making for a tree under which she often sat. It had great glossy leaves, and gorgeous flowers with a delicate but penetrating scent, and the thought of the coolness beneath its spreading branches was particularly attractive just then. After looking round and satisfying herself that she had not been pursued, she sat down and opened the book she had brought—a chronicle of the lives of the Sovereigns of Märchenland. She had read most of it already, and instead of reading any more, she found herself thinking of the contrast between their earlier Kings and Queens and the present occupiers of the throne. The former Sovereigns had had their failings; some of them had been arbitrary and wrong-headed, one or two cruel and tyrannical. But none had ever been vulgar or ridiculous. She could understand poor Mr. Wibberley-Stimpson's being so hopelessly out of his element—but it seemed strange that Queen Selina, who was the daughter of a Märchenland Prince, should not have inherited any trace of royal dignity. They were quite incapable of governing the people, who, as Daphne knew, regarded them with scarcely disguised contempt. And it was such a pity, for the good Märchenlanders had been so loyal at first! They would be loyal still, if only they had a sovereign for whom they could feel a particle of—. She had got to this point in her meditations when she was startled by a stealthy rustle in the branches overhead. The spy had been too clever for her after all! Well, she thought, with malicious amusement, if he chose to take the trouble of climbing a tree to watch her, she would keep him employed up there as long as possible and see which would tire first. He was evidently getting cramped already, for the branches were cracking quite loudly, but she would not look up or show that she was in the least aware of him. And then suddenly a heavy body fell with a flop on the open book in her lap—and she realised with terror that it was no spy she had to deal with, but an infinitely more formidable enemy. It was a huge serpent that had coiled itself swiftly on her knees, which quivered under the intolerable weight, while its tail twisted round her ankles, binding them fast, and it reared its evil flat head, crested like a peacock's, to a level with her chin. Its markings, in alternate rings of cream, vermilion, black and orange, were strangely beautiful, but she was in no mood to admire them as she sat there—spell-bound under its cold tawny eyes.

Presently it spoke words which made her wish that its speech had been unintelligible. "Yes," it said, "you are quite right to be afraid of me. I am here to kill you."

"Then don't talk about it!" said Daphne, her throat so parched that she could scarcely speak; "if you must kill me, do it at once and get it over."

"Not yet," it said malignantly. "You have an agony of terror to go through before that. When I see your eyes close I shall know that the time has come, and I shall strike my fangs into that white throat of yours, and you will recover just sense enough to feel what pain it is to die!" Daphne would very possibly have closed her eyes at once and received the death stroke rather than listen any longer to the creature's threats, but she had just become aware that help was at hand. The person she believed to be a spy was stealing up, treading noiselessly over the velvet turf, his hands already outstretched with the evident purpose of seizing the reptile from behind. If she could only engage it in conversation for a minute or two, there was still a chance for her.

"I have done you no harm," she said, after moistening her dry lips. "Why should you hate me like this?"

"Ask Xuriel, my master," replied the serpent, "who called me into being for no other purpose than to put you to death."

"But I have done Xuriel no injury."

"Then it may be you are an enemy of the Count, whose servant he is. I know not—nor is it any matter. All I know is that I have been sent here to—" and here it broke off in a dreadful strangled scream as a pair of strong hands clutched it firmly by the throat and dragged it writhing into the open. Daphne sat helplessly looking on as her rescuer struggled with the thing, which had wound its coils round his waist and leg, and was trying hard to free its head and strike. He held the venomous head at arm's-length, gripping its throat tight, while the foam slavered from its distended jaws, but it was stronger than he, and, as he recognised this, he urged Daphne to save herself while there was time.

She had already risen, as she had got over any tendency to faint, but she had no intention of leaving him to his fate. She had just seen in a pocket of his leather apron those big garden-shears which she had noticed him plying with such marked incompetence, and it occurred to her suddenly that they might be of some real service now. She ran up and, watching her opportunity, succeeded in whipping them out. Then she stepped behind the serpent, and forced the blades together just below the part of its neck that was in her champion's grasp. There was a highly unpleasant scrunch and jar as they closed, but she pressed with all her strength, until the reptile's spine was cut through and its body uncoiled itself from the young man and went writhing and rolling blindly through the grass.

Daphne dropped the shears and got out of its way in sudden panic. "It's not dead! I'm sure it isn't!" she cried to the stranger, whom she had somehow ceased to think of as a spy.

"It is harmless enough now, fair lady," he said as he tossed its crested head into the undergrowth, "thanks to your courage."

"I never killed anything before," she said. "I hated doing it, and—it seems such a silly way to kill a snake!"

"It succeeded," he said, wondering how those small slim hands could have had the strength. "I could not have held it much longer. You have saved my life."

"I couldn't have," she said, "if you hadn't saved mine first. I know now that you have only been watching and following me about as you have to see that I didn't get into any danger?"

"So you were aware that I watched you?" he said.

Daphne laughed. "How could I help being?" she replied. "And of course I guessed at once that you weren't a real gardener."

"What makes you suppose that?" he said.

"Well," she said, laughing again, "I happen to have seen you at work, you know."

"I may have little skill," he said, "nevertheless, I have obtained employment here as a gardener."

"I mustn't ask you questions," she said, "but I'm quite sure that, before you came here, you were in a very different position from any labourer's." She had noticed a refinement in his speech and manner, and also the shapeliness of his hands, which the Fairy had been considerate or forgetful enough to leave unaltered.

But Daphne's words gave him a sudden hope. Had she detected that he was a Prince? If so, he was released from his promise of silence!

"All I may tell you," he said, "is that there were reasons which obliged me to leave my own country and live here where I am unknown. But I think you have guessed more than that already!"

"I will tell you what I think," she said. "I believe you are really a student, and, whatever you had to leave your country for, it was nothing you've any cause to be ashamed of. I expect you were accused of plotting against your Government—and I don't care if you did, because you wouldn't have if they'd governed properly. Anyway, you escaped, and thought you'd be safe if you could get a post in the Royal Gardens. There! it is only a guess, of course, and you needn't tell me whether I'm right or not."

He allowed her to think she was, as it was a far more creditable explanation than any he could have invented for himself.

"It was rather clever of me to guess all that," she said. "But it would have been cleverer of you to choose something you knew a little more about than gardening, wouldn't it? And we can't be strangers after this. That thing there," and she indicated the headless serpent, which had now ceased to writhe, and lay limp in the grass, with all its brilliant colour faded to dingy grey, "introduced us, but it carelessly forgot to mention our names."

"Perhaps," he said, quite seriously, "it did not know them."

"That would account for it, certainly," agreed Daphne, with equal gravity, though her eyes danced. "Then I'd better explain that I was Princess Ruby's governess before we came here. Since then I've been a sort of lady-in-waiting—and now I'm nothing at all. I'm in disgrace, like you. My name is Daphne Heritage. Now, tell me yours ... Giroflé?... Well, I am going back to the Pavilion now. I don't feel safe anywhere else.... Yes, you can see me out of this dreadful place—just in case there should be another snake about," she conceded, for her nerves were beginning to feel a reaction, and she was glad of his protection.

So he walked humbly by her side, saying little for fear of saying too much, till they came within sight of the Pavilion and then she dismissed him. "We will say good-bye here," she said; "and you mustn't keep at a distance any more—it would be too absurd, now—you must come and speak to me, of course. Though I may be sent back to England at a moment's notice, and then you won't see me again. But if you don't, I shall never forget how bravely you risked your life for me."

She gave him her hand; he held its cool silken softness for a moment and would have raised it to his lips but for this new humility of his. Then, with a friendly but almost careless little nod, she was gone, leaving him with the conviction that it was indifferent to her whether they ever met again or not.

He felt that the Fates had not been as propitious as they might. They had permitted him to rescue her— but then he had been rescued by her immediately afterwards—a most humiliating anti-climax! There was one service he could still do her, he thought, and, cutting himself a stout stick, he made a thorough search of the groves, where however, rather to his disappointment, he discovered no serpents of any kind. But, in his anxiety for Daphne, he insisted on seeing the Court Godmother at once and warning her of the dangers to which she was exposing her protégée.

The old Fairy was secretly disconcerted, though she did not of course admit that there had been any neglect on her part. "I am not at all surprised, Mirliflor. In fact, I fully expected something of this sort to happen," she said unblushingly. "But I knew very well that there was no danger while you were there to look after her."

"But it may happen again," he urged. "That accursed Xuriel may create another serpent, and the next time I mayn't be at hand—unless you can get me excused altogether from working in the gardens."

"I shall not do that, Mirliflor," said the inflexible old Fairy. "And what you fear will not happen again. To begin with, that serpent was never created by Xuriel."

"But I heard it say that he had called it into being!"

"And have you ever known a serpent tell the truth? No, no, Mirliflor, Master Xuriel is clever enough in his way, but he couldn't make a serpent of that size. From what you tell me, it was evidently a Crested Serpent which he had got hold of and trained, and I happen to know it was the last existing.... But I will have a rope of fine silk, woven with a certain spell, laid round the Pavilion, and no snake, magic or otherwise, will be able to cross that. It's quite unnecessary, and will be extremely exhausting to me, still I'll do it, just to set your mind at ease. And I'll tell her not to go about alone in future.... But I can't have you going in there whenever you choose in future. The Head Gardener was complaining to me that you are neglecting your work, and it won't do to excite his suspicion. You must not attempt to see her till the close of the day, which will leave you ample time for your lovemaking.... No, she is not going to be sent back to England. I shall take care of that. So you can keep a good heart, Mirliflor. I consider you have made an excellent beginning!"

He was far from sure of it himself, but at least Daphne would be better protected henceforth, and even if he could no longer look after her by day, which he fully intended to do when he found an opportunity, he could at least see her every evening. It was some comfort, too, to feel that he could rely on her remaining in Märchenland.

On her next visit to the Pavilion the Court Godmother heard Daphne's version of the meeting with Giroflé. "I take an interest in the young man," she said. "Indeed I got him his place here. He seems to have behaved very creditably—for a mere gardener. Though I dare say you think him beneath your notice."

"After he had saved my life!" said Daphne indignantly. "As if I could—whoever he was! But, as you take an interest in him, Court Godmother, you must know as well as I do that he isn't really a gardener at all."

"Oh, indeed," said the Fairy suspiciously. "And how did you find that out? From him?"

"No, I guessed. And then he had to admit it."

"And what did he admit?"

"Well, that he is a student and has had to go into hiding because he was suspected of being mixed up in some plot or other. He didn't tell me any more than that."

"Ah," said the Fairy, concealing her relief, "he told you more than was prudent as it was. But I suppose he thought he could trust you with his secret."

"And don't you, Court Godmother?" flashed Daphne.

"Oh, I don't think you would betray him. You mustn't go and lose your heart to him, though. That would never do!"

Daphne laughed. "Court Godmother!" she said, "you're not really afraid of my falling in love with him, are you?"

"Well, no, my dear. Fortunately he's not good-looking enough to make me very uneasy about that. I should be much more afraid that he might fall in love with you."

"Oh, I hope he won't do that, poor fellow," said Daphne with a sudden and uneasy recollection of how he had followed her in secret. "But I'm going home so soon that I mayn't even see him again."

"You may have to stay here some time longer," said the Fairy, "so it's quite possible that he will try to see more of you. However, it will be easy for you to tell him plainly that you don't want to have anything to do with him."

"But I don't mind his speaking to me," said Daphne. "I told him he might. I should hate hurting him like that. And, after all, Court Godmother, if he should show any signs of—of what you're afraid of, he will soon see that it's no use, and be sensible about it."

"I dare say you're right, my dear, I dare say you're right," agreed the Court Godmother. "And anyhow, it will be time enough to trouble about that when it happens—which very likely it never will."

But in her heart she was more convinced than ever that Mirliflor had made a very good beginning.

CHAPTER XVI

"A CLOUD THAT'S DRAGONISH"

At the first opportunity Mirliflor had returned to the pavilion groves, where he need no longer worship from a distance. Daphne had received him graciously enough, but somehow he went away with a feeling that he had lost ground. He saw her every day after that, occasionally in the daytime, whenever he could evade the Head Gardener's eye, and always in the evening. She would talk to him from her window, or sometimes she would consent to come out and stroll with him in the golden dusk along grass-grown paths bordered with high and ragged walls of yew. And yet he parted from her with a sorer heart every evening. She had been as enchanting as ever, but quite as indifferent. It was useless to tell her how he loved her; whenever he had tried she had made him understand that, if he said any more, he would spoil the friendship between them. So he said no more.

Sometimes she had made him angry. Unfortunately he could never quite forget his rank, and he resented the airy way in which she treated him as a person of no particular importance. She would even laugh at his efforts to assert his dignity—and he was unused to being laughed at, especially as he often did not even understand why she laughed. For Fairy Princes have never been noted for their sense of humour, and poor Mirliflor was certainly no exception. Once, when she had innocently permitted herself to remark that she thought Prince Mirliflor had shown very little spirit or determination in his wooing of Princess Edna, he lost his temper so completely as to tell her that she would be wiser not to pass judgment on matters of which she knew so little. Daphne's silence showed how deeply he had offended, but he was too proud to conciliate her, and so his evening came to an abrupt end in mutual coolness. On his way back he cursed himself for his folly. He had done for himself now—she would never forgive him, never speak to him again! How could he have been so mad when his only happiness was being near her? But when he ventured back the next evening, prepared for final dismissal, he found her as frank and friendly as ever; she seemed to have forgotten that they had ever fallen out at all. Unfortunately this was rather humiliating than gratifying, since it only showed how utterly insignificant he was in her eyes.

But Daphne did not actually consider him insignificant at all. She was rather interested in this plain, ordinary-looking youth with a lofty manner and an air of authority that seemed so incongruous, and yet, even while she laughed at him for them, impressed her in spite of herself. He was not quick at seeing a joke—especially against himself—and she enjoyed teasing and provoking him as she would not have done in the case of anyone she disliked.

She knew he was absolutely devoted to her, and although she had made him understand that he must avoid any approach to sentiment, she was touched by his devotion, and sorry that she could make him no better return.

"But it's no use," she thought remorsefully, "I simply couldn't care in that way for any man who hadn't some good looks. I can't be more than a friend to Giroflé—and, luckily, I believe he's beginning to see that at last!"

Mirliflor had certainly begun to see that he was too severely handicapped to have a chance of success, and he paid a secret visit to his Godmother's apartments to tell her so. But she was deaf to all his protests, and declined to restore him to his own form until he had either won Daphne or been refused by her. He came away furious, regretting that he had ever been such a fool as to put himself at the mercy of this obstinate old Fairy's whims. If he had not, he would not have met Daphne—but better a thousand times that he had never seen her if she was not to be his!

His visit had one result. Old Baron von Eisenbänden happened to observe him leaving the tower, and it struck him as suspicious that so august a personage as the Court Godmother should have any dealings with an under-gardener. She must be using the fellow as her agent in some intrigue or other, he concluded, and, as she had not chosen to confide in him, it was clearly his duty to his Sovereigns to discover what she was about.

His cap of darkness might be of service to him here, but since the fiasco of the self-supplying tables he had been distrustful of any article supplied by the Astrologer Royal. However, it seemed as though the sudden decay of the tables had been due less to any malicious revenge on Xuriel's part than to some imperfection in his magic—for the cap proved to be as efficient as ever. So, after satisfying himself of this, the worthy Baron put it on and prowled unseen about the Court Godmother's tower. For some days his vigilance was unrewarded, but at length he saw Giroflé hurrying down a gallery that led to the Fairy's door, and immediately gave chase. Unfortunately he arrived too late to slip in behind him, and the thickness of the door made it impossible to overhear anything of the conversation till the very end of the interview. Then, as the door was open and the Court Godmother had accompanied Giroflé to the threshold, their parting words were perfectly audible.

"You are setting me an impossible task, Godmother Voldoiseau!" he heard the mysterious young under-gardener declare. "I am no nearer her than when I came. And I never shall be till you restore me to my proper self!"

"I shall do that when I see fit, Mirliflor," the Fairy replied, "and not a moment before. You have only to be patient a little longer and all will be well. I know her better than you can, remember, and, believe me, you have no cause to despair."

"So you have told me before!" he said bitterly. "But I can't and won't endure this much longer, and if you refuse to make it easier for me, I shall give up and go back to Clairdelune!"

"My dear Mirliflor," she retorted, "you won't be such a fool!"

He left her at that without another word, but the Court Chamberlain had heard enough to surprise him considerably. So this young gardener, it seemed, was really Prince Mirliflor transformed! The Baron knew that such a transformation was within the Fairy's powers, so, in spite of the total dissimilarity between the Prince and the Gardener, he never for a moment doubted that they were one and the same.

But why the Court Godmother should have chosen to act in this arbitrary manner, and how she supposed it could promote Prince Mirliflor's object, was incomprehensible.

It was only natural that he should rebel against her, and the Court Chamberlain felt so much sympathy for the ill-used young prince that he resolved to follow him to the gardens and offer his advice and assistance.

Mirliflor had already begun to rake a flower-bed with vindictive energy, when he heard himself addressed from behind, and turned to recognise the elderly official he had good cause to remember.

"Hard at work, I see," began the Baron, with a casual air intended for any witnesses of the interview. "Work," he added, cautiously lowering his voice, "which, if I may be allowed to say so, Sire, can hardly be other than distasteful to his Royal Highness Prince Mirliflor of Clairdelune."

Mirliflor noticed the purple cap which was still in the other's hand, and knew it would be useless to deny his identity. "So, Baron," he said, "you have been eavesdropping again, have you? Well, if you were in the Court Godmother's chamber just now, as I suppose you were, you know how I come to be in this position."

"I am aware, Sire," he said, "that your Royal Highness has been induced to accept it in the hope of obtaining the hand of—of a certain person whom it would perhaps be inadvisable to name."

"Certainly we will not name her," said Mirliflor, "nor need we discuss a matter that so entirely concerns myself."

"I should not permit myself the indiscretion, Sire, if I did not so ardently desire that your Royal Highness's suit may prosper. But, so long as you remain in—in the form you have deigned to assume, I cannot think you will approach your Princess with the least chance of success!"

"I agree, Baron, but as the Court Godmother happens to think otherwise, I'm powerless, you see."

"She is a most gracious and venerable lady," said the Baron; "but, though her will is as strong as ever, her mind is evidently weakening. If your Royal Highness would be guided by me, I will venture to say that you would find it more to your advantage."

"Well, Baron, and what is your suggestion?"

"I have but to inform her Majesty of the facts," he said, "and she will at once order the Court Godmother Vogelflug to restore your Royal Highness to your own form, in which, believe me, Sire, you need have no fear of refusal."

"Listen to me, Baron!" said Mirliflor, who knew very well how his old Godmother would treat such an order. "You will say nothing whatever to her Majesty of my being here—and I'll tell you why you will not. If you do, she will necessarily have to hear of your method of acquiring the information. And it's not a very creditable method, Baron!"

"I have done nothing I am ashamed of," he said doggedly; "her Majesty will recognise that I have acted solely from devotion to her interests."

"Possibly—but I fancy she will also recognise that a Court Chamberlain who uses a cap of darkness to overhear private conversations is an official whose devotion might be occasionally inconvenient. I really don't think I should mention it, Baron, if I were you."

Even he appeared to see the force of this. "Since your Royal Highness desires your presence here to remain unknown, I will observe the greatest discretion," he said stiffly; "I have the honour to leave your Royal Highness to pursue his occupation." And with this he withdrew, with very obvious affront. He left Mirliflor even more disturbed than before. The Baron, having been present unseen at his interview with his Godmother, evidently knew all about his hopes with regard to Daphne, and seemed—for some reason that Mirliflor could not fathom—anxious for his success. But, though the Court Chamberlain had promised discretion, Mirliflor doubted whether he would be able to keep such a secret long. He was quite capable of thinking that, in Mirliflor's own interests, he was justified in disclosing it. And then— Mirliflor pictured himself summoned in his present form before the whole Court—where he had last appeared as Princess Edna's suitor, the difficulty of explaining his recent behaviour—the general indignity and humiliation he would be exposed to—even if the Fairy did not repudiate all knowledge of him, which she was quite capable of doing! No, he could not stay to face all that—he must leave the Palace that very night, and without a word to his Godmother. Why should he see her when nothing he could urge would have the slightest effect? Perhaps, when she heard he was back at Clairdelune, it would bring her to her senses.

Nor would he go through any parting scene with Daphne—what was it to her whether he went or stayed? If he saw her, he might be tempted to tell her how passionately and hopelessly he loved her— and she would only laugh at him. In self-respect he would spare himself that.

He adhered to this resolution till long past their usual hour for meeting, and he had made all his preparations for departure, when he was suddenly seized with an uncontrollable longing to see her once more—whatever pain it might cost him afterwards. So, with some scorn of his own weakness, he let himself through the postern gate and went in search of her. At the end of one of the yew walks was a rusty astrolabe on a moss-grown marble pedestal, and by this he found her. Her back was towards him as she faced the western horizon, where clouds of rose and gold were sailing in a sky of warm apple-green which toned above them to a luminous silvery blue. On the edge of the slope in the foreground some cypresses were silhouetted in purplish bronze. She turned as she heard his footsteps, her face so wondrously fair in the half light that his heart ached afresh at the sight of her. "I'd quite given up expecting you, Giroflé," she said, with a nonchalance that concealed her pique at his unusual tardiness—for it must be owned that she had become a trifle exacting of late. "It's so late now that I shall have to go in very soon."

"I shall not keep you long, Daphne," he replied, determined to show himself no less indifferent than was she. "I had to prepare for my journey, as I am leaving Eswareinmal to-night, and I have only come to say good-bye."

She was not only startled but deeply hurt. If he had really been so devoted as he had seemed, she thought, he could never have spoken of leaving her in this casual tone—but she would not let him see how he had wounded her. "To-night," she repeated, "I'd no idea you meant to go so soon as this. But I dare say you are only too glad to get away."

"Is one ever sorry," he said, in spite of himself, "to get away from a place where one has suffered?" She had turned to the astrolabe again, and was idly tracing out the incisions in one of its hoops with her supple forefinger, when she next spoke. "Of course I know it must have been hard for you, Giroflé," she said, "still, I hoped—it was very foolish and conceited of me, I know—but I hoped that perhaps my being here made it more bearable."

"If you had not been here, I should never have come at all," he said; "you did not know that, Daphne, but I may tell you now. And at first, it is true, that just to see and be near you now and then, was happiness enough—but of late the hours I have spent here have brought me little but the misery of longing for what must ever be denied!"

She could no longer misunderstand. So far from his devotion having abated, it was stronger than she had ever imagined, and the discovery made her sorrier for him than ever. "Giroflé!" she cried remorsefully, "I never knew you felt it like that—I thought you understood, and were content with—with all that I could give you. Oh, why can't you be?"

"And what have you given me, Daphne? What am I to you? Nothing! Nothing!"

"You are my friend—the dearest friend I have ever had. Is that nothing, Giroflé?"

"Nothing compared with what I once hoped to be! Hoped—while, even then, I knew how impossible any hope was. And yet—and yet—what adds to my torment is that I know—yes, Daphne, I know—that—if—if by an evil fate I had not been what I am, I could have made you love me. I am very sure of that!"

She was looking at him as she spoke—and somehow she ceased to think him plain. And suddenly she knew that he had become necessary to her—so necessary that the thought of losing him was unendurable.

"And why," she said, "are you so sure that it is impossible now, Giroflé?"

"Daphne," he cried incredulously, "do you mean that you can love me—even as I am?"

She did not reply in words, but her face as she raised it to his was answer enough; and then he held her in his arms, into which she nestled with a little sigh of perfect content. He could not understand how so marvellous and unlooked for a thing could have happened to him, and Daphne herself might have been at some loss to account for her sudden surrender. But she did not try—she only knew that she had been quite powerless to help it, and did not regret it.

"And you will not go away from Eswareinmal now, Giroflé?" she said a little later, when they were sitting on a stone seat under an ilex, and the gold and silver stars were beginning to come out in the deep violet sky.

"Not alone, dearest," he replied. "But it will not be wise to stay here long. I was recognised this afternoon by that meddling old imbecile of a Court Chamberlain."

"Giroflé!" she exclaimed, clinging to him in terror, "will he give you up—can they do anything to you? If there's danger, let us escape at once—for of course I shan't let you go alone!"

"There's no danger," he said. "If he lets out that I am here, it would be—inconvenient, but no worse. And I think my—the Court Godmother will see me through it now. I will tell her our news to-morrow morning."

"I'm afraid," said Daphne, "she won't at all approve of my marrying you—she may even try to prevent it, but she won't succeed!"

"She is more likely to be on our side," he said. He refrained, even then, from telling her why; he might be already released from his promise of silence, but he no longer rebelled against it, nor had he any impatience now to regain his own form. And so they talked on far into the night, discussing their future life together, which Daphne cheerfully assumed would be humble enough for a time—and he said nothing to disabuse her. Why should he not enjoy as long as he could the sensation—denied to most princes and millionaires—of being beloved "for himself alone?"

At an early hour the next morning, after carefully ascertaining that the Baron had not yet risen, he waited on the Fairy, who heard what he had to tell with high good-humour and complacency. "Most satisfactory, my dear Mirliflor!" she said. "And everything has turned out exactly as I always told you it would. I shall visit her this morning and prepare her for the future in store for her. As for you, you must get to your work as usual, and at noon you will find us at the end of the yew walk behind the Pavilion. I shall have to change you back to yourself again, and I'm thankful to say it will be the last time I shall ever be called upon to do anything of that sort. Then I shall take you both in the stork-car to Clairdelune, and we shall hear what your Royal father thinks of the bride you have chosen. He may consider that an ex-lady-in-waiting is not—"

"He has only to see her," declared Mirliflor. "But object as he may, no thing and no one shall separate us now."

"Well, well, if it comes to that, I dare say I shall manage to overcome his objections," she said. She might have been more explicit if she had not decided to reserve the surprise of Daphne's royal descent until the final scene at Clairdelune—which would be far more effective, as well as safer.

"And don't worry yourself about that foolish old Baron," she concluded. "We shall be gone before he can give any trouble. Now be off with you—I shan't want you till noon, and a few more hours' gardening won't hurt you!"

There was no need to hurry, so she did not leave her tower till it was nearly half an hour to mid-day, when she went slowly and by unfrequented paths through the gardens and thence to the Pavilion. Daphne, who had been anxiously expecting her, saw her from the Pavilion and came to meet her, feeling and looking rather guilty.

"Have you heard?" she asked. "But I can see you have.... Well, Court Godmother?"

"Well," said the Fairy, bent on prolonging the test to the last moment, "this is a pretty thing you have done, upon my word! You to fall in love with a penniless student! If you had only had the patience to wait," she continued, as she led her towards the yew walk, "I'd have found a handsome young Prince for you. It's not too late, even now."

"I used to think I would only marry a Prince, I don't now," said Daphne. "I wouldn't change Giroflé for any Prince in the world. And what am I, after all? Just a Governess!"

"And when you have married your student, what do you suppose you are going to live on?"

"Oh, we shall manage somehow," said Daphne tranquilly. "We shall be poor, of course, but what does that matter so long as we're together?"

"Ah," said the Fairy, "but I can't understand what a beautiful girl like you can see in such an ugly young fellow!"

"He isn't ugly!" Daphne declared. "And I shouldn't mind a bit if he was! He'd still be Giroflé!"

"All the same," pursued the Fairy, "you wouldn't object to his being handsomer?"

"I don't know," replied Daphne, contracting her pretty brows, "I can't imagine him any different." And then she laughed. "It's not a bit of use trying to put me out of conceit with him, Court Godmother—so you may as well give it up!"

The Fairy was satisfied at last; Daphne had stood the test triumphantly, and the time had come for her to be told of the reward that awaited her. "I am far from wishing to lower him in your eyes, my child," she said. "On the contrary, I may now tell you that he possesses advantages you little dream of. And though true love may be inspired without the aid of wealth, rank, or good looks, there was never a maiden yet who—but I perceive," she broke off with offended dignity, "that I am not so fortunate as to have secured your attention!"

They had left the yew walk by this time and entered an avenue of ilexes, beyond which lay the valley and distant hills. "I'm so sorry, Court Godmother," said Daphne, whose eyes were fixed on the view, "but—but doesn't Drachenstolz lie over there?"

"It does," said the Fairy drily, "though I fail to see why that should interest you just now."

"I—I can see something flying," explained Daphne. "It may be only a vulture—a large vulture."

"A vulture—where?" cried the old Fairy. "Nonsense. It's your fancy, child. I see nothing."

"It is a dragon!" faltered Daphne. "Can't you see it now? It's coming towards us! And oh, I'm afraid the Count has sent it—like that snake—to—to kill me!"

A dragon was a danger which the Fairy, with all her precautions, had somehow omitted to foresee, and for a time she exhibited about as much calmness and self-possession as a hen at a fox-raid. "Heaven preserve us!" she wailed. "If we were but safe at Clairdelune! What can we do?"

"Hide," said Daphne, trembling. "Quick! In the undergrowth!"

"It would spy us out from above," groaned the Fairy. "No, we must run for the Pavilion and shelter there."

Daphne seized her hand and they ran together, but they had not gone far before the Court Godmother suddenly collapsed. "My old legs fail me!" she said, "I can go no further! Run on, child, while you can!"

"And leave you!" cried Daphne. "No, I shan't do that! But oh, can't you do anything to save us! Think!"

The Fairy rose to her feet, shaking all over. "I knew a spell once," she mumbled. "I never tried it—but if I could only remember it now, it might—But I can't—I'm too old—too old! That all my plans should have come to this!"

The dragon was forging along at a tremendous pace. It would soon be near enough to single out its prey—and still the old Fairy stood there, racking her memory in vain.

Close upon noon Mirliflor had thrown away his hoe and torn off his apron for ever. In a few minutes more he would be with his love—and yet his heart was oppressed by a certain fear that had been haunting him all the morning. The Fairy would re-transform him—but could he be sure of the effect on Daphne? What if he lost, as Mirliflor, the love that Giroflé had won? He was so absorbed in these disquieting reflections, as he alternately hastened and checked his pace down the broad walks, that he scarcely noticed a faint outcry, and sounds as though firearms were being discharged, which seemed to come from the Palace behind him. Perhaps, he thought, a revolt had broken out, but, if so, it did not concern him. His Daphne was in no danger in those grounds beyond the wall. He passed through the gate, and presently came to the astrolabe, and then the stone bench, both hallowed now by the sweetest associations. And yet it might be that those associations would be his last with her! It was almost a relief, on reaching the yew walk, to find it deserted. He went to the Pavilion, and there he elicited from Daphne's elderly duenna, who was rather hard of hearing, that, as her young mistress was certainly not indoors, he would probably find her in the grounds.

He searched all the yew walks in vain, and then, with a new and growing uneasiness, turned towards the avenue, but he had got no farther than a small pool in a marble basin when he heard a strange and dreadful noise above him. He glanced upwards, and saw the bulk of a huge dragon sailing high above the tree-tops. It was making swiftly for the valley; one of its claws held a pendent form in fluttering drapery, and he knew too well that the captive could only be she for whom he had been searching. He had saved her once from the malice of her enemies—this time he was powerless! He raved and cursed in impotent rage and despair while a sudden gust swept the pool and sent it surging over the brim, and a slender cypress that stood hard by rustled and shivered as though in terror. And as he stood there, he suddenly saw the old Court Chamberlain before him, holding in one hand his silken cap and in the other a sword and belt.

"Sire, Sire!" he stammered, "that accursed beast! It is bearing her off to Drachenstolz! But you may save her yet!"

"Show me how to get there!" said Mirliflor fiercely. "If I can't save her I can at least die with her. But those two devils shall pay for it first!"

"Follow me," said the Baron, giving him the sword and, followed by Mirliflor, he ran at a very creditable speed for his years in the direction of the Palace.

A little before noon that morning the Royal Family had collected on one of the terraces. King Sidney was pacing up and down engaged in private and apparently important conversation with the Crown Prince. The Court as usual kept a respectful distance and chattered and gossiped in whispers. The Princess Royal and Princess Ruby were sitting at a jade table playing the game that resembled Halma, while the Queen was confiding her maternal anxieties to the Court Chamberlain's sympathetic ear.

"To tell you the truth, Baron," she confessed, "I've not been at all happy lately about Princess Edna. She says nothing, but I can see she's fretting over Prince Mirliflor's silence. I hear he hasn't been seen at Clairdelune lately—taken his dismissal so much to heart that he can't appear in public, I suppose. But surely if he meant to try again he would have done so before this!"

The worthy Baron was too faithful a servant to refrain from saying something to reassure his Royal mistress, though a salutary recollection of Mirliflor's warning made him careful not to say too much.

"I can assure your Majesty from my own personal knowledge," he replied, "that his Royal Highness has by no means given up his intention of renewing his addresses to the Princess Edna."

"Then why doesn't he? There's nothing to prevent him—now."

"That, Madam," said the Baron importantly, "I am not at liberty to explain" (as a matter of fact he had no idea why Mirliflor was conducting his courtship in so eccentric a manner), "but I may say I have reason to know that at this very moment he may be nearer the Palace than is generally supposed."

"Really?" cried the Queen. "I must go and tell dear Edna that. It will cheer her up."

"I must beg of your Majesty to treat it as strictly confidential for the present," said the Baron hastily. "His Royal Highness prefers to take the Princess by surprise."

"What a dear romantic person he is!" said Queen Selina. "Then, of course, he must be humoured and I'll say nothing. But I'm so glad you told me, Baron. It's taken such a load off my mind!"

"Well," the King was telling Clarence, "those are old Goldenbergenland's terms. If you'll marry his daughter, Princess Popanza, he'll let us have all the gold we want; if you refuse, he won't even advance us a ducat. Couldn't you see your way to—to meeting him, my boy?"

"Nothing doing!" said Clarence very decidedly. "Why, Hansmeinigel was telling me the other day she's humpbacked, with a squint or something. I couldn't take it on—even if," he added gloomily, "there weren't other reasons to prevent me."

"Then," said his father, "I don't know how we're to get a fresh supply of gold—the mine's stopped working, and the confounded Council won't do anything for us."

"What's the matter with selling a few jewels?" suggested Clarence, as his eye fell on the Halma board in passing, "they must be worth a lot."

"Not here. Too common. The people think they're of no value except to kings and queens. Nothing but gold will go down in these parts. So you see, my boy, that unless you can bring yourself to—"

"I say, Guv'nor," interrupted Clarence, who seemed to welcome a distraction just then. "Look over there. That beggar Rubenfresser has let loose that poisonous dragon of his! Infernal cheek!"

"He was expressly told to keep it under control," said the King. "Most irregular!"

"It's not only loose," said Clarence, "but it's coming straight over here."

Ruby had seen it too, and sprang up delighted. "Look!" she cried, "there's darling Tützi! He's got away from his horrid master—and now he's coming to live with us! I must get some cake for him!" and she darted into the Palace.

"I'll go and tell those sentry-johnnies to take a pot at it," said Clarence, as he went down to a lower terrace, where the Palace sentinels were on duty. By the time he returned with them Tützi was almost overhead, his great wings beating with a resonant leathery clang as he flew round in ever descending circles, stretching his scaled neck and horny head in deliberate quest, until he was so low that the sunlit chalcedony slabs shed a reflected glare on his great burnished belly. "Now blaze away at it, can't you!" shouted Clarence to the sentinels, who appeared to have some difficulty in loading their antiquated pieces. "You mustn't shoot Tützi!" cried Ruby, running out at that moment with a heavily gilded slice of gingerhead, "he's only come for some cake!"

"Don't encourage the thing!" said the King, dragging her back. "Get away, you brute! Go home, Sir!"

As he spoke the monster made a sudden downward swoop at Edna, and, with a deftness that was quite extraordinary, hooked one of its steely claws in her girdle and soared rapidly aloft with her. It was fortunate that the belt, which was of stout jewel-studded leather, was able to sustain her weight.

"Stop firing, you fools!" yelled Clarence, as the sentinels opened a wild fusillade. "You'll only hit her!"

And, even if their bullets could have pierced the dragon's plated hide, it was soon out of range.

"It's carrying her off to that wretch!" screamed the distracted Queen. "Is there nothing we can do?"

"One thing, your Majesty," said the Baron eagerly. "Offer the Princess in marriage to anyone who will rescue her. It's the usual course!"

"To—to anyone?" repeated Queen Selina in despair. "Oh, Baron—must we?"

"You can safely do so, Madam," he whispered. "Mirliflor will be the man—and I know where to find him." And with this he rushed off first to his own chamber, then to the Crown Prince's apartments, and finally to the gardens in search of Giroflé.

"Sidney," said the Queen, "tell the heralds to proclaim that we will give our poor darling to anyone who succeeds in delivering her.... Don't argue about it—do as I tell you!" which King Sidney did.

As for the Court, they were too paralysed by so unexpected a calamity to be of the least assistance. The ladies-in-waiting were all in floods of tears, distressed, not only by the awful fate that had overtaken "Princess Four-eyes," but by the painful reflection that any one of them might be the dragon's next victim.

"This couldn't have happened except in a place like this!" declared the Queen, now on the verge of hysteria. "And why it should have been permitted to happen to US!—It wouldn't have, Sidney, if you had only had the sense to insist on that thing being destroyed! But you didn't—and this is the result!"

"My love," said the King, "you forget. The poor girl herself insisted on its being spared. It—it's most unfortunate!"

And it certainly was.

CHAPTER XVII

THE REWARD OF VALOUR

If the Fairy Vogelflug could only have known that it was Edna and not Daphne who was really in danger from the dragon, she would have been comparatively calm. But since she did not know this, she was, as has been already stated, entirely unnerved for a time.

Fortunately—or at least she thought it fortunate then,—just before the creature was near enough to detect them, the long-forgotten words that formed the spell recurred to her memory. It was a spell that was admirably adapted to enable any fugitive to escape discovery, but she had never had occasion to use it before, and to perform it required an amount of mental concentration from which, in ordinary circumstances, she would have shrunk. Now she must act at once or they would both perish, and so she gabbled the necessary incantations, till, though the effort took a great deal out of her, she eventually succeeded in changing Daphne into a tall and slender cypress, and herself into a circular pool in a marble basin—a double transformation which was calculated to deceive the most observant and intelligent dragon. But, changed as she was, Daphne remained perfectly conscious of her own identity and aware of all that was happening. At first she was much impressed by the Court Godmother's ingenuity and presence of mind, but as time went on, and the dragon, instead of searching for them, seemed to have swerved away towards the Palace, she began to wonder whether there had been any real need for such excessive precautions.

And then Giroflé appeared, and she gathered from his despair what must have happened to the ill-fated Edna, and that he was under the erroneous impression that she herself was the victim. Surely now the moment had come for the Fairy to reverse the spell—but, except that the surface of the pool was becoming violently disturbed, she made no sign. Daphne tried by rustling all her branches to attract his attention and assure him of her safety, but naturally failed. Even when the Court Chamberlain arrived and Giroflé had rushed away with him, she was forced to stay behind as an apparent cypress, while the Fairy still retained the semblance of a more and more agitated pool. Daphne's uneasiness and anxiety would have been even greater, but for the fact that the reason for this agitation was mercifully hidden from her. The truth was that one of those accidents had happened which are not infrequent with persons who only occasionally practise the Magic Art. The Fairy had impulsively pronounced the spell that accomplished the transformation without waiting to recall the precise formula that was needed to regain her normal appearance, and for several agonising minutes the vitally important words persisted in evading her. To Daphne it seemed an age before the marble rim began to contract and the pool dry up, and presently, to her unspeakable relief, all trace of pool and basin disappeared, and in their place stood the Fairy Godmother in a sadly shaken and exhausted condition. She had strength enough, however, to restore Daphne, which she did with many groans. "I've been trying to do this for the last quarter of an hour, child," she panted. "I was beginning to think I'd forgotten the spell altogether. And now he's gone off on a fool's errand to rescue you! But I may still be in time to stop him!"

"You won't stop Giroflé!" declared Daphne. "He will try to rescue Edna, just as he would me. And if it can be done he'll do it. I can't bear his going, Godmother—and yet I hope I shouldn't prevent him, even if I could!"

"He can't do anything!" said the Fairy. "He couldn't even get into the Castle, and he won't be so mad as to attempt it. Go you to the Pavilion, and stay there till I can find out what that old fool of a Baron is about with him."

Daphne obeyed. She would not deter Giroflé, but to encourage him in his desperate errand was more than she was equal to just then. The Court Godmother hitched up her quilted skirts, and went off at a hobbling run in the direction of the Palace Gardens.

The Baron had led Mirliflor through the Gardens, and then round to a Courtyard at the back of the Palace in which stood a massive round tower pierced with many pigeon-holes. Here he brought out a small shell-shaped car on two wheels, and at his whistle a flock of white doves fluttered down from the tower, and permitted him to attach them by collars and traces to the car. "The most gracious the Court Godmother is nowhere to be found," he explained as he did so, "but assuredly she would not grudge lending her car for such a purpose as yours, since by no other means could you hope to get over the walls of Drachenstolz. Once within them you will find the sword of inestimable service, and I doubt not that you will wield it to better effect than would its owner. I would willingly lend you this," he added, fingering the cap, "only maybe your Royal Highness would not deign to employ means which I understood you are pleased to consider discreditable?"

"Don't be an ass, Baron!" said Mirliflor, seizing the cap and stepping into the car. "Where her life is at stake I have no scruples in using anything whatever. But I've no experience in driving doves—how do I guide them?"

"They need no guidance, Sire. You have but to utter the words 'To Drachenstolz,' and they will carry you straight to the Castle and set you down within its walls. God speed you!" cried the Court Chamberlain, as the Prince gave the direction, and the birds ascended with the car. "Heaven grant you bring back your Princess unharmed!"

"Heaven grant I reach her in time!" came the answer from the dove-chariot, which, after making a few preliminary circles, flew away, to all appearances unoccupied.

It had scarcely disappeared when the Court Godmother arrived on the scene. "Where is Giroflé?" she demanded breathlessly.

"His Royal Highness Prince Mirliflor of Clairdelune," replied the Baron, "has just departed for Drachenstolz in the dove-car, which I knew you would wish to be at his disposal."

"And pray," said the old Fairy, "what made you think I should wish him to throw away his life for Princess Edna?"

"He will not fail to rescue her, never fear, Madam. No Prince ever does fail in these enterprises. And if he succeeds—he need no longer hesitate to disclose himself, for you will be gratified to hear that his Majesty has promised the Princess's hand to the person who may accomplish her rescue. At," added the Baron proudly, "my own suggestion."

"Oh, indeed?" retorted the Fairy. "Then it is high time you knew what kind of a Royal Family you have given to Märchenland!" And in a few sharp sentences she let him know the truth about the pendant which he had so rashly accepted as all-sufficient proof of Mrs. Wibberley-Stimpson's title to the throne.

The poor Baron was aghast at the information, and still more when he heard who was really entitled to the crown. "The Lady Daphne!" he cried. "But she has been sent away to that far country—and who knows where she may be now!"

"She is here still, and under my protection," said the Court Godmother. "In her own interests I had determined to keep silent as to her claims, and planned that Mirliflor should win her under the form I made him assume. All had fallen out as I expected—I had just arranged to carry them both off to Clairdelune, and leave these usurpers in possession for as long as the Country would endure them—when you blunder in, like the meddlesome idiot you are, Baron, and upset everything!"

"I have been blind indeed!" he confessed. "A traitor when I thought myself most loyal! Tell me, most Gracious Court Godmother, how I may best repair my error?"

"You can't repair it without making more mischief," she said. "The only thing you can do now is to hold your tongue about it, as I shall do myself unless I am obliged to speak out. And now we had better go and see what this precious King and Queen of yours are doing, and remember, Baron, your own safety will depend on your preserving absolute secrecy as to all the matters I have found it necessary to acquaint you with."

On the terrace meanwhile Queen Selina had implored the Marshal to do something—anything—towards the rescue of her elder daughter. He was not sanguine; "We could raise a force, your Majesty," he said, "to ride to Drachenstolz and assault the Castle walls,—but it would be quite impossible to take it by storm, even if that dragon were not among its defenders."

"We'll have a try anyway," said Clarence gallantly. "Come on, you chaps—get into your fighting kit," he cried to the Courtiers. "And two of you boys," he added to the pages, "just run and fetch me a helmet and breastplate and things—and bring me down a sword you'll find in my room somewhere. I shouldn't mind tackling even a dragon with that sword," he added to his mother, as the Courtiers and pages ran into the Palace. "It goes clean through anything."

But the pages, when they returned with the breastplate and helmet and riding-boots, reported that the sword was nowhere to be found, so Clarence had to content himself with a more ordinary weapon. At the last moment the Queen tried to detain him. "No, Clarence!" she cried, "you mustn't go. Your life is too valuable to be risked—there are enough going without you! Stay here—if only to protect us!"

"Hang it all, Mater!" he said, "you can't expect me to stay here and have them saying I shirked!" And he went off to the stables with the Marshal and other members of the Court.

"It'll be no good!" groaned King Sidney. "It's as likely as not that beast has eaten the poor girl by this time!"

"I can't believe anything quite so horrible as that has happened, Sidney," cried the Queen. "It has only delivered her into that wretch's power—which is quite horrible enough! But there's hope still. The Baron says Prince Mirliflor is quite near here—and he's sending him to rescue her. And a real prince like dear Mirliflor ought to be a match for that miserable Rubenfresser and his dragon too!"

"If he could get at them he might be," said the King lugubriously; "but that's just what he can't do!"

On finding herself borne swiftly through the air by a dragon, Edna had done what was the correct thing to do in the circumstances—she had promptly fainted. She opened her eyes to find that she had been deposited uninjured, on a truss of straw in a Courtyard. On her right was the massive front of Castle Drachenstolz; before her were its lofty walls and the grim towers that flanked its heavy gate; to the left were the stables, from the windows of which some of the black carriage horses looked out, their wrinkled lips exposing their long yellow teeth in ghastly grins. Some distance away the owner of the Castle was caressing the dragon, which lay with its huge wings compactly folded, giving its unconscious imitation of a tremendously powerful dynamo. On perceiving that she had returned to consciousness the Count came towards her, followed by the ex-Astrologer Royal, who was smirking and rubbing his hands.

"I couldn't do without you," began the Count by way of explanation, "so as I couldn't come myself I sent Tützi for you."

Edna resolved to bear herself with all the dignity of a Queen's daughter. She sat up and felt for her pince-nez, and, discovering that it was intact, she adjusted it on her nose. "Considering," she said, "that all is at an end between us, you had no right whatever to send your dragon to bring me here. It was a thing that no gentleman would have done!"

"Wouldn't that great and learned gentleman you told me of—the one whose name I always forget—have done it?" he inquired.

"Nietzsche," said Edna, instructively superior even in such a crisis; "most certainly not. Even if he had owned a dragon!"

"You told me he did," he insisted; "a great meta-something dragon that talked and said, 'Thou shalt not.' But if he wouldn't send his dragon for anybody, he would approve of my sending mine for you, because I was doing as he advised, and acting exactly as I thought fit."

She realised the hopelessness of reasoning with him. "You thought fit to act most improperly," she said severely, "and you will gain nothing by it, you know!"

"Oh, yes I shall," he said, "or I shouldn't have done it."

"You are quite mistaken," she assured him, "if you are imagining I shall ever consent to renew our engagement now I know what you are."

"I'm what you wanted me to be," he said, "a Superman."

"You're not, you're an—an Ogre. I couldn't possibly bring myself to become an Ogress!"

"You wouldn't make much of an Ogress," he said dispassionately. "You haven't the build for it. But I'm not an Ogre even yet. It's not my fault. I meant to begin with those pages of yours—but you all seemed to have some ridiculous objections. Then I've sent Tützi out to forage and pick up a small child or two, but the peasants round here are so selfish and unneighbourly that they never give him the chance—actually shutting all the children up indoors!"

"What else can you expect?" she demanded indignantly. "Surely your—your better self must see that even to attempt to devour poor helpless children is—is too perfectly disgusting for words!"

"It's disgusting when one doesn't succeed," he admitted; "I see nothing in it to object to myself. Of course the average man may, but you've taught me what to think of his opinions."

"You entirely misunderstand me," said Edna. "But I've no wish to discuss such subjects with you now—I insist on your allowing me to go home at once."

"Before I do that," he said, "you must write a letter on my behalf to your parents."

"I don't mind asking them to overlook the way you have treated me, and assuring them that you regret it and will behave yourself properly for the future," conceded Edna, "if you mean that."

"I don't mean that," he said; "I don't want to behave properly—what they would call properly. I want to lead a fuller life than I can while I'm cooped up in my own Castle. You see, it's no good having the Will to Power if you're not allowed any opportunities of exercising it. And I'm not, with guards stationed all round my walk to see that I don't get out. I might set Tützi at them, it's true, but he is the only dragon I've got, and it would be very annoying if they hurt the poor thing. So you must get the King to send me free permission to go wherever I choose and do whatever I like. Then I can make a start as an Ogre. At present I'm hampered at every turn!"

"Father and Mother," said Edna, "wouldn't hear of setting you free for such wickedness as that. It would be contrary to all their principles."

"What I think you called 'Slave-morality,' eh?" he said. "But you needn't tell them why I want to get out. Besides, I've other reasons. My carriage horses want airing, and I should like to drop in to lunch at the Palace now and then, as I used to. Not as your betrothed, you know—that's all over—but just as a friend of the family. I always enjoyed my meals at the Palace."

"Oh!" gasped Edna, "I'm sure, quite sure, they would never consent to receive you again. How could they?"

"They would," he said, "if you told them what would be the consequences if they didn't."

"And—and—what will the consequences be?" inquired Edna.

"Well," he replied darkly, "poor Tützi will never reach his full growth on his present diet. I fancy he would rather relish a change."

"You couldn't see me—me you were once engaged to—devoured by your horrible dragon!" she cried.

"Why not?" he asked cheerfully. "I am great enough now to be able to bear the sight of others' pain, as your learned What's-his-name said I ought to be."

"Listen," said the unhappy Edna. "If—if I write this letter will you promise me, on your sacred word of honour, to become a vegetarian at once?"

"Certainly," he said. "It won't bind me, you know. You might put in the letter that I've promised to. Rather a good touch! Now go and write it at once, and I'll send Tützi over with it. You can say, 'Please send answer by bearer!' Xuriel, show the Princess to a chamber and provide her with writing materials."

"If your Royal Highness will graciously come this way," said the despicable Xuriel, bowing low. Poor Edna had to follow him up a steep outside staircase to a gloomy room where deep-set windows commanded a view of the Courtyard below. He found some sheets of parchment and a reed pen, and lent her the inkhorn from his own girdle. As he was depositing these on a great oaken table, he glanced out of the window and gave a high cackling laugh.

"I fear my venerable and respected friend the worthy Court Godmother must have met with some mishap," he sniggered. "For see, Princess, her dove-chariot has just descended, without its Gracious occupant, on the roof of the bastion! Hee-hee! I trust—I sincerely trust that Tützi may not so far forget himself as to snap up any of those dear little doves!"

And, so saying, he hurried to the Courtyard. Edna was naturally concerned at any possible accident to the Court Godmother or her doves, but her letter had to be written, and it was not at all an easy letter to write. She got as far as: "Dear Father and Mother,—You will be relieved to hear that I am, so far, unhurt. But"—and there she stuck. It was really very difficult to find any plausible wording for the Ogre's preposterous terms.

Xuriel had rejoined his patron, and both were watching Tützi with interest. He had already become aware of the doves and reared his head above the level of the bastion roof, where they were strutting about unsuspicious of danger. His hideous lidless eyes regarded them intently, with a view to selecting the plumpest bird.

"Those pigeons will be quite a treat for poor Tützi," remarked Count Rubenfresser. "But what is that thing flashing there on the roof? There it is again! Can't you see it?"

Xuriel looked, and saw a thin scintillating ray of light which shifted capriciously from place to place. "It is the blade of a sword!" he said. "More—it is the blade of the enchanted sword I sold to Prince Clarence."

"Fool!" said the Count, "how can any sword be there with no hand to wield it?"

"The Crown Prince is wielding it," replied Xuriel. "He is rendered invisible by the magic cap I made for the Court Chamberlain!"

"You had no business to make such things," returned the Count, "they were very properly forbidden. But Tützi will very soon—"

Before he could say more there was another flash—a sweeping circle of light—and Tützi's head flew from his neck, which sent up a column of blood.

"The wretch!" shrieked the Count, "the cruel, cold-blooded wretch, he's killed my Tützi!"

"It will be our turn next!" cried the little Astrologer Royal, too terrified to stir.

"Help!" the Count bawled, "we are attacked! Where are you all?" A few retainers had run out to various doorways at his summons, but when they saw the dragon's great body rolling convulsively round the Courtyard, its hooked wings thrashing up the cobblestones, while its head bounded independently about, barking and snapping like a mad dog, they very prudently withdrew.

Xuriel had recovered strength to run, but he had not gone far before the head, probably quite automatically, seized his right calf and brought him down. There was another sharp glint of light—and his body was headless, like the dragon's. What with the endeavour to avoid Tützi's head, and Tützi's body, and the terrible sword flashes, all at once, the Count was kept pretty busy for the next minute or so. He rushed, leaping and yelling, roaring and dodging, from side to side and corner to corner, and then made a frantic bolt for the outer staircase, but he had only got half-way up when his head fell with a splash into a water-butt below, while his body slid down to the bottom of the steps, where it lay in a limp crumpled heap.

The noise of all these proceedings was not exactly conducive to literary composition, and Princess Edna had already been obliged to abandon her letter. In fact she had begun to realise that it would no longer be necessary to finish it. Her brother, she thought, had come to her deliverance with a promptness and energy which she would really have hardly expected of him. She put on her pince-nez again, and went out to the head of the staircase. "Clarence!" she called, "where are you?"

She was immensely surprised to encounter a plain young man in homely costume whom she had certainly never seen before. Mirliflor, who had just removed his cap and was springing up the steps in search of Daphne, was at least equally surprised at finding Edna.

"You here, Princess!" he cried breathlessly, "Tell me! Is—is Daphne safe?"

"If you refer to Miss Heritage," replied Edna, "I have not seen her for weeks, but I have no reason for believing that she is not safe—in England."

"Then," he said blankly, "the dragon carried off you—not her?"

"I should have thought that fairly obvious," said Edna frigidly. "You have evidently rescued me under a misapprehension, though, of course, I am just as much indebted to you. And I shall be glad to know who you are. In answering, kindly address me as 'Your Royal Highness.' It is more correct."

This was highly embarrassing, he thought, though he felt thankful that his Godmother had not had time to make him recognisable. "My name, your Royal Highness," he replied, "is Giroflé. I have the honour to be one of his Majesty's under-gardeners."

"Oh," said Edna, "one of them? Really. Well, you have behaved most creditably—very creditably indeed. I really don't know what mightn't have happened if you hadn't arrived just then. I have never been in such a trying situation before. And, even as it is," she added, "there doesn't seem to be any means of getting out of this odious place."

By this time Tützi's death-throes were over; his body lay extended half across the Courtyard, while the head, after having bitten one or two of the carriage horses rather severely, had also ceased from troubling. "Perhaps," said Mirliflor, "your Royal Highness will condescend to make use of the dove-car which brought me here? It will carry you back in safety to the Palace."

"It looks rather tit-uppy," said Edna, as the doves flew down with it at his call. "And it only holds one. How are you going to get away yourself?"

"I shall order some of those varlets to open the gate," he said, "and they will be wise to obey."

"Clarence's sword is a great help!" said Edna. "Then—you will be all right. And you may be sure that his Majesty will pay you a suitable reward."

"The satisfaction of having been of any service to your Royal Highness," he said, "is reward enough in itself."

"Oh, but that's such a pose!" said Edna. "Of course you expect to be paid for it!... And you will be. Must I tell these birds where to take me?... I see. Then—Home, please!"

And the doves, glad to escape from such uncongenial surroundings, whirred upwards with the car and, after a few tentative circles, took it clear over the battlements.

As for the retainers, they waited for no order to unbar the gate for Mirliflor, being all eagerness to facilitate his departure. He strode unconcernedly out, and, finding a party of the Royal guard outside, he informed them that they would find one or two severed heads within if they cared to collect them, and then, borrowing a charger, he galloped off to Eswareinmal, impatient to know what had befallen Daphne.

On the Palace terrace there had been a period of painful surprise. The Crown Prince was the first of the rescue party to return. He would have much preferred to do so by a back way, but, perceiving that he had been observed, took the manlier course. "Clarence!" shrieked the Queen as he limped up with his breastplate and hose covered with mire, a bent sword and badly dinted helmet, "is she saved?"

"Couldn't tell you, Mater," he replied heavily. "I've done all I could, and so—and so I came back."

"He's wounded!" cried Ruby tearfully. "Oh, Clarence, was it that horrid Tützi?" for she was effectually disillusioned at last.

"No, Kiddie, no," he said, "I'm all right. Took a bit of a toss, that's all."

"My poor boy," said his mother, "was it at the Castle? Did the thing attack you?"

"I never got to the Castle," he replied, "only about half-way. It was like this. That bally pendant you made me wear, Mater, got unfastened somehow, slipped down inside my breastplate and was hurting like the very deuce. So I got off and unbuckled a bit and pitched it away. When I got on again the horse was all over the shop with me in a jiffy. Couldn't hold him for toffee! And, before I knew it, I was over the brute's head. I tried to mount again, but he wouldn't let me. I tried some other gees, and none of them would. Somehow I seemed to have lost the knack all at once. So, after I'd come off once or twice more and was getting a trifle lame, I thought the best thing I could do was to leg it home."

"Hem!" said his Father. "Rather unfortunate thing to happen just now, my boy!"

"Well, Guv'nor," he replied, "I should never have got there in time, walking."

"You were quite right to come back, Clarence," said his Mother, "And—oh, look, look!" she cried suddenly, "our darling is safe after all! She's coming back in the dove-car!"

The car landed shortly after on the terrace, and Edna was frantically embraced and plied with questions. "I am quite all right, thank you," she said as soon as she had an opportunity of speaking. "Of course it was a most disagreeable thing to happen to one, and I don't feel equal to talking about it just yet—but I am very little the worse for it now."

"But how did you get that awful man to let you go?" inquired the Queen.

"He couldn't very well help himself—his head had been cut off. So had the dragon's, and that abominable little wretch Xuriel's too."

By this time not only the Marshal but the Court Godmother and the Chamberlain had joined the party.

"But who was brave enough to do all this?" asked the Queen. "Though I think I can guess!"

"I fancy he said he was one of the under-gardeners here. Of course he couldn't have done it without Clarence's sword, but still—"

"I never lent him it," said Clarence. "If I'd had it—however, perhaps it's as well he did borrow it. Jolly plucky of the beggar, I call it!"

"He behaved extremely well," Edna admitted. "You will have to reward him or something, Father."

"His Majesty," said the Marshal, with a certain gusto, "has already offered your Royal Highness's hand in marriage to whomsoever should be so fortunate as to effect your deliverance."

"Without consulting Me!" cried Edna. "Really, Father, these things aren't done nowadays! It's too absurd!"

"My love," said the Queen with a glance of secret intelligence at the embarrassed Baron, who looked another way, "the circumstances were exceptional. And a King can't go back on his word! Besides, this ex-gardener may be not such a common person as he seems—may he not, Baron?"

"But, dash it, Mater!" said Clarence, while the Baron could only blink, "an under-gardener—what!"

"I'm bound to say—" began the King, when the Queen interrupted:

"You are bound to say that you'll keep your promise, Sidney, and that is enough till the dear fellow comes to claim his reward."

It was the Marshal whose superfluous zeal led him to order Giroflé to be stopped and brought into the Royal presence as soon as he arrived at the Palace.

The Royal Family, with the Court Godmother, the Baron, and other members of the Household, had assembled in the Throne Room when the Marshal entered, leading the reluctant Giroflé, acutely conscious of looking his very worst. After him came some men-at-arms, who carried the dragon's still terrific head, with those of the Count and Xuriel, as trophies of the hero's exploit.

They caused a general but by no means unpleasant shudder to run through the beholders.

"Your Majesties," said the ex-Regent, "I have the honour to present the gallant youth who has nobly earned even such a prize as the hand of her Royal Highness."

"But—but," stammered Queen Selina, "this isn't—there's not the least resemblance! Baron, Baron, what did you mean by telling me that the Prince—?"

"I—I must have been misinformed, your Majesty," said the Court Chamberlain, having no better explanation to offer.

"You should be more careful about what you tell Us, Baron," said the Queen. "And, really, there was no need to bring those dreadful heads into our Throne Room, making all that horrible mess! It's a piece of bad taste which, perhaps—in an under gardener—please have them removed directly. Well, young man," she continued to the indignant Mirliflor, who, it need not be said, had nothing to do with the gruesome introduction of the heads, "I'm sure we are all very much obliged to you—very much obliged indeed. If you hadn't come forward as you did, it's dreadful to think what might have happened. And, though it seems you did take the liberty of borrowing the Crown Prince's sword without permission, we are the last to blame you for that. We think you are entitled to be very handsomely rewarded. But if you're expecting our daughter, the Princess Edna's hand, I think your own good sense—"

"Yes, yes," said the King; "mustn't open your mouth too wide, you know. There's a limit to all things! And a round sum of money with which you could start in business and marry some nice little woman in your own class of life would be far more useful to you."

"I ask for no reward," said Giroflé. "And the hand of a Princess is an honour to which I do not aspire, since I am already affianced!"

"That," replied the Queen, "is very satisfactory. We shall certainly send the young person a wedding-present. Who is she? One of the Royal kitchen-maids, I presume?"

"She was in your Majesty's service as a lady-in-waiting," he said, "and her name is Daphne."

"Oh," said Queen Selina. "Really? Miss Heritage? Well, you are to be congratulated, I'm sure."

"But, Mater," said Clarence, "it can't be her! I thought you'd had her sent home?"

"I had made arrangements for her return, Clarence, but it seems to have been postponed for some reason—luckily, as things have turned out. She has been given rooms in a pavilion behind the Palace Gardens, where no doubt she managed to become acquainted with this young man."

"And he may take it," said the Fairy, "that the Lady Daphne is at liberty to depart with him at once?"

"Certainly," said the Queen. "It is hardly, perhaps—but Miss Heritage is no doubt right in accepting the first offer she receives."

"Quite," said Princess Edna, "though it seems odd—even for a Governess—to think of marrying a gardener! But I'm sure I wish her every happiness."

There is no doubt that the Court Godmother should have been content with this, but her anger and disgust were too much for her discretion. She could not resist the temptation to humiliate and confound these upstarts by a sensational stroke, whatever it cost her.

"Perhaps," she said, "the Lady Daphne has made a wiser choice than any of you may imagine." With this, after muttering an incantation, she touched Giroflé with her crutch-handled staff, and in his stead Prince Mirliflor stood revealed in rich and splendid attire before them all.

The Queen was electrified for a moment, as were Edna and most present. But as soon as the shock had passed she cried: "This is a surprise! But, my dear Prince Mirliflor, why—why didn't you tell us who you were before? You see, we couldn't possibly—!"

"It was really too naughty of you to play us such a trick, Prince!" said Edna, "when, as you might have known—!"

"Never mind!" purred the Queen, "we'll forgive him—won't we, Edna?"

"Of course you only said that about Miss Heritage to tease us?" said Edna, who really believed it was so.

"I said but the truth, Princess," he replied. "She has promised to be my wife."

"And the match," put in the triumphant Fairy, addressing Queen Selina, "already has your sanction!"

"Oh," said the Queen, "but that was before—I think," she went on with a forced smile of much sweetness—"I think you and I, my dear Court Godmother, must have a little talk over this in private before I can make up my mind what I ought to do. Perhaps you will be kind enough to follow me to my Cabinet? Excuse my deserting you for a little while, my dear Mirliflor. I shall leave you to Edna, who, I know, is dying to express all the gratitude and admiration she feels."

And she swept with great stateliness out of the Throne Room towards her Cabinet, the Court Godmother following with a presentiment that her pet scheme was about to encounter some opposition, and no very definite idea how to meet it.

But that it must and should be overcome somehow she was thoroughly determined.

It should be mentioned here that, shortly after his transformation, Mirliflor found inside his rich doublet something which proved to be the Chamberlain's cap. He was about to return it, but the Baron showed so little desire to receive his property in public that the Prince decided to keep it until a better opportunity presented itself. And then he forgot all about it, for which, as things turned out, both had reason to be thankful afterwards.

CHAPTER XVIII

A PREVIOUS ENGAGEMENT

"Well, my dear Court Godmother," began the Queen, as she sank on an ivory and cloth-of-gold settee in her private Cabinet, and cooled her somewhat heated face with a jewelled ostrich-feathered fan, "I had better tell you frankly that I think both you and that designing little adventuress have behaved in a very underhand way in this business—a way that I naturally resent. Mirliflor, as you very well know, came here on darling Edna's account, and you deliberately threw that Miss Heritage in his way—I haven't the least doubt you told her who he really was!"

"That," said the Fairy, "is just what I did not do. It was part of the test I put to her. She still has no idea that he is more than a student."

"Well, you egged her on to set her cap at him, and if he cares for her at all it can be no more than a passing fancy. I cannot be a party to letting the poor, dear young fellow be entrapped into a mésalliance to please you, and I shall see that she is sent back to England at once, as, but for you, she would have been long before this."

"I don't want to lose my temper with you if I can help it," said the Fairy, with an ominous flush on her peaked old nose, "because I've been through a good deal as it is this morning, and I'm feeling very far from well in consequence. But you had better understand that Lady Daphne is not going to be sent back to England—she is going with Mirliflor and me to Clairdelune, and we shall start immediately."

"You are at liberty to go where you please, but Miss Heritage will certainly not leave the Palace except to return to her own country."

"And I tell you I intend to take her to Clairdelune with me, and you are powerless to prevent it."

"Indeed?" said the Queen, in high wrath. "Answer me this: Am I Queen of Märchenland, or am I not?"

"You are not!" retorted the Fairy, before she could prevent herself, for the opening was really too tempting. She had not meant to go so far, but, having started, she proceeded to enlighten the Queen as to her title, and the very slender evidence on which it was based.

"I don't believe a single word of it!" declared Queen Selina, as defiantly as if this were the fact. "It's a wicked plot to set up my own governess as a pretender, but there's a very short way of settling that! I shall send for the Marshal"—and she made a movement towards a handbell of exquisitely engraved crystal with a sapphire tongue. "I shall tell him what you have dared to say, and have you and that wretched girl arrested as traitors!"

The Fairy shook with mingled fury and fear, for she saw too late that she had made a wrong move. "Before you do that, listen to me," she said. "All I have said is true, and you know it is true, but it was you who forced me to say it, and I am willing to be silent so long as you permit me to convey Lady Daphne to Clairdelune. As she has no suspicion of her claims to the throne, you need have no fear that she will assert them."

"I can't trust either of you—you are much too dangerous," said the Queen, and she rang the bell.

"You had better take my warning," said the Fairy, her wrinkled mouth working with passion. "Old as I am, I have some powers left that you little suspect. Scarce an hour ago I changed myself into a pool and Lady Daphne into a cypress" (she naturally omitted to add how narrowly they had escaped having to remain so indefinitely), "and by aid of the same spell I could transform you to a shape which—which you will discover after I have caused you to assume it. And it is a shape that you will not like!"

"Pooh!" said the Queen, on whom the re-integration of the under-gardener into Mirliflor seemed to have left little impression. "Either you're trying to frighten me or you're crazy. Whichever it is, you ought to be put under restraint—and I shall see to it that you are!"

"After that I'll do what I threatened!" snarled the Court Godmother. "It may kill me—but I don't care—I'll do it!" And she mouthed words of mystic sound and import, though her jaw trembled so violently that she could scarcely pronounce them. "Now," she concluded, pointing her crutch at the Queen's breast, "become—become a—!"

But what the Queen was to become never transpired, for before the infuriated Fairy could manage to name it her features suddenly became contorted, the stick fell from her hand, and she sank down in a heap just as the attendants entered in answer to the Royal summons.

"I'm afraid," said Queen Selina, "that the Court Godmother has fainted. I daresay it's nothing serious, still one of you had better bring the Royal Apothecary at once. Be careful to keep it from the Court, as I wish to avoid unnecessary alarm." The others endeavoured to restore the afflicted Fairy, but, though still alive, she was in some kind of cataleptic condition which was beyond the ordinary remedies. The Court Apothecary arrived and applied blisters without result, and finally gave it as his opinion that, while she might survive for some time, she would in all probability never speak again.

So Queen Selina ordered her to be removed to her apartments, and the fact that she was indisposed to be suppressed for the present, after which she left her Cabinet, feeling that Providence had been more than usually judicious. Her next step was to send for the Marshal and instruct him to remove Daphne from the Pavilion to a chamber in one of the Palace towers, where she was to remain a prisoner under his guardianship. "It's only for a short time, Marshal," she said. "And of course you will see that Miss Heritage is made thoroughly comfortable."

And then, the ground having been thus cleared, she returned to the Throne Room. "Just a moment or two, my dear Mirliflor," she said suavely, "if Edna can spare you," and she drew him aside. "Well," she began, "I've been telling the dear old Court Godmother the difficulty I am in. You see, I would willingly recognise this engagement of yours—whatever I may think about it—if I only could. But really, you know, I can't possibly allow you to take Miss Heritage away until I am satisfied that your dear Father approves of her as a daughter-in-law. As her employer I feel responsible for the poor girl. And, besides, he might think I had encouraged this match, and I can't afford to put myself in such a false position as that!"

"But," he objected, "my Godmother is going with us to Clairdelune, and she will explain all."

"She has altered her plans," said the Queen, who was developing a quite unsuspected talent for diplomacy. "To tell you the truth, I fancy she is getting a little nervous about how King Tournesol may take what she has done. She feels—as I am afraid I do—that it is wiser to keep dear Miss Heritage here under her own care till you have broken the news to your Father and obtained his consent."

"My Father is certain to consent," said the Prince, "and if he did not—"

"Oh, quite so—quite so—but both your Godmother and I consider that we ought to wait till he does consent. Of course, if you can bring us a letter from him stating that he approves, all will be well. I'm sure you must quite understand that that is really as far as I can go under the circumstances. And, if you start at once, you will be back here again in a very few days, bringing, I hope, a favourable answer. We shall be most pleased to lend you any horse you like in the Royal Stables."

She was so plausible that poor Mirliflor, who, like most Fairy princes, was not very deeply versed in feminine wiles, was quite taken in. He thought her lacking in distinction for a Queen, but well meaning. And it was so like his Godmother to impose one more test on him.

"I will set forth, then," he said, "as soon as I have seen my Daphne and assured her of my speedy return."

"I'm afraid, my dear Mirliflor," said Queen Selina, "I'm afraid you can't see her before you go."

"And why not?" he asked.

"Well, you see, the dear Court Godmother—mistakenly, I think—has told her what a great person you really are, and Miss Heritage feels that she has not the right to see you again unless and until she can hear that she will be welcomed at your Father's Court. I said all I could to show her that she need not be so over scrupulous as that, but she is such an extremely sensitive girl, and feels her social inferiority so acutely that nothing would persuade her to alter her resolution. You will only be distressing her by attempting it."

He pleaded and argued as long as he could, but eventually he was convinced that it was in vain. And so, as he knew that Daphne would be safe under the Fairy's protection, he took his leave, and, choosing the best horse in the Royal stud, set out on his journey to Clairdelune. By so doing, he was only—little as he suspected it—giving his hostess time to consider how she could best deal with the girl who, she no longer doubted, was the rightful possessor of the throne. But then Miss Heritage was not aware of her birthright, which seemed to suggest more than one way of coping with the situation.

After Queen Selina and her Royal Consort, with the Crown Prince and the Princess Edna and Ruby, had waved their last adieus to the departing Mirliflor, the Marshal approached Clarence. "Allow me, Sire," he said, "to restore this jewel, which was picked up close to the spot where your Royal Highness's steed became so suddenly and unaccountably unmanageable."

Clarence reddened—for there was a covert sneer in the ex-Regent's tone which he did not like, while he was angrily conscious that it was quite undeserved. "Oh thanks, Marshal," he said as he took the pendant. "I say, Mater, no wonder the bally thing slipped down—the clasp's worn out. Whoever you bought it from ought to have put it in proper repair before he sold it. Pity you can't send it back and make him mend it!"

"Do I understand," inquired the Marshal of the Queen, "that your Majesty bought this pendant?"

"Certainly not," replied the Queen, flushing in her turn. "You're mistaken, Clarence—it—it has been in the family for years!"

"You're mixing it up with something else, Mater," he said. "Don't you remember? You wore it for the first time that evening the Baron came to fetch us. And you told us you'd bought it out of old Uncle Wibberley's legacy. I'm sure I'm right!"

"That was a different ornament altogether," said his mother; "but it's not worth discussing." Accordingly the subject was dropped, for the time, at all events, though the Marshal did not forget it. His was not a brilliant intellect—brilliant intellects being rare in Märchenland—but he had the faculty of putting two and two together, and inferring that the total was more likely to be about four than any other number. The Astrologer Royal had predicted that the Queen would be discovered in a certain spot in England, and would be identified by being the possessor of Prince Chrysopras's jewel. But the Marshal was now satisfied that she was the possessor by purchase only. The original owner—if Xuriel had read the stars correctly—was in the same locality. Was it not possible that Lady Daphne might be that owner? If so, it would explain the Queen's motive for placing her under arrest. Marshal Federhelm resolved to play a bold stroke. When in the course of his office he had next to visit his prisoner, whom he made a point of treating with all courtesy, she begged him to tell her what fresh offence she had given that she should have been condemned to solitary imprisonment.

"I know but this," said the Marshal, "her Majesty is displeased at finding that a certain jewel she purchased from you is of less value than she had been led to believe."

"But, Marshal!" protested poor Daphne, naturally imagining that the Queen had been complaining to him of the transaction, "surely it's worth at least thirty pounds! If it isn't, I'd willingly take it back and return the money. Only I can't—because I used it all to pay my bill. But I always thought that pendant was valuable, and, as it belonged to my father, I would never have sold it at all if I hadn't been obliged. What do you think I ought to do?"

"You can do nothing, Lady Daphne," he replied, "save trust that her Majesty's anger will pass away. For whatever price she may have paid for such a jewel, it is assuredly of far greater value than she is pleased to assert."

"I'm so glad to hear you say that!" said Daphne. "It would be hateful to think I had cheated her Majesty—even though I never meant to."

That was all that passed between them—but the Marshal had learnt all that he wanted to know, though he made no immediate use of his knowledge. It was enough for him to feel that he had a card which he might play to his own advantage when the opportunity came. The Court Godmother was now generally known to be hors de combat, and as for the old Baron, he could be left for the present in ignorance of his blunder.

Queen Selina meanwhile had already formed her plans. She was not a positively wicked woman, and even still thought herself irreproachable. If she had managed to separate Mirliflor and Daphne by some hard fibbing, it was only what her duty as a Queen and as a Mother demanded of her. She had never liked this Miss Heritage, and firmly believed that Daphne had alienated Mirliflor's affection from Edna to herself. And now, it seemed, she was the lawful Queen of the country, and Queen Selina had grown too habituated to power and grandeur to give them up to this inexperienced girl. Her first idea had been to carry out her original intention and have Daphne sent home to England without further delay. But this, she began to see, would expose her to considerable criticism at Court, and it occurred to her that there might be a simpler and more satisfactory way out of her difficulties.

So, full of her latest project, she went in search of Clarence, whom she found lounging with a very moody and disconsolate air in one of the balconies. Clarence was in low spirits just then, and not without reason. He had entirely lost his nerve for horsemanship, as his mounts had become as refractory as ever; he could not help perceiving that the courtiers had lost all respect for him, and received his overtures with hardly veiled impertinence; and, besides all this, there was another matter that had been weighing on his mind for some time past.

"Why, Clarence, dear boy," she began, "what are you keeping away from everybody like this for?"

"I wasn't 'keeping away' that I know of," he said. "There are times when a fellow's glad to get a quiet moment to himself, that's all."

"Perhaps," she said, "I know the real reason why you've been so mopy lately."

"What do you mean, Mater?" he asked. "You haven't—?"

"My dear Clarence, do you think I can't see that you've never got over your fondness for little Miss Heritage? I can't bear to see you looking so unhappy, and I've come to think that I may have been wrong in keeping her out of your way. So—and this is what I came to tell you—if you feel that she is necessary to your happiness, I shall not oppose you any longer—and I will see that your father doesn't."

"I wish you'd said so before, Mater!" he replied. "The Governor's been at me to propose to old Goldenenbergenland's daughter, but I had to tell him I couldn't take it on."

"Of course not, dear, I'm told she's hideous. While Miss Heritage, at all events—"

"But she's engaged to Mirliflor! Lucky chap he is to get her, too. I might have once, perhaps—if I'd had the pluck!"

"You may get her still, dear boy," said his fond Mother. "You see, she doesn't know who Mirliflor is yet— she thinks he's a student or something, pretending to be a gardener. Well, she's much too clever a little person not to get out of such an engagement as that if she knew she could be the Crown Princess." Which was no more than Queen Selina actually believed. "Trust me, Clarence," she concluded, "you've only to ask."

"I dare say you're right, Mater," he said, "only the worst of it is I'm not free to ask her."

"Not free? What do you mean?"

"I didn't like to tell you before," he said, "but—well, I—I've gone and got engaged to someone else."

"Engaged! Who to?" demanded the Queen, in her own English. "If it's anyone in my Court—!"

"It's no one you know, Mater. But she's all right, you know. At least, she's a King's daughter of sorts. Her Father's King of the Crystal Lake."

"The Crystal Lake!" cried Queen Selina. "You—you wretched boy! Don't tell me you're engaged to—to a Water-nixie!"

"Well, I suppose that's what it amounts to," he said. "I never wanted to be. I met her when I was fishing there. She came up out of the water, and we got talking and that, and I told her who I was. And after that, whenever I got to the lake, she was always popping up. I thought she was rather a jolly sort of girl if she was a trifle on the damp side, and it amused me to talk to her, but I never said a word to her that could—till her old Dad suddenly turned up and insisted on our being regularly engaged."

"And you gave way? Oh, Clarence, how could you be so weak?"

"I told him I'd see him blowed before I said yes, and he pulled me in and threatened to hold my head under water till I promised," said Clarence. "I didn't see any point in being drowned—and so—and so, sooner than have a row about it, I did say yes. What else could I say?"

"Well," said the Queen, "no engagement made under such circumstances can be binding, and you must break it off at once. Go and tell him that your Father and I refuse to hear of your engagement."

"It'll make him most awful ratty if I do," objected Clarence.

"What if it does? Clarence, you must get free. I'm extremely anxious that you should marry Miss Heritage before Mirliflor returns (if he does return) for her. It's most important, for your Sister's sake. Because, when he finds himself forsaken, he is sure to turn to Edna again. Now do you see?"

"I see," he replied lugubriously, "and I don't mind going to the Lake and trying to get the old boy to let me off—but I bet you he won't."

"Don't ask him anything. Simply inform him that your parents decline to allow such a match, and refer him to us."

"Perhaps that would be the neatest way out of it," he agreed. "Yes, I'll just tell him that—from a safe distance—and he can do what he jolly well pleases. But it won't be a pleasant job. What?"

It was some miles to the Crystal Lake, but he went on foot without any member of his suite in attendance, and in a plain cloak and slouched hat, which prevented him from being recognised as he passed through the streets of the Capital.

During his absence his Mother was engaged in long and anxious consultation with the King and Edna. "I'm surprised at Clarence," King Sidney had observed, "thought he knew his way about too well to be drawn into an entanglement of this kind!"

"He never would have been," said his mother, "if he hadn't had to choose between that and being held under water. And you can trust Clarence to make it clear that he would not be allowed to keep such a promise, even if he wanted to."

"If he marries any one," said the King, "it ought to be this Princess of Goldenenbergenland—he'll get money with her, and we want some rather badly."

"Pardon me, Sidney," said the Queen, "but I intend him to marry Miss Heritage."

"Mother!" exclaimed Edna, "Miss Heritage! What can you be thinking of?"

"I know what I am doing, my love. The poor boy is devoted to her and always has been, and, in short, I've decided that he shall have his way. It will be to your advantage that he should."

On reflection Edna saw this. Mirliflor might feel mortified for a time, but there was at least a chance of catching him on the rebound.

When Clarence returned later his entrance was hailed with an interrogatory "Well?" from his family. "Well," he replied, "I interviewed the old King. Told him you couldn't stick my marrying his daughter. He took it very quietly—better than I expected. All he said was that, if you would come to the big fountain in the Palace gardens (it's supplied from the Crystal lake, you know) at sunset, he'd be there and let you know his terms."

"Wants to blackmail us, does he?" said the King. "He won't get a farthing out of me!"

"It is like his impudence," added the Queen. "Still, it may be as well to see him."

And just before the sun's final disappearance, the four stood on the margin of a small artificial lake, from the centre of which a great column of water shot up to a colossal height against the crimson and orange sky.

"He doesn't seem to have kept his appointment," said the King. "Thought better of it, hey?" As he spoke, the tall column sank and resolved itself into a solid grey-green figure of little above the average stature, a long-bearded elderly personage in a flowing mantle which only partially covered his suit of glittering iridescent scales.

"There is the old blighter!" whispered Clarence. "This is my Father and Mother, Sir," he added aloud, "and anything you've got to propose must be settled with them."

"O King and Queen of Märchenland!" said the Lake King, in a voice like the roar of a cataract, "is it true that ye consider a daughter of mine unworthy to wed your son?"

"Without entering into personalities," replied King Sidney, "which are better avoided at all times, I may say that an alliance with a family whose nature is so—er—amphibious could not be seriously entertained by any civilised monarch."

"It would be too grotesque!" said Queen Selina, "even in a country like this!"

"I have set my heart on becoming the Father-in-law of a Prince of the Royal blood," said the Lake King, "and I will not be denied."

"Now—now—now," protested King Sidney, "what is the good of taking that tone? If we were in England I should say this was a matter that could be settled in few minutes by our respective solicitors. As it is, you had better tell us how much you'll take to compromise it. I don't admit that your daughter has suffered any material damage—still, if you're reasonable in your ideas of compensation, you'll find us disposed to meet you—as far as we can, you know, as far as we can," he added hastily, as he remembered his shrunken gold sacks.

"My terms are these," the Lake King answered. "Unless the betrothal of Prince Clarence to my daughter Forelle be proclaimed throughout the City before nightfall, the waters of the Crystal Lake shall overflow and submerge the whole land to the tops of the highest houses. It is for ye to choose."

"That would be an outrageous thing to do, if you could do it," said the Queen, "but you know very well you can't!"

"Can I not?" retorted the Lake King. "Behold if I have boasted vainly or not!" And he waved his sceptre, which was surmounted by a crystal fish. Instantly the artificial lake came pouring over its marble border, and the Royal Family were ankle-deep in water. "It's no good!" said King Sidney, as the flood spread and threatened to rise higher still, "we've got to give in."

"Nothing but the safety of our poor subjects would make me consent," declared the Queen, "but as it is, I must. Stop this horrid flood, and we'll agree to everything!"

The water flowed back into the basin at a motion of the Lake King's sceptre. "It is agreed, then," he said, smiling for the first time, "that the betrothal is to be proclaimed before nightfall, and that the nuptials shall take place within eight days?"

"Oh, very well," said Queen Selina pettishly, "I can't think your daughter will ever settle down or be really happy with us—but that is her affair, and—and I will try my best to be a Mother to her."

"It is enough," said the King of the Crystal Lake, "I have your word. Should ye retract now, what follows will be upon your own heads!" And, with these parting words, he merged into a column of water which towered up as before, its spray falling like fine bronze dust against the now purple sky.

"I don't much think I shall ever get on with him," was all Clarence could find to say, as they walked back with wet feet. "But Forelle—well, she really isn't at all bad-looking—in her way."

"Has she got the same coloured hair as her father?" inquired Edna.

"It's green," he confessed, "but a much prettier shade of green—Eau de nil, I should call it."

"And I suppose all the furniture will have to be covered in oilskin?" went on Edna. "One of the delights of having a Nixie for a sister-in-law."

"You needn't talk!" he said angrily. "You came jolly near giving me a bally ogre for a brother-in-law—what?"

"There is just this difference, Clarence," replied his sister, "I was able to break it off—which you are not."

"Well, if I'm not, it's not my fault, so you needn't nag," he said savagely, for the thought that all hope of Daphne was now irretrievably lost had just begun to gall him.

"We shall all have to change our shoes when we get in," was her answer. "And it is lucky if we escape a bad cold in the head. But I dare say," she added sweetly, "that when dear Forelle is one of us we shall soon grow inured to damp."

"What I'm thinking of," said the King sombrely, "is how the Court and the populace will take this business. It's to be hoped that the Lake King is—er—liked in these parts."

"Who could help loving him?" jeered Edna. "No doubt the wedding will excite the greatest enthusiasm—especially if the bride goes through the ceremony in a tank!"

"Oh, shut up, can't you!" cried the worried Clarence. "Don't make it out more rotten than it is!"

Queen Selina was too occupied with her own reflections to interfere. Her plan for securing the succession to the throne by a union between Clarence and Daphne was clearly no longer practicable. She had been anxious to treat the girl with consideration, and even indulgence—but events had made this impossible. It was absolutely necessary now to get Miss Heritage safely out of the way as soon as it could be managed. "I must speak to the Marshal about it," she was thinking, "and have her sent back to England in that stork-car. The poor dear Court Godmother is much too ill to be consulted just now. I have just that much to be truly thankful for!"

CHAPTER XIX

SERVANTS OF THE QUEEN

If breaking the news of Edna's engagement to Count von Rubenfresser had been a matter of some delicacy, to inform the Court and Public of Clarence's betrothal to a Water-nixie was, as his parents felt, infinitely more so. Queen Selina told the Baron first, but, rather to her surprise, he took it calmly and almost apathetically. "I'm afraid, Baron," she said, "you will think it very weak of us to allow it, but, between ourselves, there are—er—State reasons which left us no choice." To which he replied that he would much prefer to be excused from offering any opinion as to the policy their Majesties had chosen to pursue.

The Marshal, on the other hand, expressed cordial satisfaction. His lizard-like eyes sparkled as he assured his Sovereigns that he would see that the heralds proclaimed the betrothal in the City before nightfall, and that he expected it would excite heartfelt enthusiasm.

It certainly had not that effect on the Court. The ladies-in-waiting resented the prospect of having to acknowledge a new Royalty the greater part of whose existence had been spent under water. The Courtiers shrugged their shoulders with sardonic resignation. In vain the Crown Prince attempted to carry off his secret uneasiness by clapping them on the back and saying, "You haven't seen Princess Forelle yet, you know, dear boy. When you do, you'll agree that she's a regular little ripper—what?" They made it sufficiently clear that they had no wish to see the future Crown Princess. In fact, if he had not already lost all the prestige he had ever had, he would have lost it now, and his feelings were not to be envied.

Marshal Federhelm requested a private audience from the Queen, who received him in her Cabinet. He began by asking permission to absent himself for a few days on a hunting expedition in the Forest, which permission was graciously accorded.

"If the Crown Prince had not—er—ties to keep him at home," she added, "I'm sure he would be delighted to join you."

"I doubt it, your Majesty," said the Marshal. "His Royal Highness's ardour for such pursuits has languished much of late. However, he is better employed. And, ere I leave, I must ask your Majesty's wishes in regard to my prisoner, the Lady Daphne."

"Ah, I was going to talk to you about that, Marshal," said Queen Selina. "There are many reasons why it is undesirable that Miss Heritage should remain here any longer. After the underhand and ungrateful manner in which she has tried to pervert Prince Mirliflor from his attachment to Princess Edna, I feel it my duty to have her removed."

"I understand, your Majesty," he said, "and it shall be done. But I would recommend, in your Majesty's interests, that the execution should take place in private, and that the Lady Daphne's decease should be supposed to be due to sudden illness. Otherwise there may be trouble with the Court."

"Execution!" cried Queen Selina, genuinely horrified. "Good gracious me, Marshal, you don't suppose I want the poor girl put to death, do you? What do you take me for?"

"It would be a prudent course," he said with meaning, "for any Sovereign to adopt in your Majesty's situation."

"For a Märchenland Sovereign, perhaps! But I have been brought up with very different ideas. I should consider it most wicked to give orders for anybody to be killed. That is not at all what I meant in saying that I want Miss Heritage removed."

"Then I fail to understand your Majesty."

"It's perfectly simple. I merely wish to have her sent back to England. The Baron can take her in the Court Godmother's stork-car. She'll never be well enough to know of it now, poor old soul! And the dear old Baron's so devoted to Us, and has always been so anxious that Edna should marry Mirliflor, that I know I can depend on him."

"If it should be known," said the Marshal, "that your Majesty had banished Prince Mirliflor's chosen bride, there would be such an outcry that it might cost you your Kingdom."

"Oh, do you really think that, Marshal? But it is so essential that she should be sent to England! Surely it can be managed somehow without any scandal?"

"There is a way, Madam, if your Majesty is prepared to take it."

"I am prepared to do anything, Marshal—that is, almost anything. What do you advise?"

"Your Majesty should inform the Baron that, the Court Godmother being unhappily too indisposed to act as guardian to Lady Daphne, you desire him to convey her in the stork-car to Clairdelune and place her under the care of Prince Mirliflor."

"But, my dear good Marshal, that's the very last thing I desire!"

"I know, Madam, I know. But it is what he should represent to the Court and Lady Daphne, and he is more likely to do so if he believes it to be the fact. I will give him sealed instructions which he is not to open till after he is started, directing him to take her—not to Clairdelune, but to the land of her birth. Your Majesty will be good enough to write such instructions at once."

"It seems simple, and yet, Marshal, I'm not quite sure," demurred the Queen. "The Baron is an old dear, but just a bit of a chatterbox. He might let the whole thing out when he gets back!"

"He will not get back," said the Marshal. "I know a certain drug that I will administer to the storks before the journey. It is slow to act, and will not affect them until after they have reached the country that you call England. But they will never leave it again. And then it will merely be supposed that he has acted treacherously."

"I see," said Queen Selina. "Yes, I should be perfectly safe then. If there was any other way, or I didn't feel so strongly that it was really a kindness to Miss Heritage to save her from occupying a position she is so unsuited to, I really don't think I could. But I suppose I must do as you suggest."

She wrote the order, which she signed and sealed and handed to him. "I shouldn't like her to be left stranded in England without any means of support, Marshal," she said. "That would be a thing I could not reconcile to my conscience. So you will kindly see that she is supplied with a sack of gold."

"That will be a truly royal act of generosity," he said, "especially as I understand the number of sacks in your Majesty's treasury is by no means large just now."

"I was forgetting. On second thoughts, perhaps you had better make it a purse instead," she amended. "It will keep her while she is looking out for another situation."

"No doubt. And it would be wise, I think, if your Majesty would speed her departure with your good wishes in presence of the Court."

But even Queen Selina shrank from such duplicity as that. "I—I don't think I'll see her again myself," she said. "I—I'd rather not. It's most distasteful to me to have to deceive her at all, Marshal, and I shouldn't if it wasn't absolutely necessary in self-defence."

"Your Majesty has no need to assure me of that. I entirely understand," he said. "I would recommend that you send for the Baron at once, and direct him to convey Lady Daphne to Clairdelune to-morrow. Then, after I have given him the secret order, my part will be done and I shall be free to enjoy my hunting." And with that he bowed himself out.

Queen Selina followed his counsel so well that the old Court Chamberlain was completely deceived. Usurper as he now knew her to be, she was, he thought, still unaware of it, and such magnanimity to her daughter's successful rival gave him a better opinion of her. After all, he could bring himself to continue in her service, now that the Court Godmother's main object was attained. Like her, he had no wish to confess that he had been so mistaken as to saddle the Kingdom with a bogus Sovereign. So he spread the news of Lady Daphne's approaching departure with great satisfaction and the warmest eulogies of the gracious consideration Queen Selina had displayed. But even this could only partially check their disaffection, for they could not forgive her for subjecting them to the indignity of accepting a Water-nixie as their Crown Princess.

After dismissing the Baron, the Queen had felt somewhat shocked at her own talent for dissimulation. "I little thought at Gablehurst that I should ever fib like this!" she reflected. "But I wasn't a Queen then! And I can't afford to be too particular, when it's a question of keeping the Crown in the family!"

The Marshal waited until the Baron had concluded his interview with the Queen, and then visited him in his own quarters. The Court Chamberlain mentioned the instructions he had just received, and spoke in the highest terms of his Royal mistress's benevolence.

"As you say, Baron," said the Marshal, "such conduct does honour to her Majesty. She has, however, given me further instructions for you with which it is well you should be acquainted at once." And he drew out the secret order, and, after breaking the seal, presented the parchment to the Baron, who read it with honest amazement and indignation.

"I cannot believe her Majesty can have devised such wickedness!" he said. "What can be her reason—unless—unless—" and here he checked himself.

"You were about to say: Unless she knows—as you and I, my dear Baron, know beyond all doubt—that the Lady Daphne is the real Queen of Märchenland?"

"So you know that, too!" cried the Baron, recoiling in terror. "I swear to you, my lord, that I myself had no suspicion of it until it was revealed to me by the Court Godmother but two days since!"

"I accept your word for it—though whether others will do so is another matter," said the Marshal as he picked up and thrust in his doublet the document which the other had let fall. "But what I should like to know is, which of your orders you intend to execute?"

"The first, of course," exclaimed the Baron indignantly. "Lady Daphne has a higher claim to my fealty than this interloper. I shall do my duty and carry her to Clairdelune."

"You forget that Prince Mirliflor will not be there as yet to receive her. Nor is it seemly that she should quit her Kingdom without making any assertion of her claim. My plan is better than yours, Baron. Hearken: I leave the Palace to-night on the pretext of hunting in the Forest of Schlangenzweigen. I take with me a company of my own—all tried soldiers on whom I can rely. To-morrow you will set out in the car, as though to Clairdelune, and Queen Selina will naturally believe that her secret order will be obeyed. But, after having gone a certain distance, you will head your storks for the chapel of St. Morosius in the forest. There we shall be waiting to swear allegiance to our young Queen and escort her in triumph to Eswareinmal. I shall have taken measures beforehand to proclaim her title, and it is certain that the populace will rise in her favour. You cannot fail to see, my dear Baron, that your best—in fact, your only way of escaping the penalty of your folly—to call it by no harsher name—is to aid us in undoing it."

"Enough, Marshal," said the Baron, "you can count upon me."

"I am sure of it, Baron, and, as I am leaving the Palace, I will deliver the Lady Daphne into your custody. See that you say nothing to her of our scheme till the fitting moment. For the present she must be told that she is to be taken to Clairdelune. And now I must quit you, for I have much to attend to before I start, which should be within an hour. To-morrow at mid-day we shall expect you at the Chapel in the forest, and have a care for your own sake that you fail us not."

An hour later, having disposed of the business he had attended to and left everything in train for his project, he set out with a chosen band on his alleged hunting expedition. "Whether this will fall out as I calculate, or in some other way, I know not," he told himself, as they clattered out of one of the City gates and took the road to the forest of Schlangenzweigen. "But this I know—whatever happens, I shall shortly be King of Märchenland."

After he was gone the Baron began to reflect on what he had undertaken, and to feel that he would be glad of an excuse to get out of it, if he could find one. It was hardly credible that Queen Selina could have devised so treacherous a plot; it seemed far more likely that the Marshal had deceived him. After all, the secret order he had been shown might not be genuine. If it were not, the Queen was innocent, and the Baron was only too willing to leave her in peaceful permission of the throne. Before he committed himself any further he must satisfy himself on this point. His difficulty was that he could not ask her directly whether the secret order had indeed been given by her, as he might betray the Marshal, which might entail unpleasant consequences for himself. After some thought he hit upon a stratagem that was rather brilliant—for him. He obtained a private interview with the Queen, and begged her to consider whether it was altogether judicious to restore Lady Daphne to a Prince who might otherwise come forward once more as a suitor for Princess Edna. "Would it not be safer, Madam," he suggested, "to send Lady Daphne to her own country, where he would never be able to find her?"

Queen Selina was so convinced of his honesty and loyalty that she fell into his little trap without a moment's suspicion. "Now, it's really very curious you should have thought of that, my dear Baron!" she said, "very curious indeed! Because—I suppose the Marshal gave you a sealed letter from me before he left?... I thought so, and of course it isn't to be opened till after you've started. Still, I may tell you now that it contains instructions for the very identical course you suggest! I needn't say you must be careful not to mention it—but it may be a satisfaction to you to know that I've already decided on it."

"A great satisfaction indeed, your Majesty," he said, "for now my duty lies clear before me."

"And nobody, I'm sure, my dear Baron, will do it more faithfully!" was her gracious response. He proceeded to Daphne, who had heard that her Giroflé had succeeded in his attempt to rescue Edna, but knew nothing of what had happened to him afterwards. He relieved her anxiety by informing her, not only that she was to rejoin Giroflé at Clairdelune next day, but who he actually was, which last piece of information turned all her joy to dismay. Prince or no Prince, she knew that Giroflé would be true to her—but what if the King, his father, forbade him to marry anyone so far below his rank? She would have to undergo the ordeal of being presented to King Tournesol, and the thought made her heart sink with terror.

"But the Court Godmother will come with me, Baron?" she asked anxiously, only to hear why this was impossible. "Too ill even to see me!" said Daphne sadly. "And that is why her Majesty is letting me be sent to Gir—I mean, Mirliflor? It's really very good of her. I suppose, Baron, I shall be able to see her and thank her before I go?"

"Undoubtedly," he said, and, having said as much as he thought prudent, he left his prisoner to her own reflections.

Most of the Court gathered to see her off the next morning, but the only Royalty present was little Princess Ruby, who held her former Governess in close and tearful embraces. "Darling!" she said, through her sobs, "it's perfectly beastly to think you've been here all this time and I never knew it! And now you really are going and I mayn't see you for ever so long! It will be so dull, for of course I wouldn't play with the Gnomes now—even if they weren't all down with mumps. And Edna's so snappy, and Clarence is going to marry a nasty wet Water-nixie—and I wish we'd all stayed at Inglegarth, that I do!" Daphne had not heard before of Clarence's engagement and, though she naturally made no comment, she could not think he was to be congratulated on his choice. She did her best to comfort Ruby, and after taking leave of her nearly as inconsolable friends in the Household, she at length found herself seated in the car with the Baron, who had dispensed with the usual attendants. And then the Courtyard, with the mass of upturned faces and waving hands, slowly sank to the rhythmical beating of the storks' wings as they obeyed the order, "To the Palace of Clairdelune."

Clarence saw the car pass overhead from the grove in the Palace Gardens, to which he had betaken himself in his dull misery. He knew that Daphne must be on her way to rejoin her lover, and tried to console himself by the reflection that it didn't matter to him. He was done for, anyhow, whether she went or stayed. But again came the bitter thought that there had been a time when, if he had only gone the right way about it, he might have—"I thought she wasn't good enough to marry," he said to himself. "Not good enough! a girl like her! Now I'm booked to marry a Lord-knows-what with green hair. Serves me damned well right too!"

Edna also saw the car as she walked with the Queen on the terrace that commanded the City. "There goes Miss Heritage!" she said. "Delighted to recapture her Mirliflor, no doubt! I don't wish to reproach you in any way, Mother, but I can't think you've shown much consideration for my interests in packing her off to him like this!"

It was painful to Queen Selina to be so misunderstood, but she decided that the injustice must be borne for the present. "My love," she said, "I could not possibly keep her here. And perhaps," she could could not help adding, "perhaps some day you will see that I have been a better mother to you than you imagine!"

To which pathetic appeal Princess Edna merely responded by a short sniff, expressive rather of incredulity than any softer emotion.

CHAPTER XX

AT THE END OF HER TETHER

Both the Queen and Edna that morning had observed an unwonted stir in the usually quiet and sleepy streets of Eswareinmal as they looked down on them from the Terrace parapet.

The great square was black with citizens, and from it rose a faint but angry drone that was unpleasantly suggestive of the results of pitching a large stone into a hornets' nest.

"I expect," remarked Queen Selina, "they're all busy discussing this engagement of Clarence's. If we drive out this afternoon we mustn't forget to take at least two sacks of gold with us."

"I doubt if we can afford to drive out at all just now," said Edna.

"Perhaps," agreed her mother, "it would be wiser to wait till things have settled down a little. Why they should get so excited about it I can't think. It's most inconsiderate and troublesome of them—at a time, too, when, goodness knows, I've enough to worry about!"

Just then she was chiefly harassed by a doubt whether she had been wholly wise in accepting the Marshal as a confederate, and especially in committing her secret instructions to writing. What if he knew or guessed her real reasons for getting rid of Miss Heritage? But, even if that were so, he had probably acted as he had out of goodwill and desire to maintain the dynasty. He had never shown the slightest jealousy or chagrin at having been deprived of the Regency. No, on the whole, she thought he could be trusted to be silent—if only because he could not betray her without admitting his own complicity. Still, there was a danger that he might presume on his knowledge—which would be disagreeable enough. If their Majesties were reluctant to show themselves just then to the populace, the populace on the other hand were determined to be both seen and heard. The proclamation of Clarence's betrothal had served as the breaking strain to the attenuated links that still attached them to the Throne. They had murmured against the enfranchisement of the Yellow Gnomes; their deception in the matter of the self-supplying tables had weakened their loyalty seriously for a time; the projected alliance of the Princess Edna with the surviving member of a race whose scutcheon bore the taint of Ogreism had aroused their bitter resentment. But all these grievances had been redressed, and the amiable easygoing Märchenlanders were willing to forgive and forget them. Now they were called upon to put up with a humiliation beyond all endurance. The prospect of seeing the throne occupied in days to come by a creature who was not only of dubious extraction, but probably did not possess so much as the rudiments of a soul, infuriated them to madness.

So much so that the Royal Family had scarcely finished lunch when they were startled by news that the people were once more advancing en masse up the road to the Palace, and would soon be battering at the gates for admittance.

"I can't see 'em," said King Sidney peevishly, plucking at his auburn moustache. "What am I to say to them about this engagement? There's nothing to say except that it's most—"

"If you say that again, Sidney," said the Queen, "I shall throw something at you! Tell them the truth."

"I—I'd rather the Council explained it to them, my dear," he said.

"The Council have been sitting tight with closed doors all the morning," said Clarence, "like a bally lot of broody hens. I don't know, of course, but I've a notion they're discussing a Republic or something."

"If you won't speak to the people, Sidney," declared the Queen, with the courage of despair, "I must order the guards to close the Courtyard gates, and tell the mob that, if they promise to be quiet and behave themselves, I'll come out and talk to them myself."

"Good egg, Mater!" cried Clarence, "I'll come with you. It's really my show!"

"You'll only make them worse! Much better keep indoors and take no notice. More dignified," said the King. But as his wife and son paid no attention to him, he followed them out for very shame.

As they came down the front steps and advanced to within hearing distance of the crowd, which had not attempted as yet to break through the closed gates, they were received with yells and howls of execration, frantic shaking of fists and brandishing of improvised weapons. The strength of the gates and the presence of the guards gave the Queen more confidence than she might otherwise have felt.

"Now, good people!" she said in rather a tremulous voice, "it's quite impossible to speak while you're making all this noise!"

She had sent up for her crown, and perhaps this impressed them unconsciously, though she had been too nervous to put it on straight. Gradually silence was obtained.

"I know why you've come," she began, "and we quite understand your feelings about our son's engagement. In fact we share them." This provoked a renewal of the uproar and a vehement desire to know why, if that were so, the union had ever been contracted.

"If you'll only listen, I'll tell you," said the Queen. "We shouldn't have consented to it at all but for the sake of our beloved people." At this the beloved people very nearly had the gates down. "You don't understand," she shouted. "Even now, if you insist on the marriage being broken off, we are quite willing—indeed we shall be only too happy—to put a stop to it."

Here there were shouts of "We do! We do insist! Stop it! No marriage!"

"Very well then," said Queen Selina with more assurance, "only I am bound to tell you what the consequences will be. The Crystal Lake will overflow till the whole of Märchenland is under water. At least that's what the Lake King threatens. You know best whether he can do it or not."

Her hearers knew too well, and the cries and murmurs took an altered tone at once, though some voices cursed the Prince whose weakness and folly had brought them to such a dilemma.

"Weakness and folly!" cried the Queen indignantly. "How can you be so wretchedly ungrateful? When my poor, noble, unselfish boy is sacrificing himself—for you don't suppose he can have any affection for a Water-nixie?—sacrificing himself on—on the altar of his country!"

"Mater!" whispered Clarence in admiration, "you're the limit!"

"And all the reward he gets," the Queen went on, pressing her advantage, "all the reward we get—for providing that you can sleep safe and warm in your beds—instead of being drowned in them—is violence and rude remarks! Really, if you have any consciences left you ought to be thoroughly ashamed of yourselves!"

They undoubtedly were. For a moment or two there was a hush, and then the whole mob broke into tumultuous cheers—for the Queen, the King, and more particularly the Crown Prince. Never since their accession had the Royal Family been so popular.

"There now," said the Queen, when she and her family were weary of bowing their acknowledgments, "that will do. Now go quietly away, like respectable loyal persons, and tell all the other citizens what we're doing for them."

"I must say, my love," observed the King, after the crowd had melted away in a vastly different mood from that in which they had come, "you showed wonderful presence of mind. I quite thought myself we should have been massacred."

"And so we should have been, Sidney," she replied, "if I'd left it to you!"

On re-entering the Palace they heard that the Council was still sitting. "Let 'em sit!" cried Clarence. "This'll be a bit of a suck for them. What price a Republic now, eh?"

"They simply daren't depose us!" said the Queen, "now the dear people are with us heart and soul!"

Some time later, while they were sitting in the lapis-lazuli Chamber, a page entered to announce that a messenger had just arrived with tidings which he wished to communicate to their Majesties in private. "Tell him to come in," said the Queen. "I do hope it isn't some fresh trouble!"

The messenger brought grave news. The Marshal, it appeared, had been killed while hunting in the Forest. Particulars were wanting, but there was no doubt that he was dead.

"How very very sad!" exclaimed the Queen. "The poor dear Marshal! To be cut off like this in the prime of life! It must have been a wild boar, I suppose—or a bear. But, whichever it was, it is a terrible loss. I don't know exactly how long the Court ought to go into mourning for an ex-Regent—but at least a month!"

She was shocked, of course, by the suddenness of it. At the same time she could not help a renewed sense of gratitude to Providence, which had once more gone out of its way to smooth her path. "I've always said hunting these wild animals is a very dangerous sport," said King Sidney. "Glad you've given it up, my boy!"

"Fed up with it, Guv'nor. But I dare say I shall go in for it again—some day or other," Clarence replied, while he was thinking that it would have to be a day when he discovered what had become of his irresistible sword, and when he could find a horse among his numerous stud that would permit him to get on its back.

They were still discussing the Marshal's untimely end when an usher came from the Hall of Council with a message that the Councillors had ended their deliberations, and requested their Majesties to honour them by attending to hear their decision.

"I like their nerve!" remarked Clarence. "Of course, Guv'nor, you'll tell 'em they've jolly well got to come to us, what?"

"No, Sidney," said Queen Selina, flushed with her recent victory, "you will say that we are coming in presently to preside over the Council and give them our advice. I shall know how to put them in their proper places. I shall wear my crown again, and you had better put on yours, and—yes, I should certainly take your sceptre too."

She kept them waiting as long as her own dignity demanded, and then sailed into the Council Chamber, the King and Crown Prince following in her wake. The whole Council rose and remained standing until the Royal Family had taken their seats under a canopy.

The President then informed them that the Councillors had resolved to use every means to prevent a union which, if contracted, would infallibly cover the entire Kingdom with contempt.

"Oh, very well, gentlemen," said the Queen. "I should have thought even that was better than having it covered with water—but if you in your wisdom think otherwise, we bow to your superior judgment." And she explained the situation much as she had done to the mob at the gates, though with less effect, for the President's answer was that, if such were the alternatives, their Majesties would best show their anxiety for their subjects' welfare by abdicating immediately.

"I don't see that at all," she retorted. "Why in the world should we?"

"Because," was the reply, "when this so-called King of the Crystal Lake learns that your son is no longer a Prince, he will cease to desire him for his daughter."

"And may I ask, supposing we did abdicate, whom do you propose to put in our place?" inquired the Queen.

"We should appoint Marshal Federhelm as Regent once more—or even elect him Sovereign."

"A very pretty plan!" replied Queen Selina, "only there's one objection to it, as you would know if you hadn't shut yourselves up here all day. You will be sorry to hear that the poor Marshal was killed this very afternoon while hunting. So you can't get him. And, as there's no one else available, and as my husband and I feel that it would be very wrong to desert our dear people when they've just assured us of their perfect loyalty and affection—(another fact you seem to be ignorant of!)—I'm afraid, gentlemen, that, whether you like it or not, you will have to put up with us."

"It is true, O Queen!" the President admitted with a deep groan. "We can do naught except pray that Heaven may yet save this most unhappy Country from so deep a degradation!" And all the other Members of the Council groaned too, while several beat their breasts or tore their long white beards in senile wrath and despair.

"They are a cheery complimentary lot of old devils!" commented Clarence. "If I were you, Mater, I'd—what d'ye call it?—prorogue 'em."

The Queen was inclined to accept this suggestion, but at that moment a loud rapping was heard at the closed doors. "Go and see who it is, somebody," she commanded, "it may be important news." She thought it probable that an attendant had come to announce the decease of the Fairy Vogelflug, which was hourly expected.

The doors were partly opened, and then a voice she had never thought to hear again cried in weak and quavering accents: "Let me pass. I claim my right of admission as Court Godmother."

The Queen changed colour, but felt that, inopportune as the demand was, she could not refuse it without laying herself open to suspicion, and perhaps worse. "Oh, let her come in, poor old soul," she said, "and find a seat for her. I'd really no idea she was well enough to get up."

The Fairy hobbled feebly in, looking incredibly old and shrunken, and like a grim ghost of her former self in her clinging grey night-rail. Her hollow eyes glowed like live coals as she faced the Queen, and stood labouring for breath before she could speak.

"So glad to see you looking so much better, dear Court Godmother!" said Queen Selina. "But was it wise of you to come downstairs so soon?"

"I have visited the pavilion and found it untenanted," said the Fairy, without troubling to explain how she had contrived to elude her attendants and get there. "Now, answer me, what have you done with Lady Daphne?"

"Oh, haven't they told you?" replied the Queen. "I should have consulted you, of course, if I had known you were conscious; but, as it was, I did what I thought you would wish and sent her off with the Baron in the stork-car this morning—to Clairdelune."

"Is this the truth—or are you trying to deceive me by lies?"

"Really!" cried the Queen, "this is most uncalled for! I don't know what you suppose I've done with the girl?"

"You may have imprisoned—murdered her, for all I can tell. It is more likely than that you would permit her to depart so easily."

"Well," said the Queen, "if you don't believe me, you have only to make inquiries. I was not in time to see her off myself, but I believe there are members of the Court who were more fortunate."

Several Councillors corroborated this by affirming that they themselves had not only been present but had heard the Baron give the order, "To Clairdelune."

"I daresay you don't think much of us, Ma'am," said Clarence, "but after all we're English, you know, and you might give us credit for playing the game, what?"

He spoke with a resentment which convinced his Mother of her wisdom in having played her own game without seeking any co-operation from him.

The old Fairy's suspicions had been completely quelled. "I perceive," she confessed, "that I have been over ready to think evil, and can but crave your forgiveness, Madam, for having done you so great an injustice."

"Pray don't mention it!" returned the Queen. "There was some excuse for it, and we willingly forgive you, if there's anything to forgive. And now," she added, after ordering the attendants to be fetched, "you really must take more care of yourself and get back to bed at once."

"I will return to it," was the reply, "for now that my mind is at ease I am well content to die."

"Oh, but you mustn't talk like that!" protested Queen Selina, "when you've just made such a marvellous recovery! Why, you're looking ever so much brighter than any of us could have hoped. All you really need now is a good long sleep."

"That is all, and I shall have it ere long. You may rest assured," she added, with a significance which the Queen alone understood, "that henceforth your peace shall not be disturbed by any word or deed of mine."

The attendants entered and she suffered them to lead her away, while King Sidney graciously extended his sceptre for her to kiss in passing, but drew it back shamefacedly on finding this civility ignored.

"It's evidently the last flicker, poor old thing!" said the Queen, after the Fairy had retired. "I don't at all expect we shall ever see her alive again!"

If she had so expected, her conscience might have troubled her more than it did. As it was, it did not reproach her too severely. It was not nice to deceive a dying person, but it was much nicer than confessing and losing a Kingdom for it. It would have been too ridiculous to begin to be squeamish now. And, after all, it was her misfortune rather than her fault if the family interests had necessitated a slight temporary lapse from principles she still held as rigidly as ever.

She dismissed her Council, which broke up in a chastened spirit, and the Royal Family, after a light meal which was the nearest approach to afternoon tea that Märchenland afforded, went out for an airing on their favourite promenade—the terrace that overlooked Eswareinmal.

The market-place was still thronged, but such sounds as reached them were no longer menacing. "I do believe they haven't done cheering for us yet!" said the Queen. "And some of them seem to be waving flags! I shouldn't be the least surprised, Clarence, if your wedding next week goes off quite well after all!"

"I wish it would go off," he said, "but there's no chance of that now!"

"Well, it's no good being gloomy about it. Er—Forelle may turn out to be charming when we come to know her. Which reminds me, dear boy, you might tell her we should be delighted if she can come to tea here some afternoon before the ceremony."

"She could easily slip up through the fountain," suggested Edna. "I shall be anxious to see how she does her hair. Let me see—didn't you say it was green, Clarence?"

"Oh, give her hair a rest!" he replied.

"I saw before we left England," said the Queen tactfully, "that green hair was going to be quite the fashion this season. But, however strange she may be to society, we should remember, Edna, my love, that she will shortly become one of ourselves and treat her with every civility. We must avoid anything that might offend her Father."

Queen Selina was inclined that afternoon to take a more roseate view of the future. She felt herself once more secure on the throne now that all the dangers which had threatened to overturn it had been averted. The rival Queen would soon be landed in England, where, even if she ever heard of her rights, she would be powerless to claim them. Of the three persons who knew or might discover the truth, the Marshal was dead, the Court Godmother might just as well be so for all the harm she could do, and the Baron was on his way to a land from which he would never return.

As for Mirliflor, it would not be difficult to persuade him that some blunder of the Baron's must have caused the stork-car to go astray, and it was quite possible that when the Prince had abandoned all hope of recovering Miss Heritage he would return to Edna.

"Look at the dear people now!" she cried, as she looked down on the square, "they're actually forming a procession to march up to the Palace and thank us again!... Yes, they really are! It's quite wonderful the effect Clarence's self-sacrifice has had—it seems to have rallied them all round the Throne. But I knew it would, if it was put to them in the right way.... Did you hear that?" she asked later, when the procession had reached an angle of the zigzag incline which was directly below. "They're shouting for Me! I distinctly heard 'We want our Queen!' So nice and warm-hearted of them!"

The shouts had ceased, but the tramp of thousands of feet grew louder, until the sound was deadened as the demonstrators passed under the wing of the Palace on their way to the central entrance.

"Sidney, we must go in and show ourselves to them," said the Queen. "If they insist on a speech I will make it—you always manage to say the wrong thing!"

As they entered the Palace they heard a clamour which appeared to proceed from the great Entrance Hall. "Quite right to have asked them in," remarked the Queen with approval. "I shall order some refreshments for them, and then we can go up by a back way and appear at the top of the Grand Staircase." But this part of the programme was not destined to be carried out.

On attempting to pass through they were stopped, to the Queen's indignant amazement, in an inner hall by the Captain of her own Guards. "Really!" she cried, "I never heard of such a thing! What do you mean by it?"

He either could not or would not give any other explanation than that he had instructions to detain them. "Prince Hansmeinigel!" said the Queen, as she saw him approaching, "can you inform us why his Majesty and I are prevented from addressing our faithful subjects?"

"I think, Madam," he replied smoothly, "that you would find none here to address."

"How dare you tell me that, when you can hear them calling for 'their Queen' at this very moment!"

"But not for you, Madam. The Queen they are demanding is the Lady Daphne."

"Miss Heritage!" gasped Queen Selina. "Why should they want her?"

"It seems," he said, "that certain information has reached the Burgomaster and chief citizens which has convinced them of her title to the throne, and they are now in conference with the Council on the matter."

"So that treacherous old vixen of a Court Godmother had betrayed the secret after all, in spite of her promise!" concluded Queen Selina. But the battle was not lost yet by any means. She was not going to give in, when she had so many chances in her favour.

"They might have had the decency to invite us to be present," she said. "Surely we have some right to be consulted!"

"They will summon you before them presently, no doubt," he said, and almost as he spoke an official came towards them and whispered to the Captain of the Guard, who turned to the Queen:

"My orders are to bring you before the Council," he said, "if you will be good enough to follow me. We will go round by the outer corridor, so that you will be in no danger from the mob."

"What's all this about, my dear?" whispered King Sidney, as he walked with his wife and son between a strong guard. "I thought things had quieted down again."

"Oh, don't ask me, Sidney!" she returned, "you will know quite soon enough. But you needn't be uneasy. I've brought you through much worse things than this." She entered the Council Hall endeavouring to look as much like Marie Antoinette as she could. That her own Council should arraign her like this was, as she protested, most unconstitutional—they had no right whatever to do it. But, however that might be, they were doing it—a fact which even she was compelled to recognise.

The President began the proceedings by reciting the evidence of Daphne's title, which it now appeared had been put into the hands of the Burgomaster and other notables of Eswareinmal by the Marshal, just before he had gone to meet his sudden end. He then asked, in the name of the whole Tribunal, what the present occupants of the throne had to urge in their own defence.

If the Queen had possessed the legal mind she would have perceived at once that the evidence was merely hearsay—inferences that the Marshal had drawn from what Daphne had told him, and as proofs quite worthless. But she had not a legal mind; and besides she knew that the proofs were quite good enough for Märchenland—also that the allegations happened to be true.

So she did not attempt to deny them. "All I can say is," she declared, "that this is quite new to me. When we were brought here I was given to understand that the Kingdom had descended to me, and of course I accepted the responsibility. If there has been any silly mistake about it, you can't blame me or my husband either. We've tried to do our duty—even so far as consenting to our son's making a marriage we could not approve of—for the sake of saving our Country from inundation. It's not every King and Queen who would have done that."

"That peril," replied the Burgomaster, "is no longer to be feared, since the King of the Crystal Lake, on being notified of the facts in our possession, has withdrawn his demands, saying he desires no union with a family of ignoble and beggarly pretenders."

"That's a let-off!" said Clarence, "though he might have put it a bit more pleasantly, what?"

Queen Selina felt that this repudiation had put one of her heaviest guns out of action, but she was still undaunted. "I'm sure," she said, "We have no wish to be associated with such a person. And, as for being pretenders, I can only say that if the Marshal had come to me and told me what I now know, I should have been quite ready to resign in Miss Heritage's favour. But how could I, when he never breathed a word to me about it?"

"I should like to add," put in King Sidney, "that it has come as a complete surprise to me. I'm anxious to do whatever is right and proper, and if any reasonable arrangement can be come to, I won't stand in the way."

This attitude produced an immediate reaction in their favour, as was visible from the expressions on the faces of the whole Tribunal.

"Then," the President asked, "is the Council to understand that you are prepared to resign at once?"

"Certainly," said the King. "Only too pleased!"

"Not at once," said Queen Selina. "We cannot leave the Kingdom without a ruler—that would be very wrong. But as soon as Miss Heritage—or Queen Daphne, if you like to call her so—chooses to come forward to claim the crown we shall be delighted to give it up. Till then we are merely holding it in trust for her."

"And where is Queen Daphne at present?" asked the Burgomaster.

"Well," said Queen Selina, "she ought to be at Clairdelune by this time."

"She must be sent for without delay," said the President, and the order was given that messengers on swift steeds should be despatched to Clairdelune at once.

"Well, gentlemen," said the Queen, after this business had been concluded, "I hope you see that you owe us an apology for daring to put us under arrest and treat us like criminals. Until Lady Daphne arrives we are still the King and Queen of Märchenland, and you will be good enough to regard us as such."

"The Council wishes to express its deepest regret," said the President, "for having exposed your Majesties' persons to undeserved indignity."

"And now, perhaps," said Queen Selina triumphantly, "we may consider ourselves free to resume our thrones, if only to dissolve the Council?"

The guards fell back instinctively, and she and the King were proceeding to their usual seats under the canopy without any protest from the President, who was engaged at the time in deciphering the contents of a packet which had just been brought to him.

Before they had reached the steps of the dais, he looked up, and ordered them to halt in so peremptory a tone that even Queen Selina obeyed involuntarily.

"What's up now?" inquired Clarence in an undertone.

"This packet directed to myself," said the President, "was found on the body of the late Marshal. It contains an order under the Royal seal and signature, which I will now read to the Council." And he read the Queen's secret order to the Baron to convey Daphne to England, which provoked general horror and execration.

The Queen was thunderstruck as she heard this fresh proof of the Marshal's duplicity—she felt more than ever that she had been a fool to trust him—she might have known that he would take some dishonourable advantage of her confidence!

"What have you to answer to this?" the President was saying to her, and she could see that both her husband and son were waiting anxiously for her reply.

"Is it necessary for me to deny that I ever gave such an order?" she said, with a virtuous indignation that was really very well done. "Of course it was forged by that wicked Marshal!" (so fortunate, she thought, that he was dead!) "It is easy to see with what motive."

Clarence and his father breathed again. For a few dreadful minutes they had been haunted by an ugly fear—lest—but they ought to have felt assured that no member of the Wibberley-Stimpson family could be so unworthy of the name.

"It is possible," said the venerable President doubtfully, "that the handwriting may be but an imitation."

"Nay," struck in the sturdy Burgomaster, "it is hers, sure enough. There can be no doubt to my mind that both our unlawful sovereigns and their son have plotted to deport our true Queen, the Lady Daphne, and that their vile design has succeeded but too well!"

"You're quite out of it, old cock!" shouted Clarence, through the roar of assent that greeted the Burgomaster's speech. "Why should we plot against her, when we hadn't an idea she had a right to the throne?"

"So you allege," said the Burgomaster. "But this order speaks for itself, and if the Council will take my advice it will order all three of the prisoners to be executed at once in the City Square, in sight of the people they have wronged and deceived."

This suggestion evidently commended itself to the majority, but the President demurred. "We must not act too hastily," he said, "lest we find too late that we have been misled by appearances. It may be that Queen Daphne has reached Clairdelune in safety, but of that we cannot have sure knowledge until our messengers return. In the meantime our prisoners must not be regarded as though they were proved guilty. I shall order that they be removed to apartments in the North Tower, where they are to be given honourable treatment and every indulgence save their liberty. Should it be found that they are innocent, due reparation shall be made them."

"And what if we hear that our Queen is not at Clairdelune?" asked the Burgomaster.

"Then they shall receive no mercy," replied the President. "Their heads shall be struck off that same day, in the great square of the Capital."

"Good!" said the Burgomaster. "I will have the scaffold put up the moment I return."

"I just want to say this, Gentlemen," said Clarence before he was led away: "if we were really guilty of trying to get rid of poor little Lady Daphne, we should be such a set of rotters that we should jolly well deserve losing our heads for it. But you'll find we're not."

"I can answer for my poor wife as for myself," said King Sidney. "She is far too much of a lady to dream of doing anything that isn't strictly correct."

Queen Selina said nothing—she was not feeling well enough just then.

"Not half bad!" remarked Clarence, as he went through the suites of rooms that were to form their prison. "Pleasant look-out from all the windows, and the rooms jolly comfortable, considering. We shall do very well here for a day or two."

"Don't talk in that light way, Clarence," said his mother, "or you'll drive me mad!"

"Why, there's nothing to be down in the mouth about, Mater. We may have to stick this longer, of course—depends how long those chaps take getting back from Clairdelune. But as soon as they do get back we shall be let out, and I shouldn't wonder if the Country gave us a thundering good pension. It's no more than it ought to."

"You—you mustn't count on that. You—we must all of us prepare for the worst, the very worst."

"What skittles, Mater! What can they do to us, unless, of course, Daphne wasn't sent to Clairdelune. But I saw her in the car myself."

"It—it doesn't follow that—that she got there, Clarence."

"Why on earth shouldn't she?"

"The Baron might—might have missed the way somehow."

"Not he! He may be an old foozle, but the storks know their job, anyhow."

"We mustn't make too sure—of anything," said his mother, who had the best reasons for knowing that Miss Heritage would never be found either in Clairdelune or Märchenland, and that a shameful and probably exceedingly painful death on the scaffold was their inevitable fate.

It was terrible to think that she, the acknowledged head and master-mind of the family, had brought them to such an end as this—more terrible still to see both her son and husband so utterly unprepared for it. Her nerves were jarred and fretted by King Sidney's apathy and Clarence's light-hearted optimism, and the impossibility of arousing them to a proper sense of their position. She could only do that by confessing what she had done—and she shuddered at the mere thought. If it would save them—but nothing would do that now! No, she could not lower herself so immeasurably in their esteem; she would carry her secret with her to the block itself!

"Now, Mater," said Clarence, "you mustn't give way to the blues like this. You can take it from me that we're as right as rain. So cheer up, and let's see you smiling again."

The unhappy Queen made a heroic attempt at a smile, but the result was so extraordinarily ghastly that it disheartened even Clarence.

"Oh, very well, Mater," he said, "you needn't—if it hurts you as much as all that. But you've been so plucky up to now, I never thought you'd come out as a wet blanket!"

Even Marie Antoinette herself, thought Queen Selina bitterly, had never had to bear being called a wet blanket!

CHAPTER XXI

"WHOSE LIGHTS ARE FLED, WHOSE GARLANDS DEAD"

Daphne had taken her seat in the car with somewhat conflicting feelings. She was going to Clairdelune, where she would be reunited to Giroflé—an altogether joyous prospect, if she could hope to find the Giroflé with whom she had last parted. But he was now the magnificent young Prince Mirliflor, and it was quite uncertain whether she would even be able to recognise him. It would be dreadful if she discovered that she did not care for him any longer! Perhaps it was anxiety, but still more probably the fact of her Fairy blood that prevented her from being overcome by the somnolence that none of purely British birth seemed able to resist for long after entering that magic car.

Daphne was not in the least drowsy, and thus was startled, after the Palace and Eswareinmal had vanished out of sight, by hearing the Baron suddenly order the storks to go to the Chapel in the forest of Schlangenzweigen, and seeing them wheel in a direction she knew was not that of their original destination. "What are you doing, Baron?" she cried. "I thought you were to take me straight to Clairdelune?"

The Baron put his hand to his heart (which he had once more been obliged to compress by a metal hoop) before he could speak. "It is now time," he began, "that you should be told who you are, Madam, and the glorious future that awaits you." And, with a prolixity that may here be avoided, he informed her of her right to the crown of Märchenland and of the Marshal's arrangements for placing her on the throne.

"But I don't want to be placed on the throne!" said Daphne. "Do you really think I should turn out these poor Wibberley-Stimpsons now—when they behaved so decently in letting me go? It would be too horribly mean of me if I did."

At this he thought it his duty to enlighten her upon Queen Selina's perfidy, which naturally altered Daphne's opinion, but did not shake her determination.

"If she is so keen about her crown she may keep it," she said. "All I care for now is to get to Clairdelune and see Giroflé—I mean Mirliflor."

"But," objected the Baron, employing the Marshal's argument, "we should arrive there days before the Prince."

"Then," said Daphne imperiously, "tell the storks to take us to him—wherever he is."

"If I did so," he objected, "the Marshal's plan would fall through!"

"And what if it does? How do you know that he's to be trusted? I always thought myself he had a bad face, and I don't feel at all inclined to put myself in his power. So you will please not be a pig, Baron, but do as I say."

No doubt her diction should have been more on a level with her dignity, but then it must be remembered that she had not been brought up as a prospective Fairy Queen.

"I am convinced," he persisted, "that the Marshal's devotion to your Majesty's cause is beyond suspicion."

"And I'm quite sure that it isn't," retorted Daphne. "If, as you tell me, Baron, I am your Queen, it's your duty to obey my orders, and I order you to take me to Mirliflor." He did not venture to oppose her any longer, so he gave the necessary command, and the great birds wheeled round once more towards Clairdelune.

Mirliflor had discovered, after accomplishing a third of his journey, that his horse had suddenly gone so lame that it was unable to proceed at any pace but a walk. He had dismounted, and was leading it until he could reach a hostelry and provide himself with a fresh steed, when he heard a loud throbbing in the air behind him. The next moment a large flight of storks passed over his head and descended with a car on a spot some yards in advance of him. He saw at once that one of the occupants was Daphne, and leaving his horse by the wayside he went forward to meet her, not without some constraint and uncertainty, however, for his fear that she would love him no longer had not ceased to haunt him.

She had alighted and was standing still, her face expressing wonder and something of alarm. Could this splendid gallant cavalier really be her homely Giroflé? she was thinking, and if he were, how could he help her to overcome this paralysing sense of his being a stranger? He came towards her, feeling almost as shy as she.

"Daphne! my dearest!" he said, stretching out his arms, "am I so changed that you can't care for me any more?" And, as she heard his voice, all her doubts and apprehensions suddenly fled.

"No," she murmured, placing a fair hand on each of his broad shoulders and looking fearlessly up into his face. "You are just the same, really. My very own Giroflé! And, oh, I'm so glad!"

"And you forgive me for deceiving you, dearest?" he asked when the first rapture of meeting and reassurance was over. "I was bound in honour to tell you nothing."

"I know," she said; "the Court Godmother is to blame for that—not you. And I was prepared to find you changed, Gir—Mirliflor—only—not quite so changed as this."

"If you would love me better as I was, darling," he said, "tell me so, and I will make her transform me again. I will become Giroflé for the rest of my life—rather than lose you!"

"I don't think she is well enough to be asked to do that now," replied Daphne. "And, besides"—and here she held him from her at arm's length—"besides, now I look at you, you really are rather nice, you know! No, darling, I won't have you altered again."

After all, this was only in accordance with Märchenland's precedents. Did Beauty, for instance, resent her Beast's emergence into a Prince? All the same, Daphne was a little ashamed of herself for the increasing satisfaction she felt in Mirliflor's good looks—it seemed almost an infidelity to Giroflé—but she could not help it, and did not even try.

The Baron had tactfully remained with the storks until, in his opinion, it was time to interrupt the lovers, when he stepped towards them, cracking loudly.

"Sire," he said, "accept my congratulations on a good fortune that is perchance even greater than you yet know. You have won a lady who is not only lovely, but, as I shall show you, no other than the daughter of our late Prince Chrysopras, and thus rightfully entitled to the crown of Märchenland."

"And you knew this, Daphne?" cried Mirliflor when the Baron had concluded. "Why did you say nothing to me about it?"

"I only heard of it myself just now in the car," she said. "And what does it matter? I don't want to claim the crown—all I want is to live at Clairdelune with you."

But he told her it was her duty to her Country to assert her just rights, and, on being informed of the appointment with the Marshal, he was in favour of keeping it. "He will be useful," he said, "if he is an honest supporter of your cause."

"But I'm quite certain he isn't!" said Daphne.

"We can only make sure by meeting him," he replied, "and as of course I shall be with you, you will be in no danger."

He had no weapon but the sword that had served him so well at Drachenstolz, which he had brought away with him rather as a souvenir than with any idea that he might need it on his journey, but Daphne felt that, so long as Mirliflor was at her side, she had nothing to fear, and so she readily consented to re-enter the car and be taken to the Chapel in the forest, where the Marshal in all probability was awaiting her arrival.

As the car neared the borders of the forest, Mirliflor took out the silk cap which the Baron had lent him. "I meant to have returned this to you, Baron," he said, "but I find I have it still. With your permission, I will keep it a little longer, as I fancy it may be useful. Don't be alarmed, darling," he added to Daphne, "if you don't see me when I put this on. Remember that, though I shall be invisible, I shall be near you all the time."

"I'll try to remember, Mirliflor," said Daphne. "But—but don't stay invisible longer than you can possibly help."

The Chapel stood in a clearing in the very middle of the forest, and the storks calculated their descent with such nicety that they brought the car up in front of the door.

The Marshal, in his plumed helmet, golden cuirass, and high boots of gilded leather, was waiting, and now came forward to help Daphne to alight. His vizor was raised, but the company of knights with him wore theirs down, so that it was impossible for her to know who they were or whether they intended her good or ill.

"We expected you long ere this, Lady Daphne," said the Marshal as he handed her out.

"Did you, Marshal?" she said, trying to appear unconcerned. "We went a little out of our way." She noticed that, either by accident or design, several of the knights had interposed themselves between herself and the Baron.

"We have the less time at our disposal," said the Marshal, "so I will come to the point at once. You have no doubt been already informed of your rights, and that I and my companions are here to place you on the throne, provided you accept my conditions?"

"I—I was not told of any conditions," said Daphne.

"There is but one," he said, and at this the Chapel door was thrown open and a priest of extremely disreputable exterior appeared on the threshold, with the lighted altar as his background. "Wed me— and you shall be Queen of Märchenland."

"I've no wish to be that," she replied, "and, as you know, Marshal, I have already promised to marry Prince Mirliflor."

"You may dismiss all thought of that," he said blandly, "for if you refuse my hand, both you and the Baron will meet with instant death, the car and birds will also be destroyed and buried, and I have so arranged that it will be believed that her Majesty Queen Selina has had you removed to the distant land from which you came."

"Marshal," pleaded Daphne, trying hard to remember that Mirliflor was really by her side, "I must have time—time to think over your—your proposal."

"It may help you to decide, Lady Daphne," he said, "if you reflect that, in any case, you will never again behold Prince Mirliflor of Clairdelune."

"And why not, Marshal?" said Mirliflor, as he flung away the cap of darkness and stepped in front of his beloved.

The Marshal knew at once that his fate was sealed. He stood no chance whatever against a Prince who had slain a dragon singlehanded. The knights also seemed to recognise this, or else their sympathy had veered to Daphne's side, for they stood back in a circle without attempting to interfere, while the priest, who perhaps had not till then understood that the marriage ceremony was to be compulsory, promptly re-entered the little Chapel and blew out all the candles.

The combat was over in a second or two—as any combat would necessarily be in which one of the antagonists was equipped with an irresistible sword. Mirliflor, to be sure, did not know that he possessed this somewhat unsportsmanlike advantage, and had disdained to shelter himself, as he might have done, under the cap. But it is more than possible that if he had known more about the sword, he would have stretched the point of honour in this particular case. As has already been seen, he had occasional lapses from the ideals the Fairy had bestowed on him at his baptism, and he was quite incapable of troubling himself about them when Daphne's life was at stake. Perhaps he ought to have been more consistently punctilious, but he was not—which was fortunate for both of them.

As soon as the knights saw the Marshal fall, they hastened to protest their loyalty to their young Queen and offer their congratulations, which Daphne thought it politic to accept at their face value. Horses were found for her and Mirliflor, who decided to make, with a picked body of the knights, for a village a league from Eswareinmal and await developments there. Of the rest of the party, some were instructed to go back to the Palace and report the Marshal's death while hunting, the rest remained to bury his body, and it was one of these who found the packet, and, most unluckily for Queen Selina, thought it necessary to deliver it in hot haste to its addressee.

The Baron was directed to go on in the car to Clairdelune and inform King Tournesol that his son had found a bride at last.

On reaching the village near Eswareinmal, Mirliflor had sent on two of his escort into the city to ascertain the state of feeling there. They brought back the unexpected news that all the citizens now knew that the Lady Daphne was entitled to the Crown and were demanding her; that Queen Selina, with her husband and son, had been imprisoned on suspicion of having made away with her, and, if she were not forthcoming by an early date, would be executed publicly without fail.

In the heat of his resentment at the treachery which had so nearly succeeded in parting him from Daphne for ever, Mirliflor declared that they should be left to the doom which they would certainly meet if Daphne's return were kept secret for a few days.

"Mirliflor said that—not Giroflé," she told him. "Giroflé would never be so horribly cold-blooded. But even Mirliflor didn't really mean it! Of course we can't let these Stimpson people be executed. Besides, I know—I can't say how, but I do know—that Mr. Stimpson and Clarence, at any rate, haven't been parties to any plot to get rid of me. And as for Mrs. Stimpson, I dislike her, and I want to go on disliking her—which I couldn't possibly do after she had her head cut off! So we'll go into Eswareinmal at once, Mirliflor, and do what we can for the poor things."

"I spoke in haste, dearest," said Mirliflor. "I was wrong, and you are right as usual."

"And now we're both going to be right, darling!" said Daphne.

"I wish," Clarence remarked later the same day, "I wish these windows looked out on the front. We might see her coming back in that blessed stork-car. She'll be sure to come the quickest way when she hears we're in the soup like this—don't you think so, Mater?"

"I'm sure I don't know!" said the tortured Queen Selina. "She mayn't come back at all. I mean, she may keep the messengers and leave us to perish. It is only what I should expect of her!"

"No, dash it all, Mater, she's too much of a sport for that," he said. "She'll either turn up or send word that she's all right."

"Don't deceive yourself, Clarence!" said his mother. "I know better than you can, and I tell you that she will do neither."

"Not when it's to save our lives?" he replied. "She's bound to—unless—unless anything has happened to her. I'm a bit worried about that, because—well, time's getting on, you know—what?"

"I trust, my boy," said his father, "we shall not be brought to the—er—scaffold by any mistake of that kind. If that occurred, it would be most un—" he caught his wife's eye and substituted "unsatisfactory. I'm not sure," he added, "but I fancy I hear shouting. Seems to come from below."

"It certainly is shouting," said Clarence, "and it's getting louder. They're coming this way. I—I hope I'm wrong—but I've a strong impression that we're going to get it in the neck after all!"

"Sidney! Clarence!" cried Queen Selina, as she sank on her knees, unable to bear her guilty burden any longer. "I—I can't die without asking you to forgive me for—for what I have brought on you!"

"It's no fault of yours, Mater," said Clarence. "Just the family luck, that's all!"

"Ah, but listen—listen!" implored his Mother; but, before she could proceed, the door was suddenly unlocked, and Prince Tapfer von Schneiderleinheimer entered with every sign of respect.

"I am charged by her Majesty Queen Daphne to desire your attendance in the Throne Room," he said, "and to convey her and Prince Mirliflor's regret that you should have been subjected to any inconvenience by having permitted her departure to Clairdelune."

Queen Selina—or rather Mrs. Wibberley-Stimpson, as she was now once more—hastily rose from her knees. So the Baron had disobeyed his orders, and Miss Heritage did not even know that they had been given! This was indeed an unhoped-for deliverance. What a mercy, she thought, that it had come just before she had spoken words she could never have recalled! "Kindly assure—your Mistress," she said, with all the dignity of fallen grandeur, "that while we cannot but feel that we have been most unjustly suspected, we are willing to make every allowance for the circumstances, and shall have much pleasure in coming down to offer our congratulations presently. But first I want to see the Princess Royal and Princess Ruby if they are well enough to leave their dungeons."

"Your daughters, Madam, have merely been required to remain in their own apartments, and are in perfect health," he replied; "I will have them conducted to you immediately."

"Oh, Mummy!" exclaimed Ruby a little later, as she ran to her Mother's arms, "is it really true? Aren't you and Daddy King and Queen any more?"

"No, my darling," said Mrs. Wibberley-Stimpson, "it seems the people would rather have Miss Heritage."

"Oh, I don't mind so much if it's Daphne. And will Prince Mirliflor be King?"

"I really can't say how they will arrange it—nor does it interest me what they may do."

"It does me," said Ruby. "I hope they'll let us stay here with them."

"I consider it most unlikely—even if I were willing to be a guest in my own Palace. But I've no doubt they will make some suitable provision for us."

"Speaking for myself, Mother," said Edna, "I should be far happier leading a simple life in retirement than ever I've been in this pretentious place. And, though I never cared much about being a Princess, we can scarcely be treated as commoners after what we have been."

"I shall settle all these matters myself with Miss Herit—Queen Daphne, I suppose I ought to call her, but it's so difficult to get into just at once. And now I think we will all go down to the Throne Room.

Remember on no account to show the slightest ill-feeling. Let her see that, if we have lost everything else, we still retain our manners."

She was herself so far from betraying any ill-feeling when she entered the Throne Room that she was almost overwhelmingly affectionate.

"My dear child!" she said, advancing to Daphne, who was standing in the centre of the room with Mirliflor, "so pleased to see you both back! but we're all of us that! And, as I was saying to His—to my husband—only a few minutes ago, 'I'm sure, Sidney,' I said, 'there's no person in the world I would give up my crown to so willingly as I would to dear Miss Heritage!'"

"Most happy," said her husband. "We've abdicated already, your—your Majesty—both of us—as soon as we knew the facts."

"I—I'm most awfully glad to see your Majesty back again," said Clarence, noting the flush on her cheeks and the sparkle in her eyes as she glanced at Mirliflor, whom he envied more than ever. "I was beginning to think I—er—shouldn't—you ran things a trifle close."

"Perhaps I did," said Daphne, "but you see, I thought it was wiser to try to find Mirliflor, before being taken to—to Clairdelune." She said this quite simply, for she could see that, as she had been sure of from the first, both Clarence and his father were no parties to Mrs. Stimpson's design, and she was anxious to spare them all knowledge of it if she could.

Her words only confirmed Mrs. Wibberley-Stimpson's sense of security; Daphne evidently suspected nothing, probably because the false Marshal had never handed the Baron his secret instructions. "Much the best plan, I'm sure, your Majesty!" she agreed, "though it was fortunate for us that you found dear Prince Mirliflor so soon. However, it has all ended happily, so we will say no more about it. And now I want to beg that you mustn't consider Us. If you would like to have possession of the Palace at once, you have only to say so. Or if I could be of any use to you by staying on for a little, just to show you how things ought to be done—?"

Daphne forced herself to be civil to her for her family's sake, not her own.

"It is very good of you," she said, "but I'm afraid it won't be possible for you to stay here."

"Well," said Mrs. Wibberley-Stimpson, "we shall be perfectly satisfied with any residence—if it's only quite a moderate-sized castle—that your Majesty is good enough to put at our disposal. Not too far from here, or poor Ruby"—here she glanced at her younger daughter, who had taken possession of one of Daphne's hands, which she was kissing and fondling—"would be quite inconsolable at losing her dearest friend!"

But her remarks were lost on Daphne, for just then, to Mrs. Stimpson's surprise and secret dismay, the entrance was formally announced of the Court Godmother, whom she had imagined to be at least moribund, if not dead. She came in, looking frail and feeble, but still with much of the energy and vitality that had seemed to have departed for ever.

"Really," thought the disgusted Mrs. Wibberley-Stimpson, "Mother Hubbard's dog is a fool to her!"

Daphne had already gone to greet her and lead her to a seat. "I'm much better, my child—in fact almost as well as ever. A day or two ago I thought I was dying—but a little rest and the good news of your return have quite set me up again. I begin to think I shall see my second century out yet!"

"It is indeed a marvellous recovery, my dear Court Godmother!" chimed in Mrs. Wibberley-Stimpson. "We've all been so anxious! We should have sent to inquire, only we couldn't—because—well, you'll hardly believe it, but we've been imprisoned (and very nearly executed, too!) on a ridiculous charge of having made away with our dear young Queen here! When, as you know, I had actually gone out of my way to have her sent to Clairdelune as soon as I found you were too ill to see to it yourself."

"And well for you that you did so!" said the grim old Fairy, "for if you had played—or even sought to play—her false, I would have seen to it—old and ailing as I am—that such treason did not go unpunished!"

Mrs. Wibberley-Stimpson shivered inwardly under the implacable old eyes; she knew well that she could expect no mercy if the Fairy discovered that these secret orders had ever been handed to the Baron. Only, as the Baron had never received them, he could tell her nothing, and as the Council now believed them to be a forgery of the Marshal's, Mrs. Stimpson felt herself fairly safe.

"Yes, dear Court Godmother," she said sweetly; "but you see, I haven't—so we needn't discuss that now, need we? When you came in just now, I was just telling her Majesty that we had no desire to stay on at the Palace longer than is unavoidable, but that, naturally, we were anxious to know where accommodation would be found for us—nothing grand, of course, any fairly large château would suit us."

"I'm sorry," said Daphne, after stooping to kiss Ruby, "but that is quite impossible."

"Impossible?" cried Mrs. Wibberley-Stimpson. "I can't believe that your Majesty would turn us out of our own Palace, without a home to go to!"

"You have 'Inglegarth,'" said Daphne, "and as soon as the Baron returns with the car he shall take you there."

"I am much obliged to your Majesty," returned Mrs. Wibberley-Stimpson, her complexion deepening to a rich purple, "very much obliged for such truly generous treatment! Some people might think that, considering that you wouldn't be Queen at all but for our kindness in taking you with us, when we were brought here—by no seeking of ours—to reign over this ridiculous country—I say, some people might call this rather shabby and ungrateful. Especially when we gave way the moment we were told there had been a mistake—sooner than make any fuss or trouble—as few Sovereigns in our position would have done! And now it seems we're to be rewarded by being bundled back to a suburban residence which, whatever else may be said for it, is absurdly inadequate for any retired Royalties! But you will find we are not to be got rid of quite so easily. I absolutely decline to go back to Gablehurst to be an ordinary nobody after what I have been. Nothing in the world shall induce me to!"

"My love," said her husband, "we can't stay here if we're not wanted."

"No, Mater," said Clarence, "we've got to clear."

"I shall be thankful to get away myself," added Edna. "What is Märchenland, after all?—just a petty little Kingdom that nobody even knows is in existence!"

"You may go if you please," Mrs. Stimpson declared. "I shall stay—if I have to sit and starve to death at the Palace Gates! And a pretty scandal that will be!"

"If you were allowed to starve," said the Fairy Vogelflug—"which you wouldn't be, you'd get food enough—but no sympathy. So I should advise you myself to return to your own Country, where you are probably held in more esteem than you are here. And now," she added to Daphne, "I must ask your Majesty's leave to withdraw to my own apartments. I shall be obliged if you would send the Baron to me as soon as he arrives from Clairdelune." And with this, and a stiff but stately curtsey to the young Queen, she hobbled out of the Throne Room.

"I shall maintain to my dying breath," declared Mrs. Stimpson vehemently, "that, after governing this Country as we have done, we have earned the right to stay in it. I consider we are not only entitled to that, but to a suitable establishment and pension. Your Majesty can surely spare us something out of all we have given up!"

Daphne intimated that she wished to reply to Mrs. Stimpson in private, whereupon the others withdrew out of hearing and left them together.

"I hate having to say it," she began in a low voice, "but you really can't stay here on any terms, Mrs. Stimpson—I think I needn't tell you why."

"Your Majesty surely doesn't suspect me of any—?"

"I don't suspect," said Daphne, "I know how you tried to part me from Prince Mirliflor for ever—and how nearly you succeeded. He knows, too.... Oh, you are in no danger from us—we shall say nothing. But there is someone else who might."

"Not—not the Baron?" cried Mrs. Wibberley-Stimpson, so thrown off her guard that she failed to see how completely the question gave her away.

"Yes," said Daphne gravely, "the Baron. You heard what the Court Godmother said about seeing him as soon as he returns? We have forbidden him to speak—but it's quite possible that she will get the truth out of him—and that might be rather disagreeable for you, mightn't it?"

"Very," agreed the trembling Mrs. Stimpson. "She'd have no mercy on me—on any of us!"

"I'm afraid not," said Daphne, "and she might not listen even to me. So—don't you think it would be wiser to change your mind about staying and go back to Gablehurst before she does see him?"

"Much," said Mrs. Wibberley-Stimpson in a half-choked voice—"much! if—if it can be arranged."

"I think it can. The journey to Clairdelune and back won't tire the storks—they will be quite able to take you over to England as soon as you are ready to start."

"We'll go and get ready at once," said Mrs. Stimpson, "so as not to keep the car waiting."

"You have plenty of time. It can't be here for some hours yet."

"Oh, I hope the Baron will make haste—and—and if your Majesty could only prevent him from seeing the Court Godmother till after we are gone!"

"She will probably be asleep," said Daphne, "but in any case he shall have instructions to take you home the very moment he arrives at the Palace. I think," she added, "that is all we had to say to one another."

"Except," said Mrs. Wibberley-Stimpson, "that your Majesty really must allow me to express my deep sense of the very handsome—"

"No, please!" said Daphne, turning away, for she felt that she had had as much of Mrs. Stimpson as she could stand just then.

That good lady, having partially recovered her equanimity, retreated to her husband and family.

"I've been talking it over with her Majesty, Sidney," she announced, "and she has quite brought me to see that, under the circumstances, we shall really be more comfortable in dear old England. So she has kindly arranged for us to be taken home in the car directly it gets back from Clairdelune."

"Glad to hear it, my love," said the ex-Monarch. "Personally, I much prefer 'Inglegarth' to this sort of thing."

"But I say," Clarence put in, glancing down at his fantastic attire, "I don't quite see myself going back to Gablehurst in this get up. Wish I knew what had become of the kit we came in!"

It was now the hour when the Court was accustomed to go up and change their costumes before dinner, and Daphne felt a difficulty as to the proper course to pursue with the Wibberley-Stimpsons. Could she without indelicacy invite them to sit as guests at what had lately been their own table? And yet it seemed hardly human to leave them out. She decided that the former course was on the whole less open to objection.

"I hope," she said to Mrs. Stimpson, with a touch of shyness, "that you will all give me the pleasure of dining with us this evening? You see, you must have something to eat before such a long journey."

"Your Majesty is most kind," said Mrs. Stimpson in a great flurry, "but, if you will excuse us from accepting what—no one knows better than I—is really a command, I—I really don't think we should have time to sit through a long dinner. We—we might miss the car—and besides, there's the question of dressing. If we could have a few sandwiches and a little wine in one of the vestibules while we are waiting for the car, that will be all we shall require!"

"You shall do exactly as you please about it," replied Daphne. She was greatly relieved, as one reason for her hesitation in asking them had been the dread that Mr. Stimpson might think himself called upon to make an after-dinner speech.

Her ladies-in-waiting were already in her Tiring-Chamber, highly delighted by the prospect of arraying a Queen whom, even when she had been nominally one of themselves, they had always not merely admired but adored.

It had suddenly occurred to Daphne that the Stimpson family might find themselves on their return to Gablehurst in certain difficulties against which she felt bound to do what she could to protect them.

She thought over the best means of doing this, which took so much time to carry out that the business of arraying her for her first banquet as a Royal Hostess had to be got through more hurriedly than her ladies of the Bedchamber thought at all decorous.

But she knew that Mirliflor would be well content with her, however she looked—and as a matter of fact he not only was, but had every reason to be so.

The Wibberley-Stimpsons had already ascertained that the clothes they had worn on their arrival in Märchenland had been carefully laid up in one of the Royal wardrobes, from which they were brought at their earnest request. They put them on in frantic haste, and, in deadly fear of being surprised by the Royal Household, they stole down the great Staircase to an antechamber by the Entrance Hall. There they found a table set with every description of tempting food, to which all did justice but Mrs. Stimpson, the state of whose nerves had entirely taken away her appetite. She was continually starting up and saying, "Listen! I'm sure I hear these storks!"

"You'd better eat something, Mater," Clarence said. "It's the last dinner we shall ever have in Märchenland."

"I can't," she replied, "I don't know how any of you can.... There go the silver trumpets! She's going into the Banqueting Hall now. On Prince Mirliflor's arm, most likely! How she can have the heart when she must know we are still here!"

"She did ask us to dinner, my love," Mr. Stimpson mildly reminded her.

"She had the execrable taste to do that, Sidney," replied his wife, "and I think the manner in which I declined must have been a lesson to her.... Dear me, is that car never coming?"

She said that many times during the evening, as they sat on in the ebony and ivory chamber, while the strains of music reached them faintly from the distant Ballroom.

Clarence thought gloomily of the dance on the night of the Coronation, and how his mother had forbidden him to choose Daphne as his partner. Perhaps, if he had insisted on having his own way—if he had not limited himself to a merely morganatic alliance, she might have—but it was too late to grouse about that now! He endeavoured to cheer himself by the thought that he would very soon be in a civilised land of cigarettes.

It was getting late, and the music had now ceased, from which they gathered that the Queen and Court had already retired. "She might have had the common civility to say good-bye to us!" complained Mrs. Stimpson, "but of course she is too grand now to condescend so far! Not that I have any desire to see her again. On the contrary!"

The doors of the Vestibule were thrown open here and one of the ushers announced: "Her Majesty the Queen and His Royal Highness Prince Mirliflor."

"Coming here to triumph over us!" was Mrs. Stimpson's comment as she rose.

"We came to wish you a pleasant journey to Gablehurst," explained Daphne, as she entered, followed by Mirliflor. "I hope you won't have to wait for the car much longer, but I've told the attendants in the Hall to let you know the minute it is here."

She was looking radiantly lovely and girlish—and queenly as well, in spite of the fact that she was still uncrowned. But if she had had the right to wear her crown, she was incapable of doing so just then.

Mrs. Wibberley-Stimpson made a curtsey that might have been lower if she had had any practice—but all the curtseying previously had been done to herself. "We thank your Majesty," she said. "I too hope there will be no more of this delay. I am getting worn out with all this waiting. Oh, while I think of it," she went on (the desire to be offensive overcoming any fear of the consequences), "of course we are not in a position now to give really valuable wedding presents—and I'm afraid mine must be a very humble offering, particularly as it needs repairing. However, such as it is, perhaps your Majesty will honour me by accepting it with our congratulations and very best wishes?" And she offered the jewel which she had formerly acquired from Daphne. Daphne's eyebrows contracted for an instant, but the next moment she laughed.

"I really couldn't, Mrs. Wibberley-Stimpson!" she said. "You see, you have already given it to Clarence, and I mustn't deprive him of it."

"Won't you accept it from me, then?" he said awkwardly. "I—I shan't have any use for it now."

She shook her head. "You will please me so much better by keeping it," she said gently—"in memory of Märchenland."

It was true that it had once belonged to her father—the father she had never known—but then it had also belonged to Mrs. Wibberley-Stimpson, and Daphne was conscious now of an invincible unwillingness to accept any gift from that lady.

"I—I'd do anything to please you," said Clarence, taking the pendant from his mother and slipping it into the pocket of his dinner-jacket.

Ruby, in the white silk frock she had last worn at "Inglegarth," was clinging to Daphne. "I don't want to go back!" she wailed, "I want to stay here with you. Won't you send for me some day? Say you will; do say you will!"

Daphne stooped to caress and comfort her, and also to hide her own emotion. "I wish I could, darling," she said tenderly, "but I'm afraid, I'm afraid I mustn't make any promises that I'm not sure of being able to keep."

"Then say you will—perhaps!" entreated Ruby, but her mother promptly interposed.

"Ruby, my dear," she said, "you're forgetting how far her Majesty is now our superior. A Palace is no longer a fit place for any of us to visit, and I consider it best we should remain in future strictly in our respective spheres."

"Then I will go to mine at once," said Daphne, smiling. "Good-bye, Mrs. Wibberley-Stimpson. Good-bye, Edna." She held out her hand to both of them, but they curtsied formally without offering to take it. "Good-bye, dearest little Ruby—I hope your next governess will love you nearly as much as I do—she can't quite! Good-bye, Mr. Stimpson—I think you will be rather glad to be back in the City again, won't you?"

"I shall, indeed, your Majesty," he said. "To tell you the honest truth, I don't think I was ever cut out for a monarch."

It was Clarence's turn next, and when he saw her offering him her hand with the old frank friendliness, he had a renewed sense of his own unworthiness.

"No," he said in a low voice, "you can't want to shake hands with—with such a hopeless rotter as I've been!"

"I shouldn't," she replied, "if I weren't sure that you could be something very much better if you chose. And I know you will choose."

"I will," he said, "I swear I will—if I ever get the chance!"

"Your chance will come. Quite soon, perhaps. And when it does, remember that I believe in you—and, good-bye, Clarence."

"Good-bye—Daphne," he said brokenly. As he took her hand he thought with a keen pang that he had never held it before, and never would again. And the time had been—or so at least he imagined—when he might have made that hand his own for ever!

"Good night, Mirliflor," said Daphne, as he held aside the hangings for her. "We shall meet to-morrow."

She passed into the great Hall with a dignity the more charming for being so natural and unconscious—and that was the last Clarence was ever destined to see of her.

He turned to Mirliflor, whose eyes still betrayed the pride he felt in his beloved. "I don't mind telling you, old chap—er—Prince Mirliflor, that I took to you from the start, and—as I can't be the lucky man myself, I'm jolly glad it's to be you!"

"Thank you," said Mirliflor, who was less given to florid phrases than the average Fairy Prince. "So am I."

"I dare say," Clarence went on, as he realised the contrast between his own clothes and the magnificent costume that the old Fairy had provided for her royal godson, "I dare say you're thinking we're not looking very smart?"

Mirliflor was honestly able to disclaim having any impressions on the subject.

"Well, these togs must seem a bit rummy to you—but I can assure you that, for informal occasions like the present, they're quite the right thing in England." (He had a momentary impulse to except his father's white tie, but, after all, why should he say anything about that when Mirliflor knew no better? So he decided to pass it), "Worn by the very best Society."

Mirliflor politely accepted this information, and then made his farewells. Edna's good wishes were couched in a spirit of frigid magnanimity. She had too much self-respect to let him perceive that she resented his fickleness.

They were now alone in the antechamber. From time to time Mrs. Wibberley-Stimpson would rise impatiently and peer out into the vast hall, now only lit by one or two flickering cressets, to see if the stork-car had arrived—but the attendants in waiting always assured her that it had not, and, after some fussing and fretting, she lay down on a divan and fell into an uneasy slumber.

Her husband was snoring placidly; Ruby had cried herself to sleep long before; Edna had brought down her lecture-notes, and was conscientiously employing the time in polishing up her knowledge of English Literature.

Her notes on Nietzsche's philosophy had been torn out after the rupture with the Count. Somehow the Nietzschean theories did not seem to work quite well when carried into practice. But, after deciphering a very few Literature notes, Edna found herself too drowsy to continue.

Clarence remained awake longest. He had wandered restlessly out into the hall just to look at the great Staircase half lost in the gloom. Daphne had ascended it a little while since. To-morrow she would come down, fresh and radiant, to meet Mirliflor. Before long they would be married and crowned, and live happy ever after in the good old Märchenland way. Well, he wouldn't have to look on and see them doing it, which was some consolation. He went back to the antechamber and regarded the sleeping forms of his family with disillusioned eyes. "We look like Royalties—I don't think!" he said to himself. "No wonder they've booted us out. Why, a bally rabbit-warren would!"

But this depressing reflection soon ceased to trouble him, unless it still continued to shadow his dreams.

CHAPTER XXII

SQUARING ACCOUNTS

Almost simultaneously Mr. Wibberley-Stimpson and his son and daughters opened their eyes, then rubbed them, and sat up and looked about them with a bewilderment that gradually gave way to intense relief. For, although the light had faded, their surroundings were reassuringly familiar. They were in their own drawing-room at "Inglegarth." It occurred at once to most of them that they had never actually left it—an impression that was pleasantly confirmed by Mrs. Wibberley-Stimpson's first remark as she awoke later.

"Why, hasn't the dinner-gong gone yet?" she inquired crossly. "Cook gets more and more unpunctual!"

"I don't think it can be eight o'clock yet, my dear," said her husband, "it's quite light still."

"Nonsense, Sidney, it must be long past dinner-time! I've been so lost in my own thoughts that somehow I"

"Now, Mother, you know you've been asleep and only just woke up!" said Edna, from one of the chintz couches.

"Have I? Perhaps I did drop off just for a few seconds. In fact I must have done—for I begin to recollect having quite a curious dream. I dreamed that you and I, Sidney, were King and Queen of some absurd fairy Kingdom or other, and that—well, it was not at all a pleasant dream."

"It's a most singular coincidence, Selina," he said, "but I've been dreaming much the same sort of thing myself!"

The others looked at one another, but none of them ventured to express just yet what was in all their minds.

"Have you?" said his wife languidly. "I suppose it was telepathy or something of that kind. Ring for Mitchell, Clarence—I hope dinner has not been allowed to get cold. And—and Miss Heritage seems to have left the drawing-room. Run up, Ruby, and tell her to come down."

"I don't believe she's upstairs at all, mummy," said Ruby. "No, of course she can't be. We left her in the Palace—don't you remember? She's Queen now, you know?"

"Queen! Miss Heritage! Why, you don't mean to tell me you've been dreaming that too?"

"So have I, as far as that goes, mater," said Clarence. "If it was a dream, and not—not—"

"How could it be anything else? Besides, here we all are, exactly as we were!"

"We've got our cloaks and things on, though," said Ruby. "I know how it was! We've been brought here in the stork-car while we were fast asleep. We sat up ever so long waiting for it."

"It can't be! I won't believe anything so absurd. Draw the curtains, somebody, and pull up the blinds.... It's odd, but it certainly looks more like early morning than any other time. Clarence, go out and strike the gong. Perhaps the maids haven't finished dressing yet."

Clarence went out accordingly. The gong bellowed and boomed from the hall, but there was no sound of stirring above. "I say," he reported, "I've just looked into the dining-room, and all the chairs are upside down on the table. That looks rather as if we'd been away for a bit—what?"

"Clarence! You're not beginning to think that—that all that about our having been a Royal Family may be true?"

"Well, Mater," he said, "if we haven't been in Märchenland, where have we been? Oh yes, we've been Royalties right enough—and a pretty rotten job we made of it!"

At this time there was a deprecatory knock at the drawing-room door. "Mitchell!" cried her mistress, "don't you know better than to—?" However, it was not Mitchell that entered—but a person unknown—a respectable-looking elderly female, who seemed to have made a hasty toilette.

"Askin' your pardons," she said, "but if you were wishing to see the family, they're away just now."

"We are the family," replied Mrs. Wibberley-Stimpson. "We have been—er—abroad, but have returned. And we should be glad of breakfast at once."

"I can git you a cup of tea as soon as the kittle's on the boil," she said, "but I'm only put in as caretaker like, and I've nothink in the 'ouse except bread and butter. The shops'll be opening now, so if you don't object to waiting a little, I could go out and get you a naddick and eggs and such like."

"Yes, buck up, old lady!" said Clarence, "and I say, see if you can get a Daily Mail or a paper of some sort."

"What are you so anxious to see the paper for?" inquired Edna after the caretaker had departed.

"Only wanted to know what month we're in," he said. "It would have looked so silly to ask her what day it is. We must have been—over there—a good long time."

"At least a year!" said Mrs. Wibberley-Stimpson, no longer able to sustain the dream theory. "More. When we left it was quite early Spring—and now all the trees are out! Sidney, what will your firm say to your having been away so long without letting them know where you were?"

"I can't say, my love. I'm afraid they might make it a ground for a dissolution of partnership—unless I can give them a satisfactory explanation of my absence."

"The difficulty will be to find one!" said his wife. "As for you, Clarence, they will be too glad to see you back again at the Insurance Office to ask any questions."

"I dare say they would, Mater, only—it didn't seem worth mentioning before—but, as a matter of fact, I—er—resigned the day we left."

"Then it seems," said Mrs. Wibberley-Stimpson bitterly, "we have been sent back here to find ourselves in comparative poverty! I hope and trust"—she felt furtively in her bead handbag before continuing more cheerfully—"that we shall be able to struggle through somehow."

She knew now that they would not be without resources. She could feel them through the handkerchief in which they had been wrapped—two pieces which she had had the presence of mind to pick up from the Halma board as she passed through Edna's and Ruby's chamber the evening before. One was carved from a ruby, the other from a diamond, and each of them was worth a small fortune. Her one regret now was that she had not pocketed several more while she was about it. But, although she would have been perfectly within her rights in doing so—for were they not her own property?—she had thought at the time that it would be risky to take any number that could be noticed. There was always the chance that Miss Heritage might count them!

However, she said nothing about this to her family just then; it would be a pleasant surprise for them later on.

"But," she continued, "I do think it might have occurred to Miss Heritage—I can't and won't call her by any other name—that, as she was known to be in my employment when we left 'Inglegarth,' our returning without her may expose us to very unpleasant remarks. People may think I've discharged her—left her stranded in foreign parts—or I don't know what!"

"That is what she calculated on, no doubt!" said Edna.

"Oh, stop it, Edna!" said her brother, "you ought to know her better than that!"

"Oh, of course she's an angel—in your estimation! But she could have saved mother from being misunderstood if she'd wanted to—and since she hasn't—well, I'll leave you to draw the obvious inference!"

Ruby, who had been roving about the room during this conversation, now broke in:

"Mummy," she cried, "there's a letter here for you, and it looks like darling Queen Daphne's writing!" And she brought it to her mother. It was enclosed in a folded square of parchment—envelopes, like other modern conveniences, being unknown in Märchenland—and fastened with the royal signet, which Mrs. Wibberley-Stimpson broke with a melancholy reminiscence of the satisfaction it had given her to use the seal herself.

"Dear Mrs. Wibberley-Stimpson," she read aloud—"As I am about to be married here very shortly, my return with you to England will naturally be impossible. It is a great grief to me to have to part from my dear little pupil Ruby, to whom I have become so deeply and sincerely attached. Will you please tell her from me that I shall never forget her, and miss her very much indeed.—Believe me, very truly yours,

DAPHNE HERITAGE."

"Well," commented Mrs. Stimpson, while poor Ruby's tears began to flow afresh, "that is certainly a letter which I could show to anybody. Though I notice she doesn't say anything about being grieved to part with anyone but Ruby. A deliberate slight to the rest of us! And then the meanness of turning us out without the slightest return for all we've done for her! It does show such petty ingratitude!"

"Easy on, Mater!" said Clarence. "She don't seem to have let us go away quite empty-handed after all. I mean to say there's a box or something over there that I fancy I've seen before in the Palace."

He went up to examine it as he spoke. It was an oblong case, rather deeper and squarer than a backgammon box, covered with faded orange velvet and fitted with clasps and corners of finely wrought silver set with precious stones.

Inside were the emerald and opal "halma" board and ruby and diamond pieces, and with them a slip of parchment with Daphne's handwriting. "I thought perhaps," she had written, "you might care to have this. Princess Rapunzelhauser tells me she is afraid two of the men are missing, but I hope she is mistaken and they are really all there.—D."

"I shall never play with them!" declared Ruby breaking down once more. "I—I couldn't bear to, without Her!"

"Of course you will never play with them, my dear," said her mother, "they are far too valuable for that."

A very inadequate impression of Mrs. Wibberley-Stimpson's strength of character must have been given if anyone expects that this gift would cause her the slightest degree of shame or contrition; on the contrary, it only served to justify her in her own eyes—not that she needed any justification—for having appropriated those two pieces. She had merely anticipated—and nothing would be easier than to put them back in the box without being observed.

"A magnificent present!" pronounced Mr. Stimpson. "Really what I should call very handsome indeed of her. If we ever had to sell this set they'd fetch a colossal sum—here—simply colossal!"

"And a minute ago, Mater," said Clarence, "you accused her of being mean!"

"Well," she replied, "and what are these things, when all is said, to the riches we've surrendered to her? A mere trifle—which she'll never even miss!"

"You're forgetting they were hers—not ours—all the time. And we've left her precious little gold to go on with. It makes me sick to hear you running her down, when, when ... well, anyhow, Mater, I'll be glad if you won't—in my hearing!"

"There's no occasion to use that tone to me, Clarence. I have my own opinion of Miss Heritage, and I am not likely to alter it now. But if you choose to keep your illusions about her, I shall say nothing to disturb them."

"You may be very clever, Clarence," said Edna, "I know you think you are, but there's one subject at all events you're hopelessly ignorant about—and that's Women!"

"I don't mind owning it," he retorted. "I'd have taken my oath once that a highly superior cultivated English girl like you could never have cottoned to any Johnny in the Ogre line of business. But you've shown me my mistake!"

Edna, who was scarlet with wrath, would no doubt have made an obvious rejoinder had not a diversion been caused by the caretaker, who appeared with that morning's Daily Mail.

"Ah, so you managed to get a paper?" cried Clarence. "Good!" and he took it from her hands and opened it. "I say," he announced as soon as they were alone, "we haven't been away so long as we thought. We're still in 1914. Saturday, twenty-fifth of July."

"Is that all?" said his mother. "But I remember now that tiresome old Court Godmother saying that Time went quicker in Märchenland than it does here. I don't understand how—but there's evidently some difference. The twenty-fifth of July? Dear me, the Pageant must be over and done with long ago! Not of course that I should have cared to take part in it now!"

"Well, my boy," said Mr. Stimpson as Clarence ran through the columns of the paper, "and what's the latest news?"

"First defeat of Middlesex," replied Clarence; "Surrey's at the head of the table now for the Championship! Fine batting by Gloucester at Nottingham yesterday—319 to Notts 299 first innings, and 75 for three wickets!"

"Capital!" said his father without enthusiasm, "and what about Politics? Got Home Rule yet?"

"I'll tell you in a minute.... Looks as if they hadn't. Breakdown of Home Rule Conference at Buckingham Palace. Wonder what the Government will do now."

"They've only to be firm," said Mr. Stimpson, in his character as ex-autocrat. "If Ulster chooses to resent the will of the People as expressed in the last General Election, well, she must be put down, or what's our Army for, I should like to know. Any other news?"

"Nothing much, except that Austria's just sent an ultimatum to Servia. Seems the Austrian Grand Duke's been assassinated, and Austria believes the Servians were in it. Anyhow, they've got to knuckle down by six o'clock to-night or they'll be jolly well walloped. But of course they'll give in when they're up against Austria.... I see these writing chaps are doing their best to work up a scare, though. Here's one of 'em actually saying it may 'plunge all Europe into War.' Good old Armageddon coming off at last, I suppose. How they can write such tommy-rot!"

"It's only to send up their circulation," said Mr. Wibberley-Stimpson. "Depend upon it, there'll be no War. None of the Powers want it—too expensive in these days. They'll see that it's settled without fighting. And even if they can't, we shan't be dragged in—we shall just let 'em fight it out among themselves, and when it's over we shall come in for a share of the pickings!"

"Well," said Clarence, as he crumpled the paper into a ball and tossed it away, "we needn't worry ourselves about Armageddon—got something more serious to think about."

"What do you mean, Clarence?" inquired his mother uneasily.

"Why," he said, "it seems we've been away about four months. We can explain now why Miss Heritage hasn't come back with us. She's made that all right by her letter—and a trump she was to think of it! But what are we going to say when people want to know—and you can bet they will—where we've been all this time and what we've been doing?"

"We can simply tell them we have been temporarily occupying exalted positions in a foreign country which we are not at liberty to mention," suggested Mrs. Wibberley-Stimpson hopefully.

"We could," he said; "and the reply we should get would probably be 'Rats.' They might put it more politely—but that's what it would amount to. Believe me, you'll never make people here swallow you and the governor as the late King and Queen of Fairyland—it's a jolly sight too thick! Besides, there's nothing particular in what we've done there to brag about—what?"

"I at least have nothing to reproach myself with," said his mother virtuously. "Still I agree with you, Clarence, that perhaps it would be better if we could give some account of ourselves which would sound a little less improbable."

"We shall have to invent one. And as soon as we've done breakfast I vote we put our heads together and fake something up. But, whatever it is, we must all remember to stick to it!"

And after long and strenuous cogitation, the Stimpson family managed to construct a fairly plausible story of an unexpected summons to a remote part of the world, in which they were obliged by circumstances to remain without any facilities for informing their friends of their situation.

There was one danger which Mrs. Wibberley-Stimpson foresaw. At any time she might encounter the Duchess of Gleneagles or Lady Muscombe in Society. However, she decided that the risk was almost negligible. After all, their respective circles could not be said to intersect and, if she ever should come across either of these distinguished ladies, it would be easy to deny all recollection of ever having met them before.

And thus reassured, she was able to support the official version of the family adventures so whole-heartedly that she ended by accepting it as the only authentic one.

Ruby, it is true, confided a widely different account in secret to one or two of her most intimate friends.

But Ruby's story met with the fate that is only too certain to befall this veracious and absolutely unexaggerated narrative—nobody was ever found to believe a single word of it!

EPILOGUE

The re-appearance of the Wibberley-Stimpsons, coupled with the circumstantial explanations they gave of their mysterious absence abroad, provided their friends and neighbours with very nearly the proverbial nine days' wonder. It might have done so even longer, but for that fateful beginning of August, when, with appalling suddenness, the blow was dealt which shattered the peace of Europe and convulsed the whole world.

Then the Fools' Paradise in which England had so long luxuriated crumbled beneath her feet, and left her face to face with stern realities. Nothing was the same, or ever would be the same, again. Issues, causes, topics, which scarcely a week before had seemed of such vital and engrossing importance, shrivelled into insignificance or extinction under the scorching blast of war.

And so it followed that Gablehurst entirely forgot its previous curiosity concerning the private affairs of the Wibberley-Stimpson family, thereby relieving them from a strain on their inventive powers which they had begun to find extremely wearing.

The crisis afforded Mr. Stimpson a long-desired occasion for taking a spirited part in politics. At the suggestion of his wife, who reasoned that in so Conservative a neighbourhood it would be popular to condemn any steps a Radical Government had taken, he summoned a public meeting to protest against the British Ultimatum to Germany, on the ground that England's safety and interests alike depended on her preserving the strictest neutrality under any circumstances whatever. As his sole supporter on the platform was a recently naturalised British subject with a pronounced German accent, the result of this patriotic endeavour was, as he admitted afterwards, "a little unfortunate." Mrs. Wibberley-Stimpson herself was compelled to recognise, as she led him home with two black eyes and only one coat-tail, that she had been less correct than usual in estimating the local sentiment, though, of course, she ascribed his treatment entirely to the lack of tact and ability with which he had handled his subject. However, they have long since succeeded in living all that down. Mr. Stimpson very soon recognised that his views of the situation had been mistaken, and made haste to publish his conviction of the righteousness of our cause. No one now enlarges with more fervour on the ruin and disgrace that would have overtaken us if we had been induced to stand aside by persons he refers to as "those infernal cranks and pacifists."

Moreover, he acquired further merit by his generous contribution of two thousand pounds to the Prince of Wales' Fund—a contribution which caused a sensation among many who could give a fairly shrewd guess at the income he drew as a partner in the firm of Cramphorn, Stimpson, & Thistleton.

But then they did not know that, shortly before, he had disposed of two exquisitely carved pieces—one diamond, and the other ruby—by private contract to an American millionaire, for a sum which would have covered an even more princely donation. He has several more of these curiosities, but is reserving them for times when they are more likely to fetch their proper value.

As for his wife and elder daughter, they have already achieved the distinction of sitting on more War Committees, and talking more at every one of them, than any other ladies in Gablehurst.

It is unnecessary to say that they have also knitted a prodigious quantity of garments, or at least did until they were requested to abandon their colour-schemes for the regulation khaki wool—which perceptibly cooled their enthusiasm.

But, after all, the greatest exhibition of self-denial was given by Ruby, who parted with her latest and best-beloved acquisitions—two tree-frogs and an axolotl—and sent the proceeds of their sale to the Red Cross Society.

Clarence had made several applications for such vacant berths as he could hear of in the City which seemed to combine the advantages of light work and a heavy salary, but somehow the principals he interviewed could not be brought to share his own conviction that he was exactly the person to suit them. He had referred them to his previous employers, but even that had led to no favourable result.

The war had not gone on long, however, when it was forcibly borne in upon him that, if there was no particular demand in business circles for his services, they were needed rather urgently just then by his King and Country.

And so, one evening before dinner, he strolled casually into the drawing-room at "Inglegarth" and electrified his family by mentioning that he had offered himself that afternoon to a certain Cavalry regiment, and been pronounced physically fit after examination.

His mother was naturally the most deeply affected by the news, though, after the first shock was over, she was sustained by recollecting that she had caught herself secretly envying a neighbour, whom she had never looked upon as a social equal, but whose boy had just obtained a commission in the Territorials.

"You might have prepared us for this, Clarence!" she said, as soon as she could speak. "It's a heavy blow to me—to us all. Still, if you feel it your duty to go, I hope your Father and I are not the parents to hold you back. If I'm not on one of the same committees as Lady Harriet," she added more brightly, "I really think I must call and let her know. She would be so interested to hear that you are now a Cavalry officer."

"You might make it a Field-Marshal, Mater, while you're about it!" he returned. "But, if you want to be accurate, you'd better describe me as a bally trooper, because that's all I am, or likely to be."

"A trooper!" exclaimed his horrified mother. "Clarence, you can't mean to tell us you've enlisted as an ordinary common soldier! I couldn't possibly permit you to throw yourself away like that, nor, I am sure, will your Father! Sidney, of course you will insist on Clarence's explaining at once to the Colonel, or whoever accepted him, that he finds we object so strongly to his joining that he is obliged to withdraw his offer."

"Certainly," said Mr. Stimpson. "Certainly. It's not too late yet, my boy. You've only to say that we can't allow it—you're more badly wanted at home—and they're sure to let you off."

"Can't quite see myself telling 'em that, Guv'nor. Even if I wanted to be let off—which I don't."

"After the way you've been brought up and everything!" cried Mrs. Wibberley-Stimpson. "To sink to this! Has it occurred to you that you would have to associate entirely with persons of the very lowest class?"

"You wouldn't say that if you'd seen some of the Johnnies who passed the Vet with me," he replied. "And, as to classes, all that tosh is done away with now. There's only one class a fellow can't afford to associate with—the slackers who ought to be in khaki and aren't. I couldn't have stuck being in that crowd any longer, and I'm jolly lucky to have got well out of it!"

"All the same, Clarence," lamented his Mother, "you must see what a terrible come-down it is for you, who not so very long ago were a Crown Prince!"

"I thought we'd agreed to forget all that, Mater," he said, wincing slightly. "Anyway, if I don't turn out a better Tommy than I did a Prince, they won't have me in the regiment long. But I'm not going to get the push this time, if I can help it. Come, Mater," he concluded, "don't worry any more over what's done and can't be undone—just try and make the best of it!"

But this was beyond Mrs. Wibberley-Stimpson's philosophy just then. If he had been leaving his comfortable home with a commission as sub-lieutenant, she might have been able to find some slight consolation in announcing the fact to her friends. Now she would have to make the humiliating admission that he was nothing more than a common trooper—after which she felt she would never be able to hold up her head again!

As things turned out, these apprehensions proved unfounded. For it seemed that other young Gablehurst men belonging to families in as good a position as her own had enlisted as privates, and, so far from being considered to have brought discredit on their parentage, were regarded with general approval.

And the pride with which their mothers spoke of them encouraged Mrs. Wibberley-Stimpson to be even prouder of Clarence, as the only one who had joined a Cavalry regiment.

When he was undergoing the necessary training with the reserve regiment and first had to enter the Riding-School, he was prepared, remembering how suddenly and completely his control of Märchenland horses had left him, for some highly unpleasant experiences.

Daphne's pendant had been left in safe custody at Inglegarth, and, even if he had had any idea that it had assisted his horsemanship (which he was far from suspecting), he would not have brought it with him, lest he should lose a thing which Daphne had said he would please her by keeping.

Probably, had he brought and been allowed to wear the token, it would not have made any impression whatever on the mind of a British charger—but fortunately no talisman was needed.

All the riding in Märchenland, while his horses continued docile, had not been without some good result after all. At least he found that he had quite as good a seat as any of his fellow-recruits, and a very much better one than most of them.

And the months of training passed, not unhappily. He made friends, not all of them in his own class; he set himself to learn his job as quickly and thoroughly as he could, and his sergeant-major spoke of him, though not in his presence, as a smart young chap who showed more sense than some he had to do with.

He had not been many weeks in the regiment before he got his first stripe, and when he came home on furlough he was able to inform his family that he had just been promoted to be a full-blown Corporal. It was a farewell visit, as he was being sent out in a day or two with a draft to his regiment at the Front. He had grown broader across the chest, and looked extremely brown and fit, while his family noticed that he no longer ended his remarks with "what?" Once or twice he expressed his satisfaction at getting the chance at last of having a go at the Bosches—but he said very little about the future, and seemed more interested in hearing about Ruby's new school and Edna's ambulance class.

Then he left them, and for months after that they had to endure the long strain of constant anxiety and suspense which few British households have escaped in these dark times. Clarence had always been a poor correspondent—and his letters, though fairly regular, were short and wanting in details. But he said the regiment was doing dismounted work in the trenches; that he was acquiring the habit of sleeping quite soundly under shell-fire; that he had been much cut up by losing some of his best pals, but so far had not been hit himself, though he had had several narrow shaves; he kept pretty fit, but was a bit fed up with trench work, though he didn't see an earthly of riding in a cavalry charge at present.

The last letter was dated February. After that came a silence, which was explained by an official letter stating that he was in a field hospital, severely wounded. Inglegarth remained for days in helpless misery, dreading the worst, till they were relieved by the news that he was now in a base hospital and going on well.

But it was some weeks before he could be moved to London, and longer still before he was convalescent enough to be taken to his own home, where the joy of seeing him recover so rapidly was checked by the knowledge that he would only leave them the sooner.

He was much the same slangy and casual Clarence they had known, though rather subdued, but he had moods of sombre silence at times which none of them dared to interrupt, when his eyes seemed to be looking upon sights they had seen and would fain forget. As to his own doings he said but little, though he told them something of his experiences during his last week at the front—how the regiment had been rushed up in motor-buses from Bleu to Ypres; how they had marched to the Reformatory which they had defended for five days under heavy fire; how they had then dug caverns and occupied trenches to the south of the Menin road, and how the trenches had been mined by the enemy, and five officers killed and sixty-four casualties, of which latter he was one.

Before he was pronounced fit for active service again he heard that he had been recommended for a commission, and given one in another cavalry regiment which had very nearly the same prestige and traditions as his own, though he would have been the last to admit it till then.

Thus was Mrs. Wibberley-Stimpson's dearest desire at last attained; she could now inform her friends and acquaintances that her boy was actually a subaltern, while, even in conversation with strangers, it was always possible to lead up to the fact by enlarging on the heavy cost of a cavalry officer's kit.

And yet, in fairness to her, it may be said that, with all her striving after social distinction, if she had been required to choose between her son returning to the front with a commission and keeping him at home with no higher rank than that of a corporal, she would have chosen the latter without a moment's hesitation.

But since the choice was not given her, Clarence's promotion did much to console her for his approaching departure—at least until the day arrived, when she turned blindly away from the platform with an aching dread that the train was bearing him out of her life for ever.

That was several months ago, and Second-Lieutenant Stimpson (he dropped the "Wibberley" when he first enlisted) has been at the front ever since.

There is a certain endless road, bordered by splintered stumps which once were poplars, and pitted in places with deep shell-holes, that he knows only too well; having taken his troop along it many a night to relieve the party in the trenches.

Even now, when he comes to the group of ruined cottages at which he has to leave the road and strike across country into the danger-zone, he is unpleasantly conscious of a sinking at his heart at the prospect of another week or so of that infernal existence of shattering noise, flying death-splinters, and sickening sights and smells. There he will have to be constantly on the watch, meals and sleep can only be snatched at precarious intervals, and seldom without disturbance; if there is anything more nerve-racking than the scream of shells and the hail of shrapnel it is the lull that follows, when he waits for the enemy's rush to begin. And yet, the moment he finds himself back in the trench again, he becomes acclimatised; his men speak of him as a cool and resourceful young officer under any difficulties, while on more than one occasion he has done some daring and very useful reconnoitring work that may even earn him mention in despatches.

But at present he is enjoying one of his hard-earned rests, being billeted in a farmhouse well away from the firing-line.

Here, having no duties or responsibilities to fix all his thoughts on the present, he can allow them to dwell on the future for a while.

This desperate and relentless war will come to an end in time—how soon he knows no more than anyone, but that it will end in victory for England and her Allies he has no doubt whatever. He is equally sure, though he could not account for his certainty, that, unlike many a better fellow than himself, he will live to see his country at peace once more. But what is he to do then? Even if an opening in the City presented itself, he could never stick an office again after this. On the other hand, even if he gets another step or two, he will find it difficult to live on his pay in a crack cavalry regiment. However, the Governor will no doubt give him an allowance that will enable him to stay in the Service—the Mater can be safely trusted to see to that!

So, this question being satisfactorily disposed of, his thoughts, as usual on these occasions, drift back to Märchenland, and particularly to Daphne's parting words on the night he left the Palace.

Would she think, he wonders, that he has done something to justify her belief in him?

At least she might be pleased if she knew that he could not fairly be described any longer as a useless rotter.

"Only," he tells himself disconsolately, "she never will know. England's no country of hers now, and she wouldn't feel enough interest in it even to send the Baron across in the stork-car for a daily paper. If she did, she'd be none the wiser, because he'd be sure to bring The Poultry-Fancier's Journal or The Financial News, or something of that sort. And, after all, if she had any idea of the ghastly business that has been going on in this old world for the last year, she's too much heart to be happy—even in Märchenland. But now she'll go on being happy for the rest of her life, bless her! and if she gives me a thought now and then—well, it will be a jolly sight more than I deserve!"

F. Anstey – A Concise Bibliography

Vice Versa (1882)
The Black Poodle And Other Tales (1884)
The Giant's Robe (1884)
The Tinted Venus (1885)
A Fallen Idol (1886)
Burglar Bill And Other Pieces (1888)
The Pariah (1889)
Voces Populi (1890)
Tourmalin's Time Cheques (1891)
Mr. Punch's Model Music-Hall Songs And Dramas (1892)
The Talking Horse And Other Tales (1892)
The Travelling Companions (1892)
The Man From Blankley's And Other Sketches (1893)
Mr. Punch's Pocket Ibsen (1893)
Under the Rose (1894)
Lyre and Lancet (1895)
The Statement of Stella Maberly, Written By Herself (1896)
Baboo Jabberjee, B. A. (1897)
Puppets At Large (1897)
Love Among The Lions (1898)

Paleface And Redskin (1898)
The Brass Bottle (1900)
A Bayard From Bengal (1902)
Only Toys! (1903)
Salted Almonds (1906)
Winnie, An Everyday Story (1909)
In Brief Authority (1915)
Percy and Others (1915)
The Last Load (1925)
The Would-Be Gentleman (Adapted From Molière's Le Bourgeois gentilhomme) (1927)
The Imaginary Invalid (Adapted From Molière's Le Malade imaginaire) (1929)
Humour and Fantasy (1931)
A Long Retrospect (1936)

www.ingramcontent.com/pod-product-compliance
Lightning Source LLC
Chambersburg PA
CBHW072055170626
46813CB00004B/1369